Additional Prai

THE LAMPLIG

"Crystal J. Bell's *The Lamplighter* is an eerie and unsettling debut that sucks you in from the first page. Both quiet yet intensely haunting, this dark, powerful horror mystery will keep you up at night. The rich setting comes alive, and its flawed characters and complicated relationships in a small whaling village will make you question everything you thought you knew about fog and lampposts. This is a debut you don't want to miss."

—Colby Wilkens, author of *If I Stopped Haunting You*

"Atmospheric and haunting, *The Lamplighter* is the kind of book made to be read at midnight as the candles flicker and the wind howls—a masterpiece in folkloric horror. Tempe is a fiercely relatable protagonist, one for whom every girl who has ever felt her voice has been unfairly silenced will love. Each element of this story adds to the deliciously spooky horror of the world Bell has crafted: the slow-burn rising tension; the lush, spine-chilling descriptions of the small whaling town and the mysterious fog stealing away the souls of those unlucky enough to be caught in the dark when it arrives; the tension between madness and morality we see Tempe struggle with as she is drawn further and further into Warbler's web; all culminating in a climactic finale that will leave the reader awestruck and horror-stricken, desperate to know more. A must-read for mystery and horror lovers!"

—Christy Healy, author of *Unbound*

"Crystal J. Bell has conjured a lush maritime tale with a churning sense of dread that builds to a stunning conclusion. I absolutely devoured this Gothic story of haunted New England forests, family secrets, girls fighting the patriarchy, and the darker side of magic."

—Megan Cooley Peterson, author of *The Liar's Daughter*

"Atmospheric and riveting, Bell's debut is a lushly imagined feminist tale of confronting the monsters that lurk within. *The Lamplighter* will creep inside your bones just as sinuously as the fog in Warbler."

—Kate Anderson, author of *Here Lies Olive*

"Dripping with atmosphere and suffused with a slowly creeping dread, Bell's deliciously dark debut is a fog-wreathed delight."

—Amy Goldsmith, author of *Those We Drown* and *Our Wicked Histories*

THE LAMPLIGHTER

CRYSTAL J. BELL

Mendota Heights, Minnesota

First Edition
Second Printing, 2024

Book design by Karli Kruse
Cover design by Karli Kruse
Cover illustration by Grace Aldrich

Flux, an imprint of North Star Editions, Inc.

Library of Congress Cataloging-in-Publication Data
Names: Bell, Crystal J., 1988- author.
Title: The lamplighter / Crystal J. Bell.
Description: First edition. | Mendota Heights, Minnesota: Flux, 2024. | Audience: Grades 10–12.
Identifiers: LCCN 2023059585 (print) | LCCN 2023059586 (ebook) | ISBN 9781635830989 (paperback) | ISBN 9781635830996 (pdf)
Subjects: CYAC: Missing persons--Fiction. | Sisters--Fiction. | Supernatural--Fiction. | Fantasy. | Horror. | LCGFT: Fantasy fiction. | Horror fiction. | Historical fiction. | Novels.
Classification: LCC PZ7.1.B451455 Lam 2024 (print) | LCC PZ7.1.B451455 (ebook) | DDC [Fic]--dc23
LC record available at https://lccn.loc.gov/2023059585
LC ebook record available at https://lccn.loc.gov/2023059586

Flux
North Star Editions, Inc.
2297 Waters Drive
Mendota Heights, MN 55120
www.fluxnow.com

Printed in Canada

Dedicated to my boys:

Mogget, who was with me from the beginning,

Rowan, who was always by my side,

and Patrick, whom I love madly.

A NOTE ABOUT THE CONTENT

The Lamplighter contains discussions and/or depictions of sexual assault, suicide, the death of a parent, strong language, and violence.

While this book is set in the mid-nineteenth century in New England, creative license was taken with some historical facts in order to craft this story.

CHAPTER 1

They found Da hanging from the northwest lamppost, neck bent, ladder fallen useless in the dirt.

It doesn't matter how much time has passed. Day and night, I find myself struggling beneath the weight of that moment each time I approach the lamppost. And this evening is no different. The cast iron is rusted in parts, but it stands solidly, waiting for the wick in its glass cage to be lit. Its presence holds me frozen to the ground as I recall that terrible morning: the creak of the rope as Da's body swayed in the breeze, the whispers loud as a swarm of bees, the cloying fog a voyeur.

Laughter down the street, a deep guttural sound, shakes me from my stasis. I blink as two men pass by, dipping their hats in greeting. After acknowledging them with a nod of my own, I look back to the lamppost. It is just that: a lone lamppost. The creaking remains like a dying echo from my memory, but it's only the ships in the river. Da's not here. He died four years ago. I clear my throat, and with it some sense falls back into place, grounding me in the present. I grip my glowing lantern and shrug my bag farther up my shoulder, ignoring the ache that is my constant companion.

My heartbeat slows as I pass the lamppost, leaving it for last.

In the distance, high above the trees, masts shift and sway. The whaling ships protest their restraints before being lulled into complacency by the gentle swell of the harbor water. Fog, a living, breathing creature in the dying light of the setting sun, will soon roll out of the woods, creep down the streets, pour onto the wharf, and smother Warbler Seaport entirely. Buildings and ships will become mere suggestions. And the villagers themselves? Wraiths forever adrift in the murk.

But not on my watch.

First, though, the bell.

It hangs in the middle of the courtyard in front of the town hall. The wooden arch holding it—designed by Gideon, Warbler's infamous ship carver—is constructed of black locust. Etched into the hardy wood is the chase between a whaling ship and a whale through turbulent, crashing waves. As young children, Josiah and I would trace the whale with our fingertips for good luck.

My fingers find their old route across the wood, the edges smoothed over by years of the tradition. I took it up again nearly six months ago. Josiah would laugh at me were he to find out. Even so, I trace the whale once more for good measure before ringing the bell.

Just before sunset, Warbler is alerted, and my shift begins.

The sound is pure, resonating through the chill air in joyful triumph. Three times it calls out beside me, the vibrations of its song spreading down the rope and into my hand. I leave its bold signal behind—a reassurance to the constables that Henry need not be sent to do my work in my stead—and unlock the door to the shed beside the town hall. Inside, I retrieve the ladder and a bag containing a cloth for cleaning, extra wicks, Da's wick trimmer, a glass scraper, and other odds and ends should I need them. It's best to prepare for anything.

The first lamppost is a stone's throw away from Warbler's Bell; its blossom of light will be a guide for any villagers near the town hall, the schoolhouse, or the church. Three buildings to a lamppost. I prop the ladder against the lamppost, climb, open the glass door, scrape and wipe any residue off the panes and tin reflectors, trim and light the wick. Then it's on to the next one down the street. And the next. After each lamppost is lit, an audible sigh follows in my wake and with it smiles from anyone nearby. Light is comfort. Safety. Hope. Patterns and routine keep the people of Warbler, Connecticut, at ease.

Knowing I get to be the one to do that for them keeps my chin up in this solitude.

Before long, I've reached the Green. Gardens surround the benches at its center. Their once-bright colors are muted, their leaves crisping up in the autumn air. Not many people frequent the park after dark, except Benjamin, the local drunk. He has taken up his usual position on one of the benches nearest the lamppost in the circular courtyard. The smell of manure and sweat wafts from his, thankfully, sleeping form. I'm saved from his drunken mutterings and the awful sound of his tongue licking his cracked lips as he watches me work.

The fog arrives silent as the dead.

It pours from the smattering of trees to the northwest of the Green, then climbs over the creek before spilling between the dry flower stalks and into the courtyard. I frown. It's earlier than usual. If Benjamin awakens, he may believe he is still in the slumbers of a dream, floating on a cloud.

While the fog generally arrives around the same time each evening, it isn't something Warbler can set its clocks to. Therein lies the importance of the bell. It's best to head home at its song, but should the fog creep out before expected, Warbler knows I'm not far behind. Lighting the way for all.

Movement catches my eye.

Two young women cross over the stone bridge into the Green, drifting toward me like ghosts. The fog and their blue skirts have concealed their feet. They reach me right as I step off the ladder. The taller of the two, Molly, carries a woven basket filled with colored fabric and lace. Her smile is welcoming as always. "Hello, Temperance."

I nod. "Good evening, Molly. Susannah."

Both of them are around Pru's age of sixteen summers, though I don't believe Pru interacts with them often. The two young women are in a more well-off position than our family has ever been. Molly's father is Warbler's single druggist, while Susannah's is the most successful merchant in our seaport.

Susannah nods abruptly at my acknowledgment, nose scrunched as she gives Benjamin a sidelong glance. His lecherous gaze remains hooded by sleep.

I remove my cap and re-pin my copper braid around my head. It had loosened while I scraped off a particularly stubborn mark on the back pane of glass. Molly's basket catches my eye once more. The blue silk ribbon gleams in the light. My fingers itch to touch the smooth fabric. I put my cap back on and rub my sooty hands along my rough trousers. "A visit to the seamstress, I see. Special occasion?"

"Oh yes." Molly tugs absentmindedly at a strip of white lace. "It's for the Gathering on Friday. Will you be attending?"

The Gathering is all anyone has been able to talk about for the last fortnight. Even Pru has been trilling away at the possibility of finally meeting the mysterious beau who began writing her at the beginning of the summer. If I had a shilling for every time she brought him up, she, Mother, and I could live comfortably for the rest of our days. I must admit, I too am anxious to learn his identity. Romantic letters may sweep my sister off her feet, but I am not so easily swayed. In my experience, there is usually an ulterior motive when a man is involved.

Why else wouldn't he be up-front about his identity?

"Temperance couldn't possibly go, Molly." Susannah's

haughty tone pulls me out of my troubled thoughts and back into the park. She lifts a dark eyebrow, gaze measuring me, rising from my scuffed boots and patched and dirty trousers, to my worn jacket and the cap on my head. "There is a dress code, after all."

Heat floods my cheeks. "I do own other clothes."

"There isn't a dress code." Molly's elbow finds Susannah's side. "You just don't want anyone there who may draw attention from yourself and limit any offers of courtship you may now receive."

Susannah releases an unladylike snort she wouldn't be caught dead doing in front of her gaggle of admirers. "Not likely . . ."

I clear my throat. Susannah's priorities are different from my own. Her world revolves around finding a suitable match for herself to begin a family. Why she thinks I am any sort of threat is beyond me. I understand the need to protect aspirations, though maybe not at the cost of decency and etiquette.

But I don't have time for snobbery. As we've been speaking, the fog has climbed up to our knees. The lampposts in the business district are next on my route. No doubt the fog has already reached the wharf. My toes tap impatiently beneath the murk.

"It is no matter. I will join while I can, but lighting the lampposts takes precedence over dancing and socializing." I stare hard at Susannah, who meets my gaze without flinching.

"Oh, but it won't take you all night to light them all, surely." Molly pouts, drawing my attention away from Susannah and her rolling eyes. "You should spend time celebrating with the rest of us."

Of course it won't take me all night to light the lampposts. From start to finish, it takes perhaps two hours. But the girls don't know any better. They don't have jobs to do in order to support their comatose mother and make sure their sister doesn't want for anything. They are free to think of only themselves. I can no longer allow myself to wonder what that must be like. To allow myself to dream about another life.

Someday, maybe. Hopefully.

"And besides," Molly continues, unaware of the ache in my heart. "Isn't the *Miriam* supposed to return? I'm sure Josiah would appreciate celebrating with you."

Susannah glares at her. The girl could teach a class on disdain and its many expressions.

But even her negativity cannot stop the rush flooding my system. The mere mention of Josiah has my lips curving into a smile and fireflies warming my belly.

"Yes, the *Miriam* is due back, but we'll see. You know as much as I how temperamental the Atlantic can be." The tremor in my voice cannot be helped. Our whaling schooner required a cooper before it departed in the spring, and Josiah was quick to sign up for the opportunity. The mere thought of his ship not returning on schedule threatens to shatter my control completely. Tucking away any and all thoughts of Josiah until his return has been the only way to maintain my sanity. But it isn't always easy.

I make a show of grabbing my ladder. "I apologize, but I really must be going now."

Susannah's skirts brush me as she passes by without a word. Molly only sighs, and then smiles sweetly at me. A light brown curl has escaped from her bonnet, softening her face. "Well, I hope you'll reconsider coming. Tell Prudence I say hello."

With their exit through the trees, silence returns to the park. Well, nearly. Benjamin's sporadic snores continue to grate the air as the leaves rustle in the branches above.

The sun has set and twilight reigns, but soon dusk will be upon us. I shift the ladder beneath my arm to a more comfortable position. Lantern in hand, I continue at a quick pace from the Green to the storefronts. As expected, the fog has reached the business district, and is slowly consuming the façades of the cooperage, smithy, and hoop shop in its greedy appetite. Shadows come alive, and I am almost fooled into believing there is something out here with me.

Superstitious whispers plague our seaport as bugs to a carcass. They don't only come from our elders. With so many different nationalities coming through, I've heard rumors of kelpies in the river, African water spirits that followed ships into port, or vilas on the hunt to drown a man. Spirits of whalers lost at sea coming to take the lives of those who survived the passage. One of our locals insists finding a pearl in our river oysters is the only talisman to keep you safe from danger.

Each superstition is as far-fetched as the last.

I will not deny, though, that the fog does love to play tricks. It trails my every step. Encouraging me to tread where I should not.

But I could walk this village blindfolded and still know where I am. I've done just that before, in fact. A game Josiah and I used to play before he began his apprenticeship at the cooperage. He'd take a sash and tie it over my eyes, spin me round, and tell me a location to walk to. I never once stepped wrong.

"How do you do it, Tempe? You magic or something?" His voice carried awe.

"Of course not. There's no such thing." I remember even now the heat of pleasure warming my cheeks. "Besides it's not a useful skill."

"You know that isn't true."

Josiah was right. When nighttime comes and inevitably the fog with it, it is only the lampposts that guide the villagers—a semblance of safety in a place where people easily, and all too often, disappear without a trace. If a body is found, we have answers and can address the issue. But that is a scrap our seaport is rarely thrown, a black mark we will never be free of. The fog descends from the woods north of town, a tidal wave of anonymity rolling over Warbler, and if you don't hold steady to the lampposts, you're lost forever. But I will always know my way. Da made sure of it.

Even if I didn't know where I was, the boisterous laughter and shouting from the tavern would alert me to its location. British, Dutch, and Spanish accents intermix with others I do not recognize. The lamppost out front stands a frozen interloper as a small group cajole and hit each other's arms, throwing heads back to swallow their drinks. More revelers—a mix of black, brown, and white men—pour out of the tavern and onto the street like spilled marbles. I only vaguely recognize some of them, having seen these newcomers the last few nights.

This particular group's whaling ship arrived earlier this week from New Bedford, not too far north of us. Word has spread through the seaport that a few weeks before they were to set sail, the figurehead crowning the front of their ship cracked. A bad omen. As they are a superstitious lot, rather than chance sailing the seas with bad luck, they sent a messenger to Warbler, commissioning our ship carver for a new figurehead. When the ship set sail, the captain directed it here to receive the figurehead before they head back out on their hunt.

Lucky figureheads are the one positive thing Warbler Seaport is known for.

And while Gideon finishes the new figurehead, our tavern entertains the whaling crew. More so than the ships constructed or repaired in our shipyard, it's the visiting whaling ships that bring considerable currency to our village. We generally put up with their crews' drunken gaiety, albeit reluctantly. I stick to the edge of the walkway, not wanting to draw too much attention to myself.

David, a local fisherman, catches my eye when I stop at the lamppost. He leans against the wall, a smoking pipe perched in his gnarled hand. He tips his head, leathery skin softened by a large, unkempt beard. "Evening, Temperance."

"David." I nod.

One of the whalers turns toward me, bringing his cup away from his lips. He towers over the others, a mountain of a man. I bet he could hold his arms around four of his mates without difficulty. Probably lift them up too. His gaze has my stomach twisting. The intensity of it can only bring unwanted attention. I pull my cap down as far as it will go before propping the ladder and climbing it.

"Temperance? A man with a g'hals name?" His voice sounds exactly how I thought it would. Deep, sardonic, and predatory. The responding chortles float above the tavern like vultures.

"That ain't a man, Leonard." Someone else laughs.

I glance over my shoulder at David as the whalers argue my sex. It's a tired song and dance brought on by the mere sight of me in trousers, but I am used to it from strangers. David puffs on his pipe and rolls his eyes. I smile and refocus on the glass.

A hand squeezes my buttock.

I jerk forward, into the post, a gasp ripping my throat. The ladder wobbles beneath my shifting weight.

"Blimey! Well, either that man has the softest ass this side of New England or they're a woman!"

I hear someone's drink spraying the air, coughing, exploding laughter. Rage burns my skin.

Always think before you react, Tempe.

The memory of Da's voice is soft, the lilt soothing, but someone else is controlling my body now. I grip the neck of the lamppost and kick out behind me. I halfheartedly hope I miss.

I don't.

My boot hits something solid before glancing off. Most likely the whaler Leonard's shoulder. There is a brief second of silence wherein I don't think anyone moves or breathes. My own heart has stopped, taken aback at my boldness.

Leonard's roar starts it again. "You bitch!"

I jump from the ladder. A jolt shoots through my legs upon landing, and the weight of my bag yanks down my shoulder. The fog recoils from me. I make it only a few steps before fingers scrabble at my back. More shouting. The air smells of sour breath and whiskey.

His hand catches the back of my jacket and I'm whipped around. Our eyes meet—his bloodshot brown, mine blue—as his ham-hock-sized fist pulls back to strike me.

A shrill whistle pierces the air from down the street.

The whaler freezes in place, chest heaving with his breaths. My heartbeat pounds in my ears, matching the rhythmic click of the constable's boots as he jogs over.

"Step away from each other *right* now," Henry's voice booms. He raises his arm up, a silent message to the gathering group of drunken whalers to back off. Unexpectedly, they listen.

Leonard's eyes gleam as a muscle flexes in his ruddy cheek. His anger is unjustified and merely adding oil to my own burning temper.

Henry reaches us, tucking his hat under his arm, then toying with the baton on his hip. "What's going on here?"

"She kicked me!" A few drops of spit fly from Leonard's mouth. Shouts of affirmation come from his friends at the tavern entrance.

"Only after he groped me," I grit out through my teeth. They begin to ache with the pressure, no other options available to me as an outlet for my anger. What he did was wrong.

And yet, it takes all my willpower not to apologize.

"Is this true, David?" Henry looks at David, who puffs once on his pipe. Nods.

Leonard scowls at me, disgust curling his lip. "Did I hurt ya? No. And what are you doing walking around dressed like a boy, anyway?"

The drunken throng all shout in agreement behind him, their words slurred, laughter taking the forefront. Henry merely sighs, and in it, I hear the repercussions he might have given Leonard die away. My shoulders drop as Henry releases his baton with a shrug. "He isn't from around here, Temperance. He doesn't know any better."

I bite the inside of my cheek, the copper taste as unwelcome as this whaler's presence.

"Temperance is the lamplighter." Henry turns back to Leonard. "I don't know about you, but I imagine constantly climbing up and down ladders proves difficult in a dress."

"Well, it ain't right. It's a man's job."

More copper in my mouth.

"What's important here is that you lot stay on the wharf." It seems Henry doesn't feel the need to correct Leonard as he turns to the entire group. "It's dangerous to travel in the fog, particularly when you aren't familiar with our village or if the lights aren't yet lit."

One misstep into the void in a drunken stupor could easily send someone toppling into the creek or river. Drownings, broken necks, split-open heads. Crimson red splashed upon the rocks. It has happened before and will likely happen again. The handful of times I've gone out to douse the lights and found bodies will forever be branded in my memory.

Thankfully, people are drawn to light like moths, and as long as I keep the lampposts lit, accidents rarely happen.

"You are expected to respect the rules of our seaport. That includes staying out of the lamplighter's way." Henry's gaze flicks to Leonard before returning back to me. "Why don't you two go your separate ways and we'll call it even."

He smiles at me as if he's done *me* the favor and Leonard is on the outside of some private understanding between us. I clench my jaw to keep from saying words I cannot take back.

"Remember, you lot are not to leave the wharf . . ." Henry's voice quiets to a dull grumble as he turns away, hand guiding the tosspot toward the rest of his friends. I breathe through my nose, fists clenched, shaking. I close my eyes and count to three before opening them again. Same world. Nothing has changed.

He doesn't know any better.

I'd be willing to bet a month's wages if I had been a man, Leonard would have received no such leniency.

Once I light the wick in the lamppost, the front of the tavern becomes a sick haze in the thickening fog. I gather up my ladder and lantern and hurry past it, refusing to give in to the shiver going up my spine. I feel the whalers' eyes on me, and for a moment, I wish the wind would pick up and blow out the light, shroud me in the ether.

But no. There is no running. There is no hiding. I mustn't show fear.

I move up the street to the print shop, general store, and seamstress without incident. Prop, climb, open, clean, trim, light. Only once I've passed the inn do I look over my shoulder. The whalers are grouped together once more before the tavern, merry in their oblivious worlds. The notes of a fiddle from within accompany their raucous laughter. One whaler stands apart from the rest, a giant of a man. He watches me, ignoring calls from his mates. He clenches and unclenches his fists.

I swallow down the unease tightening my throat as I turn the corner and Leonard disappears.

The stars are gone, rubbed away by a milky haze. Beyond the shipyard and wharf, all sound has been swallowed. The air is still, fog thick enough now I can't even see the branches reaching out overhead from the smattering of trees lining the street. There's nothing to be seen. No landmarks. No movement. Just a fuzzy absence. Perhaps I'll walk forever in this nothing, no beginning, no end, until one day my heart finally gives out and it all becomes black.

I whistle one of Pru's favorite tunes to break up the nothing. Let anyone still outside know I'm here, the light with me. You shouldn't give power to the unknown.

Rather than alleviate the feeling of solitude, my solemn whistle echoes back to me, confirming how alone I am out here. I stop and look behind me, listening for any sounds of following footsteps. Eyes searching for a dark silhouette.

Satisfied, I continue on once more. Though the light from my lantern is a marker for anyone out at this hour, it still is not strong enough to break up the gloom or give life to my shadow. I could be swallowed up with no one the wiser. Well, except for Pru. But how long would it take before she realized something was wrong? Would she be too late?

Like we were with Da?

My stomach growls, interrupting the dark path my thoughts are taking. I pick up the pace, knowing there's a hot bowl of Pru's clam chowder waiting for me at home. Winter has already begun to test autumn's waters, and by the time I come around to extinguish the lights and refill their oil wells tomorrow at dawn, frost will crunch beneath my feet.

With thoughts of the sweet bite of onion and creamy milk and clam keeping me moving, I reach the two buildings connecting the business district with the residential district: the home and workshop of Warbler's renowned ship carver,

Gideon. I take a deep breath, instilling calm into my body to contain my anxious nerves. I imagine myself floating in water, cradled and at peace. The fog is too great for me to discern the buildings, but I know they're there. After a few more steps, the iron fence appears before me, but nothing else. No lights glow in the murk. Gideon's windows are either shuttered for the night or, even better, he isn't home.

A welcome reprieve.

The lamppost is near the entrance of his workshop. As I take the time to scrape and clean it, my arm muscles burn as my thoughts wander. Though I'm grateful to have avoided Gideon's piercing gaze and dark interest, I do hope he finishes this new siren commission sooner than later. I'd rather not have to deal with drunken and belligerent whalers like Leonard longer than necessary.

Gideon's workshop houses numerous figureheads. Angels, mermaids, knights, animals. But everyone knows he will take special commissions for one of his sirens should a captain have the purse for it. His siren figureheads are known for their good luck, which is the reason we often have so many visiting whaling ships.

When he isn't working on figureheads, he can be found carving nameboards, trail boards, and tafferels for the ships being built in the shipyard. Or hired for smaller projects around the seaport like the bell's arch.

Gideon is truly an artist.

I glance over my shoulder toward the workshop, flesh crawling, but I remain alone, only Da's words to keep me company.

Stay away from Gideon.

It isn't too long before I finish cleaning the glass and reflectors, light the wick, and am back on the ground. I shove my cleaning cloth in my bag, pick up the ladder and my lantern, and hurry on my way. Only the lampposts in the residential district to go.

The first lamppost peeks through the fog, a black slash in an otherwise blurry world. Prop, climb, open, clean, trim, light. Glowing windows watch me as I walk by, busybodies to the ongoing of life passing by on the street. Thankfully, most everyone returns home at the sound of the bell, in case the fog creeps out before I can light most of the lampposts.

Some, however, use the early fog to their advantage.

It is not an easy life aboard a whaling ship, and word has spread of our unnaturally foggy seaport. Abandoning a ship post is not unheard of, and oftentimes a captain will come to find a disgruntled member of his crew does not show up the morning they are to set sail. Whalers are notorious for disappearing in Warbler, our fog providing the perfect opportunity for them. If it weren't for our figureheads and shipyard, I don't believe many captains would take the risk to stop here.

Real unease crawls through Warbler when one of our own goes missing, however, rare as that is.

I finish lighting and cleaning all of the neighborhood's lampposts—but for one. My chest is already tightening. All light is gone from the sky, nighttime settling down with the blanket of fog. Another ten yards along the street and I will reach the northwest lamppost. My steps are heavy, as if each of my feet has been tied to a brick. It never gets easier. I hold my hand out into the nothingness, slowing down.

Cold iron presses into my fingers. I flinch. Does it recognize the grooves and lines in my fingertips? Feel the blood pumping through my veins, the warmth in my skin? Does it know I am from Da?

Superstitions and folklore will never surpass the horror of truth.

I release a breath, the anticipation always the worst. I look up and wince. Glancing away, I blink at the wetness in my eyes. I still see him. The furrowing of the skin of his neck. The rope embedded deep. I remember thinking how indecent it was that his tongue stuck out. Then how horrible that was the first thought that came to mind.

I shake my head, clear my throat, and the lamppost stands, alone, waiting for the burning fire of my light.

Within minutes, the warm glow pools into the air and I can just hear Da below me, holding the ladder solid. "Atta girl, Tempe. It's an honor to bring light to the dark. You're a natural."

"Thanks, Da." I remember laughing. "But it's not hard."

"Oh, you'd be surprised, m'dear. You'd be surprised."

I never knew when things began changing for him. I had no idea he was lost in the dark. He'd never let on. The only reason I can imagine is that he didn't want to worry us.

Why didn't he give us a chance? I don't know if I could have helped. But leaving me in the dark, and Mother, Pru . . . it went against everything he was. Everything he valued. It made me question everything I thought I knew.

Someone screams.

The sound lodges an invisible hook in my navel, and I jerk back. The ladder wobbles beneath my unsteady weight, and I jump down before it can fall. My heart hammers in my rib cage. I stumble toward the sound, boots scuffing the cobblestones. "Hello?"

The scream came from the east. I run to the neighboring lamppost, and then the next. "Is anyone out here?"

All is calm. I close my eyes, listening for any sort of sound to guide me. There is only the soft rasp of my panting and the smell of wet earth. Did I imagine the scream?

It sounded so real.

I open my eyes to the hazy glow of the lights down the street and from the windows of the houses nearby. No one has glanced outside to investigate. The world has stopped, not a single thing out of place. I wait a minute before drifting back to my tools. I walk slowly, ears perked, pausing to look over my shoulder once more.

Nothing.

No wraiths in the fog.

Only me and the lamppost and the memory of Da hanging there while everyone gawked. In the single space between heartbeats, hope had shattered in my chest. The glass shards embedded into my lungs, and grief bled through me. A scream poured out of me, the final wail of childhood innocence as the constables rushed forward, turning me away from Da's body. Henry shouting at Matthew, "You were supposed to cut him down!"

The scream I heard tonight must have been in my head. A memory hovering in the air of my present. I release a deep breath as well as the suspicion and fear from my thoughts. A dark chuckle escapes my lips.

Pru always cautions me before I leave for work. *Be careful out there, Tempe. Even lamplighters fall victim to the fog.* As if I don't know.

But she's right—not that I would ever admit it to her. I peer down the street one last time. Maybe it wasn't so much that a person could get lost in our fog. Disappear.

Maybe it was that, if you weren't careful, the fog wore you down. Subtle. Day by day. Year after year.

Is that what happened to you, Da?

I lay my hand on the post, squeeze gently. The growl in my stomach urges me onward toward home and Pru's supper.

It's quiet the whole walk home, the scream just another memory to be absorbed in the fog. Yet I am unable to completely ignore the small splinter of doubt embedded into my skin. I glance over my shoulder. It is a splinter that will, no doubt, work itself out in time.

Surely.

CHAPTER 2

"You have immaculate timing," Pru chimes from beside the hearth.

Though I left the ladder on the front stoop, the rest of my tools have their place in the entryway beside the oil cannister I will use in the morning. I douse my lantern, set it down with my bag, then swing off my jacket and hang it on the peg on the wall along with my cap. "You know I'm helpless against the siren call of your chowder."

Pru grins, a pleased blush filling her cheeks. Mother is already seated at the table, a steaming bowl in front of her. The warm fire coaxes me over after I've washed my hands in the wash basin. I hold my hands over the lazy flames while Pru finishes ladling chowder from the hanging pot and into our bowls. Her hair is up in a simple bun, but the firelight sets it aglow like gold as she hums the tune to an old Irish song, one of Da's favorites.

It used to sadden me, these little breadcrumbs of the life we once had and how we've had to patch ourselves back up. But it would be worse if we didn't have them, I suppose. Da would hum this song in particular anytime he and Mother swayed in front of the fire, foreheads touching, hands clasped. Pru and I would giggle behind our hands, but they never seemed to care. Content in their own moment together.

In no time the heat of the fire chases away the unease and chill from earlier. As I take my seat, Pru sets our bowls in front of us and holds her hands out to Mother and me. My growling stomach competes with her murmured prayer as the heat from the chowder rises up to taunt me.

"Amen," Pru says, squeezing my hand.

I attack my bowl, the potato and clam chunks perfectly tender. The warmth and richness are a treat after the dry oatcakes I had midday. The saltiness of the clam is tame enough not to overpower, but strong enough to take me to the ocean and her endless possibilities. In no time at all, my spoon scrapes the bottom of the bowl. "This is delicious."

Pru nudges Mother. As if Pru's touch pulls her from a dream, Mother shifts and slowly reaches out for her spoon. Her nails are long, unchipped, and clean, courtesy of the attentiveness of her youngest daughter. They are so unlike my own, which are often covered in soot with a faint odor of oil. Pru's fingers are calloused from her constant sewing, washing, and gardening. Mother's hands belong to someone who doesn't participate. Beautiful hands of a ghost.

My sister clears her throat, and I look up into her frowning face. She jerks her head once, in warning, and shame sours the bite in my mouth. Two years my junior and yet she can still properly chastise me for thinking negatively of Mother. I turn my attention back to my bowl, tucking the soft slurp of Mother eating her chowder away.

"How was it tonight?" Pru prompts after I've returned to the table with a second helping from the pot.

"Not entirely uneventful. I ran into Susannah and Molly. Molly says hello."

Pru nods, but it's clear she isn't the least bit interested. She is sitting on the edge of her chair, practically vibrating: the crackle of a wick being lit. Her chowder remains untouched. I swallow another bite, but the intensity of her glittering stare has me wiping a drip from my chin.

After Da died, Pru took it upon herself to make up for the silence and loss in our house. Constantly on the move—working, planning, chatting without expecting a response, being excited and positive—Pru was a hummingbird. A wonder to watch and generally a pleasure to be around, she nonetheless could be exhausting. A year ago, she thankfully put some of her energy toward starting a book club. She and a handful of other women in the village now get together once a week, the club providing an escape from the monotony of everyday life as they discuss the books they read and the themes there within. Still, the amount of energy in her repertoire could wear down a saint.

If only it were possible to harness her energy, we wouldn't need to send out our ships to hunt down whales for lantern fuel. We'd merely light the way with Pru. The outlandish notion has me giggling into my chowder with slaphappy exhaustion.

Pru doesn't even register it. It couldn't be more obvious there is something on her mind. I swallow another bite of potato, taking my sweet time to chew it before I set the spoon down and lean back in the chair. "And how has your night been?"

"He's coming." She blurts out the news, belatedly biting her lip to control her grin.

"Who's coming?"

"My secret admirer. Tomorrow!" She reaches into her pocket and extracts a letter with the excited tenderness of a child with a new doll.

Her enthusiasm and joy ignite a smile on my own face. Around Pru, it's easy to forget the shadows in the world. She is my sun.

Nonetheless, my breath hitches, unbidden. This young man, whomever he is, is serious. It is no longer a safe flirtation through correspondence. At least we shall know his identity now, and I'll have a better notion of the right course of action. I hold my hand out for her letter, and she places it into my palm and sits back down, all but bouncing in her seat. The seal of black wax gleams like hot tar. "He doesn't want to wait until the Gathering?"

The parchment unfolds beneath my hands with a whisper. The calligraphy is fine and looping. Sentences sensical. A learned man. I glance over the beginning. Pru does not rush me as I work through each sentence, though her hands fidget in her lap. My eyes push past the eloquent descriptions of life in Warbler and tender compliments about Pru's person to the end.

In truth, my heart cannot wear this mask any longer. I must see you. If you agree, leave the front gate open to your home as a signal. I will present myself to you on the morrow, at the rising of the sun—and hopefully the beginning of the next chapter of our lives, should your family permit it.

Forever Yours

I read the letter twice and blink back tears. Josiah would never write me a love letter such as this, let alone a letter at all. But we've known each other since we were children; there never was a need for a courtship between us. I swallow down an unwelcome twinge in my gut. This is no time for petty thoughts.

Someone truly sees Pru and just might love her in the way she deserves. And he obviously is respectful enough to value our family's opinion, despite the lack of a male head of household. Warbler, while more open than other villages in New England—I, a woman, am the lamplighter after all—is still quite old-fashioned. Tradition and protocol are valued. Da always said if you don't tie a proper knot in a rope, it unravels. Once something is tried and true, some people aren't always open to trying something new.

But these admirable qualities don't account for this man's secrecy. Every fortnight he has written her a letter, the first one delivered over four months ago. Pru keeps each of his letters in the trunk at the end of her bed, pulling the latest out each morning with a smile and a sigh. I found myself waiting for the week the letter wouldn't arrive and her heart would break as he lost interest, his anonymity permitting him an escape.

After tomorrow, there is no backing out.

Was this all a ploy to make sure she fell in love with him before finding out his true identity? Is he a man with drinking problems? Debts? An outcast?

Pru's grin is gone as I lift my gaze. It's replaced by a nervous energy, worry shining her eyes. I see the reflection of my pragmatic and critical self in them and am suddenly filled with so much anger at our parents for turning me into this cynical person. Supper turns in my stomach. I take a deep breath through my nose to try and settle it.

By the sinking of Pru's shoulders, she reads this as a refusal.

I fold the letter up and my own doubts and fears with it. For how could I deny her a chance at a future?

I clear my throat. It's difficult to maintain a straight face, but I keep my expression in check. The light in her eyes fades as I toss the letter onto the table, though her back remains ramrod straight. I wait just long enough to flirt with torture before smiling. "Well, what do you plan on wearing?"

A joyous squeak and happy jig later, we debate the merits of her blue dress that emphasizes the blue of her eyes, versus the cream dress with the lace trim that emphasizes the gold in her hair. We giggle and laugh while Mother watches behind empty eyes. Pru reiterates the many qualities she has inferred from his letters: *There are no ink stains or blots, so he must either know exactly what he wants to say or have the wherewithal to wait before making decisions. He hardly speaks of himself, so he certainly isn't vain. The quality of paper means he may come from wealth. Can you imagine not having to worry about having enough food?* I indulge her by pretending she hasn't been repeating the same words for the last few months.

As she continues to expound on her admirer's virtues, I remove the pins holding up my braid. The twists quickly unravel. I rub a few strands of hair between my fingers, and they shine in the light of the fire. I may wear trousers and my hands may often be dirty, but my hair is the one feminine feature I maintain. The one thing Mother and I have in common. Long, thick, copper hair. There was a time she would run her fingers through it and massage my scalp when my head ached. Every time I start a braid, I feel the kiss of her fingertips on my own hands when she taught me as a child. For a moment, the backs of my eyes tickle.

I glance over at her, but she is staring at something neither Pru nor I can see. She has never found her way out of her grief over Da, even with the passage of so many years. Forever lost in the refuge her heart burrowed into.

Saddened, I clear my throat and add more logs to the flames as Pru gathers up the dishes. There's a break in her joyous rambles as she takes a breath, and I'm able to toss out a question. "What will you do if he is unattractive?"

She rolls her eyes. "I do not believe that will be the case. And even if he were, I don't care about appearances. I've fallen in love with the man, not his looks."

The conviction with which she speaks is reassuring. It also sticks me in the gut. She grew up so fast.

He'd better not hurt her.

I squeeze her hand when she reaches out to grab my bowl, pausing her in her fluttering motion. "I am quite happy for you."

Her cheeks ball up with pleasure as she squeezes back.

CRACK.

We both jump into the air, spinning toward the sound. Pru holds her hand to her throat as we look to the window. A dark shape clatters against it, withdraws, and cracks again. The shutter has come loose from its tie. The wind whistles through the fireplace, stirring the embers up, confirming it is only that. Mere wind. But my heart continues to pound against my rib cage.

"Good heavens." Pru laughs nervously, shaking her head.

I hurry outside to secure the loose shutter and make quick work of checking the others around the house. The wind has thinned the fog enough I can see down the road by at least two lampposts. The air is a cloudy river in constant motion. A draft blows my hair across my face, and my ladder clatters to the ground. Curling up beneath my quilt and listening to the wind whistle and moan outside the house sounds beyond appealing, especially with my full belly. But if the wind can loosen our shutter ties, there's a possibility a lamppost door has been blown open. I always double-check the doors are shut tight, but Mother Nature isn't to be trifled with.

The lights cannot go out.

Part of my duties as lamplighter is to provide at least one patrol through the village after lighting the lampposts, to ensure the lights are still burning bright. I step back inside and begin the process of braiding my long hair back up and into a coil around my head.

"Already?" Pru winces.

I nod before grabbing my cap and yanking it on, using one of the pins to hold it tight to my scalp. She places the dishes into the wash basin as I swing my jacket back on. "Would you like help before I go?"

"Of course not. Mother and I will take care of the dishes." She pats Mother's arm as if she would actually get a response, and I turn away before she sees me grimace.

Outside, I catch the door before it slams against the side of the house. The wind races by and through the trees with a rustling growl. Leaves skitter and scratch the cobblestone road in earnest, torn from their perches in the branches. Each lamppost on my path glows like a beacon in the night, mirroring the light of my own lantern. Yet somehow, the light makes the night feel even darker. I prop my ladder against each one and check the latch on the door to be sure it won't blow open. At this time of night, most people are safe indoors, finishing their meals or already tucked in bed, but I cannot take a chance. My concern is justified when I turn onto Silt Lane.

A lamppost is out.

My heart races with my feet as I hurry through the blurry void and find, to my surprise, the door is clearly shut. A quick inspection reveals nothing. All of the glass panes are intact, not a crack in sight. I don't understand how the light could have gone out. I unlatch the door, and it swings open easily. The wick is still there, plenty of whale oil left.

Strange.

A poorly shaped wick can affect the light, so perhaps that

was the cause. I pull Da's wick trimmer from my bag and use it, ensuring the wick's shape is just right for a brighter and cleaner burn. The material lights up without a hitch when I'm done, and I'm confident it will still be burning when I come to extinguish it in the morning.

Finished, I climb down the ladder and continue on my path. Despite the wind, the surrounding area proves as uninteresting as usual. Nothing amiss.

But the next lamppost before the Green is lifeless too.

Just like with the other, there is no hint or suggestion of what might have extinguished the light. Nothing appears to be tampered with or broken. The wick too appears normal, though I want to blame it, same as the other. Unease crawls over my skin like a tide creeping up the shore. I know I lit them both. I lit this side of the Green prior to running into Molly and Susannah, so it wasn't as if I had been distracted. I glance over my shoulder and try to peer through the fog, see something that isn't there.

I don't know what I'm looking for.

The tree branches sway violently in the wind, sounding like the roar of a waterfall. They dip in and out of my pocket of light, picking at my imagination. The memory of the scream I heard earlier surfaces, and I grip the lamppost neck tighter. Could the scream have been real? Movement out of the corner of my eye, low to the ground, makes me suck in a breath. I'm not alone. Whoever it is creeps just outside the cusp of my line of sight. I swallow my heart down and lift my lantern. Two silver eyes glow back at me.

A raccoon.

I take three deep breaths and force my shoulders to drop. Getting worked up over nothing isn't healthy. Relighting the lamppost and getting out of this ambiguity is a priority. I trim the wick of this lantern as well, and hurriedly light it. There are people counting on me. Granted, most of them are likely inebriated, if the shouting and cheering pushing through the fog has any say about it, but they'll be grateful as they stumble either home or back to the inn from the tavern.

Don't lose yourself in the fog, Tempe.

My heart pounds as I continue down the stretch. I hold my breath when I take the turn. A small flame flickers in the lamppost at the beginning of the business district. I release my breath and with it the tension in my chest. Only two lampposts were out, which is certainly concerning, but not terrible. The wind must have had a hand in it.

No reason to draw anyone else's attention to it. That's just asking for unnecessary trouble. Henry did not have my back during the confrontation with Leonard, so I cannot expect him to do so here. Best I handle it myself.

As expected, the tavern is just as lively as if not more so than earlier. One man loses his cap to the wind and goes stumbling down the street after it while his mates laugh raucously. The lamppost appears untouched by the wind, however, and I'm of half a mind to bypass it and the drunken revelry taking place near its base entirely. Except it would bother me and sleep would escape me if I did.

With a quick scan of the area, it's clear Leonard is absent. Reassured, I check the lamppost and am on my way down the street with no one the wiser. The rest of the lampposts along the business district glow in the night, great eyes watching me move about. Not a single light out and good thing because the wind is stirring up the river like a witch her cauldron. Water smacks up against the wharf, and the shadows of the ships look like dancing giants. If anyone fell in, they wouldn't get back out.

After I turn off the wharf, Gideon's workshop awaits me. The door is cast wide, a cave of light in the dark, aiding not only the reach of the luminous lamppost but also my disappointment.

He's home.

A wooden sign hangs above the entrance, creaking as

it sways. Warbler Wood Shop. Each black letter is its own carved piece of wood attached to the white sign. The *R* at the end of *Warbler* had come off at some point and never been replaced, so now it reads as "Warble."

The sound of rhythmic scraping grows with each step as my path takes me closer to the building. In my head, I see the scraping plane sliding along wood. Slowly, hands emerge, gripping the handle of the tool, with long fingers sporting calluses, nails short. The forearms are next, corded with muscle, blue veins pulsing beneath pale skin. They disappear into a fine cotton shirt, the sleeves rolled up to the elbows.

At the lamppost, I prop my ladder as quietly as possible. But my bag slips off my shoulder. I wince as it clatters onto the cobblestones. The woodshop goes quiet. I climb the ladder rungs with the hairs rising on the back of my neck.

A resounding silence crawls inside me with my breath and settles like a festering sickness. Goose bumps spread up my arms within my jacket. I don't need to look behind me. I know he is there, watching. Expressionless blue eyes wrapping me up and assessing every inch.

The lamppost flame burns bright, its door secure. I climb down, situate my ladder, bag, and lantern, and hasten away, feigning ignorance of his presence. But curiosity has me glancing over my shoulder as I make my way up the street. My breath catches. Gideon stands in the workshop doorway, a laceration in the warm light. His soft voice manages its way across the yard like a whisper in my ear. "Pleasant night, Temperance."

My lips turn up in acknowledgment, but there is no substance to it.

Before the fog consumes the workshop, I can just make out the prone form on Gideon's worktable. A frightened thought races through me before reason catches up. Bathed in lantern light, the wooden figurehead lies like a body set out for a wake with Gideon its dark sentinel. I shake my head. This strange evening is fraying my sensibility.

Thankfully, I finish checking the rest of the lampposts without incident, and a gentle breeze is all that remains of the wind by the time I reach Da's lamppost. It appears as unaffected as most of the others. After I check the door, I step off the ladder with a sigh. Da would have known why the lights went out and what to do to ensure it didn't happen again. There's a sudden ache behind my eyes, and I pinch the bridge of my nose.

At least no one need know about them. And only I was here to see them out.

A quiet creaking skulks just above me. Experience tells me to just ignore it, but of course I look up anyway. A rope is tied just under the lantern cage, the iron arms supporting it. It continues to creak as Da's body sways. His eyes watch me, bloodred. Spittle rolls down his chin as he rasps something I cannot hear. His arms and feet spasm, boots clacking against each other.

As I clench my eyes closed, a whimper spills out of me. My body shudders, and I mutter, "Stop it, Tempe. Stop it now."

The mantra repeats in my head, over and over, as his clacking boots grow quieter and quieter until all is silence once again. I peer under my eyelids at the apparition, but there's only the lamppost.

I take a deep, shaky breath and release it while my eyes flit over the small glowing space. The church says suicides go to Hell. I don't know exactly what I believe, but out here my imagination easily takes over. I haven't told Pru about the waking nightmares I have had since the day I saw Da's body.

Perhaps he is being punished for his actions. Doomed to hang from the lamppost for all eternity on some ethereal plane. I suppose whatever I choose to believe, Heaven or

Hell, Da *is* watching me. I cannot say there is always comfort in that. Especially when the goose bumps spreading up my arms tell me there is someone else watching me right now.

My fear waits just this side of the wall of fog like prey listening for a predator. "Who's out there?"

I lift my lantern, wait for a response.

The shushing of the leaves ceases as thick tendrils of fog continue to reach out from among the trees.

For once I find myself entertaining the superstitions of old seafarers. Perhaps there *is* an entity in the fog. Some otherworldly creature or malevolent spirit biding its time before snatching up unexpecting victims. Without a body, how are we ever to truly know what happens to Warbler's missing? Ghosts don't make any noise, do they?

I whip around and hasten down the street, heart galloping in my chest. They're still there. Whoever or whatever watches. Not a racoon this time. I know it. But through the rasp of my breath, I hear no signs of a pursuit.

It doesn't stop me from locking the front door when I arrive home.

CHAPTER 3

As I turn to the open room, the warmth of the fire envelops me completely, chasing not only the chill away but also my fears. Being home with Pru is the only place I feel truly safe. She catches my eye from her chair, where she is darning my socks. I ask her to leave it until morning, but she waves me off.

For a brief moment I'm nine years old again and Mother is laughing over her embroidery as she shoos me to go play because I'm standing in her light. But the memory is gone just as quickly as it appeared, and I head to our room, passing by Mother in her rocker. The repetitive creaking grates my nerves.

I splash water from the basin on my face and wash my hands with a small wedge of lavender soap. Pru makes it special for me. So long as I scrub hard, it does a decent job of masking the fishy oil odor. After that's done, I wet a small cloth and scrub it over my teeth. We're out of charcoal. I'll have to grab some from the general store this week. Once I've stripped out of my clothes and into my shift, I undo my coronet braid, copper strands falling down to my navel. I glide my fingers through my tresses and onto my head with a groan. There's something entirely soothing about rubbing the tension out of your scalp.

The bed creaks beneath my weight. The end of a goose feather pricks my cheek. I pluck it from the pillow, roll the soft down between my finger and thumb. On the other side of the wall is Pru's gentle tone as she talks to Mother. The rhythm of the rocking chair remains a constant.

I'm not sure how Pru is able to act so normal around her. As if having a mother who doesn't participate is a natural occurrence in a family. Nothing tarnishes Pru's sweet nature and optimism. Or at least, she is a master at hiding any dark thoughts. The very contemplation of Pru concealing her feelings puts a sour taste in my mouth. I never want Pru to feel like she should hide anything from me.

Will she continue to be open with me once she's married?

At the thought of her marrying and getting to start her life—forgetting about me?—I cannot deny the envy sitting on my shoulders. She has the opportunity to become an adult woman without worrying about the care of anyone else.

Leaving Mother to me.

As the eldest, it's only fair. I would never push Mother on Pru and her new life. Her future husband—I'd better get used to saying it, I suppose, but it's like hearing some of the whalers speak from other countries: foreign—won't want to take on Mother, and who could blame him? Pru's helped out enough as it is, and I don't want anything ruining her chances with her new suitor. If there is one lesson I've learned, it's that you can't count on others to stick around when life becomes difficult. You can only count on yourself.

Josiah knows Mother is nonnegotiable. Could she be the reason he hasn't asked me to marry him yet? Or perhaps it is both her *and* Pru. Coopers make a comfortable living in their trade, and with my extra income, we should be able to take on any hardships. Now that Pru will be taken care of, perhaps that will incite him to start our life together. I know it encourages me.

I'm thinking too far ahead and must rein in my hope. Tuck it away to safety. Josiah isn't home yet. Warbler is a whaling seaport, and he's on a whaling ship. All of us know how treacherous whaling can be. How easily people can lose their lives.

I remind myself to take a deep breath.

The room blurs as Pru's muffled voice soaks through the wall and into my thoughts. My pulse continues in my ears, as does the gentle rustle of the sheets over my shifting feet. The darkness is warm, a deep embrace pulling me down, down, down. Sore and tired muscles relax as the mattress swallows me up.

A deep red saturates the dark. The soothing black of closed eyes is gone. Something is wrong. I open my eyes. A roar fills my ears. I'm sitting in one of our kitchen chairs. But I'm not in the house. A frenzied wind rips at my hair, my shift. I'm frozen in place, my hands folded in my lap. I can't move. It's nighttime, but the river is aglow in the darkness. I can only watch as confusion courses through me and my face begins to burn beneath the heat.

Ivory River is on fire.

Raging wind blows over its surface, stirring up the flames. The river groans a deep and hoarse sound as the flames part like torn flesh and a dark mass pours out. A ship. A ship is coming through. I try to scream at it to stop. Warn someone it is going to catch fire. But my jaw is locked.

Still the ship comes, no signs of slowing down. Straight for me. Smoke curls up its hull, sliding over the figurehead like a caress. The figurehead's mouth is open impossibly large. So large she could swallow me up. She continues to come my way. Growing in size. The fire crawls up the shoreline with her. I cannot move. It's louder. The flames snarl; the hull growls as it rushes up onto the rocky shore, wood scraping and splintering. And the figurehead closing in. She is so close I can see her eyes. They blink.

She's screaming.

I'm screaming.

"Tempe!"

A jolt like lightning rushes through me. My eyes flutter, and the black is now a soft blue. Pru stands beside me, a ghost in her white shift, the soft light from the window reflected in her large eyes. My shoulder hurts. She's squeezing it.

"What . . . what is it?" I sit up, leaning back on the headboard of my bed. The small hairs and curls at my temple are wet with sweat. The image of the screaming figurehead is gone. The angry red of fire drowned in the quiet blue of early morning.

Pru wraps her arms around herself and bites her lower lip. "You were having a nightmare."

Laughter dies before reaching my lips. A nightmare.

Such a simple word for something so terrible.

My heart belatedly accepts the fact, its rhythm of terror stumbling back into normal pace. I smack my tongue around my dry mouth. Water trickles as Pru pours a glass for me out of the pitcher. The cool glass in my hand grounds me even further as I wet my thirst. I feel Pru's gaze on me still and plaster a smile on my face for her benefit. "I'm all right now. Truly. Go back to sleep. Looks like I need to get up anyway."

She nods and patters back to her bed, crawling into the sheets. She opens her mouth as if to say something, but instead closes it, shaking her head so subtly I wonder if she even realizes she did it. I tuck her blue quilt over her, a wave of tranquility, and she closes her eyes. In only moments her breath evens out.

Dawn burns away the fog. Only an afterthought of it remains as I begin my morning shift, extinguishing each lamppost, refilling the tanks with the whale oil from my cannister, replacing wicks as needed. The air is damp and chilly, removing any dregs of sleep from my body.

With a tilt of their heads, fishermen and crabbers pass

me by while I'm on my ladder. Poles and nets flung over their shoulders, beards warming their faces as they head to the river. We are the early risers, the greeters of the new day. All doing our part to preserve and complete life in Warbler. As I climb down, a flash of red flits past me. A cardinal. The bird's dominant trill is returned by another deep in the trees. Most of the birds have already begun to migrate for the winter, but the cardinals are present year-round.

Morning is my favorite time of day. The claustrophobia of night evaporates, leaving so many possibilities. Breathing comes easier, and a sense of freedom and choice pervades the senses. Like a single tree in the forest, the idea that you are only one small part of something great is comforting.

We all have our part to play in this life.

In Ireland, Great-Grandad was the first lamplighter in our family. He passed the position down to his son, who then taught Da the trade. When Grandad died, Da left Dublin for America in search of a new home. Warbler didn't have a lamplighter, simply relying on volunteers. Da convinced the council to hire him for a trial period. Sure enough, after seeing the benefit of a dependable employee who knew what they were doing, the council made the position permanent. Warbler didn't pay as much as the big cities, but no one else was in need and Da refused to do anything else. He took pride in providing light and guidance for others. It was a family legacy he cherished.

Now it is mine to preserve.

The sharp blue and pink of sunrise softens into a peach glow as I continue to work on the lampposts. Households are awakening as smoke floats lazily out of chimneys. Feed is placed for animals, the farming families already deep into their chores when I dampen their lights.

My breath billows ahead of me, but I already feel warm enough to loosen my scarf. I tug at the scratchy fabric as I wind my way east through the residential district and head toward the lamppost just ahead of the Green. For a moment, it looks like the wick is out again and my heart skips a beat. But in the light of day, the glow is weak, and I realize all my worry is for naught.

With each lamppost, my oil canister grows lighter and more manageable, and by the time I reach the business district, Warbler is wide awake, humming with activity. Shouts echo from the docks as crabbers pull in their catches from their traps, the chime above the general store rings a greeting, children laugh as they run by to the schoolyard. Ruby, Josiah's dog, barks from the cooperage, and I pause to give her a good ear scratch. She must miss him as much as I do, if not more.

He raised her from a pup after finding her in a barn. Her mother had suffered a complication and died while giving birth, and Ruby was the only puppy delivered. Josiah retrieved milk from the cows and hand-nursed her until she was old enough to take water. Now, the yellow dog is nearly twelve years old. She didn't understand why Josiah left without taking her.

She stays in the cooperage while he is away on the *Miriam*, in a bed he made for her out of a barrel. Pru sewed a red cushion for her that we placed inside. My contribution was to pet her to within an inch of her life.

I think she liked my gift best.

"He'll be home soon, girl." I run my fingernails along her snout, scratching the silver hairs and grinning into her big brown eyes.

"Morning, Temperance." George looks up from his stool across the cooperage, croze tool in hand. The bucket he is cutting the groove into is propped in front of him. "She's ready for her father to be home."

"We all are."

"I can't deny it'll be great to have his help once more. I could use another cooper round here who knows what he's doing." George nods none-too-subtly over his shoulder to his new apprentice and two frowning boys in the back of the shop. "Say hello to Prudence and your mother for me."

I wave goodbye and shoo Ruby off as she tries to follow me, nails clicking on the wood walkway. On the wharf, the tavern is empty of customers but for one slumped-over form at the end of the boardwalk, head drooped over a bucket. Benjamin. The whalers would have returned to their ship, most likely to sleep off their carousing. One or two may have stayed at the inn, if they had the penny for it.

I douse the flame in the tavern's lamppost and am just finishing filling the oil well when a voice calls to me from behind. It's Henry, a pained smile on his face.

Odd. Lamppost closed up, I climb down, careful not to misstep. "I feel like we've been here before."

"Temperance, I wish that were so. I'll take a drunken whaler over a missing girl any day."

The smile slips from my lips. "Missing girl?"

He rubs a hand over his face, highlighting the exhaustion of a difficult night shift. "Mr. Fairchild reported it late last night. His daughter never came home."

"Molly? Molly Fairchild is missing?" A weight drops into my stomach, and I have to take a deep breath. God, Molly's poor family. "But I saw her yesterday. She was fine."

"When was that?" He pulls out his book and looks up at me, eyes refocused.

"I ran into her and Susannah Culver in the Green. Just before six. I was lighting the lamppost." Molly's welcoming smile flashes before me, the basket of lace and silk ribbons in her small hands.

Henry makes a quick mark and nods. I cross my arms and step closer to him; I'm not sure why. Perhaps it's that in moments of concern, there is comfort in the presence of another. "Have you spoken to Susannah?"

"Yes, she said they parted ways at her house right after

seeing you in the Green. Molly forgot her gloves at the seamstress's and mentioned possibly returning there to retrieve them. She never made it, though. Did you notice anything strange last night? Out of place? Susannah mentioned a drunk man in the Green."

Of course, she wouldn't know his name. I nod toward the still slumped-over form. "Benjamin. He was asleep at the time."

Henry scratches notes onto the paper. I know he's going to talk to Benjamin nonetheless. Good.

"Well, if you think of anything, please let me know. Or Matthew. He's going to be on shift soon." Tipping his head toward me, Henry begins to turn around, reminding me of last night.

"Have you looked into those new whalers? The one who assaulted me? Leonard?" I feel the ghost of a hand on my buttock and wince. The thought of Leonard laying a hand on Molly sets a raging fire in my blood.

But Henry is already shaking his head. "Leonard was taken onto his ship not long after your confrontation. The ship's captain confirmed his whereabouts."

I frown, mind racing. "*Not long after?* That could mean anything."

"He was three sheets to the wind last night. I truly doubt he was involved. But I promise to look closer into it."

The whaler didn't appear completely inebriated to me. I still feel the intensity of his stare, the violence in his eyes as I left. I wouldn't put it past him to retaliate if he could . . .

It hits me so quickly my breath catches in my lungs. The scream in the fog. I thought it had been in my head. But maybe it wasn't. Oh God, had it been Molly? What if Leonard went looking for me and found Molly instead? And then there was the feeling I was being followed.

Henry frowns and takes a step closer to me. "Temperance?"

I swallow and mentally kick myself. "I heard a scream last night."

Henry flinches. "A scream?"

"Yes."

All concern for my welfare leaches from his face, replaced by a curt professionalism. "When? Where?"

"I was at Da's—the northwest lamppost. The last stop on my shift. I thought it came from the east, but you know how easily the fog carries and disguises distance and location. I ran back along the street to the other two lampposts but didn't see or hear anything else. No one stepped outside of their home when it sounded. I thought maybe I imagined it. Or maybe the fog was playing tricks on me."

"You should have reported it, Temperance." Henry shakes his head, scribbling in his notes. "You know better."

I deserve the bite in his tone. "I apologize. I wasn't thinking."

"Well, this changes things." He frowns and runs his hand over his face once more, palm scratching the whiskers on his chin.

"Please look into Leonard again, Henry. He would have struck me if you hadn't arrived when you did. What if he went looking for me and found her instead?"

"I'll look into it. But like I said, the captain corroborated his alibi."

"But—"

"Until we find Molly," he interjects, "please be careful. Best be on your way unless you can think of anything else."

My eyes widen as words threaten to spill from my lips.

Henry lifts an eyebrow. "Yes?"

I should tell him about the lampposts being out, but self-preservation halts my tongue. The scream suggests she isn't missing on account of being lost in the fog, because it came before the lampposts went out. The windstorm didn't occur until much later. Besides, the scream came from a completely different direction. If I allow Henry to believe Molly got lost because of my lampposts, my livelihood would be threatened.

If I lost my job, Pru and Mother would be destitute. I do not have the skill set for another occupation. Warbler is a small whaling seaport. There isn't exactly an abundance of positions to be filled. Besides, I don't want to do anything else. The position of lamplighter has been held by my family for generations. It's in my blood.

It doesn't change the fact that I'm a woman, however. I had a difficult enough time convincing the council to let me take on Da's job at fourteen, and now this? I won't receive the clemency given to Da when people went missing under his watch. It's why I chose to not report the extinguished lamps in the first place. If I had any proof or assurance something was truly amiss, of course I would have.

But now one of Warbler's own has disappeared. Molly.

"Something on your mind?" Henry's eyes search my own, and I realize too much time has passed.

"I'm sorry. I just—" I can't say anything. Not yet. Only when I know for sure it's necessary. "I had just seen her. It's difficult to conceive how she could be missing all of a sudden."

Henry's eyes narrow ever so slightly, but he nods. "Yes, well . . ." He clears his throat and steps back. "Rest assured we will find her."

He may say the words out loud, but we both know he cannot guarantee it. Such optimism does not exist in Warbler. No one missing has ever been found alive.

I pick up the ladder and oil cannister and smile at the constable. It's more of a grimace, though. Survival has stayed my hand. I would never keep away details from an investigation if I knew they would help. But at this point, telling Henry about the lampposts will do more harm than good. It might send him on a wild goose chase when it sounds like there is actually something or someone more menacing than an extinguished lamppost.

Out of the corner of my eye, I see Henry's gaze follow me as I continue down the wharf. There are people all around, calls of fresh fish, mallets hammering from the shipyard, the creak of the docks shifting with the current, the dong of the church bell, the splash of nets. All reassuring sounds of life in Warbler Seaport, like on every other day.

Except that not everyone woke up to enjoy it.

I wince and shake my head. No, do not assume the worst yet. To dwell on such dark assumptions may give life to them. And yet, in my heart, I feel like we may never see Molly again. The worst that can happen often does. If we prepare ourselves for it, it is a kindness to our spirit should it occur.

Upon reentering the residential district, it is clear word has spread. Neighbors speak to each other over picket fencing, swapping theories and offering pained expressions of sympathy in the direction of the Fairchild household. Through the broken bits and pieces of conversation I hear as I pass by, it becomes apparent Mr. Fairchild has set out with Molly's older brother and volunteers to check the woods and creek running through Warbler.

Please, God, don't let them find her body in the river. The image will be carved into every waking moment of their lives like a love note from Death himself on the bark of a tree, a scar never to heal. No amount of time can make it go away. And the loss would reflect on their faces for anyone and everyone to see. They would forever be associated with the tragedy of their lost loved one.

There's an ache in my stomach, and I press my fingers into it. The morning light brings everything into sharp focus. The crisp lines of the autumn leaves losing their grip on the branches, the dusting of frost on the grass and windows. The pale grays and blues of villagers' cloaks and clothing pop in this rust-colored, brown world. The lampposts are dark skeletons piercing the horizon.

Concern travels down the streets and up the walkways, intent on making its presence known. Superstitious utterances sneak up like roots through dirt. It is no surprise and something I am far too familiar with as I extinguish the last lamppost, Da's, recalling the whispers that trailed me as Henry led me to his body.

"They made him do it, aye. The spirits."

"Shadowed his footsteps they did."

". . . couldn't take it no more."

Before leaving, I lay my hand against the neck of the lamppost. Frost melts beneath my warm skin, and I feel no ill will in the air. No fear. The brutal memory of Da isn't as easily retrieved in the light of day. It's just an old lamppost.

Only, now I hear Molly's scream. Last night I couldn't decipher who it was. Today I hear her terror. Her helplessness.

You heard her after you lit the lampposts, Tempe. This isn't on you. My reassurances don't tamp down the guilt. Because involved or not, as lamplighter I serve as a sort of watchman. I didn't report the scream and I have kept information from Henry.

My stomach twists. I need to go home. Eat something. Regroup and see what I can do to help the Fairchilds.

First, however, I return my equipment to the shed beside the town hall. If for whatever reason I do not ring the bell in the evening to start my shift, Henry can retrieve everything to light the lampposts for me. The only thing I keep at home is a single oil cannister, which I refill from the reserves in the shed each morning after my shift. That way, every morning, I can begin dousing the lights and refilling the wells on the lampposts starting on my street. Whale oil is an expensive commodity, so part of my contract is to extinguish the lights as soon as safely possible each morning.

With everything in its place, I return home with the

refilled cannister, the warmth of the morning sun a welcome companion. The gate is open when I reach our fence, the pathway up to the door swept of all leaves. The green of the lettuce and green onions catches my eye in the front garden. While the lettuce won't last, the onions will. Every little bit helps.

Once inside, my shoulders sag from the weight of the morning. It's not yet eight, and I'm already exhausted. I need warm food in my belly. To see Pru's smile. This small haven is a safe place for me. "Pru, I've some terrible news."

After setting the cannister down, I pull off my boots and look up into the warm room, where Mother is already at the table with her tea and Pru is beaming in front of the fire, working her magic over whatever new bread recipe she's trying out.

Except there is someone else standing in front of the fire beside her.

Gideon.

The ship carver's hands are clasped behind his back, hat dangling loosely from his fingertips. He turns toward me as Pru stops midsentence. His blue eyes pierce into me, stripping me of my clothes, skin, muscle, blood, and bones until I'm not even here anymore. Like the whales hunted in the ocean and dragged onto the boats. Carved and used up.

Stay away from Gideon.

A predator is in our home.

I swallow down the knot of fear, only taking my eyes away from him when Pru appears suddenly beside me, squeezing my hands, hope and thrill lighting up her smooth face. "Can you believe it, Tempe? Gideon is my secret admirer."

CHAPTER 4

A cannonball has hit my chest. I inhale sharply, releasing the pressure.

My heart continues to beat, blood courses through my veins, my stomach growls for food. My eyes take in the shadows and light of the room, ears listen to the crackling flames and creaking of the house. Everything is doing what it is meant to do, and yet it all feels slightly off. Like an embroidered picture just off center in the hoop. Gideon isn't supposed to be here. There should be a young man standing here, cheeks flushed with nerves. Or one of the shipbuilders, hands calloused from hard work. A crabber even, the smell of fish stuck to his skin.

Gideon's decision to remain nameless this summer makes sense now. The snake.

His dark hair is pulled back by a leather strip, but a loose strand has fallen on each side of his thin face, accentuating his goatee and mustache. He dips his head toward me. "Temperance. An absolute pleasure, as usual."

His voice is quiet and calm, the measured cadence never faltering. While his tone is low, he speaks clearly, each word enunciated and given the special thought and care one gives a pet. There could be a lively debate occurring in the town hall, impassioned and angry people shouting over each other, throwing words like harpoons. But the moment Gideon spoke, the entire room would go quiet, pulled toward him like swimmers in a riptide. Gideon knows how to command an audience.

And two years ago, that included a young woman still grieving the loss of her da and the security she once knew. I swallow back both bile and memory.

Breathe, Tempe.

This is my home. My safe place. He is in my territory, under my roof. The roof Da and Mother helped build with their own hands. Pru is the one person who means most to me in the world. I will protect her with everything I have. He has no power here if I do not allow it.

I lift my head high and cross my arms. "You've been the one writing my sister?"

He nods.

Pru's frown feels like a hot brand as she squeezes my arm. "How about we all sit down and have a cup of tea? Please, Tempe."

I head to the table but refuse to take my eyes off Gideon. His movements are slow. Deliberate. He places his hat on the mantel, fingertips pausing on the red cedar. It's worn down and damaged, a discarded piece from the lumberyard my parents could afford. We have a likeness of Da propped on it, a shillelagh, and the dried-out flowers Da gave Mother on their wedding day. It isn't anything like the fine mantels Gideon carves for the more affluent families. Yet there is appreciation in his perusal. A quiet contemplation.

He turns from the mantel, eyes flitting between Pru and myself. Only after Pru clears her throat do I realize he's waiting for us to sit. I do so, perching on the edge of my chair while Pru pours tea from the kettle into our best china set, refilling Mother's cup. She gives herself the chipped cup. Gideon watches every move she makes, his chest barely rising with his breath. He only sits once Pru has seated herself.

"I'm sorry, we don't have any sugar." Pru reddens, gaze dropping to the table as her fingers grip her cup.

My stomach twists at her unfamiliar shame.

"That is quite all right. I do not take sugar." His smile is quiet and unassuming, and instantly Pru brightens.

I take a sip of my tea, not tasting it, despising every second of this performance. I want him out of our house, but as he is a guest invited into our home, I am required to offer up a modicum of civility. It's the proper thing to do, after all. Just because our budget doesn't allow for sugar this week does not mean we are without manners.

Why am I defending myself? I curl my hands around my cup, allowing the heat to steadily climb and burn my palms. Ground me.

Why did Pru's secret admirer have to be him?

"How is your new commission progressing?" Pru's voice pulls me out of myself. I set my cup down. I am, in fact, interested in his answer. Whether Henry thinks Leonard and his shipmates had anything to do with Molly's disappearance or not, the sooner they are gone, the better.

"Very well. It should be finished and attached by the Gathering."

Pru's eyes widen. "So soon. Can you tell us what it is? It was a special commission, correct?"

Gideon places his tea back on the saucer, the delicate *tink* of his cup absurdly loud to my ears. Mother flinches. Pru doesn't see because she has eyes only for Gideon, who responds about a special bough he removed from his grove and molded into a captivating siren, his usual when it comes to commissions. Soon the conversation drifts to the other pieces he is working on. A sign for the shipping office, spindles for the mayor's staircase, and a new figurehead: a mermaid with swirling hair.

I'm only listening with half an ear, my attention on Mother. Her gaze is on Gideon. Not only that, but she is actually *looking* at him. She's processing his movements, taking in his words. She is completely present.

It's been four years since she's looked at anyone with any sort of interest. My heartbeat pulses loudly in my ears.

"A beautiful mermaid out to sea, fighting the waves and storms to find her love." Pru sighs. "It's all so incredibly romantic. Isn't that right, Tempe?"

Pru nudges my foot beneath the table, requiring me to drag my gaze from Mother. I retrace the conversation, catch up to the topic at hand. "I believe a mermaid figurehead to be sad."

Pru frowns. "Whyever so?"

Gideon's gaze is on me, unblinking, his expression neutral. I take a sip of my bitter tea to stall while I attempt to calm the electricity suddenly coursing through me at Mother's unexpected engagement. "You've created a mystical, beautiful creature, yes, but she will spend her life forever trapped above the water. Every day she will watch the sea go by, feel the spray hit her face, but she'll never be where she wants to be. She's being used."

I swear Gideon's pupils change shape. Sending tiny dark chutes from it like broken blood vessels. But when I blink, they're the same as always. Piercing and unmoved.

"I suppose I didn't think of it like that." Pru grimaces, gazing back at Gideon. "I like my version more."

"As do I." Gideon looks away from me and inclines his head with a sweet smile. The same smile he gave me two years ago as he slid his fingers through my hair while my body screamed at me to run and Da's warning whispered in my ears.

I cannot maintain this calm farce any longer. A spider nest could burst at my feet, thousands of baby spiders crawling beneath my clothes and over my skin, and I would be more at ease than this moment. My cup clatters against the saucer. "May we get on with this? It's been a trying morning."

"Tempe!" Pru scolds.

I can only shake my head. "Molly Fairchild is missing. She never came home last night."

The irritation falls from Pru's face as she leans back in her chair. "Oh no. How terrible. Do they have any thoughts on what might have happened?"

Gideon's eyes widen, and the corner of his mouth lifts ever so slightly. "Was a lamppost out?"

The air leaves my lungs.

It is the same look he gave me the day after Josiah and I broke into his workshop as children. Josiah wanted to look at the figureheads hanging on the walls. He appreciated the woodwork and gushed about the skill Gideon had to create such expression in wood. At the time, Josiah was George's apprentice, and his life revolved around wood. I was more concerned with being caught and placed myself near the door as lookout. It was strange seeing such realistic creatures and people be so still. For a moment I forgot they were made of wood. The silence of so many immobile eyes raised the hairs on the back of my neck. I was certain any minute the figureheads would climb off their perches and chase after me.

When I encountered Gideon outside the general store the next day, I worried that just by looking at me, he would know I'd snuck into the workshop. Gideon never said anything, but there was something about his expression when our eyes met.

Like now.

My heart gallops in my chest and sweat gathers beneath my arms. It's a reasonable enough question for Gideon to ask. Yet out of his mouth, it doesn't feel like a question.

"Henry and Matthew are working on it." I choose to ignore him entirely and shift my eyes back to Pru. To safety. "Her father is gathering volunteers to look for her now."

Gideon's chair scrapes the floor as he pushes it back

and stands up. Pru and I follow suit. "Perhaps it's best I go and see if they can use another volunteer. Check the grove. This isn't quite the way I saw this morning going. Under the circumstances, would it be all right if we continue this at another time?"

"That won't be necessary." The response slips out of my mouth before I can stop it. I bite my lip almost immediately. *Don't back down. Don't back down.*

Three sets of eyes look at me while the fire continues to crackle. Mother is still present. I clear my throat, willing away the wobble in my voice, somehow managing to make eye contact with Gideon. "You cannot marry Prudence. I do not give my permission."

Gideon traces his thumb along his jaw. Beside him, Mother drops her gaze.

"Tempe! How can you be so unreasonable?" Pru hurries toward me, grabbing my hands. The corner of Gideon's mouth lifts up, but he turns away before I can be certain I saw it.

"Ouch!" Pru's nails dig into my palms. I don't think she even realizes she's hurting me.

"This isn't like you, Tempe. You cannot make this decision so lightly. It's only right you at least mull things over."

Gideon retrieves his hat from the mantel, then walks over to us. He's shorter than Josiah, but it does nothing to take away from the intensity of his gaze and the sharp lines of his cheekbones, the perfect shave of his facial hair. "I respect the concern and wariness you possess, watching over your family. It's an admirable trait. I ask only that you think on it a little more before making your decision. Certainly, with emotions high under the current circumstances, you can see how a rash decision shouldn't be reached."

The gall! I manage to bite my tongue should I say anything, in fact, *rash*.

"I will wait until the Gathering before asking again." He glances at Pru, giving a supportive smile I want to rip off his face. "But know for you, my dear Prudence, I will wait as long as I need to. And I'm good at waiting."

He nods his head at the three of us separately, a rock falling into the pit of my stomach when he looks at me, and then Pru walks him out. I watch through the window with the intensity of the village busybody and suddenly feel so old and disgusting I turn away, clenching my eyes closed. My jacket is too tight, heat climbing up my neck, head pounding. I yank it off and throw it over a chair. I fan air onto my face, bracing for the hurricane that will be Pru.

As she steps back inside, however, she doesn't utter a word. She doesn't even glance my way, blatantly ignoring me as she makes a wide berth around my person. Our bedroom door shuts behind her with a gentle click.

Her silence is so much worse than her anger.

Mother, still at the table, picks up her cup. She takes a sip and sets it back down before turning to glance at the fire. The flames have died down since my arrival. I hurry over and feed them another piece of wood, watching as the bright orange of the embers changes ever so subtly, like the roll of the water in the river. Flames stoked up once more, I sit back down in my chair.

I glance at Mother as the fire reflects in her gray eyes. It isn't often I'm alone with her. Hope dares to peek out of the wooden chest I had tucked it into a long time ago. "Mother?"

I reach out and squeeze her arm. Maybe she will look at me. Alert. Present. "Mother?"

She turns in her chair, and my breath catches. Her eyes are watching something behind my head, completely disregarding me in front of her. I don't know what happened to her earlier. What woke her up. Whatever it was, it's gone now. And so is the hope of a marriage for Pru and for me and Josiah. At least anytime soon. I refuse to cry and instead ball up my fists.

The ocean will dry up before I allow Gideon to marry Pru.

I make quick work of cleaning the tea set and pace in front of the fire while I wait for Pru to emerge. Knocking on the door does nothing, and no amount of pleading will pull her out. Mother has moved to her rocker, the floor creaking with each backward and forward motion. The fire crackles, the pendulum swings in the clock, and suddenly these minuscule sounds are too much. Emphasizing the intolerable quiet and missing presence of Pru and her warmth.

There is movement beyond the front curtains. People passing by on the street. I should help, if I can, with Molly. It's the least I can do. And as much as I wish to explain everything to her, Pru needs space right now. Someday she will understand. She must.

Molly's name is an echo across the seaport. Every person I pass moves at a sedate pace, their eyes alert, hoping to see any sign of the missing young woman. Our elderly minister offers a prayer to an assembly of volunteers before breaking them into two groups. One to search the fields south of town, the trees gutted over forty years ago to establish Warbler and fill the lumber mill. Their search shouldn't take long. The other group is to investigate the woods to the northwest, a more arduous challenge.

The minister leans heavily on a walking stick made of twisted apple bough, a wood Josiah is fond of using on account of its hardiness. Down the street, a fisherman makes the sign of the cross after someone calls Molly's name. A prayer, maybe. More likely a shield against any spirits he presumes at fault.

Whatever the case may be, someone is to blame. But not me. And not my lampposts.

I wince. The ugliness of my thoughts, no matter how justified, is shameful. Molly is missing, and here I am excusing myself.

As I walk the business district, my eyes are drawn to the whalers retrieving supplies for their upcoming journey. Like minnows in the water, they move to and fro, preparing for success and survival in the precarious Atlantic and beyond. If any of them had hurt Molly, would it be noticeable, like items of clothing announcing one's profession? Would he move a little bit different from the others? Slow with regret? Antsy with the fear of being caught? Would he be unable to meet anyone's eye?

The clunk of a mallet draws my attention, and I head over to the cooperage. George is working on what looks like a quarter cask, most likely for whiskey. He is situating the wooden staves perfectly, enabling the withies to hold them together. Josiah used to talk me through his projects when we were younger. Unlike others, I have a familiar eye for what takes place in the cooperage. The smell of fresh wood shavings feels like coming home.

I clear my throat in the doorway. "George?"

The older man looks over his shoulder and smiles as Ruby opens her eyes, emitting a protective huff before realizing it's me. She pulls herself to her feet and trots over.

"May I borrow Ruby? I just thought what with everything going on in the village, maybe she can help out with the search?"

The sun spots on George's forehead are swallowed in his frown. "Aye, I heard. Terrible. Well, I don't know how helpful the old girl will be, but couldn't hurt."

I slap my thigh and Ruby follows me out, wearing the only smile to be found in Warbler.

In the late afternoon, the white oak trees are lit up like flames. Their red leaves glow, like splashes of blood under light. The off-orange and rust of the beech trees break up the intensity, while other trees have already dropped their lackluster leaves. At most, we have one week left of the stunning colors, before it all fades into disregard and every living being prepares for the harsh winter.

It's impossible to move quietly in the underbrush, the leaves forming a crunchy rug. Ruby's tail is high and wagging as she follows her nose, nudging the detritus of the forest as she finds interesting smells. There are enough shouts of Molly's name beneath the trees that I find no need to add my voice. Instead, I listen. To the whispering leaves, crunching footsteps, worried voices, the rustling of forest animals looking for safety, the snuffling of Ruby.

There are so many sounds it's hard to pinpoint them all. Something can be so easily missed. A whimper, a gasp.

Ruby stops, her tail going still. I pause, following her lead, but I cannot see anything through the brush beyond a giant white oak, its color darkening. "What is it, girl?"

I take a step toward Ruby, heart pounding. She bolts, disappearing into the underbrush before I get a word out. Branches scratch at my cheeks as I give chase. They tear at my sleeves, my legs. Like arms reaching out to grab me, stop me from going farther. From seeing. "Ruby!"

I can barely hear her path through the racket of my pursuit. A branch tugs at my hair, catching in the ties. I slap at it, pushing forward to get through the thick foliage. Brittle leaves crumble beneath my hands and shatter beneath my boots.

The smell hits me first. A rancid cloud. I fall back a step as if the odor were an impenetrable wall. Ruby sniffs and snorts, excitement shaking her old legs as she circles her find. I reach forward and pull her back by her excess neck skin before disgust takes hold of me.

The fox's abdomen is split open, organs already eaten. It's hard to say whether a predator got to it or it died of some sickness and the woods have had their way.

The skin is sallow, skeleton pushing up against it. The once-brilliant fur is dull, the vibrancy long lost with life. White teeth gleam midsnarl. I wave my hand in front of my nose as a breeze nudges the fur on its tail, traveling over its rot and brushing against Ruby and me in macabre greeting.

"Molly! Where are you? Molly!" Echoes in the woods.

I tug at Ruby, trying to pull her back as she makes to roll over the carcass. "No, Ruby."

Before I turn away, something catches my eye. A sapling juts out of the center of the fox. Sprouting right out of its guts. The oddity of life blooming out of death gives me pause. I cannot say I've ever seen such a sight before. The state of decay suggests the fox died recently, but the sapling must be six months old.

The poor creature more than likely curled up at the sapling's base to die. It's just coincidence the fox deteriorated in such a way that it looks like . . . what?

Like the tree is eating it.

A shiver runs through my body that doesn't quite make it to my skin. I turn my back on the corpse, ignoring the creeping fingers up my spine, and pull a reluctant Ruby alongside me.

I mustn't allow myself to entertain absurd notions. I'm no superstitious whaler or elder villager with fantastical and violent tales of monsters living among us in Warbler. No. I'm the lamplighter. I'm here to bring light. To show the way.

The once-glowing woods are darkening; the earlier blue of the sky has been swallowed by cloud. It won't be long before the fog begins to crawl among the tree roots and start its nighttime stroll. It isn't safe to be out here anymore, and I have work to do. Molly's name trails Ruby and me as we make our way out of the woods and back into the village.

Footsteps crunch from my peripheral, behind me, in front of me. Ruby's tail is wagging once more, but her pace is more leisurely. Out of age or an awareness that she is going back to an empty home, I'm not sure. However, we all are returning, our footsteps a little slower, no one having won this day. I pick out Gideon's voice among the others, trailing from the private grove of trees he owns to the northeast.

No one is permitted entrance. Begging ignorance is impossible with the multiple signs that read *Private Property*. Years ago, Gideon managed to convince the council to preserve a substantial portion of Warbler's remaining woods, giving guardianship of nearly thirty acres to him. It wasn't a hard decision for them to make, recognizing the woods' value after the popularity of Gideon's commissions.

Unless we want other ship carvers to get their hands on Gideon's secrets and specialty wood, the grove will remain private, per the council's decree. Because Gideon always gets what he wants.

Now he wants Pru.

My bad mood sours further.

Men in power do not like hearing no, but I must stand my ground. Truth is, I'm not worried about Gideon, though. Not completely. The bigger battle is to be with Pru. It's the ones you love who can wound the deepest.

And in her eyes, I've struck first.

CHAPTER 5

Coming home should feel like loosening the stays of a corset.

Instead, it's as if I've tightened them. Letting down my guard, relaxing, is impossible. I hesitate before each move I make, each thing I say. Walking on a frozen pond couldn't be more stressful than walking into this unstable house.

I find Pru out of her room, resuming her daily activities. There is no welcome for me. The amount of energy and acknowledgment offered toward me is on par with Mother's contribution.

I want to scream.

That base instinct will get me nowhere. I'm the adult here and should act as such. "Pru? May we please speak about what happened this morning?"

She ignores me, sweeping her way through the sitting room. It's the room Da and Mother used to entertain guests. We've only a settee and side table left in here. If it weren't for the colorful quilts hung on the walls—sewn by Mother and her mother before her—it would be quite dreary indeed. The *swish swish* of the broom is somehow soothing and irritating at the same time. Pru's acting like a child, but there's no way I can say that. There would be a wooden door between the two of us quicker than a candle can be snuffed out.

"How about this." I drop down onto the settee and cross my ankles. A leaf crumbles from the bottom of one of my boots, small pieces falling to the wooden floor. There are leaves stuck to my trousers, unnoticed until now, and mud droplets near the hemline. Any other day, Pru would scold me for my carelessness. Today she gives me nothing.

I clasp my fingers together. “I’m going to speak, and I hope you give me the courtesy of listening. It is all I ask.”

She sniffs, but at least she’s still here. Her sweeping path brings her close, and she hits my boot with the broom stick, nudging me. I lift my feet as she cleans up my mess. So far so good.

“I’m sorry for spoiling everything for you. Truly. Believe me when I say I want nothing but your happiness above anything else in the world.”

Swish swish.

“But I cannot in good conscience say yes to a match with Gideon.”

“Why?” She spins around, clenching the broom handle with both hands, knuckles white.

“Because of Da.”

Pru takes a step back. I certainly have her attention now. The corners of her mouth turn down. “I don’t understand.”

I lean forward, perching my elbows on my knees, hands squeezing tightly together. I look up, and I’m inside my memory with Da. The cool shadow of the room is gone, replaced by the golden warmth of late afternoon. Beside me, Da is fidgeting with his hat. The wool keeps catching on the rough skin of his palms. The blond hairs on his fingers glint in the light with each fidget. He smells of oil and smoke, which for some wouldn’t be a pleasant combination, but to me is distinctly Da.

“I need you to promise me something, Tempe.” His voice is low, hesitant, like he’s second-guessing whether he should be saying anything at all.

Mother is outside with Pru, weeding the garden. I wish I was with them, feeling the dirt under my fingernails as I hunt for the potatoes we planted in the spring. The sweet, light smell of autumn clematis floats in through the open window. A delicate, white bloom peeks over the sill. Pru giggles, followed by Mother's contagious laugh.

Da clears his throat, pulling me back into the sitting room. There is a strangeness around Da, a nervous energy completely unlike him. "I want you to steer clear of Gideon."

"Gideon? The ship carver?" It isn't at all what I expected.

Da nods.

"Whyever so?" Gideon has always been nothing but kind to me. Just this morning, while I was out with Da, Gideon complimented me on my smile. Josiah never said such things, so it was nice to hear it from someone, even someone as old as Da.

Da jumps up to his feet. He briskly rubs a hand over his hair and pulls his cap back on. His usually jovial face is folded into deep lines more pronounced this year than ever. Some of the hair at his temples has begun to go gray. He turns and looks at me with unblinking, tired eyes. "Just listen to your da, all right? You stay away from Gideon."

"Those are strong words, Da." I laugh gently, hoping to put an end to his strange intensity.

"Promise me."

I would have said anything to soften his expression. "Of course. I promise."

"Tempe?"

I blink as Pru's voice pulls me back. The amber light of memory is swallowed in shades of evening.

She stands with Da's same intensity as I recount to her his urgent message to stay away from Gideon. When I finish, the understanding I hoped to receive is absent. Instead, Pru expels her frustrated expression with a laugh, shaking her head at me.

"Surely that cannot be the reason you're forbidding my union with Gideon. A promise to Da four years ago? He was more than likely being protective. Didn't want his daughter getting mixed up with any men before getting married. Not that Gideon would have done anything, I'm sure."

A different memory struggles against its restraints, and my chest tightens. I still feel Gideon's touch like a burn.

Pru chuckles as if this is all a misunderstanding on my part, and it takes everything in me not to get up and shake her. "It doesn't matter if it was four years ago, Pru. Da had his reasons, and I'm going to stand by them."

"He had his reasons for killing himself too. Do you stand by those as well?"

I inhale sharply. Pru winces and rushes over, but as her fingers squeeze my own, they could be sticks for all the comfort they provide. I want to pull away from her, bolt from the house, and run until there is no pain. Instead, I sit here, breathing and existing because it's all I know and there is nowhere to run to. I'm trapped.

"That was cruel of me to say, Tempe. I apologize."

I hear Da's noose creaking.

"I'm just . . . upset. I've the opportunity to start a life with Gideon, and you won't give me your blessing. You're not only my sister, but my best friend. And letting the warning of a protective father, without any substantial proof, stop me from being happy feels like a betrayal. What I feel for Gideon is no mere infatuation. Do you have so little faith in my judgment?"

I know before looking up at her she is crying. But no amount of her tears will move me. Hurt feelings have no place when safety is at stake. Experience and intuition are rattling me as fierce as the shutters did in the windstorm last night. Her tears are rain to my ocean.

"Pru." A knot tangles in my throat, and I swallow it down as my pulse begins to race. I understand her doubt. I do. I was warned of Gideon once, and I didn't listen either. She wants substantial proof. "Two years ago, Gideon and I—"

Her eyes widen, and I can see the pulse in her neck. How do I explain what happened to me and make her understand? I've pushed the shame of that encounter into the deepest and darkest recesses of my core, where I don't have to see it.

Fingers so like mine fidget on the broom handle; she never breaks eye contact. "Two years ago, you what?"

I know my sister. If she thinks she was Gideon's second choice, the beautiful optimism she has will crack. She'll distort her worth and tear herself down. How do I keep her safe without hurting her?

"I kissed him." The partial truth turns my stomach.

Pru's lip trembles. "What?"

"I wasn't thinking clearly." The words stumble out as shame and confusion blossom anew in me. Recalling what happened that evening is like holding on to a used matchstick. The flame is gone, but I know it burned my finger. The details come and go, doubt blurring the lines. First the kiss, then Gideon's response as regret and shock swirled inside me like a typhoon.

I remember how it all felt. Clearly. But the images in my head. The physical memory doesn't make sense . . . has time skewed my recollection?

"You weren't thinking clearly?" Shock elevates Pru's voice, ripping me from reflection. "What's there to misunderstand? You kissed a man."

"Yes, but . . ." Pru is far more responsible and mature than other young women her age. But she's only sixteen. It isn't that she lacks judgment, but experience. She's vulnerable to predators. Of being taken advantage of. Like I was.

I *was* taken advantage of, right? It's been two years, but the echo of panic hits me all the same.

"Then what happened?" Pru shifts her feet, eyes wide, as she attempts and fails to maintain a stiff upper lip. Already, insecurity is stripping her self-worth.

This isn't what I wanted.

"Then what?" she insists. "Did he reject you?"

I latch onto the lifeline like a man overboard. "Yes. Yes, he did."

The lie burns my eyes as I release a quivering breath. I brush the tears roughly away and stare at the floor, willing myself to regain my composure, letting Pru see only what I want her to see. When I look back up at her, some of the weight has lifted from her shoulders.

"I don't understand." She sniffs. Even this shadowed acknowledgment has hurt her, but maybe it is enough. "You won't let me be with him because you are embarrassed by his rejection?"

"No. I mean—yes." I shake my head, more tired than I have ever been. What a mess I've made. "Even if Gideon hadn't rejected me, there was something not right about . . ."

"About what?"

"How he handled it." I cannot say it aloud, as what actually happened doesn't make sense even to me. I know in my heart this is important, though. "I'm not sure how to explain exactly. It felt wrong. I need you to trust me."

"A feeling? You were rejected and had a bad feeling?" Her jaw clenches. My stumbling attempts aren't succeeding.

"Yes. A feeling. And Da's warning, which I ignored, and shouldn't have." I reach out to squeeze her arm. If only touch could relay truth wherein words fail. "Know it hurts me to see you unhappy, but you cannot marry Gideon."

She pulls away, eyes flashing, temper rising. She paces back and forth before she stops, eyes widening. "I think you're jealous that *you* haven't married yet."

I snort, not even bothering to hide the incredulity from my face.

My reaction does not give her one second of pause. "And what's more? Every time you see Gideon, not only do you recall his rejection, but you know if Josiah ever found out, it would break his heart."

Her cold words punch through my gut, the impact rocking me backward. The safe place where I keep Josiah tucked in my head splits open, and there he is, vulnerable to every frightening and horrible possibility. This conversation is not going the way I had hoped. I shake my head, searching for words, but nothing surfaces.

"I know you feel stuck having to give up your own happiness to help care for me and Mother. Life has done that to you. To us. But this?" She shakes her head. "This corner you walked into by kissing Gideon is on you. And it is selfish to make me pay for your mistakes."

Who is this person? Never have I seen this side of my sister before. Her accusation burns like fire. Soon I won't be me anymore, but mere ash to be swept away with her broom. How can she say such terrible things and with so much conviction?

Anger draws me to my feet. At this nonsense. This threat. All because of Gideon. Curse him. "I don't take care of you because I feel stuck. I take care of you because I love you. It's what family does. And because I love you, I'm telling you Gideon is dangerous and you need to stay away from him. Da warned me and I ignored him, and I will regret my mistake for as long as I live."

The clock chimes through the house. Half past the hour. My shift is starting.

I brush past her and out of the sitting room, and nearly run into Mother. The worn rug muffles her steps as she turns away and glides back to the fire. Was she eavesdropping? I tuck this curious response away with the others. There's been no time to think them over.

"You cannot stop Gideon and me from seeing each other." Pru is on my heels.

My lantern waits on the table for me as I pull my gloves out of my jacket and put them on. Next, I jam my cap onto my head, not bothering to pin it. "Things haven't always gone my way either, Pru. But it doesn't mean I lose all my senses and throw a tantrum."

"I am a grown woman, Tempe!" All she'd need to do is stomp her foot and she'd be five years old again. "I too had to grow up fast. Just like you. Stop acting like a victim."

"Stop behaving like a child," I snap, striking a match to light my lantern with more force than necessary.

"Then stop treating me like one."

All my good intentions have shattered, the shards reflecting Pru's ugly accusations back. I take a deep breath before letting it out slowly. "Everything I do, every decision I make, is with your best interest at heart. It's all been for you."

"And I don't need another parent." The stubborn tilt to her head reflects my own. I can make out the small freckles on her cheeks before she wipes away her tears. "I just want my sister."

We stand at a stalemate, both refusing to budge.

It's like we're little girls again, fighting over who gets the last piece of cake. But Da isn't here to tell a joke, make us laugh at how silly we're being. And Mother couldn't care less about anything as she rocks in her chair in the corner. I'm the big sister here. It doesn't matter how deep Pru's words cut, I refuse to cut her back.

And the lampposts are waiting.

I sigh. "I wish you would respect me enough when I tell you I don't like Gideon. You are grown, yes. But you still are young enough and inexperienced enough to ignore things that you shouldn't." I raise my hand as she opens her mouth to retort. "And the same goes for me. I know I'm not perfect."

If I were, Molly wouldn't still be missing. I should have alerted Henry the moment I heard the scream. I can no longer disregard the most inherent survival instinct that is intuition.

"I do not trust him, Pru. I cannot." *Stay away from Gideon.* Da's voice is a whisper.

So were Gideon's fingers in my hair, before they curled into a fist.

My entire body shudders, rejecting the memory.

Pru doesn't stop me as I leave, lantern in hand, the click of the door putting an end to our conversation. The evening air is cool, a relief to my heated skin. I take a deep breath, grateful to be alone. The relief lasts only until the end of the path, however, where Henry is waiting for me.

"Why didn't you report them, Temperance?" he barks at me.

Except for a sharp inhalation, I somehow manage to keep my reaction in check. I nod in greeting to a couple passing by, waiting until they're out of earshot. "Report what?"

"Don't play coy with me. You're better than that." His tone is as cold as a winter wind, and it stings my pride.

I don't want to see the blame and anger in Henry's eyes, but refusing to look at him is cowardly and only supports the notion of guilt. In withholding the detail about the lampposts, I did nothing wrong. I stand by that.

I look into his harried face. "I heard the scream while I was out lighting the lampposts. It sounded close by me, where the lampposts were lit. So a couple of unlit lampposts near the Green hours later couldn't be to blame. I thought it through, Henry."

"Did you?"

"Of course I did." I continue down the street, only stopping when I reach Warbler's Bell.

I pull the rope tied to the clapper and ring the bell once, twice, three times. Going through the motions of my routine is what keeps me from unraveling completely. I quickly gather my equipment from the shed and find Henry waiting for me at the lamppost across the courtyard. I hook the ladder up onto the post's horizontal bar.

"How do you know the lights went out hours later?" he presses.

Unable to stop myself, I glare at him. This veiled chastising is becoming old quickly. "That's when the windstorm kicked up. It's the reason I went to check on the lampposts in the first place."

Henry's brass buttons gleam in the light of my flame. Somewhere nearby, a door slams shut. Wagon wheels groan and clack against the cobblestones. Everyone is returning home. Henry crosses his arms and looks at me with an expression that makes me feel like a child again. I'm instantly ashamed and angered. "Benjamin found the lampposts unlit before he stopped back in at the tavern around seven."

Benjamin. The town lush. It's a miracle the man hasn't been counted among the missing over Warbler's dark history, fallen into the river on account of a drunken stupor. I don't even bother to hide my scoff. "Alcohol has replaced the blood running through Benjamin's veins, Henry. You know just as much as I how unreliable he is. Can you really believe he saw the lampposts out?"

"Considering he's the only reason I knew about the dead lanterns in the first place? Yes." He isn't shouting, but I cannot help but flinch all the same.

I'm cornered. There is nowhere to go but up. I climb the ladder, away from his accusations, to trim the wick. The respect Henry once had for me has diminished so much he has taken a drunk's word over my own. A lecherous drunk, at that.

My eyes widen, a theory tugging at my gut. "What if Benjamin is involved?"

"What do you mean?"

"Every female in Warbler knows to avoid him. He's inappropriate with all of us once he's too far into his drink, which is almost always, and rarely is anything ever done about it."

I know I shouldn't poke Henry, especially in the mood he is in, but it slips out.

"Who's to say he didn't hurt Molly in a drunken fit?" My grip tightens on the ladder, the theory ringing true the more I play it over in my head. "He wouldn't remember it, so of course he wouldn't say anything to you."

"He has never once hurt anyone."

"Doesn't mean we should have to put up with his behavior," I mumble. My skin crawls at the thought of him smacking his lips and watching the young girls of Warbler. Molly. Pru.

"You and Susannah confirmed the time you saw him in the Green. David confirmed when he came into the tavern, and he never left. You saw him out front this morning. Besides, in my *experience*"—Henry puts his hands on his hips—"inebriated people are messy. If he attacked Molly, we would have found her by now. Perhaps your time is better spent on the lampposts than on obtuse theories."

My hand shakes so badly it takes multiple tries to light the lamppost. My reputation has become a wick, consumed by a hungry flame. Soon, everything I've worked for will burn out into nothing.

I shut the door and climb back down, swinging my bag onto my shoulder and ripping the ladder from the post. Henry follows me to the next one. The fog is already to my knees, mocking me, proving how inadequate I am at my own job in front of the constable. I'm running behind.

I know it is cowardly to not look at Henry, but I just can't see the disappointment right now. I need to keep busy. Keep moving. Prop, climb, open, clean, trim, light. Move to the next.

My voice shakes when I finally gather the courage to speak. "I didn't mean any harm by not reporting the unlit lampposts."

"It's part of your job."

"I knew you would give it too much attention. Exactly what you are doing currently. Spending unnecessary time on something completely separate from the issue at hand is a waste of your time and Warbler's resources."

"Are you a constable?"

"No."

"Then how would you know what is or isn't imperative to an investigation?"

"She screamed!" I spin around, arms out, lantern swinging. "Proving someone attacked her. Not that she got lost in the fog on account of my lampposts."

My breath is hurried, and while I raised my voice, I don't regret the volume. I'm fighting for myself here. There's no one else to do so.

"You know better than most how mystifying the fog is." Henry lowers his voice as if the fog itself eavesdropped on our conversation. "You said it yourself this morning. The scream sounded close by, but it could have been blocks away for all you knew. Someone could have tampered with the lampposts so they wouldn't be seen when they grabbed Molly. Had you told me where the lights were out, I could have started looking there first. Found any clues. Did that ever occur to you?"

My face goes hot at his patronizing tone. Nonetheless, his words are a punch to my gut. Because no. No, it hadn't.

"You want to be respected as the lamplighter? Then respect others enough to do their jobs as well. I expected better of you."

Shame draws my gaze to the fog creeping beneath us, coiling around our legs like a snake. There's nothing I can say on the matter. He's right. "I apologize, Henry. I should have told you."

"There's a chance you'll be stripped of your position now."

My stomach drops.

I tear my eyes from the fog's ceaseless ambiguity and back to his face. "What do you mean?"

"Because of your actions, the question of your continued employment as lamplighter has been put on the town council's docket for tomorrow morning." Henry shrugs. "I had to report it. We need to trust everyone in our community is law-abiding, and with the safety of our villagers at stake, we can't take any chances someone won't do their job. The lamplighter is to light the streets of Warbler and serve as a watchman while on shift, reporting anything suspicious to the proper authorities. Me."

Henry's outline becomes fuzzy. I cannot catch my breath, and a wave of heat spreads over my skin. This cannot be happening. I've devoted everything to being Warbler's lamplighter. It's not only a part of me but my family, as well. Without it . . .

Before panic hooks into me completely, I breathe in through my nose and exhale out my mouth several times. No longer lightheaded, I take a step closer to him. "If I lose my position, how do you expect my family to survive? This is all we have."

He doesn't budge.

"It was one mistake, Henry. One. If it were anyone else, you wouldn't be doing this."

There is a hard glint in his eye. I've pushed him too far. "A young girl is missing. Don't you believe your priorities are a bit misguided?"

I hate that my lip is wobbling. That there is nothing I can possibly do to exonerate my failure to report the lampposts. Henry will never understand what it is like to be in my position. How could he? But we're past that now. My decision was made, and it looks like it was the wrong one. I failed my family by making one mistake, ironically in the name of self-preservation.

Da is watching from somewhere, head shaking with disapproval.

Unable to be still, I grab my ladder and brush past Henry. My business with him is done. Standing here with nothing of consequence to say is as useful as bleeding out from a wound and hoping it will merely stop on its own.

I quicken my pace to make up for lost time. I will not give the council any more reasons to steal away my livelihood. I have to work harder than most, but I'm willing to do so as long as needed. Giving up when life becomes difficult is not an option.

Not for me.

CHAPTER 6

I make good time bringing light to the rest of Warbler. The night is especially cold; my breath clouds around my face. There is hardly anyone around. Even the tavern is quiet, everyone warm at home. It's only me out here. Noticed only when I've made a mistake and never for the hard work I've put in.

The thought gives me pause, the anger rising out on my breath, ingested by the fog. Is Henry correct? Have I misguided priorities?

Once I reach Gideon's lamppost, I leave the notion behind. Prop, climb, open, clean, trim, light. I shake my head as I climb back down, hurrying to grab my tools and head toward the next lamppost. No, I do not. Family always comes first.

A shiver trails down my spine, but I refuse to look behind me at Gideon's workshop and his attentive silhouette. I shove thoughts of him far away. There is no room for him right now. Or ever.

The fog beckons me to the next lamppost, cajoling me silently with each step, erasing me until I light the wick. I cannot leave my fate to the whims of Warbler's men. I have to speak up at the council meeting tomorrow. Pru's and Mother's lives depend on it. We need the wages I bring home to pay for our food, for the light in our home, the fuel for our fire. There are no open positions in Warbler that pay as well as the lamplighter post for a woman. I cannot ask

Pru to do more than she already does, caring for Mother, cooking, cleaning, maintaining the house and my sanity.

I'm all we've got.

And the thought of someone else taking Da's position is like finding him hanging all over again.

The next morning, the frost has melted away by the time I finish my shift. There is an unprecedented warmth for October. The blue sky is a never-ending calm at odds with the turbulent nerves coursing within me as I prepare my arguments for the council meeting, such as: In the four years of my employment as the lamplighter, this is the first time a lantern has gone out. And more importantly, none of our villagers have gone missing or been found dead. Visiting whalers, yes. But none of our people.

Unlike the four women lost during Da's service.

I hurry home with the filled cannister, eager to speak with Pru. Despite our fight, she needs to know the situation I put us in. I never got the chance last night, as she had gone to bed early by the time I finished my first shift. When I too fell asleep, tossing and turning for what felt like hours, I found myself plunged back into my recurring nightmare of the burning river, the ship, and the screaming figurehead, instilling a dread within me so heavy I thought I would drown in it.

Even now it is hard to shake the feeling of helplessness away. My heart pounds as I return home to ready myself for the council. I believe I've managed a calm expression when I step inside, but I know I've failed completely when Pru looks up from the table. Alarm wipes away her residual anger from our fight. "Tempe? What's wrong?"

It is nearly impossible hiding how I feel from her. I don't have a lot of practice.

As I change into a clean dress, I explain what happened with the lampposts and their possible, however unlikely, connection to Molly's disappearance. Yet somehow, it's Pru reassuring me it will all work out in the end. I'm supposed to be here for her. Not the other way around.

"You won't lose your position, Tempe." She finishes pinning my hair up into a modest knot and then ties my bonnet over top. "Everything is going to work out. Wait and see."

I cannot say I believe her false sense of positivity, but I appreciate the effort all the same, her inherent ability to rise above the storm and offer comfort. It's an attribute I sorely lack. With a reassuring smile, she sees me off. For a moment, I think everything really will come together as the crisp smell of leaves and the perfume of the autumn clematises and freesia greet me when I reach the town hall.

But a closed door greets me too.

My stomach turns to knots when Matthew, standing watch, bars my entry. He agrees to let them know I wish to speak. When he returns, he gestures to one of the outdoor benches with a shrug. The council's discussion of my fate is muffled through the thick doors. After nearly an hour, my eyelids have grown heavy as the sun holds me to my bench, the adrenaline having long faded away.

The doors swing open, jolting me and shattering the stillness of the courtyard.

Why wasn't I given the opportunity to speak?

I jump to my feet and rush over as the leading members of Warbler file out, hoping the irritation is not too apparent on my face. Some members are in conversation, others hurrying to get back to their day. Molly's father is among them. Disappointment and fear weigh down his eyelids and deepen the lines of his face. Then he sees me. His expression darkens as he makes a sudden step toward me. Henry appears out of nowhere, placing his hand on the druggist's arm.

Molly's father shakes his head, chin set firmly. "Your silence might have cost me my daughter. Can you live with that?"

The venom in his voice burns deep into my soul. Striking me would have hurt less.

He shakes Henry's arm off and brushes past me none too gently, footsteps heavy on the brickwork. The rest of the crowd disperses after saying farewell to the beating heart of our town's leadership: Gideon. He wears a clean collared work shirt, brown suspenders that hold his tan trousers up, and large boots. Despite his facial hair and rough dress, amid the satins and smooth faces of the wealthy merchants, he appears as the only one of worth.

Our eyes meet, and a weight falls into my stomach. He doesn't smile, no, but there is pleasure in his gaze as his head tilts to the left. An unconscious movement, maybe. But it feels deliberate, as if he's measuring me. A piece of wood to be weighed. My scalp itches with each passing second.

I turn away with effort, giving my attention back to Henry.

He has been joined by Mayor Albright, who now steps close to me. A short man with a round belly, he has no trouble making himself heard. Perhaps compensating for his lack of physical prowess, his clipped tones are sharp as a blade and clear as water. "We will tolerate no more mistakes, Mistress Byrne. Your careless actions might have caused the loss of a valuable member to our community. However, we the council have decided to give you a second chance." He lifts his finger, narrowing his eyes at me. "One more mistake, and you're stripped of your duties."

My corset is too tight. I'm roasting within. I open my mouth to explain, but Henry shakes his head quickly behind the man. I swallow hard, fists clenched in unspent anger. Mayor Albright looks down his long nose at me, expectation in the arch of his brow. I somehow manage to curtsy but cannot bring myself to look up at him as I mutter, "Thank you."

Pacified by my demure response, he grunts. "Not everyone is so lucky to always have a benefactor in their corner."

Before I can ask him what he means, he ambles away, clapping another man on the back as they wander off to congratulate each other on their prestige.

I turn to Henry, looking for an explanation.

He exhales. "Molly's father wanted you gone, but Gideon spoke up for you. His opinion holds more clout than most of the men who were in attendance, even under the circumstances."

"Gideon?" The ship carver stands out of earshot and eyeline, and yet I feel a tug as if a fishhook is embedded into my neck, Gideon at the other end of the line.

"He spoke of your years of service without incident. But even still, it was agreed that should Molly be found under suspicious circumstances, your pardon will be revoked." Henry props his bowler cap back on. "Don't make any mistakes."

I nod because I'm not in a position to argue. But something about the mayor's comment still doesn't sit right with me. "The mayor said I always have a benefactor in my corner. I don't understand."

"What do you mean?"

"Gideon stood up for me in there, but how does that make him my benefactor?" I frown. "He hasn't *always* been in my corner."

"I'm not sure. Maybe you should ask him." Henry shrugs and departs. No one looks at me as the courtyard clears.

I should be grateful to Gideon for speaking in my defense. Offering up all the reasons I would have for myself had I been allowed to—had I been a man. Instead, all I feel is his hook in my flesh.

I do not want my life entangled with Gideon's, and yet he keeps implanting himself at every turn. And I can't exactly be mad at him for doing so because he just might have saved me. Us. Mother and Pru. But it doesn't mean he won't eventually put us in peril. Or hurt Pru.

Being indebted to anyone is unacceptable. Especially to Gideon. Surely, he expects this debt to be repaid?

My stomach drops. I peer past Henry's retreating back, looking for Gideon's quiet progress. There, not yet at the end of the street. My boots slap the ground as I run. I hold up my skirts, not giving a damn about who sees me. I reach him at the church, ignoring the minister's disapproving look as he sweeps the steps. "Gideon?"

He slows down, a precision in his movements as he turns. His blue eyes lock on to me.

"This doesn't change anything," I blurt out.

His hand pulls my attention, thumb stroking the side of his pointer finger. I drag my gaze away to meet his sparkling eyes once more. He's laughing at me. "I'm afraid I don't understand."

"You deciding to speak up for me. Helping me keep my appointment as the lamplighter. I appreciate it, but it doesn't change anything."

"I didn't do it for you." He speaks gently, as if chastising a child. "I did it for Prudence."

I bite my tongue as embarrassment consumes me, then swallow down my pride with the copper taste of blood. Of course, he did it for Prudence.

Stay away from Gideon.

Da's warning forever ringing through me like a bell. Have I turned this whole situation into something bigger than it is? Da isn't here anymore. Perhaps Pru was right: I give too much credit to a man who left us by choice.

I've changed considerably in the last few years. Perhaps so has Gideon.

Gideon tips an invisible hat and turns away as if we had simply been discussing the warmth of the day, rather than my incorrect assumptions. I watch him go, realizing I forgot to ask him about the mayor's comment. I catch myself running my thumb along my pointer finger as he did, and shove my hand into my pocket.

Whispers draw my attention from his retreating back, pecking at me like seagulls over chum. I turn toward the sidewalk. Susannah and a girl whose name I cannot remember are watching, dropping their hands from shielding their mouths. Not even bothering to look ashamed at having been caught eavesdropping. Susannah's eyebrow rises; her lip curls. Accusations and disdain written in her snarl.

She's not worth my time.

Pru asked me before I left to pick up items from the general store while I was out. With no other plan for my day, I make my way, my steps lighter than earlier, but still not entirely at ease. I carry a new weight.

I'll be watched like a hawk from now on. Any wrong move, any minor mistake, will be used against me.

At least I've been given time.

The wharf greets me with the familiar smell of drying cod, and the docks brim with activity. Supplies are loaded onto a ship, the *Elizabeth,* set to sail next week. It is the third and largest of the Silver Star Whaling Company's fleet. The entire fleet is owned by Andrew Culver, the wealthiest man in Warbler. Where Gideon commands respect for his talent, prestige, and presence, Andrew commands it for his wealth. Susannah, who is currently burning a hole into my back with her glare, is his only child.

The *Elizabeth* is large enough that she could be out to sea for a few years if Mr. Culver so ordered it. Word has it the ships have had to go out farther than ever before to find the whales. The creatures have begun to abandon their usual feeding and breeding grounds. I can't help but wonder if they've been hunted for so long their numbers are simply dwindling. Like harvesting raspberries. The bushes don't produce forever. Eventually there aren't any more berries to pick.

Hopefully the whales will repopulate, in time. Nantucket has all but decimated the sperm whale population closer to the coast, forcing ships to sail farther away into either the colder waters up north or the warmer waters in the south. I heard some of the crew from the visiting whaling ship say they were off for warmer waters as soon as they could be. Cape Horn, maybe. I can't imagine a place that doesn't change with the seasons. Would it feel like time has stopped? Like being trapped in the same moment forever?

A solid chunk of Warbler's population consists of whaling crews, so it isn't uncommon for many of our men to be gone. Their absence gives the women left behind more power and say in our choices. I think this was one of the reasons I was allowed my position as the lamplighter. That, and the town council can pay me less.

Perhaps, I should make *that* argument next time the council tries to take away my job.

Shouts draw my attention to the dock leading to the *Elizabeth*. A young whaler has dropped a crate, the contents are shattered and spilled everywhere. What a waste. The ship's captain, as red as a turnip, is yelling at the whaler.

I pull my gaze away from the mortified boy and step into the general store, the chime of the bell announcing my entrance. The inside smells of beeswax and tea leaves. A small boy is restocking the flour in the corner, but otherwise the shelves are all full. The owner must have anticipated the *Elizabeth*'s departure and double ordered on everything.

Mr. Landon is bald but for the wisps of gray hair encircling his head like seagulls. Small spectacles balance on the tip of his fine nose, threatening to fall off. He stands straight, not much taller than me, and picks up his pen, poising it over his pad of paper. "Afternoon, Temperance. What can I help you with today?"

"Just the basics. A can of Hyson, two candles, and charcoal, if you please."

He nods as he jots my items down, then moves along the back wall to scoop out the tea leaves before grabbing my other items. He picks the beeswax candles, knowing I cannot afford the spermaceti. By the looks of it, the store is running low as it is. I imagine, should the *Miriam* return from a successful trip, the shop will soon be restocked with the coveted candles. They burn longer, cleaner, and brighter than beeswax or tallow candles. They also do not smell as bad. They are made from the oil in sperm whales and are not as easy to come by, especially in a smaller whaling community like Warbler.

The bell chimes above the entrance, clearing all thoughts of whaling from my head. A man steps through the doorway, and the nerves I had just begun to calm steep in dread.

Leonard.

CHAPTER 7

He fills the doorway, light barely slipping past his frame. His gaze roams up my body, lips curving until he gets to my face. His appreciative countenance hardens with recognition. "You."

I turn back to the counter and fiddle with the money in my pocket.

"I'll be with you in just a moment!" Mr. Landon shouts from the back corner, where he is wrapping my brown candles.

The floor creaks beneath Leonard's approaching footsteps. A sour smell covers me as he stops at my side. Entirely too close, his chest all but touching my right shoulder. But I refuse to step away. He's waiting for me to look up at him.

I clear my throat. "Take a step back."

"Going to kick me again?"

I clench my teeth and try to picture trees swaying in a breeze. The snap of flint and the following spark, the lazy trickle of the creek. Anywhere and anything else.

"I don't mind it rough, ya know." His rank breath oozes out with his whisper. "Might even teach you some manners while I'm at it."

Before I can retort, he's grabbed my arm, hand encircling it completely. I jerk back, but his grip is a manacle. Leonard's face fills my vision. My ears buzz, and my lips part to scream. Just like Molly did.

"Do we have a problem here?" Mr. Landon steps into my peripheral, setting my wares on the counter.

Leonard's grip tightens and his nostrils flare before his thin lips slit open into a grin; all the while his eyes never leave me. "Course not."

"Then I suggest you unhand Mistress Byrne and leave before I give you one."

Leonard lets go, and I stumble back into the counter, arm throbbing in tandem with my heartbeat. Touch should not be associated with violence, and yet that seems to be all touch is. All that I can attain. Little-girl dreams of fairy-tale princes and respect are so easily shattered by reality. My hand trembles as I turn and count out my coin. The numbers mix in my head, and I'm forced to recount multiple times. I want to go. I need to be out of here.

"Let me." Mr. Landon holds his palm up, and I set my coin purse there. He unhooks the latch and counts out what I owe him before handing my purse back. "Would you like me to escort you home?"

The knave shifts beside me, and I can imagine his look of incredulity as he gazes down at the slight, elderly Mr. Landon. I shake my head, grateful. He's always been a kind man. "That isn't necessary, but thank you."

My muscles are stiff as a board, and a sharp ache has begun behind my eyes, but I manage to grab my merchandise and shove it into the pockets Pru sewed into my dress. I didn't think to bring a handbag to carry it all. Before I can go, Mr. Landon sets his hand on the counter, stopping me. He turns to Leonard. "I believe I told you to leave. You're not welcome in my store."

Leonard huffs like a bull, but Mr. Landon doesn't blink. The bell chimes a moment later as the whaler departs. I release my breath.

"The sooner that lot has set sail, the better. They're nothing but trouble." Mr. Landon shakes his head as he watches Leonard out the front window. "Usually don't have much difficulty, but this batch has been worse than normal."

I'm sure he is only speaking to give me time to compose myself. He couldn't possibly know of my interest in Leonard and his crew. Will Mr. Landon still treat me with kindness after learning of my actions the night Molly disappeared?

To calm my nerves, I pull at the hem of my sleeves and clear my throat. "Did you ever see any of them interact with Molly?"

"No, cannot say that I did." The older man shifts his attention back to me. He pauses, as if deciding whether to say anything more. "To be frank, while I've seen a number of ruffians come and go with the ships through the years, none of them hold a candle to what's in the fog."

I frown, unsure whether I heard him correctly. "Pardon?"

"There should be no need for me to explain it to you, Mistress Byrne." His eyes narrow. "You're in it every night. Like something's watching you out there, right? Waiting. Playing with your thoughts."

A smothering cold crawls over me, and I rub my arms. "Imagination has a large part to play, Mr. Landon. I try my best not to let it get to me."

He tuts as he removes his glasses, wipes them on his apron, and replaces them on his face, the lenses enlarging his bright brown eyes. "Your bell doesn't just notify the constables of the beginning of your shift. It reminds the rest of us to be on our guard. To get home while we can—*before* it begins its hunt. Those of us who know better, anyhow."

My frown deepens. I didn't know that Mr. Landon sided with Warbler's eccentric crowd. "Before what begins its hunt?"

"I couldn't tell you. I'm still here, aren't I?" He doesn't blink as he flips his notepad closed. "But a lot of people have disappeared over the years. Such a tragedy for it to happen to a good girl like Molly."

I do not care for the finality in his voice. "Perhaps she will still be found."

"I've owned the general store here a long time. No one is ever found. Least not alive." He speaks the truth, but I don't want to accept it. "Inattentiveness and running off only go so far to explain everything that happens in the fog. You be careful out there. We know the courage it takes to do what you do."

The credit bestowed upon me after what has happened with Molly feels wrong. Unjustified. But I cannot contain the pleased blush burning my cheeks. Bestowing a grateful smile, I exit the store, take a deep breath of fresh air, and allow the sounds of the wharf to wash over me. The flap of canvas, the splash of oars, the clop of hooves on the cobblestones. I turn and smack into someone, unable to contain an exclamation.

Susannah's large brown eyes blink up at me. Her surprise melts into lip-curling disgust. There's no getting around interacting with her now.

I remind myself she's just lost her friend. She's on her own. With a sigh, I wince. "I'm sorry to hear about Molly. Has there been any news?"

"No, no thanks to you." Her voice cuts the air between us.

"Excuse me?"

"My best friend is missing because of your carelessness."

Emotions already high after the encounter with Leonard, and now realizing how quickly word has spread, my hackles rise. I am nowhere near as benevolent as Pru. "You're acting quite haughty for someone who is out shopping while her best friend is missing."

Her eyes flash, and a crimson hue climbs up her slender neck. For a second, I regret my cutting words. Then she holds her chin up, eyeing me from head to toe with disdain. "No, you're not careless. You're arrogant. With Gideon in your pocket, you don't have to concern yourself with any consequences for your actions. Must be nice."

My mouth goes dry as the giant fist of her implication lands in my gut. I only just catch myself from gagging. Susannah has, in all probability, lost her friend and is merely unable to control her emotions. She's lashing out because, like me, she is becoming fully aware there isn't anything she can do about her circumstances.

Accusing me of being involved with Gideon, however, is crossing the line.

Before I can say anything though, she steps forward, crowding into my personal space. "If you were anyone else, your house would have been taken away. You, Prudence, and your mother would be out on the streets. You're receiving special treatment no one else would."

Susannah's ignorance is going to get her into trouble one of these days. "You are sorely mistaken. I have not, nor have I ever, received any such special treatment. And no one can just take our house from us. It's my parents' home."

Susannah gazes up at me with pity, tutting as she shakes her head. "You want to play make-believe? All right, we'll pretend there's nothing suspicious about Gideon owning the house you live in. Or speaking up for you during the council meeting. My father told me what he did."

My jaw drops.

Not everyone is so lucky to always have a benefactor in their corner.

Footsteps approach me from behind as my mind races, trying to untangle myself from this new information. Susannah's unkind smile softens immediately. "Good afternoon, sir."

"It is now."

She doesn't notice me stiffen; all her attention is on Leonard, who has stepped entirely too close to me. Again. I grit my teeth and depart without saying a word. I shouldn't leave Susannah with him, but with each step I take, my body moves quicker until I am almost running. As the sound of their flirtatious laughter fades away, my eyes begin to tickle.

Gideon owns our home?

Everything is too close. The blue sky reaches out to the far edges of my sight, pressing down just as the cobblestones and river and woods grow upward, sandwiching me in between. I stumble to a halt, close my eyes, and take a deep breath. Let it out, wipe away the tears. I open my eyes back to the bright sky, and everything is as it should be. I need to go home. Eat something. I make my way off the main street, alongside the activity of the shipyard. Ruby, resting in front of the cooperage, hurries up the road when she sees me. Giving her a quick pat, I whisper words of comfort to her as if she can actually understand me. She doesn't say otherwise.

It isn't until I get to the end of the street and see Pru in her blue dress in front of Gideon's workshop, her hand on his arm, that I think I might truly lose all of my composure. The shaking begins deep within my bones, reverberating outward like a stone dropped into water, the ripples reaching farther and farther out. I clench my hands together to control their trembling, my heart pounding so loud it's a wonder they haven't heard me all the way across the street.

Then Gideon glances over Pru's head toward me. The hook tugs. Our eyes meet, and I'm thrown backward two years into memory—

—and off my feet. The wind blows across the river with the power of a steam train, making it difficult to regain my footing on the icy cobblestones. My backside aches, and a hint of red gleams through the fresh tear in my glove. I look up through tears, eyes narrowed against the biting air. The lamppost remains lit, despite my sudden fall. The wind shut the door for me.

My teeth chatter and my palms burn as I attempt to stand.

Suddenly, there is a hand on my arm pulling me up. The wind roars like a great monster, tugging me one way as the stranger pulls the other. Abruptly, all resistance ceases. There is warmth and light. A door slams shut. Remnants of the wind moan through the workshop's walls.

Gideon turns to me from the closed door. "Quite the storm out there. Perhaps you should wait it out for a few minutes. Get warm."

Da's warning reverberates in my head, but his words feel far away from the promise of immediate warmth. Gideon offers me a strip of jerky and a slice of bread with jam from his plate. I'm not even ashamed when I scarf it up, having not eaten all day. With a satisfied sigh I turn back to Gideon, remembering my manners.

I inhale sharply, not realizing how close he has come up to me. He reaches out, tenderly grabs my hand, and turns it over to inspect the cuts on my palm. His grip is steady. Soothing. He places his other hand along my cheek. The bold movement shocks me completely, freezing me. The smell of husky wood and fresh paint surrounds me. His thumb brushes away something from my lips. I don't know what. A crumb, maybe.

Josiah hasn't even touched my lips yet. His courage has only manifested itself in taking hold of my hand while we walk.

But I so long to be held by someone. To not be the strong one, even if it is just for a minute.

Stay away from Gideon.

Da's words are drowned out by the whoosh of blood rushing through my ears. The brightness of Gideon's eyes is so opposite the deep warmth of Josiah's. Gideon's eyes are the crisp frost of a blue dawn. He is so close to me I can see the pulse in his neck. Only a hand's span away. For a single moment, there is finally warmth. Safety. Touch. Things so far from my reach. Before I can stop myself, I press my lips against his. So tender and soft. A timid whisper between two people.

My first kiss.

I had always thought it would be with Josiah.

Guilt sweeps through me, cold as the wind outside. Josiah. What am I doing?

I open my eyes and gasp. Gideon's pupils are splintering into the gray-blue of his irises.

Then Gideon slams me into the wall.

Stars burst before my eyes. Fingers slide through my hair, tug my already messy coronet braid free. At first they're gentle, exploring. Then they curl in, yanking sharply. I cry out.

This was a mistake.

My back and head ache. He leans against me, pinning me, hair fisted in his hand. His mouth brutalizes my own, teeth biting my lip. The taste of blood is on my tongue.

This isn't what I wanted.

I whimper, petrified and unable to do anything else. Gideon pulls back, lips wet, breath ragged. My heart pounds, and I know he can hear it. Feel the thrum. Our eyes meet again. A stabbing sensation begins in my palm—from what, I don't know. A nail?

This doesn't make sense.

His pupils begin to grow, to swirl. Like fog. Thicker and thicker. Thick enough to drown in. To be lost in.

But I am the lamplighter. I can't get lost. I have to get out of here. Leave.

Immediately.

Tears blur my vision. His hand tightens in my hair, tugging it painfully from my scalp. A few strands fall into my eyes, splicing my view of him. My hand is on fire.

Shoving Gideon's chest with my free hand proves futile. He could be made of wood for how much he budges. Escape isn't an option, with the workshop wall against my back and his grip an unbreakable vise. There is only one thing I can do.

I spit on him.

Gideon blinks, releases me. The stinging in my scalp spreads, then weakens. My gob of saliva crawls down his cheek. I draw my arms in to hug my torso, hands shaking, the heat abating.

I spit on a man. One of the most respected men in Warbler.

Gideon blinks again. The swirling black is gone, a panicked figment of my imagination. He steps back, a strange look on his face. He wipes the wetness from his cheek, eyes simultaneously bewildered and intrigued.

"Forgive me, Temperance. I do not know what I was thinking."

Cheeks burning, I only run when he turns from me. I fling the door open, and the screaming wind takes me into its open arms. Its dull roar can't drown out my internal scream. Nor can its icy touch freeze the fear shaking my limbs at Gideon's violence, my brazenness of kissing him in the first place, the shame of them both. But most of all, the tugging uncertainty something very wrong just happened.

Pru's laugh pulls me back to the present. Gideon is looking down at her with tenderness, his chuckle soft. I shake my head as if it'll dispel the memory from me forever. It doesn't. When I got home that night, two years ago, Pru wondered why my hair was in disarray. How I came by a knot on the back of my head and bleeding hands. *Fell from my ladder in the windstorm. Yes, I'm fine. Stop fussing.* At fourteen summers, Pru was still naïve to the desires of the flesh. A few days later, I asked her to stay away from Gideon. She agreed easily without question, thinking nothing of it, blindly trusting. Not a suspicious bone in her body.

She forgot that conversation.

I gave Josiah the same excuse of falling, the lie coming

easily upon retelling. He could never know I kissed Gideon first. It would break him. No one could know. My reputation would be ruined. I would lose my job. I would be punished.

No. All I could do was hope Gideon would keep our secret.

And he did. For two years, Gideon and I steered clear of each other. I never stayed at his lamppost longer than necessary, and he was courteous in public when etiquette required it. Beyond that, we had no interactions. Until this past summer, when I felt his gaze find me once again on my shifts.

And now that gaze is on Pru.

I turn my back on the two of them and make my way home to Mother the long way, unable to do anything about Pru. Like she said, I cannot actually prevent her from seeing him. But the memory of Gideon's assault and the ache in my arm from Leonard's grip fuel my racing heart all the way home. No one understands, and no one can help me. Helpless tears cool my flushed face. There is nothing I can do about either man, and there never was. I'm losing what control I thought I had. Any moment, I could fall to the ground, my body bursting into fog, unable to do anything but watch as people walk through me.

CHAPTER 8

Four days have passed since Molly's disappearance, and there continues to be no sign of her.

There are more volunteers each day, usually led by Mr. Fairchild or our minister, which should have instilled a kinship of unity and optimism in Warbler. Instead, as the echoes of "Molly" slide in and out of the trees, through the farms, over the fields, and across the water, all I can think of is dropping a pebble down a well. Wondering how long it could possibly fall before the inevitable splash.

I know I'm not the only one. Whispers have begun to slip into conversations. Suspicions. Trepidation. Surly interactions with the visiting whalers. No one says it in front of Mr. Fairchild, but it's clear by their sideways glances what they are thinking. It would seem there are a great number of others in the same frame of thought as Mr. Landon. That Molly may never be found.

Just like those who went missing under Da's watch, and so many more before.

Some people ask questions about what I heard. If I saw anything. Others disregard me completely. I am unreliable. A pariah for daring to look out for myself. The constables are harried and ill-tempered. Henry shakes his head at me anytime I approach with a questioning gaze. I am grateful for my work. Sitting idle while rumors and fearmongering spread is the worst sort of torture. Focusing on physical tasks, having purpose, keeps me sharp.

Because of the council's threat, I've taken to two

nighttime patrols through Warbler after lighting the lampposts instead of my usual one. I listen for anything suspicious and keep my eyes open for anything amiss in the fog. But so far there has been nothing out of the ordinary. That is, except for the few villagers who watch me light the lanterns, standing near enough to let me know they're there. One fisherman goes so far as to pull out a stool and have a closer inspection of my work after I finish.

Rather than lash out at the rude man, I offer a pained smile and speak through gritted teeth. "May I help you?"

"Doesn't look properly closed."

"It is," I snap.

He snorts, eyes the door for an agonizing minute, then steps back down with a self-assured nod. My lantern handle bites into my palm I grip it so tightly, watching the fisherman carry on down the wharf. More often than not, I turn to see eyes upon me. Skeptical expressions as I carry on with my work. Doubt.

This feeling follows me even now, increasing once I've entered the Green. When I turn, I find it is only Benjamin, haunting his usual bench. "Yes, Benjamin?"

"'Elp a man out?" He reaches his trembling hand out for coin, causing my pulse to pound painfully in my ears. Did Molly offer him money? Did he snatch at her wrist and yank her down? Did he hurt her?

I shake my head and turn my back on his grumbling, glancing over my shoulder to make sure he isn't advancing on me. But he is lying down already, talking to himself, how I usually find him.

Only once during my second patrol do I believe I see a suspicious figure, but I blink and there is nothing but the trunk of a young tree, its naked branches reaching toward me. For the briefest of moments, I think I see one of the branches move. Shifting back into place. That can't be, however, as there is no breeze, the air still as a post.

I know imagination and exhaustion are playing tricks on me. Pulling these extra patrols may be doing more harm than good. I wish I had never asked Mr. Landon about the whalers. His belief that something is in the fog shadows me with each step, forcing me to make a conscious effort to shake it off.

Despite the constant glancing over my shoulder and pausing to listen for following footsteps, I encounter no one. I am completely and utterly alone in the fog.

Just like Da was.

The sun has just begun to peek over the horizon as I stifle a yawn. My usual promptness in snuffing out the lampposts is falling short each morning. The dark circles under my eyes are answer enough should anyone ask me about it.

Upon reaching the wharf, I hear the bell of a ship calling out over the water, a ghost in the dissipating haze. It's as if we all walk in an underwater world, the air a gentle blue, mist blurring any hard lines. The bell tolls once more, confirming a ship is coming into dock. A few of the crabbers pause, all of us waiting. She arrives a moment later, an apparition from another world.

The familiar silhouette ignites a thrill that has me all but levitating off the ground.

"Josiah." His name lifts my lips into a smile so large, my cheeks ache. He's home. He's finally home.

A crabber draws my attention with a triumphant whistle. I grin at him over my shoulder. Gladness is spreading along the wharf among us early risers, as quick as a warm breeze. I turn back to the river as the figurehead glides out of the fog, the dark hull of Josiah's ship behind her. My breath catches.

It's the figurehead from my nightmares.

For a moment, the blue begins to bleed. Fire curls up from the water as the sky darkens. I mash my eyes closed and take a deep breath. My ears pick out sounds in the darkness. The shouting of orders from the deck, the steps of the crew's boots, the creaks and groans of the wood, the river current trickling against the rocks, the splash of an anchor.

Grounded, I open my eyes to find the *Miriam* has stopped, giant white sails like clouds being furled. The ship sits deep in the water with its weight, a sign the trip was successful. Men move about the deck like ants on their hill. The haze in the air is just enough I am unable to discern individual faces. My eyes are pulled to the figurehead. Named and carved for a woman who disappeared over ten years ago, Miriam holds her mouth open, singing a song from the depths to any who would hear. The thought in Greek folklore is that sirens sing sailors to their deaths. But for us, here on a whaling ship, she sings the whales to theirs.

With difficulty, I wrench my gaze from the figurehead and scan the upper deck. One of those anonymous figures is Josiah. Home at last. I try to discern any unique movement, some sort of sign that will show me which one he is. Somehow catch sight of his ambling gait or hear his boisterous laugh. But the crew of the *Miriam* is all business until they've come ashore and unloaded her. Thoughts of being with Josiah once again help propel me on my way, anxious to be done with my shift.

Finally, some stability in my world.

Ruby's excited barks and whines alert me to Josiah's presence before my eyes do. I stop just inside the cooperage entrance, catching George's eye from his stool in front of the stove. He nods at me and shakes his head at Ruby's antics. The old dog's body is one giant wiggle as she unsuccessfully tries to jump up to Josiah on her hind legs. He squats down and wraps his arms around her, an attempt at a hug she cannot quite handle in her excitement. Her high-pitched whines tug at my heart.

Josiah runs his huge hands over her, chuckling under his breath. His smile splits his tan face, bright teeth peeking through the unruly brown beard. His deep brown eyes, so like the syrup extracted from the maple trees, crinkle at the edges. He's lost weight, some of the elasticity of his skin missing. He looks harder because of it, the usual gentle plush to his face gone.

But he's still my Josiah.

A smile tugs at my lips. When Josiah finally gets a moment to glance up beyond the yellow bundle of energy, all the weight of the past few days drops off my chest. In a single heartbeat, he's up and I'm in his arms.

George coughs from his stool. Josiah sets me down and steps back, beaming. Ruby wiggles her way in between us, nearly knocking me over. Josiah gives her another pat before straightening again. He hooks his thumbs behind the straps of his suspenders, rocks onto the balls of his feet, and whistles. "You look fine."

"Well, I did put on a dress specially for you." I gesture down at my gray dress, lace sewn into the collar and cuffs.

"Did you steal it from Pru?" He grins, his gregarious laugh filling the cooperage.

There's the Josiah I know so well. "I happen to own a few dresses, thank you very much. In fact, I actually enjoy wearing them from time to time."

His eyebrows rise, opening his eyes wide. "Oh, is that so?"

I punctuate my agreement with a swift nod and reach down to stroke Ruby's head, as she pants between the two of us, tail thwacking my shins through my skirt.

"Well"—he pats his flat stomach—"let's eat while I regale you with tales of my heroic deeds." He ignores my snort and slaps his hat to his thigh, sending Ruby into a new dance of excitement. "I've a hankering for something sweet."

Josiah buys a whole apple pie from the general store, as well as a wedge of cheese. The odd combination will receive no complaints on my part. I cannot imagine what I would crave after six months at sea. He amuses me with tales of their chases of giant whales with tails as large as a house. Sailing through summer storms that threatened to swallow them up. The songs the men came up with to pass the time when there was no wind. The rancid and horrendous smell of boiling whale blubber after they rowed a carcass to the side of the ship, and then began to bring it up, piece by piece.

We cross the bridge and take our food to the Green, Ruby keeping pace at our heels. Two benches in the courtyard are occupied. An elderly couple sit together, their attention on the three small children chasing one another around the faded flower beds. The children's mother looks to be enjoying a moment of peace on her own bench. Water trickles over the rocks in the creek, a barrier separating the business district from this quiet, soothing place.

Ruby makes her way to a beautiful rowan tree. The small leaves are a rich orange color, dappled by vibrant red berries. It stands out among the rest of the trees in the Green like a beautiful flame. I spread my skirt out around me before sitting at its base, a feeling of comfort and protection overcoming me. Thankfully, the fallen leaves respond with a satisfying crunch rather than a pliant silence upon contact. You can't brush off wet. Crisp detritus floats up like dust motes in a ray of sun breaking through the branches.

For just a moment, I imagine everything in my world is as it should be. Pru is happy and married to a wonderful man. Molly is home safe. Leonard and his shipmates are gone. I am no longer glared at by the citizens of Warbler on my rounds. There's a ring on my finger, and Josiah and I are enjoying a beautiful afternoon while we discuss the possibility of—what? Anything and everything.

The cider Josiah brought with us washes down the lump in my throat, and I wince at its tartness. The truth of the matter is so long as I am a woman doing a man's job, I will never truly be respected. Pru has fallen in love with someone who unsettles me. And even now, Molly's name is a brittle leaf soon to be blown away by the wind. The determination with which I move about each day has become shadowed.

"Is something wrong?"

I bring myself back to Josiah, force a smile on my face. "Tell me more about your adventures."

"Honestly, Tempe? I'm glad to be home. When I wasn't inspecting and fashioning the casks, it was all I could think about." He reaches into his pocket. "Give me your hand."

I do, and he places a giant tooth in my palm. I run my thumb over the carved design breaking up the smooth surface. "Is this scrimshaw? Josiah, this is lovely."

He nods. "One of the older whalers taught me how. I've got three more."

I turn the yellow whale tooth over in my fingers. He's carved a mini-Warbler into the surface, lampposts and all. He even managed to get Ruby in there. It reminds me of the etching on the arch holding Warbler's Bell, and I smile.

"I've been flapping my jaw all this time," he chuckles, and pops a wedge of cheese into his mouth before tossing one to Ruby. It reminds me of childhood, when we tried to see who could stuff the most bread into our mouths, resembling little chipmunks. Eyes sparkling, he tosses another one in, a knowing grin on his face. "What have I missed around here?"

Warbler looks so tranquil on the tooth. Idyllic. There is no fog. There are no people. No past, judgments, regrets. No danger. I hand the scrimshaw back to him with a sigh, fingers brushing his own. It strangely takes no time at all to tell him of the conflicts and anxieties of the last week. It almost sounds trivial when spoken aloud, but Josiah's expression darkens the more I tell. Takes on an edge I've not seen before. One more reminder that we aren't children anymore.

"Your position is safe now, correct?" he confirms.

"For the time being," I mumble as I pick up a leaf, turning it over to inspect the tiny lines laced through it.

He takes my hand, the leaf crumpling between our palms. "I don't understand your dislike of Gideon, but if you don't want Pru to marry him, I support you. And once we are married, I'll take care of all of you. Whether you lose your position will be obsolete."

"Once we marry?" I raise an eyebrow.

"Yes." He clears his throat. "It's why I signed on as the *Miriam*'s cooper. The pay was substantial. With it and the money I make in the cooperage, you won't have to work because I can properly support a family. Our family, after you've become my wife."

It's then I realize Josiah is holding his breath. My heart doesn't even skip a beat. I had hoped for so long to hear these words out of his mouth. Dreamed about the safety, comfort, and peace of being asked to marry my best friend. And yet his words, while sensible, somehow lack the shine I had expected. The flush of nerves and joy never hits. The breeze is gone. The cheese is too potent, its stink combatting the sweetness of the pie and the punch of its cinnamon. Ruby chews a stick, cracking and crunching her way through it with determined huffs. A baby cries from its pram. What is wrong with me?

Except there is nothing wrong. The picture in one's mind always differs from reality. The truth is there are many scenarios to consider before taking such a step as marriage. Ones I mustn't ignore no matter how much I wish to.

Josiah continues to look at me earnestly, and I squeeze his hand reassuringly, heart pounding, before I speak. "I can't, Josiah. At least, not yet."

"Why not?" His grip on my hand loosens, his chest rising.

"You may not care whether I lose my job. But I do. I don't ever want to chance being put in the position where we are left financially wanting. We will have Mother to care for, after all, and any number of other mouths to feed, whomever the future brings into our family. And now after all that has occurred with Pru, I want to make sure she is happy and settled, as well. She's earned it."

"So have you." He frowns, and I have to restrain myself from kissing his scratchy cheek.

I nod to appease him instead. "But it's different. I will worry about her until it happens."

"Why do we need to wait to marry until she is wed?" He chuckles, not unkindly. "Are you not allowed your own happiness?"

"Of course I am. But it would feel as if I were rubbing it in her face after taking away a chance at her own with Gideon." Not that he would have provided her happiness. She'll never realize that, though.

"I don't think Pru would see it that way. Give her more credit than that."

"Maybe so, but it doesn't stop me from feeling that way." I grimace. It's hard to explain to someone who has never grown up with siblings. There is a power dynamic interwoven in the relationship, even more so now that I am the head of our household. "It's important to me that you and I have as clean a slate as possible when our life begins together. If I can eliminate messy feelings that might affect us, I think it's worth it."

He seems to mull it over as he takes another forkful of the apple pie, his free hand still touching mine.

"Besides—" It's important I circle back to my first point. Be as clear as possible with him. "I like my job. So right now, I need to focus on ensuring I do not lose it."

"After everything that has happened with Molly, and the way the council and Warbler have treated you? How could you possibly still care for it?" Josiah shakes his head and sits back, and I feel the loss of his touch like an empty trap to a starving crabber.

"I enjoy the sense of purpose in my work. The freedom it gives me. Usually," I offer belatedly, recalling the fisherman inspecting my work the other day.

He sighs and rubs a hand over his jaw.

"And I don't want to rely on you to support me. If you became injured, or sick, or heaven help me, died, I would be at the mercy of fate. Keeping my position gives me peace of mind. Surely you must understand how important that is to me."

"Would accepting my support be so bad?" There are lines between his brows, and I realize how my words have wounded him, however unintentionally. Why is it never easy to explain one's own feelings? I know it isn't selfish of me, and yet I can't help but second guess all of it as he sighs. "I wish you would let me take care of you, Tempe."

Josiah has worked hard his entire life. He wasn't born into wealth like Susannah or the other merchant families. He started his apprenticeship for George quite young, and when he became a journeyman cooper, his parents left their small house to him in order to move closer to Hartford for his father's health. Josiah knows the pride in putting in a hard day's work. He knows what it means to stretch the budget. But for all the obstacles he has overcome to be successful, he has never had his life upended like I have. I don't know what he would do if it was. I don't ever want to have to find out.

Da's lifeless face flashes before my eyes.

I reach out and squeeze Josiah's hand. When he doesn't

respond, I tug gently until he looks over at me. "I love you. I want the next part of my life to be tied with yours. But not yet. The time isn't right, and it needs to be for us to work."

I muster every bit of earnestness I contain into my expression. I need him to believe me. The thought of not having him in my life is painful. It isn't comprehendible. "Will you wait for me?"

He uses his fork to push around the crust on his plate. My heartbeat speeds up before he glances up at me. His warm eyes glow in the amber light of the late afternoon. The corner of his mouth twitches within his beard. "So you're saying if I find Pru a husband, you'll marry me?"

Once I clear the laugh in my throat, I make my face serious. "It would speed the process up a bit."

He jumps up, startling me, and waves his hand along an invisible sign. "Josiah Dermot. Cooper and matchmaker extraordinaire."

Laughter spills out of me. He glares, and I suck in my lips, eyes wide.

One hand on his hip, he strokes his chin with the other while pacing in front of me. "So what should I be looking for? A man? Two legs, two arms, successful profession, good hygiene . . . ?"

"Indeed, that is a good start. A decent personality would also be preferable. Kind, gracious, possessing a sense of humor . . ."

"Whoa." He shakes his head and waves his hands. "Personalities are where I draw the line."

I laugh and lift my hand toward him. "Help me up?"

He pulls me up easily, his hands rough, my breath catching. We stand so close I feel the rise and fall of his chest, and I nearly lean in to kiss him. What would he do if I did? For a long moment, neither of us lets go.

Then a child screams. I start, releasing Josiah. The child is fine, merely having scraped his knee after falling. His mother coos and reassures him, wiping away his tears. We clean up our impromptu picnic and Josiah offers to escort me home.

The moment is lost.

Everyone we pass welcomes Josiah back, offering a hand or smile. He is a welcome shield against the glares I'm becoming accustomed to, though not one I want to have to rely on. I understand completely, though. It isn't hard to like Josiah with his genuine and gracious nature. His arm brushes against my shoulder as we walk, and I bump him with my hip. When we were younger, we would try to knock the other off their feet. Now the game has an ulterior motive. Touching one another, simply for the sake of pleasure.

"May I ask why you do not approve of Gideon? Is it his age?"

I groan, my good mood on the cusp of vanishing. "The age difference is uncomfortable, but not the reason."

"I'm still waiting."

"Did you know he owns our home?" I can barely get the words out without wincing. While I was alone with Mother yesterday, I confronted her about it. Of course, I didn't expect her to respond, but I'd still hoped for an explanation. I received none.

"No, I didn't."

"How? How was he able to take our home?"

Josiah won't look at me. "Probably after your father, well, you know."

I stop, reaching out to his arm, eyebrows rising in question.

When he finally glances at me, he shifts uncomfortably. "Women can't own property."

I hear the words coming out of his mouth, but they don't make any sense to me. In fact, they are utterly ridiculous. "But it's Da and Mother's house. Mother is still alive. Why wouldn't we get to keep it? It's our home."

"Did he have a will?"

I bite my lip, mortification shaking my twisting hands. "I don't know. No one said anything. I just assumed . . ."

I've been doing everything I can to support us financially, barely making ends meet. Yet I'm continuously blinded by my own naivety. I wipe my arm across my eyes, embarrassed over the tears filling them.

"Someone should have told you. You had a right to know as the head of your family." He squeezes my arm, but I feel no pity in his touch. Only resolution and respect. It gives me strength. "Someday it won't be like this. I'm just not sure what to do about it right now. I'm sorry, Tempe."

I release a ragged breath, staring at the threading on his muslin shirt. Pru and I care for Mother and our house. We contribute to this village. But because of our sex, we cannot own our home, and no one even bothered to tell me.

The injustice of it all is absolutely asinine.

As if reading my thoughts, Josiah says, "Gideon never mentioned he owns your home?"

I shake my head.

"He's been letting you live there for free." He raises his hands in defense when I glare at him. "*Letting* isn't the best word, but you know what I mean."

Gideon should have told us. I would have found a way to make payments. Somehow. I bite my lip.

Josiah shrugs. "Someone like that doesn't sound so bad to me."

How do I make him understand that even though it sounds good, it feels wrong? There is an imbalance of power with Gideon that cannot be overcome as is. For now I decide to share my most pressing fear. Josiah is a full head taller than me, but I take a step closer, craning my head to look up at him. "I'm scared he might hurt her, Josiah."

"That's a natural feeling. You love her." He squeezes my shoulder, oblivious to my connotation. "But you have to take a chance eventually. Pru is a grown woman. You have to let her go."

Though I love Josiah with my whole being, he doesn't understand what life is like for a woman. If we are unhappy with someone, we do not have the option to try someone else. Our fates are sealed the moment we marry as if we are chattel. Or if we never marry, we are branded as spinsters.

"Hearts can be mended, Tempe. They're resilient."

Pru's heart being hurt isn't what I am worried about. I don't bother to correct him, though. "You speak of it as if you know."

He takes his hat off and holds it to his heart. "I've had one great love in my long life—"

"Of twenty years," I interject.

"Of twenty years," he consents. "And today she broke my heart by saying no to my proposal."

I roll my eyes at his theatrics. "You didn't actually propose, and I merely asked you to wait."

"'Tis one and the same." He pulls his hat back on, releasing a heavy sigh of one accepting their terrible fate.

Josiah jests with ease, but I know behind his smile there is a seed of hurt. Best to steer the conversation away from us. "I would like to wait and see if there is a better match for Pru. She's only just come of an appropriate age for marriage, and there hasn't been any time for her to get to know anyone. Her time is consumed with Mother and the house. Oh, and she has her book club as well. We usually have around eight women who come to the house once a week and they either read or talk about books."

"Oh? What are they reading right now?"

I don't have the slightest idea, often leaving the house as guests arrive. I was never much of a reader, having struggled in school. That, and I become antsy sitting still so long. I much prefer being outdoors and on the move. I'm not the social butterfly that Pru is. Large groups make me feel like

I'm on display, my every move watched and judged. Like the morning I came upon Da hanging from the lamppost. Neighbors' whispers burrowing into my ears, growing like weeds, and spreading through my chest. Squeezing my lungs until I was gasping for breath.

No, Pru's reading group is not for me.

"Jane Austen, no doubt." Josiah's voice pulls me out before I sink too deep. "The ladies must resort to the romance in novels as there aren't a great many eligible bachelors here. I'm the best of the lot, so I suppose Pru's out of luck."

"Humble, I see."

He shrugs. "Merely reminding you what you're missing out on."

"Then perhaps a whaler who comes in for supplies. Someone new who knows nothing about Warbler. You never know, Josiah. I just want someone different for her."

"A whaler, eh?" His eyes harden.

"Sure. Why not?"

Josiah nods over my shoulder.

I turn around. The beauty of the golden hour does nothing to soften the situation occurring at the end of the street. Pru is trying to step around a large man, but he keeps blocking her. The breeze carries his cajoling tone all the way to us. I recognize it at the same moment his profile becomes clear.

Leonard.

Pru's expression shifts between harried and apologetic, lines on her forehead, half smile, half grimace. No matter the situation, Pru never fails to be courteous. It can be maddening at times. I'm not sure where she got this quality from. But in a situation such as this, good manners only provide ample opportunity for someone like Leonard to take advantage of her. As she attempts to step around him once more, he grabs her instead.

My vision narrows. I'm moving so quickly, it's a moment

before I hear Josiah's footsteps catch up to me. Leonard says something, and Pru's face goes red. Before I can even fathom what terrible thing he might have said, someone steps between the two.

My periphery a blur, it's as if Gideon climbed out of the air itself. Josiah grabs my arm, stopping my progress, the momentum of my skirt still moving forward. I glare at him, but he holds his hand up. "Just wait."

Down the street, Leonard releases Pru and laughs, unaffected by the new arrival. She rubs her arm, and my own bruised arm aches in response. My stomach twists with the effort it takes to prevent myself from rushing over. I should be with her. Protecting her.

Leonard's broad back is to us, so I cannot see his face, nor see what Gideon is doing in front of him, but with no warning, the general ease with which Leonard is holding himself is gone. Like a rabbit noticing a predator, every muscle in his body appears to stiffen.

He takes a cautious step back. Another. Then he turns around completely and hurries down the street. He doesn't even acknowledge us as he passes. When he makes it to the corner, he looks over his shoulder at Gideon, a disturbed expression tugging at his weather-worn skin.

I turn around and catch Gideon and Pru squeezing each other's hands. He nods at Josiah and me before walking down a path between the houses. When Pru catches sight of us, she squeals and hurries toward us, skirt swinging, eyes on Josiah, who has all but been a big brother to her her entire life.

Josiah looks at me out of the corner of his eye. "Gideon doesn't seem so bad to me, Tempe."

The ship carver's abrupt arrival and departure leave me lost for words. There one second, gone the next. Like a ghost. It seems there are no obstacles the man cannot get through. He gets whatever it is he wants.

I lift my head a notch. *Almost* everything.

When Pru reaches us, she squeezes Josiah's hands, all but begging for him to join us for dinner so she can hear all about his adventures. "Mother will be so pleased to see you. I just know it."

I follow behind the two and their joyful banter, and yet the peace I should feel at having Pru and Josiah to myself has been overshadowed by my curiosity. What did Gideon say to Leonard to make him look so fearful? What would make a man like that walk away?

CHAPTER 9

Though I am not keen on talking with Pru about Gideon, I cannot shake from my head what I saw yesterday. It's a scratch I awoke with this morning that must be itched. After I've extinguished all the lampposts and refilled the oil wells, I return home to find Pru ironing her dress for the Gathering later this evening.

"Morning, Tempe. There's hot bread for you over here." She nods to the hearth, where a cut of soda bread rests on a plate.

A flat iron sits on a trivet set close to the fire while Pru works with a second iron, rubbing its smooth side over the wrinkled cotton of her green dress. Silk dresses are all any of the women can talk about among the upper class, but there is no possible way for us to afford one. Her dress does have the desired V-neck and narrow bodice, so she won't be completely out of style.

She wouldn't have to go without if she married Gideon, though.

The thought pulls at me like the undertow. I run a finger over the soft needlework on Pru's dress—dainty leaves along the hemline, collar, and wrists done in a golden thread that glows if the light hits it just right. She has a beautiful matching shawl of golds, browns, and greens to wear with it.

Pru folds another pleat, sending the iron over its long stretch. Her dress, elegant in its simplicity, inspires thoughts of Ireland. I have never seen it with my own eyes, but Da told us enough stories I feel like I have been there. I can still hear the deep brogue in his voice as he told us stories of Tír na nÓg, fairy circles, puca, and banshees. Mother scolded him once for telling me about the banshees right before bed. I had nightmares for weeks of a keening woman who foretold the death of a family member.

For all my fears of a banshee's sorrowful wails, I never heard her. Of course, I do not believe in such myths. Though the fanciful part of me, the part that is distinctly Da, wonders if I *had* heard her . . . could I have stopped him? Perhaps she had cried out to us from across the Atlantic, but we could not hear her warning.

Pru begins humming one of his songs, and I have to blink back the wetness in my eyes. The song is soothing in its duet with the iron's soft whisper over the cotton. After a minute, she swaps flat irons, the one in her hand no longer hot enough to smooth any wrinkles.

The plate of bread she set near the fire warms my stiff fingers as I pick it up and take it to the table. After pouring myself a glass of water from the pitcher, I cut a small piece of butter off the butter dish and smear it onto the bread. The heat of it is a warm cloud, and I enjoy a comforting bite while Pru continues her song. Mother sits in her rocker, stroking her fingers along a green ribbon stretched out over her lap. For a moment, I can only see Molly's small hands gripping her basket of ribbon and lace. I blink twice before the image fades, and the memory of her scream dries out my mouth, the bread becoming tasteless mush.

"Pru?"

She glances up at me, song silent. "Hmm?"

"What happened yesterday with Leonard?"

She frowns and switches out irons once more. "Who?"

I set the bread back down. "The whaler who was giving you trouble before Gideon showed up. His name is Leonard."

"Oh." She winces. "He was unpleasant."

I pull my chair closer to her and adjust my feet nearer

to the fire. I flex them and then point them, the motion distributing the heat more evenly. "Unpleasant, indeed. I had a similar run-in with him earlier this week. What did he want?"

"He asked if I would go for a walk."

Warning bells ring in my head, and an image of Molly disappearing into the fog fills my vision. A knot twists in my stomach.

"When I said no, he wouldn't let me pass. He became quite crass. Thankfully, Gideon arrived." She bites her lip as her eyes flit my way and then back down.

"I saw that. I'm glad he stepped in." Even more so now, knowing Leonard tried to take her somewhere. I need to check in with Henry. He ought to know.

The iron stops moving, resting on a pleat. Pru widens her eyes. "Really?"

I heave a sigh and sit up, the knot unraveling a bit. I lean my elbows on my thighs and pick at my trousers for a moment before glancing up at her. I don't want to admit it, but it's true. Despite my reservations, watching Gideon step in for Pru eased some of my unsettled spirit. "Of course, Pru. It was a good thing to do."

She offers a small smile before moving the iron. With a little patience and give and take, this rift between us over Gideon might be mended. I still do not want them to be together, but if I've learned anything in my eighteen years, it is though we can never know what might happen, we can prepare for the worst and hope for the best.

"What did Gideon say?" I encourage her to continue. "Leonard retreated hastily after they spoke."

Pru shrugs. "Gideon introduced himself and explained he knew Leonard's captain and asked if he needed to have a word with him."

It is a valid enough threat to warn Leonard off, but I

didn't peg him as the type to back down so easily. "That was all?"

She nods. "Then he left."

The pendulum whooshes on the wall as resignation settles in my limbs. I was reading into their interaction too much, I suppose. But why did it leave me feeling unsettled?

"Well." Pru's voice pulls me back. "Gideon also shook his hand."

"A standard greeting."

"Yes, but I think Gideon has quite the grip." She smiles in appreciation. "Leonard flinched and pulled away as soon as he could." Pru shrugs and sets the iron down. She picks the dress up, flips it, lays it down again, and begins to iron the back side.

Leonard pulled away after Gideon touched him, but that doesn't necessarily mean anything. Yet my thoughts immediately jump to the night two years ago when Gideon grabbed me. There was something to it, a strangeness that froze me completely. I search for recognition, but time has blurred my recall.

"What are you wearing to the Gathering?" Pru asks, reeling me in from memory. "Shall I iron a dress for you? The blue one, perhaps?"

I shake my head, pushing my present disappointments away. "I won't be attending this year. There is too much to do."

The cast iron clanks onto the trivet. Pru turns to look at me, her expression unamused. "You aren't working all night. You can join the festivities for a little while at least. You always have before."

I swallow the lump in my throat, this conversation not unfamiliar. Pru stands in front of me, a frown on her face. But the hard lines of her go soft, and suddenly all I see is Molly with her basket, a curl escaped from her bonnet, kindness in her hopeful smile as she speaks nearly the same sentiment. What must her family be feeling right now? Warbler is to celebrate a productive season and dance, eat, and be merry while their daughter is nowhere to be found. How can I enjoy the Gathering when her absence is partially my fault because I never reported the scream, nor the lights going out?

"Josiah will be expecting you. He told me he was looking forward to dancing with you." Pru shakes her head at me, chastising in place of Mother.

I shrug helplessly.

"After all that has happened this week, I believe you've earned the right to enjoy yourself. Don't you?"

"It is *because* of what has transpired this week that I need to keep an eye on Warbler. I'm treading a fine line, and should anything happen to anyone during the Gathering . . ." I trail off, leaving her to speculate on her own as I run my hand over my face. What could happen? I do not know, but it feels like there is a risk here. Like a window is open, and if I don't keep an eye out, there could be a storm and the water will rush in.

"The Gathering starts a half hour before you even need to light the lampposts, Tempe."

I nod begrudgingly at the fact.

"I appreciate what you've done for us and all you feel you must do . . ." Her voice slows as if bracing herself.

"All I feel I must do?" The words come out haltingly through my laughter. When Pru doesn't respond, I see she isn't jesting. The knots return to my stomach. "What are you saying?"

She places her hands on her hips and looks at me straight. I might have respected her directness, a strength so few possess when it comes to discussing difficult matters. But immediately I feel myself going on the defensive.

"You take on too much." She glares at me when I scoff and raises her voice. "Unnecessarily, I might add."

"I do not take on more than I need to. Besides"—I gesture at Mother—"I don't want to burden you with more than you already have to handle."

"How do you know how much I can handle? Why must you bear the weight of everything when you have me to help share the load? I'm your sister, or did you forget?"

"You don't understand."

Pru throws her hands up. "Help me, then."

I groan, rubbing my pointer fingers against my thumbs in agitation.

"I can take one of your patrols to make sure the lights are still lit so you can catch up on sleep. Or you can confide in me with whatever worries come up. I'm great at brainstorming solutions to problems." She takes an eager step forward. "It isn't as if I don't have the time. I've had help with things at home, so I'm not sure why you think I cannot help you, even if it is with an emotional burden."

"You've had help?" That certainly was not something I expected to hear. "What do you mean?"

"If I need someone to keep an eye on Mother so I can run errands, or if I need help with a recipe, a second set of hands for garden or housework, the women from my book club are there. Most importantly, though, they've been a refuge for my own thoughts and ideas. They've helped bolster me when I needed it, given me perspectives I hadn't considered, and valued my opinions." Her eyes brighten; all the while jealousy burns my skin as if she'd taken the iron to it. "They've been a great comfort to me."

"Because I'm not around to help."

"That isn't what I'm saying."

"I bet that's what they think, though. Have you spoken to them about me?"

She bites her lip, confidence chased away by uncertainty. "Yes."

I gesture for her to continue, mentally bracing myself.

"You work so hard for us, but I can't be your excuse to not go after what you want." She smooths her skirt down, though it does not need it. "If you aren't careful, you'll lose your chance and end up a spinster."

There it is. I picture them all in here with their romance books in their laps, drinking their tea, gossiping about me and my apparently misdirected priorities as a woman. It takes everything in me not to scream. "The only way to be happy in this life is to be married. That's what you and your friends believe? That I'm wasting my time working rather than chasing down a man?"

"Of course not. Everyone admires your tenacity to fight for your position. Me most of all." She smiles with pride, which I couldn't care less about at this point. "But marriage, love, is just as much of a valid path toward happiness. One I believe you'd like to take with Josiah but are neglecting entirely."

"I'm done with this conversation." I stand up and head toward our bedroom. "I'm going to lie down for a while."

It isn't exactly a retreat. I was up for multiple patrols throughout the night and could use the sleep. When the door closes behind me, I expel my breath. The mirror catches my reflection, drawing my attention. My stern expression is bereft of any softness, frown lines tucked in pale skin. There is no sign of vulnerability. High cheekbones emphasize the darkness beneath my tired blue eyes. I cannot recall what I look like wearing a carefree smile.

I try to picture my hair down. The dark clothes and cap of the lamplighter replaced with a soft lilac gown and ribbon as I dance amid others. Laughter and gaiety.

Right now, she is an untouchable version of myself, a dream. In truth, amid the dancers I will be in my lamplighter gear, hair pinned up, eyes observant, and stance solid. No opportunity to do more. A rock among diamonds. I narrow my gaze at my reflection and see exhaustion, anxiety, frustration. I lift my chin.

There is also strength and determination.

In truth, I do not like how Pru's words cut me. I'm glad she can confide in her friends and am grateful they have helped her. But why wouldn't she confide in me? Does she think I cannot help? Shame chases the heat of jealousy at the very thought. Or is she unwilling to shoulder me with more, believing it too much a burden for me?

Well, isn't that the pot calling the kettle black.

Is she right, though? Have I lost myself so completely in my work and in supporting our family that I've lost an important part of myself? I know she means well, but her words have wounded me to my core. True or not, it's as if she couldn't care less how much of myself I've given to her, to ensure her health and happiness.

She thinks the only way to happiness is marriage. That the worst to occur is to become a spinster. I suppose if there is one thing I've done right, it's provided for her well enough that rather than fear there won't be enough food on the table, she's more worried about courtship. And if that is what will make her happy, I aim to do what I can so that she has it. I've *been* doing so all along, in fact, causing an imbalance in my own wants and needs.

Have I been misguided in my choices?

I turn away from the mirror to strip off my clothes and doubts. They fall to the floor in a heap. There is nothing wrong with being cautious for what storms life brings. Preparing. I would love to attend the Gathering. To set my cap and bag down to dance the night away with Josiah in a gown to truly set Susannah's envy alight, just for the sheer pleasure of it.

A spinster, indeed.

I splash cold water onto my face and wash the grime from my hands in the basin. The bed creaks as I climb in and pull the quilt over my head. The cold blankets, so welcome in the summer, send a shiver from my toes all the way up to my neck. I curl up, waiting for my body to heat them.

How does one manage to tuck their concerns and duties away in order to truly let go and enjoy themselves? There are a great number of people in Warbler, men and women alike, who have taken to telling me how I should be living my life, without understanding the ramifications of what that would mean for me. I know the right path for myself. But so many people shaking their heads at me, all the disappointment—they give me pause. I draw the quilt up over my head to block out the light. The doubts.

All I've done is trapped them in closer. Whispers in my ears.

It is no surprise my sleep is fitful and short. Staying home provides no outlet for my thoughts, and so I dress and make my way to the waterfront, where preparation is being made for the Gathering. Tables are fashioned from boards laid out together over barrels, with tablecloths thrown on top. These are placed in long lines in front of the businesses. The light from within the establishments will illuminate the makeshift tables. Everyone contributes to the celebration. Linens, flowers, games for the children, breads, pies, chowders, ale, cider, even fresh fruit. The village's musicians will rotate playing, taking turns eating and celebrating before they all come together to play the second half of the night.

Josiah and George have already rolled out barrels from the cooperage with the help of others. These barrels establish the perimeter for the Gathering. Oil lamps are interspersed on the barrel heads, along with gourds and leaves. Normally, such a large use of whale oil wouldn't be permitted. But as the celebration is known to go late into the night, for safety reasons there needs to be as much light as possible.

I recall previous Gatherings with pleasure. Children snuck around beneath the tables, trying to steal sweets while the adults weren't looking. Dogs ran back and forth, ready to pounce on any dropped food. The sweet scent of hot pies mingled with the tobacco of those partaking of their smoke pipes. Everyone wore their finest clothes and was in the highest of spirits. As couples danced in the glowing fog, I liked to pretend the Sidhe—fairy folk—had stepped out of Da's stories to join us humans for a night.

The hammering of mallets pulls my attention from the memory of twirling couples to the dock. Scaffolding has been suspended off the bow of the foreign whaling ship. Two men stand on it, while another three stand on deck, reaching over with tools and offering more support for the figurehead. One of the men, Gideon, perches on the scaffolding with ease, one hand grasping the figurehead's shoulder as he hammers into the wood with his other hand.

He has finished his new siren.

She has long curls, her arms down at her sides, wrists exposed and turned outward, lips parted as if she's at the end of a breath. From where I stand on the waterfront, the detail is astounding. I can only imagine what she looks like up close. The captain watches from the dock, hands on his hips, nodding in what I imagine is approval.

With the sound of woodworking and the splash of fishermen behind me, I enter the general store. Mr. Landon grabs the wicks I need and takes note of the new barrel of oil to be delivered to the town hall shed so that I can refill my cannister each morning. Warbler pays for my supplies, and Mr. Landon keeps a tally of how much I use. I've never used more than the quota established at the beginning of each year. I know my lamp lights.

Back outside, Josiah catches me. "Tempe!"

His eyes are bright, sleeves rolled up, right forearm boasting a long white scar. He received it the sixth year of his apprenticeship with George. While shaping the inside of a barrel stave, he lost the grip of his jigger drawknife. Later, when I saw his wrapped arm and blood-covered apron, I felt as if I had plunged headfirst into the river during winter. Rather than seek attention for his injury, he all but pushed me away, ashamed to have made such a mistake.

With any other apprentice, a mistake so dangerous might have shaken their confidence, but Josiah embraced the incident. He told me once that he always thought of it anytime he was in a hurry. It reminded him to take a breath, slow down. Have patience. I can't recall him ever making a mistake of the like since.

Though the memory of that stocky, young boy is clear as crystal in my mind's eye, there is only the man standing before me. Josiah has a hardness to his body that has been shaped and molded after so many years—the final touch from his travels on the *Miriam.* It sets my heart thumping in a way I don't dare admit aloud, though I know Pru would approve.

Instead, I gesture at the decorated wharf. "It all looks wonderful."

"It's coming along, that's for sure." He wipes his forearm along his head, clearing the beads of sweat. He grins and clears his throat, an almost bashful drop in his gaze before he lifts it once more to my own. "I'm looking forward to dancing with you."

"Oh." I don't need to feign a grimace. "I'm not coming."

His shoulders sag with disappointment. "Why not? Is your mother ill? Pru?"

"No, but I'm going to patrol after I've lit the lampposts."

"Well, what about before your shift? Surely there is time to stop by."

"It hardly seems worth it for so short a time." He flinches, but I continue on. "Truth is, I cannot risk it."

Silence sits between us, a third member, for far too long before the concern washes from his face, replaced by exasperation. "Risk what?"

"Josiah, are you serious?" He crosses his arms in response to my tone, clearly annoyed with me. But how can he not understand? "I have to work. I cannot make another mistake, and the Gathering is the perfect storm for me. People imbibing too much and not paying attention on their way home. I told you what I've been dealing with. Have you already forgotten?"

As I speak, his expression hardens further until he could be a figurehead himself. A perfect replica of irritation and disappointment towering over anyone confident enough in themselves to approach. He might be able to intimidate most, but I am the ocean. I cannot be moved.

"This panic over losing your job is all for naught." All trace of the previous kindness and concern has left his voice. Frustration lowers his volume. "Take a breath. You'll run yourself ragged for no reason. Surely you can join the Gathering for a little while. Dance with me."

This is maddening. First Pru, and now Josiah. I grit my teeth. "Are you purposely being obtuse? This isn't a jest. It's my life, my family's life. My livelihood. You cannot understand what it is like to have your every move watched and be uncertain of your future."

"It doesn't have to be that way." He speaks softly, the implication loud. Rejecting his marriage offer is still an open wound.

"I thought you of all people would understand, or at least try." I lift my chin, pulse racing for a different reason. "All you're doing is making life harder for me."

Hurt flashes in his eyes, and I want more than anything to take my accusatory words back. He blinks, and the hardness resumes—a look I am becoming all too familiar with these days.

"You're right. I'll leave you be." Josiah departs so quickly all I can do is stutter at his absence, mouth open with no one here to listen to my justifications. I turn my back on the chatter and laughter on the wharf. A group of girls run past me, the leader holding a long pink ribbon like a flag as they go.

A hollowness takes up inside me as I recall Molly and her basket of ribbon.

Regret and guilt are fierce scavengers, and I am easy prey. I haven't dedicated near enough energy into helping find out what happened to Molly. I had a part to play in her disappearance, however unintended, and in all probability was the last person to hear her. I failed her as the lamplighter, but I refuse to fail her as a woman and a neighbor.

After I take the fresh batch of wicks to the supply shed, I make my way over the bridge and into the Green. I pass by one of Pru's friends from book club—Sara, I think?—who greets me with a smile. I nod, but do not stop. I imagine her shaking her head after I pass, and it takes quite a bit of effort not to check over my shoulder. She's oblivious to my intentions, spinster that I am.

I'm not sure if it's the village's traditional notions, Josiah's inability to put himself in my shoes, or Pru's lack of appreciation, but a determination to not only set them straight but prove to myself I know what I'm doing provides an extra wind to my sails.

The Green is the last place I saw Molly. I step beside the lamppost, imagining myself with her, a shadow as she walks home. Eyes closed, I take a deep breath of the crisp air and then reopen them. The residential district is laid out before me as the fog of that night creeps through the streets, spilling out beneath the smattering of trees. I take one step and then another, paying special attention to what is around me, aware all the while that Leonard was out here that night as well.

Pru's voice rings in my ears. *He asked if I would go for a walk.*

There shouldn't be anything interesting about this path, but knowing it was possibly Molly's last walk instills an ominous air to it. The first set of homes are smaller, the shutters in need of paint, piles of leaves and brittle stalks of plants unacknowledged. I nod at the villagers passing me by, not all of whom return it. Most everyone is excited for the celebration tonight and the short respite it will offer them after months of hard toil.

The houses are larger on the far west side of the village, the fencing and architecture more intricate. These are the homes of not only our merchants, but also the farming families. The land behind these homes is a patchwork quilt of farms that supply our village with produce.

Thankfully, no one appears to be about when I reach Susannah's home. Avoiding any sort of confrontation with her is high on my list. I think through what Henry found out from Susannah—that Molly had forgotten her gloves at the seamstress and had considered walking back. How long did Molly linger here with Susannah? Did she even head back for the seamstress's, or did she instead head home?

I decide to proceed to Molly's home first. I haven't any idea what I'm looking for and find my earlier resolve lagging behind. Of course, Henry and the others would have done this already. I'm not sure what I thought I might find that they didn't. Upon reaching Molly's white house with blue shutters and ivy crawling up the sides, I sigh, disappointment weighing me down. Nothing. There are two lampposts between Molly's and Susannah's homes, and neither one of them had been extinguished the night she disappeared.

She must have believed she had time to return to Celia's for her gloves and headed that way instead.

Did something grab her attention? Or someone? I heard the scream closer to Da's lamppost, so there is a possibility something along the way there may strike a chord. As I pass each house, I run through theories about each villager and their possible relationship with Molly. How it could possibly sour. With each one I entertain, the more uncomfortable I feel. The very thought that a neighbor, someone I know, could possibly harm Molly has me wanting to rinse off in the icy river, shock my system back to a time when the world made sense.

If she did head back across the seaport, there is a chance she could have run into Leonard. The timing would have matched up with when I left him. Yet Henry and Matthew, our own constables, haven't found any substantial evidence to support this. How can I? Good intentions only go so far. With a heavy heart and zero answers, and feeling more than a little foolish, I turn around to return home.

That is, until a familiar face turns onto my path. The moment I see him, I laugh aloud at the obviousness of it all. I could kick myself.

Benjamin, a man I find suspect, and the drunkard who blew the whistle on me.

CHAPTER 10

Eyes red and sweat beading down his head, he maneuvers a wheelbarrow to a stop beside a pile of horse manure in the middle of the street.

While I am certain Benjamin is always drunk to some degree, he does manage to function around midday. Cleaning up the horse manure from our community stable and streets, while not a coveted position, is valued. No one wants to walk through it or deal with the smell if they can help it. As part of an initiative to care for Warbler, the council voted to create the position, and while the assumption was that a child would fill it, it was Benjamin who stepped up.

The drunk needed to support his habit somehow.

"Good afternoon, Benjamin," I call out.

Benjamin jerks, causing his shovel to hit the cobblestones, missing the pile of manure at his feet completely. We both wince at the sharp *cling*. I'm sure it is more painful for him, if the squinting of his cloudy eyes and shaking of his hands is any indication of his state right now.

"Oh, I apologize. I didn't mean to startle you." I smile, and then do everything in my power not to wrinkle my nose as I stop beside him. The man is rank. Somehow, he manages to smell worse than the steaming pile awaiting his shovel. I proceed to breathe through my mouth. "I was hoping to ask you about the other night. You know, when Molly went missing."

He pushes the limp hair from his eyes only to have it fall back into place and licks his lips twice over. "Awful thing."

I nod. "I know you told the constable about seeing the lamppost lights out, and I was wondering if you saw anything else odd. It's just, I know I lit them, and I'm trying to figure out what caused them to go out."

Benjamin's eyes connect with mine briefly before slipping downward, as if losing focus. If I hadn't found the lampposts out myself, I would be hard-pressed to believe this man actually saw what he saw. His hands shake as he sways, and I can't help but think Henry is probably correct. Benjamin couldn't easily manage climbing a lamppost to extinguish it, let alone restraining a healthy young woman, while in his usual state of inebriation.

But it's not impossible.

Nevertheless, the concern I might have had about being alone with him lessens. I lift my eyebrows, awaiting his response.

He lets out a breath of air, his stained and darkened teeth like rancid corn kernels. "I didn't see nothing."

I don't bother hiding my disappointment. It was a long shot. Benjamin rubs his lip with a filthy hand, mouth smacking, already anticipating a drink. It's a wonder he isn't already at the tavern, which gets me thinking. "What made you enter the residential district?"

"Didn't."

A frown pulls at me as my pulse begins to race. The tavern is directly east of the Green, the opposite direction of the unlit lampposts. "Then how did you know the lights were out?"

"Was told."

My jaw nearly drops to the ground.

I didn't see nothing. Could a detail so small as the nuance in conversation be the key to all of this? Henry must have asked him if anything strange had happened, and for him it would be the lights being out. Benjamin was just repeating what he'd been told, failing to make the distinction he had not actually seen them himself. He had in fact seen nothing. So, Henry moved on.

Benjamin may be lying to send me on a false lead, but wouldn't he have told Henry the same lie? I cannot help but grapple for this new information as if I had a fish on a line. I grip his thin shoulders, excitement coursing through me. "Who? Who told you about the lampposts?"

He doesn't seem to mind, thin eyebrows rising up in mild interest. He shrugs. "Woke up to get a drink. Voice said two lights is out and I was going the wrong way. Sure 'nough I was on the wrong bridge. Turned my ass round and took the other."

"Did you recognize who it was?"

Benjamin steps back from me, eyes shifting. "Was the fog. Watching me, speaking to me."

A leaf skitters across the cobblestones. The cold breeze blows Benjamin's long scraggly hair even farther into his eyes. I clear my throat and release his arms. "Excuse me?"

"Always there, they are. The spirits. They keep an eye on good ol' Ben, though. Always do." His eyes glaze over as he stares at something behind me. I spare a glance, but there is nothing. Only the trees, branches shifting back into place as the breeze dies. I swallow and look back to find his attention on me once again. Direct. Unblinking. "Yearning for what they lost while at sea."

He is speaking of the whalers dead in the ocean. A common story passed over ale at the tavern that often dissuades visitors from making Warbler their permanent home. It's one I've never considered credible. But I indulge his fantasy nonetheless in the hopes of deciphering some truth in clarification. "And what did they lose?"

"Their loves."

Navigating Benjamin is like rowing a boat with my hands as the oars. "So the voice, the fog, it sounded like a man, then?"

He nods.

"You're positive you cannot recall more than that? If you did, you might be able to help us figure out what happened to Molly."

"Awful thing what happened to her."

My shoulders drop as his attention shifts, looping back around like the wavering path he takes each night from the tavern. I'm not going to get any further with him. The small glimmer of hope I had is scraped up and thrown into the wheelbarrow with the rest of the manure.

All I know for sure is there could have been a man out there, hidden in the fog, but he remains just as much a shadow as before. Why did he tell Benjamin about the lampposts? I do not believe it was for altruistic reasons. I rub at the chill rushing through my arms. Once Henry found out about the lampposts, all attention was shifted toward me, despite the scream being nowhere near those posts.

They must have been a diversion. Perhaps I was the original target?

With a nod, I leave Benjamin to his work, feeling a little worse for wear. I drop by the constables' office to share what I've learned from Benjamin, though I don't know what good it'll do. Matthew is on shift and writes everything down before dismissing me to make his rounds. I suppose I shouldn't expect more.

I sit at the table alone. Mother and Pru left for the Gathering a quarter of an hour past. Excited, high-pitched voices trail each other down the street, the click of heels on cobblestones leading them onward, the clap of closing gates left behind. Soon it will only be myself, the pulsing embers, the swinging pendulum, and the aching memory of a different time.

The afternoon light won't falter for at least another hour.

I trace my fingernails along the grooves in the wood, lost in the monotonous motion while emotions churn within me, a wayward storm encased in glass. The heat in the embers brightens before darkening. Brightens again. Pulsing like a heart.

The fire screen scrapes the ground as I drag it in front of the fireplace, the burning embers safely tucked behind its guard. The soft curtain is but a whisper as I pull it aside to gaze at the empty street. Everyone has left.

What am I doing?

The council's lack of confidence in my ability and Pru's friends' opinions of my person have shaken me. So much so I am allowing them to dictate the choices I make. Proving everyone wrong has been at the forefront of my decisions. The truth is I have nothing to prove. I am enough and always have been. I learn from my mistakes and become stronger because of them. The epiphany pushes into place like the cork in a barrel.

I don't need anyone's validation.

I stand up, pride pulling my shoulders back, a cleansing breath filling my lungs. I'm the lamplighter. Me. No one else. I find the path through the dark because no one else can.

"It's my life to live."

I snatch my hat off the wall and pin it to my head with the hairpins I keep in my pockets, my hair already braided up. Jacket on, I grab my lantern for later, shut the door behind me, and inhale deeply of the crisp autumn air as I make my way down the street. The haunting notes of a violin guide me, and with each step I take, a weight begins to lift. Deep amber light pours through the tree branches reaching out overhead. The creek trickles as I hurry across the bridge, my pace quickening as more jubilant sounds surface through the still setting.

Excitement courses through me, the dam broken, and for a silly moment I nearly skip. I laugh aloud, thinking of the look on Josiah's and Pru's faces if they saw me skipping along the wharf, looking like I'd lost my mind.

I turn the corner onto the wharf. The Gathering is a crowd of colors; swirling eddies of laughter, chatter, song; wholesome smells of stews and chowders; and a decadent sweet-smelling cloud of cinnamon. Small groups stand outside the barreled perimeter, children chasing one another in circles as dogs bark merrily behind them, men smoking their pipes, whalers and fishermen gesturing to the ships anchored along the river like wooden sentinels. I set my lantern on a barrel in front of the tavern and make my way through the crowd.

My eyes search through the throng, drawn to the tall figure of Josiah. I try to contain my smile, but already my cheeks hurt. The crowd opens up, and he twirls through with a dance partner. His left hand rests on Susannah's lower back, his right cupping her small hand as her other rests on his chest. She stares up at him like a pink flower taking in the sun.

The Gathering darkens suddenly, the sun dipping behind the woods across the river.

There is a delighted shout to my right. Pru draws my eye, waving, face beaming. I can no longer see Josiah and Susannah, but I still feel them moving just out of eyesight, like the heat of a fire in the hearth when you're across the room. You know exactly where the flames are.

Pru throws her arms around me when I reach her and Mother, who is perched on a chair, a plate of food sitting in her lap. She glances up at me but says nothing. Pru pulls away, a sprig of baby's breath tucked behind her ear. "You're here! Whatever changed your mind?"

I shrug, smiling weakly. It's all I can manage at the moment.

"Are you going to dance with Josiah?" Her cheeks are

rosy as she sways to the rhythm of the music, always in motion. I don't even think she realizes she's doing it.

"He's currently engaged." It's apparent by Pru's frown I failed to hide the hurt in my tone. I clear my throat and gesture out. "Quite the turnout this year."

As to be expected, Pru ignores me, standing on her toes to look over my shoulder, eyes narrowed. I snatch a clam cake from Mother's plate and pop it into my mouth, chewing the hot morsel with a ravenous fervor. It all but melts in my mouth. I recognize it as Celia's recipe. She makes them every year.

Did she give Molly's gloves back to her family?

I reach out for another clam cake, sadness threatening to knock me off balance, but Mother shifts to the left, my hand glancing against her knee instead. Did she truly just guard her plate against me? A surprised laugh skips out of me before I can stop it. I look up at her face, a fragile hope unfurling inside me. She's looking away, down the wharf, unaware of my presence.

"Pleasure seeing you, Temperance."

I drag my gaze away from Mother and swallow the final bit of clam cake in my mouth, the pleasurable taste gone. "Hello, Gideon."

The ship carver wears a black frock coat that ends at his thighs, a short waist coat of blue, and long black trousers tucked into boots. Per usual, his long hair is pulled back. A black top hat is perched atop his head, elongating his stature. His straight posture appears unperturbed, at ease. The intensity in his gaze, however, suggests dark interest.

I flinch as someone squeezes my arm.

"Surely you aren't jealous over Susannah?" Pru's chiding tone interjects into the space that has become small in mere moments.

"Of course not." She doesn't appear to notice my sudden

discomfort as I shift closer to her. It is a struggle, but I manage to place an imaginary barrier between myself and Gideon. Pretend the only people here are Pru and myself talking about a love interest. Everything is normal.

"Then I suggest you make your presence known. Besides—" She reaches out for Gideon, who steps close, breaking my barrier as if it were mere water and he an anchor. Her arm hooks through his, and I take a deep breath through my nose. "I'd like to dance with Gideon."

"Go ahead. I'll stay with Mother." I refuse to look at Gideon, heat coursing up my neck, no doubt a splotchy red breaking up my fair skin.

"Please, enjoy yourself," he murmurs.

"Mother is fine, Tempe. Go. Josiah is too kind to refuse Susannah. By the looks of it, she's quite content to stay with him the entire night." Pru nods toward the dancers. There is a gap in the crowd. Josiah is smiling indulgently down at Susannah, who is batting her eyelashes, a coy smile on her lips as a new song begins.

It is silly to believe Josiah would wait for me, especially considering my refusal to participate in the celebration. He's allowed to dance with whomever he would like. Jealousy and irritation are two emotions that have no place here. I've stooped low, acting like a lovesick schoolgirl. Even under the circumstances, this sort of response is unnatural for me, jumping to conclusions and acting on them without a moment's hesitation. I sneak a glance back at Gideon and Pru, my vision narrowing in on their tightly clasped hands.

Pru is happy. When I look back into her eyes, they sparkle with eagerness. A hopeful smile tugs at her pink lips. She's happy, yes, but not only for herself. For me. For us. I showed up when I said I would not and we are talking about Josiah, whom she knows holds my heart.

Is this what it is like to be carefree? To laugh with your sister and focus on something other than the debilitating fear of losing your job and being unable to care for your family? Of being stripped of the part of your life that makes you proud?

I've been so intent on shouldering all the weight alone, perhaps I have deprived Pru's and my relationship of something pivotal. Connection—in all things, but particularly joy. An emotion lacking in our home for the last four years. She's right. Would entertaining the notion of better things be so bad?

A little girl's scream of delight pulls my attention. Her father wraps her up in his arms, a doll clutched in her hand, and swings her over his shoulder. The wharf abounds with echoing sounds. Tankards of ale clank against one another in cheers. Young women titter as eligible bachelors strut past them. Chowder slops into bowls and villagers bite into apples with a crisp crunch. A group of children stand to the side of the dance area, playing a game of graces, the wooden hoop trailing blue and green ribbon as it flies through the air and is caught on the wooden dowel of a little girl with a missing front tooth.

The evening is filled with gladness. A reason to shrug off hardship and responsibility—for most of us, anyway—and be joyful. To remember we are a community. Josiah and the other whalers from the *Miriam* have been out at sea for six months, and their friends and family are happy to have them home. Grateful for their safe return and a successful journey. It has been a plentiful harvest and decent year. While Molly's disappearance is a dark mark against the time, the world cannot stop. It might feel like it does to her family, however. Their absence has not escaped me. But life does not stop. It goes on.

Even without people like Molly.

Like Da.

Everyone is relaxed and celebrating with one another, including the council. They do not appear troubled in the least, their cheeks ruddy already with drink, an obvious food stain on the mayor's shirt. The tension ebbs from my shoulders. I'm a part of this too. I can be here. I should be here.

Pru's smile is all but beaming.

I wind my way through people in conversation, a few tapping their heels, and pass dancing couples until I reach Josiah and Susannah. Josiah's eyes widen. I frown and gesture at Susannah, whose back is to me, and his deep brown eyes suddenly sparkle with humor. He shrugs helplessly, laughter barely contained.

I clear my throat. "May I cut in?"

Susannah looks over her shoulder, all joviality leeching out of her smile when she catches sight of me. She turns back to Josiah, curls bouncing with the movement. "Surely you won't deny me the rest of our dance."

The whiny pitch in her tone makes it clear she is pouting. I cross my arms and barely refrain from tapping my toe.

"I promise to finish our dance later tonight, Susannah. Tempe makes her rounds soon. I wouldn't want to miss this opportunity to dance with her." He has a knack for civility.

She sighs. "Promise me two dances, at least?"

Josiah is to be congratulated on maintaining a straight face before her beseeching tone. I can only roll my eyes.

"Looking forward to them both." He smiles kindly as she dips into a shallow curtsy.

Someone bumps into me. The crowd swirls as I turn around and find myself inches away from a huge chest. I look up.

"Don't you have somewhere to be, lamplighter?" Leonard smirks down at me, hate in his gaze.

CHAPTER 11

Josiah's hand slips into my own and squeezes, reminding me that I am not alone. It says *I'm here.* It's all the reassurance I need.

"I'm right where I'm supposed to be," I reply through gritted teeth. Josiah squeezes my hand again, a silent question.

Leonard's smile is full of malice. "Wouldn't want any more lights to go out, now, would we?"

Susannah has been tittering behind her hand at my discomfort. Now the gleeful delight on her face flickers at the same time I'm hit with the weight of his words. My mind races back to what Benjamin said. The voice in the fog. The spirits of dead whalers. If he had recognized the voice, if it had come from one of our villagers, he would have said so. Right? He doesn't know Leonard, though, a foreigner to our seaport.

My imagination spins in tandem with the couples dancing around us. But my postulations are supported by nothing of true substance. Theories as insubstantial as the fog. Henry said he would look into Leonard. I'm sure if he found something suspicious, Leonard wouldn't be here. It doesn't stop me from thinking about causing a scene. But even through my rage, I can see the concentrated stillness in the whaler. The expectation in his dark eyes. And the pride. I embarrassed the man back at the tavern. Now he's baiting me.

Lifting an eyebrow, I allow a bored look to cross my face. Throw in a yawn for good measure.

Red patches bloom up Leonard's neck as I mentally congratulate myself, not at all ashamed of this spite. It's oddly satisfying until the giant man takes a step forward.

I gasp as Josiah takes me into his arms and spins us away. Leonard disappears, my peripheral a blur of colors. Any minute, we'll take off into flight like the seabirds trailing the ships down the river from the ocean. I never have been a good dancer. Neither of us are. But there is security in his arms, and any misstep I make is echoed by one of his own lumbering feet. We laugh together in our ease, and all thoughts of Leonard are whisked away.

Josiah's calloused hand grips my own, the other squeezes my waist through my coarse jacket. Does he wish it were more like the soft silk of Susannah's dress? I do.

His firm upper arm provides my hand a solid grip as we swing past others in our meandering path. Laughter spills out of me unchecked, and everything falls away for this brief chaotic moment of balance, foot placement, navigation, and merriment. The lively song ends with an abrupt high note, and the crowd erupts into applause.

I fan the heat from my face as a new musician steps in, an elderly gentleman. He pulls his bow confidently over the strings of his violin, a poignant note commanding all of our attention. He closes his eyes and leans into his instrument with tenderness, and suddenly it seems wrong to be standing still. Josiah takes hold of me once more, his touch gentle, and we begin to move.

At a more sedate pace, I am able to truly look at Josiah, close enough to see the small red hairs in his dark beard. What would it feel like beneath my fingers? Would surprise flicker in his eyes at my touch? Or would a warmth suffuse his features, a wanting I've seen in couples who courted each other. Of course, I could never make such a forward move with nearly all of Warbler here to witness.

Such affection wouldn't be a problem if we were married.

The longer he holds me and the world sways past, the harder it is to remind myself why I've asked him to wait. Just as the doubt begins to settle in, reason arrives. I need to secure my position as Warbler's lamplighter. It allows me to maintain my autonomy if something were to happen to Josiah, and it also preserves Da's legacy.

If I were a man, this would not be questioned, but such is the way of the world. It does not mean I plan on accepting it, however. I will play the game as needed to survive, but I will push when I can, and I swear to go down fighting if it becomes necessary.

There is another reason that hits differently, however. Pru's safety and happiness. How could I possibly allow myself such joy while she has none? The guilt alone would be too much. She worries about me becoming a spinster, but after what we went through losing Da and then Mother, all we are *going* through now, it wouldn't feel right putting my happiness first.

But she has found happiness, Tempe.

Can I trust that Gideon has changed? I close my eyes, concentrate on the movement of Josiah's and my bodies, place all my trust in his arms. We've so little time on this earth, and who knows what could happen? Would Da have done things differently had he known what his future held? Yet here I am asking Josiah to wait. He will wait for me. Right?

Did Susannah notice the red in his beard?

"Something on your mind?" Josiah's voice is soft, in deference to the haunting song.

I open my eyes to his curious expression. "Didn't take you long to find a dance partner."

"Well, I am one of Warbler's most eligible bachelors." The corner of his mouth lifts, his gaze direct. It soon falls, a frown taking up position on his face, when I fail to respond to his cajoling. "Are you upset with me?"

The confusion in his tone has an edge, an echo of our last conversation. I sigh and shake my head. I don't want to go back there. "No, of course not. I'm just . . ."

"Jealous of Susannah?"

"Incapable of managing all of my insecurities," I mumble, refusing to acknowledge the actual word that seems inconsequential for the volume of hurt it causes. Over his shoulder, I see Leonard whispering in Susannah's ear. She nods and reaches up to affectionately squeeze his arm. She's good, I'll give her that. It's a shame her judgment is so terrible.

Leonard leads her away. A shiver rolls through me as the crowd swallows them up. She needs no keeper, but with Molly still missing, shouldn't we be keeping a better eye on one another?

Josiah squeezes my hand, redirecting my attention back to us and his soft smile. All of the worries hooked into my heart concerning him disappear. I *was* jealous. I'm merely human after all. But there is no room for resentment where Josiah and I are concerned. That's never been us. He has always been my soft place to fall.

We move together on the crooning notes of the violin, the sweet smells of desserts meandering around us and the other dancers. I allow myself to step closer into him, imagining the warmth of his neck and chest against my cheek, inhaling the scent of cedar on his cotton shirt. All around, lights flicker to life. Lanterns are being lit as the sun sinks beneath the tree line, her golden reflection swallowed in the cold current of the Ivory River. I try not to let Josiah see the disappointment on my face when the final violin note reaches out to the approaching evening, tucking itself in with the last light of day.

The applause breaks my cocoon of safety within Josiah's arms. Someone calls out to him from across the way. Josiah turns to me. "Will you be back later?"

"Maybe."

"I'll look forward to it, then." He smiles his lopsided grin and moves through the crowd, a head taller than most.

As Josiah disappears, I turn and find myself under scrutiny. Through the crowd, three council members watch me, identical frowns on their faces as they speak out of the corners of their mouths. I lift my chin. My shift hasn't started, yet they still manage to make me feel guilt for tarrying. Da always managed a few dances with Mother at the Gathering before his shift. Not once was he judged for it, I'm sure.

I glance across the crowd to Mother. Gertrude, a friend of Pru's, sits beside her, toe tapping to the new song. Mother appears to be watching the dancers, but I know she isn't really seeing them. Is she recalling her dances with Da? How he seemed to have rhythm in every part of his body? How he made anyone look good who danced with him?

Do the memories bring her peace or pain?

I return to the barrel in front of the tavern to retrieve my lantern, a barely discernable reluctance in my steps. I am glad that I came, a lightness of spirit I have not felt in over a week reinvigorating me. Pru was right to press me, though she'll never hear it from my lips. No doubt she'll let me know, as little sisters are wont to do. With one more glance over my shoulder at the festivities, I turn and come face-to-face with Gideon. I gasp, all traces of newfound ease ripped away.

"My apologies. I didn't mean to startle you." His eyes are contrite. "I merely hoped for a word with you."

"Another time? I need to start my shift." With so much to think about, I want nothing but to hold on to the good feeling I felt with Josiah. Just enough to get me through my shift. But cordiality does not come naturally when Gideon is involved.

"Of course." He gestures his hand out for me to proceed. "Might I walk with you instead?"

The taste of copper spreads through my mouth as I bite the inside of my cheek. I'm not exactly sure how to bow out of this. My eyes flit down the cobbled street and back as I rock my weight between my feet.

Gideon lifts his hands in supplication. "It distresses me so, the consternation my presence causes you. I am ashamed of . . ."—here he hesitates while he clasps his fingers together and looks intently at me—"that night . . ."

With a sharp shake of my head, I cut him off. I cannot believe he is doing this here. Over my shoulder, there is no sign of Pru amid the other dancers. She must be retrieving food or speaking with some of the other villagers along the perimeter.

I nod for him to follow after me. Hearing him speak the words aloud, this secret, is like watching oil spill out of a lantern and being unable to do anything about it. Any stray spark could mean devastation. I don't want to chance anyone overhearing. The damage it would cause . . .

Gideon puts his hands behind his back as he keeps pace beside me. "It was wrong what happened. But I would like to move on from the past and hope you will let us."

A weight lodges into the pit of my stomach. I'm not *not* letting us move on. That isn't at all what this has been.

"I care deeply for Prudence and believe I could provide more for her than anyone here. I will take care of her and, more importantly, love her." I glance over at his profile, the sharp lines to his face. He must feel my gaze, but he never looks over at me. "I know you would never consider your family a burden, but I know how difficult the years have been for you since your father's passing. I ask nothing from you, other than Prudence's hand in marriage."

I ask nothing from you. He doesn't specify, but it's clear he's addressing the shocking information dropped in my lap the other day. Gideon could easily kick us out of our home if I do not give in to his demands. Well, his request, I suppose. He could use it to his advantage. Yet he doesn't seem to be taking that route. He's taking the amicable, respectful path despite the situation we are in. Choosing to treat Pru as a person, rather than an object to be bartered, as he could . . .

Gideon just wants Pru. She is enough.

We've reached the bell at the town hall. I ring it three times, grateful to do something with my hands, to focus on routine. I unlock the shed to retrieve my ladder and bag, lock it back up, and hurry to the first lamppost. Out of the corner of my eye, I see Gideon trail his fingers along the carving in the bell's arch. Somehow, the action seems intimate. Like a caress. I feel my cheeks redden, and I quickly look away before he notices.

I prop my ladder and pull out a match to light my lantern. It hisses after I strike it, flickers and blossoms to life, and quickly lights the wick. Gideon stops a few steps away from me. Not too close, but close enough I can see the shine of his boots and hear his soft tone as if he whispered into my ear. "You've had to put your life on hold, Temperance. I know your mother's unique situation."

Caught off guard, I clear my throat and stand up with my lantern. The flame throws light across the planes of his face and dances in his eyes.

"Without Pru to help take on some of the burden, it will be difficult for you to work while caring for your mother. I do not know you very well, but I do know you enjoy your work and the connection it provides to your father. I understand."

The more he speaks, the tighter my skin begins to

feel. How is it possible this man can be so understanding of my motivation? Something even Josiah doesn't seem to recognize? I've steered clear of Gideon, and yet it's as if it were all for nothing. He sees me. But rather than feeling relieved, an uneasiness itches my scalp, my arms, my everything.

"That is why Prudence and I have discussed our wish to have your mother live with us. Once we are married, of course."

I fall back a step. Pru wants to bring Mother with her? Gideon is all right with it? I'm the eldest. Mother is supposed to be my responsibility. Not Pru's.

I frown. "I could never do that to Pru. It isn't right."

"What's not right about it?" Gideon tilts his head. "Whether it's you or Prudence, your mother will be with family. Taken care of. I can easily afford extra help should Prudence wish it. She worries about your happiness just as much as you do hers."

For so long, I've been leading our family. Making all of the decisions for us. I suppose Pru is correct. I haven't given her the credit she deserves. In her own way, she has been supporting me the best she can.

"This is her gift to you." He emphasizes this with a nod, and for some reason the word sounds off. Too light amid the heaviness of the situation.

A gift. If I didn't know Pru was pure of heart, I would believe this a dirty trick. Bribery. Perhaps Gideon . . .

As if he plucks the very thought from my mind, he shakes his head. "This was entirely Prudence's idea, and I support her wishes."

Behind Gideon, fog winds around the trees and creeps over the courtyard. Low to the ground, like growing roots. It's early tonight. As the minute hand continues its unceasing journey around the clock, the fog will grow into a slow-moving tidal wave, swallowing Warbler up. Gideon follows my gaze, quiet in his contemplations.

Unease nestles up alongside my ribs.

The wispy fog reaches us, disappearing our feet and continuing past us on its slow hunt. The corner of Gideon's mouth turns up. I cannot imagine what goes through his mind. The man is an enigma.

One who I was warned about. One who loves my sister. "Why?"

"Excuse me?" He frowns.

"Why Pru? Why did you begin writing to her in the first place?"

There is no hesitation before he responds. Only a crinkling of his eyes as his soft voice caresses the air. "Her devotion caught my eye first. I would see her at church every Sunday with your mother. Helping her, guiding her. Not once did she complain about being unable to converse with others after the sermon. She did not gossip like the others, your mother's comfort her top priority."

His words weigh heavily on me. Pru is only sixteen. She should be with other girls her age, dreaming and laughing. Yet somehow, she's adapted, creating a book club and hosting it in our home instead of out socializing with the other girls. Her optimism and ability to make any situation better is so beautiful. Something I never really stopped to think about, too busy pushing my own bitterness away, embracing the independence my work provided, and letting Pru take care of Mother. Because in truth? I don't want to deal with her.

Gideon continues, oblivious to my guilt, looking far younger than his age decrees. "I would pass Prudence on the street or see her shop, and she was kind to everyone she met. Her energy is astounding, as she would pop up at one shop or the other with her mother and check in on different neighbors. I believe she sacrifices her own happiness for others, and yet to her eyes it is not a sacrifice. She is good through and through and the type of woman I wish to spend my life with. To someday raise my children."

I fidget, shifting from foot to foot with every bit of praise he gives my sister. Compliments I should have been telling her. Standing still while the fog grows feels like waiting to drown as the water gets higher and higher. He isn't wrong. Everything he said is as true as the sun shines. The shield I keep between Gideon and Pru wavers ever so slightly as his words threaten to wash away my resolve.

Gideon clears his throat. "Please consider our offer. I know it would make Prudence happy. Not only for our union, but to know she could contribute to the family in her own way."

He makes to turn away, but I stop him with a question. "Why couldn't she tell me herself?"

"I asked if I might speak to you in her stead. Considering our history, I want very much for you to see who I have become. Not who I was."

"And who are you now?"

"A man looking to remedy my past with a better future." Gideon tips his head and turns away from me, our conversation over. The fog curls up around his calves like the barn cats that rub up against a visitor's legs. He maintains a sedate pace as if he hadn't a single care in the world as he disappears down the street.

A barrage of thoughts hammer the inside of my skull, a maelstrom of possibilities. Doubts. Hopes. Am I really beginning to consider this? I turn back to the lamppost, inhaling the cold, wet air. I climb up the ladder and above my previous concerns. After a quick wipe down of the glass, I trim and light the wick. A bloom of heat wafts out, caressing my face. Gaiety and song echo in the distance. Amid it stands Pru, happier than I've seen her in the last few years. Not that she isn't usually happy, but there is excitement and pleasure in her smiles. Progress is finally happening for her. If I allow it.

And also, therein waits Josiah. Always Josiah. If Pru married Gideon and took Mother with her, there would be no reason anything should stand in the way of a strong union between Josiah and myself. Well, so long as nothing else occurs on my shifts and I prove to the council I am still qualified to be the lamplighter. Beyond that, this could work.

Losing the house will no longer be a concern. Josiah and I won't have to tamp down our affection for each other in front of Pru because she will have her own love. Mother will be cared for. There will no longer be a need to worry about my family. It will be a fresh beginning for Josiah and me to build our life together as he creates in the cooperage and I light the way for Warbler. Respected and appreciated once again, I can uphold the Byrne lineage of lamplighters.

This is everything I've wanted.

I climb back down, the fog swirling around my feet as my boots hit the cobblestones. The light is quickly fading, and the lampposts are waiting. I allowed myself time to enjoy a bit of the Gathering, but now it is time to get to work. No one is going to go missing on my watch tonight. And I have much to think about.

With each lamppost I bring to life, it becomes clearer what my decision should be. There is still a small check in my spirit, but I don't think it will ever go away. It is possible people can change. They can also make mistakes. I'm aware of it now more than ever. I think back on the lampposts that went out the night Molly disappeared.

The past will always hold regrets.

But fear and sadness have been taking control of my decision-making. It's hard to accept Pru isn't going to be just mine anymore. We will no longer share the same room. She won't be the first person I see when I wake up, the last when I go to sleep. Her smiles and optimism will be missing. But I'm not some sort of oyster hiding a pearl away from the world. She deserves her own life. It's time she makes her own choices.

Gideon is one of them.

When I finish lighting the last lamppost, Da's, I return to Gideon's workshop. Dull light peeks out from the windows, though his house is dark. He must have retired early from the Gathering to finish some work. I'd rather not speak to him here, but if I've an opportunity to let him know my decision without any eavesdropping, I'll take it.

I set my bag and lantern down before propping my ladder on the lamppost. "Gideon?"

He doesn't answer. I approach the workshop door and knock, only to have it creak open at my touch. There is no sign of movement through the crack in the door. I call out his name once more, and he doesn't respond. This could work in my benefit. Leaving a note is more appealing than speaking to him in person. Especially here. This way, he'll have my official blessing, but I can tell Pru on my own.

Already I can imagine her delighted shout and large grin.

I swing the door wide and hesitate in the doorway. Gideon's workshop stares back at me, an interloper, with silent vigilance. The light is coming from Gideon's drafting table along the back wall. There should be a pen and paper there I can use. Keeping my eyes on the glowing light of the lantern as I move through the room, I avoid the shadowed gazes of the numerous figureheads staring down at me from the walls. The child in me wants to run out of here, afraid of being caught.

The woman in me wants to, as well.

The forest fog has snuck in behind me, consuming the floor. In combination with the poor light, I feel like I'm walking in a strange dream. The swirling fog at my feet is the ocean. Wooden griffins, mermaids, and other sea creatures watch hungrily from the shadowy depths, waiting to pull me under. The hairs stand up on the back of my neck, and I quickly glance over my shoulder. The doorway yawns toward me, much farther away than how far I've actually walked. I turn back to the lantern, a lighthouse among the dangerous waters.

Now I'm just being silly.

I let out my breath when I finally reach Gideon's drafting table, feel the hard wood beneath my fingertips. It grounds me. The doorway is just over my shoulder, a stone's throw away. Nothing to concern myself with. Soon enough, I find an inkwell tucked into a compartment with pen and paper. I dip the pen and tap the excess ink from it onto the side of the little jar with a delicate *tink tink*. My heartbeat pounds in my ears once more, my body's way of racing to catch up to my decision. There are only the wooden figureheads here to witness my hesitation.

The quill scratches against the paper. Ink bleeds through with finality as I accept Gideon's proposal to marry Pru. The ink gleams in the lanternlight, a rich black. It is done. I run my finger along the edge of my name, smudging the fine line, then grimace at my blunder. I should throw some pounce powder down to dry the ink. The small drawers in the drafting table prove fruitless. Surely Gideon has some.

I squat down in front of the row of cabinets running perpendicular to the table. The first one opens silently at my touch. The lantern light gleams off something inside, and I reach in. My ink-stained finger caresses soft fabric, tracing it to a smooth handle of what feels like woven sticks. My vision narrows. Time itself slows. I withdraw the item out of the cabinet, arm heavy and movement slow.

Recognition holds me captive.

I can't move. Can't breathe. Blue silk ribbon and white

lace lay on folded fabric. Its intended use was for a young girl's dress for the Gathering.

Yet here it sits, forgotten. No, not forgotten. *Hidden.*

Molly's basket. The one she carried the night she disappeared.

It's here.

Hidden away by Gideon.

CHAPTER 12

Shock carries me out of the workshop and sends me running down the street, leaving my supplies behind at the lamppost. There is no time to waste.

Molly clearly had been with Gideon the night of her disappearance.

Why else would he be hiding her basket? Why not report it? I cannot believe I allowed myself to believe the man. He had sounded so contrite for what he did to me two years ago. He certainly fooled me. Da's warning rings in my ears, a constant drone as shame twists inside my stomach like a pile of copperhead snakes. I ignored my instincts.

I know better.

The fog has risen into the branches of the trees when I reach the wharf. Tendrils stretch out to the silent night sky, like the fingers of a drowning victim. The fog is extra thick tonight, as if it wishes to work against me. To slow me down, prevent me from unveiling the truth.

I hear the music down at the Gathering first, its merry tone a slap to the situation I've discovered. When the dim glow of the lanterns peer through the fog, the knowledge I am walking toward both danger and safety disorients my steps. For a moment I falter, the lights deceiving my brain as it all seems to shift, like the deck of a ship angling at the mercy of the waves.

As I step through the lit perimeter, the appearance of the crowd overwhelms my focus. So many faces. Everyone looks the same. My heart thrums in my chest, and my mouth goes dry. Gideon was wearing a top hat. That specificity should help me find the danger. The anticipation of seeing that black shape, however, continues to build and build with no release. Gideon and his top hat are nowhere to be seen.

"Tempe?"

I gasp, spinning, as a hand squeezes my arm. It's Josiah. Relief turns my muscles into water, and I barely manage not to fold into him and completely fall apart. Words tumble out of my mouth uncontrolled. Of Gideon's workshop, finding Molly's basket. I'm not sure if any of it makes sense, but I have to find Pru. God help me if Gideon has hurt her . . .

"Tempe. What are you doing?" Josiah's grip tightens as he pulls me back to him. Around us the dancers' eyes are wide. They've paused, interest piqued by my lost composure.

"We have to find Gideon." I peer over my shoulder, my breaths harsh in my ears. "Where is Pru?"

"She's dancing with George." Josiah nods toward the tavern. A small weight lifts away at the sight of her blonde curls and the golden fringe of her shawl floating out behind her as the elderly cooper spins her. Josiah's calm cadence is steeped in concern. "She's safe. I need you to take a deep breath, though. Don't look at me like that. Just do it. Please."

I do as he says, but all it does is feed my urgency. "We need to find Henry."

The song ends abruptly with a boisterous shout by the band, and the crowd erupts into applause. Josiah smiles widely at the few dancers still watching, acknowledging them with a nod of reassurance. When the final one shrugs and looks away, Josiah leans into me, his voice low. "Of course I'll help you. But we cannot cause a panic right now. If you accuse Gideon in public, it may not go well."

My jaw drops. "You don't believe me?"

"Of course I do." He frowns, the hurt in his eyes evidence I misjudged him. "But if word gets out, the Gathering could quickly turn into a mob."

"Gideon did something to Molly. Would a mob be so bad?"

"If Gideon is attacked, we may never find out what happened to her. Or maybe there's more to the story and you're accusing an innocent man. What then?"

I scoff. "Innocent?"

He's so close I can see the tiny freckles on his neck, the bead of sweat glistening at his temple. "You will have destroyed his life and have to live with guilt the rest of your own. Perhaps have your own reputation damaged when the truth comes out." He sighs heavily. "Too much is at stake. You know better than to react without the facts. Do not be unreasonable."

His words echo Pru's when I first denied her union with Gideon, and once again I feel the restraint of society's opinions and regulations. I take a deep breath, knowing I'm not wrong. Gideon has done something, but Josiah does have a point. I need to go about it the right way. I cannot make any mistakes.

More importantly, Molly must be found and Pru kept safe.

Josiah watches me intently, eyes waiting. When I nod, he releases me. Everyone around us has moved on with their conversations and dances, a slower song wrapping them up in romantic notes, my frantic gesticulating and raised tone long forgotten with Josiah's encouragement. Together, we wind our way through the crowd, on the hunt for Henry but eyes peeled for Gideon. After asking around, we find the constable on the south end of the Gathering, speaking with the minister, a rare smile on his face.

I don't bother to wait until the conversation is over before interrupting. Our minister frowns at me but excuses himself. Henry stills as I step close with Josiah. "Gideon has Molly's basket. The one she had the night she disappeared."

Fog lazily twists around us, giving off some semblance

of privacy away from the weak lantern light of the barrels. Henry looks me up and down, bringing my attention to my disheveled appearance. My unbuttoned jacket, braid threatening to come undone from pins loosened as I ran, sweat dripping from my temples. My appearance alone could dissuade someone from taking me seriously.

But a second later, Henry nods. "How do you know?" he asks, managing to keep his usually booming voice low.

Henry isn't a bad man. He may not always see the world as I do, but he has always tried to give people a chance. To listen. I'm grateful my mistakes have not completely lost me his trust.

"I found it in his workshop. Just now. You need to take him into custody." I clench my fists, nails digging into my palms at my barely restrained nerves. I must portray some semblance of control. "Question him. Before he might hurt someone else."

Henry runs his hand over his chin, shifting weight between his feet. His gaze searches my face for any jest or trick before he looks over to Josiah. "You saw it too?"

Josiah shakes his head. "No, I was here."

"I'll show you." I'm unable to remove the urgency from my voice. Each second we stand here feels like an eternity. While Henry processes the situation, I keep an eye on the Gathering. No sign of Gideon. Finally, the constable nods and gestures for us to follow. He asks me questions as we go: What does the basket look like? When exactly did I see Molly with it? What was I doing in Gideon's workshop?

I answer clearly and succinctly, keeping calm so as not to suggest I am letting emotions guide me. As to why I was in Gideon's workshop? The door was open. When I went to close it, the basket caught my eye. Simple.

Josiah and Henry are a step behind but keep my pace as we travel down the street. The lampposts are glowing eyes through the gloom of the wharf, watching us and waiting.

Witnesses to all of Warbler's misfortunes. They were the last to see the souls of the lost, missing, and dead. Da flashes before my eyes, body limp, rope embedded in his neck. I jerk briefly, but the men don't seem to notice.

I shake it off, hoping fate will be far kinder to Molly. As we turn away from the wharf and traverse down another street, a darkness grows behind the thickening fog. The forest. I am sure-footed the entire way, the glow of the lampposts reassuring, but I barely control the urge to run. We are so close to finding Molly and my own redemption.

Gideon's lamppost awaits us, fog swirling in the bloom of light as tree branches stretch out above us like cracks in a gray abyss. The confidence I carry falters when we reach the workshop.

The door is closed.

I distinctly remember leaving it open upon my hasty departure. Rather than go straight for it, Henry turns and walks up the brick path to Gideon's house with its bloodred shutters. Unlike earlier, light now shines from the windows.

"What are you doing?" I call out to Henry while looking at Josiah for support. "It's in his workshop."

"I must check if Gideon is home before entering his property, Temperance. He isn't guilty of anything right now. I'd like to hear what he has to say." Henry raises his eyebrows at me before turning back to the front door. It takes Gideon only a few moments to respond to Henry's pounding fist.

"Constable." Gideon steps from the shadows within his doorway. I can just barely make out the frown on his face from where I stand with Josiah at the front gate. "To what do I owe the pleasure of your company?"

"Unpleasant business, I'm afraid." Henry looks over his shoulder at me, drawing Gideon's attention. Mild interest shines from the ship carver's face. Nothing more. Yet the moment our eyes meet, the line he's hooked into me tugs. Josiah and Henry fade away like smoke as a frigid current runs through me. There is a sound. A hum. Just there. On the outside of conscious awareness, like the reverberation of Warbler's Bell long after it's sounded.

Gideon looks back at Henry, and something releases. I can breathe once more, a sharp gasp piercing my lungs. I did not realize I had stopped breathing in the first place.

"Are you all right?" Josiah steps close, his warmth comforting.

"Could I have a look in your workshop?" Henry's loud voice is polite, but it is clear this is no request.

"Of course." Gideon holds his hand out for Henry to precede him down the path before he shuts the door. He is still wearing the clothes from earlier, excluding the top hat. He nods to Josiah as he and Henry pass. I look away and hurry to pick up my lantern. It glows at the foot of the workshop's lamppost.

The door to the workshop swings open. Light blooms from within after Gideon strikes a match and places it to the wick of an oil lamp. He replaces the glass over the flame, then turns the knob to brighten it. The heady smell of oil soaks into the earthy oak. The figureheads are exposed, half their faces in darkness, the other half awash in light, the grains in the wood discernable. Gideon straightens, only a hint of a frown on his face.

Henry turns to me. "Temperance?"

There are too many eyes on me, not all of them real. My heartbeat pounds in my ears. I move toward the back of the workshop, my lantern light chasing away the shadows here at the end of the room. The truth too will finally be exposed. One small detail Gideon did not think significant enough to conceal. A detail so irrelevant as a girl's ribbon and lace.

I open the cupboard, expectations breathing down my back. Roles of string are stacked atop each other, a wooden bucket with a variety of chisels and gouges. No basket. Tools and rolls clatter as I push through them. I look in the next cupboard. Nothing. Where is it? I stand up, retrace my steps earlier. The only sound in the room is the burning of the fuel in the lamps. Gideon must have seen it when he came home, after I left. It was why the door was closed, the lantern out. How could I be so senseless to leave it all in the open?

"Well?" Henry's gruff voice arrives at my side.

"It isn't here," I mutter.

"You're sure?"

"I left the basket right here. He must have moved it, Henry. He must have." I glance at him and try not to wince at the disappointment I see there.

"Might I offer some assistance?"

We turn at Gideon's question. He stands beside Josiah, two men who work with wood, and yet remarkably different. Even slouched, Josiah is taller than Gideon. His unkempt beard and rumpled clothes are endearing. An open, encouraging expression lives on his face; warmth extending from him like a gift. Josiah is a red maple.

The ship carver, on the other hand, is a birch. Standing straight, unyielding, smothering its surroundings as it takes over silently. Everything about Gideon is deliberate. Yet it is impossible to assess what little he offers of himself. Dark possibility shrouds him.

His question is directed toward Henry, but his eyes are on me, his gaze a spider crawling up my spine. I look past him at a large, twisted bough of wood propped against the wall. As my eyes trace the lines of it, Henry's explanation for Gideon sounds a long way away, muffled. I can't seem to look away from the wood, frustration clenching my teeth together.

The basket was here. I know what I saw.

The fresh smell of cedar loosens the shell around me, like water through cracks in a rock. Josiah nudges my elbow, his tall frame a pillar of comfort shielding me from the trouble at hand. I shake my arms and roll my head on my neck, as if removing the weight of an invisible cloak.

"I have no baskets or ribbons here. You must have imagined it," Gideon explains. I take a deep breath before stepping out from behind Josiah to look Gideon in his unblinking eyes. He winces, shaking his head. "Frankly, I'm offended you could think I would have anything to do with what happened to Molly."

"I didn't imagine it." I lift my chin. "You must have moved it when you came home from the Gathering."

"After leaving the Gathering, I came directly home. There was no need to enter my workshop tonight." Gideon sighs. "I can understand your error. You have been under an unfathomable amount of stress lately, after all, what with Molly's disappearance and the pressure from the council."

I know without a doubt Josiah and Henry hear only compassion, consideration. Their ears are not attuned to the patronizing undertone laced inside each word. Nor do they notice the subtle change in their perception of my worth as Gideon carves into my person. "Perhaps my timing in asking for Prudence's hand in marriage has not been ideal with everything going on. Especially considering our history."

Josiah's head whips toward Gideon, and my stomach drops.

"But I would never have believed you could stoop to such a level as this."

Each word uttered from his mouth hollows me out until I am nothing but an empty husk. A husk about to burst into flames and take everything down with me. "How dare you!"

Henry frowns at Gideon but holds his arm out to prevent me from advancing. "I'd like you to leave, Temperance. We will talk later."

He nods to Josiah, an unspoken command to remove me. All I can do is sputter. So easily have I been dismissed. What's worse, I see the betrayal in Josiah's face. The hardening of the trust and compassion so easily given. Gideon has punctured a hole inside the boat carrying Josiah's and my relationship.

"But now that I'm here"—Henry's voice plows ahead as we depart—"I'm sure you will not protest my having a look around your workshop?"

"Of course not," Gideon murmurs. "You're welcome to. I've nothing to hide."

Josiah exits, jaw clenched, the muscle in his cheek flexing. There is no need to pull me out of the workshop. I have to trust Henry will find something. And if he doesn't, well . . . he will. I know what I saw. If there had been some sort of explanation for the basket, anything at all, I like to think I'd be willing to hear it out before placing judgment.

But Gideon hid it. Why would he do so if he were innocent?

Josiah waits for me to grab my bag and ladder before we begin our walk into the fog, hints of light in the distance mere suggestions. He doesn't look at me.

"The Gathering is that way." I nod in the opposite direction.

"I'm walking you home. Then I'll retrieve Pru and your mother."

"We should get them first."

"Damnit, Tempe!" he barks, shoulders rising to his ears.

I flinch, instant heat flooding my body. Josiah has never raised his voice to me before. I picture Gideon's face, stoic, watching me through the fog, pupils filled with chaos. My fingers twitch at the thought of clawing out his eyes.

The fog wets my face as we continue on Josiah's chosen path, small droplets gathering together until they are heavy enough to drip down my cheeks and tuck inside the crease of my lips. They taste of salt.

"What did Gideon mean about your history?" Josiah asks.

How do I explain? I never thought I would need to. I

never wanted to discuss what occurred between Gideon and myself in his workshop. How do you tell someone you love that in a moment of weakness you reached out for someone else? How would Josiah get past it to even hear what transpired after? At the time it happened, I believed I was at fault. For kissing Gideon, and then being unable to handle his aggressive physicality. Unprepared, inexperienced.

I know better now, but at the time I had no one to talk to who had any experience. No one I could trust. It didn't matter. I kissed him; I have seen women shamed for less, shunned by the rest of society. I couldn't take a chance two years ago that Josiah would look past my actions and at what Gideon did. He might have abandoned me right then and there, heartbroken.

I'm still not ready to risk it.

"Does Pru know?" In my hesitation, it seems Josiah has already assumed the worst.

"It isn't like that, Josiah. At all. Don't you see what Gideon is doing? He's trying to redirect everyone's attention away from himself. Ruin my reputation so no one will believe I can be objective." I try to grab Josiah's arm, but he jerks out of my grasp. "Why are you acting like this?"

Josiah marches ahead, and I jog to keep up. The turmoil churning through me is an ocean, and another tidal wave rolls through me as we reach Da's lamppost. I skid to a stop, vision narrowing in on the base of the lamppost. A high tinny sound fills my ears, and I forget to breathe. In my peripheral, I see two boots kicking together. Da's.

I wasn't there to see him strangle to death, but it matters not. Coming upon his body was all my imagination needed to paint the picture. It's burned into my brain by an iron brand. No matter what I do, I cannot seem to break the cycle once the images begin. All I can do is clench my eyes closed and wait for the sounds of his struggling to quiet.

"Tempe?" Josiah's voice is soft. Close by.

"Don't." I jerk away from the kiss of his fingers on my arm. When I look up at the glowing cage, Da's ghost is gone. I lean my forehead against the post and inhale the odor of wet metal.

"What's wrong?"

Da is only visible to me. For that I am grateful, but for the first time, a crack of doubt splits open my confidence. Is my mind playing tricks on me? Is guilt guiding my hand? I could not help Da, and so I see his ghost every night. I did not help Molly, and now I see her basket.

I peer sideways at Josiah. The anger is gone from his face, leaving behind only pain. He may be a man, but that doesn't mean he's free from doubt or vulnerability. He glances up at the light, confusion and concern knitting his brows together, before he looks down at me.

In this pocket of light there is only us, the swirling wall of fog barring anyone else from sight. The woods, our only spectators. My heart races as I shove all my concerns away and take a leap I have never done before. After setting everything down, I lift my hand and place it against his cheek. His eyes widen, but he does not pull away.

The stiff curls of his beard tickle the lower half of my palm. "There is nothing going on between Gideon and myself. There never has been." I rub my thumb atop his cheekbone. "I have loved you and only you."

He leans into my hand, eyes searching for something in my own. I'm not sure what. All I can do is instill every speck of love I feel for this wonderful man into the very air he breathes. Into the skin running beneath my fingers and thumb as I caress the sharp planes of his face.

"I don't understand what is going on." He gestures around us, and I think he means Da's lamppost. "With Gideon and Molly. With Pru and yourself. But I care about you deeply. I always have and always will."

Our sinking boat steadies, the hole plugged up. For now, it is enough.

I bite my lip, willing the wetness in my eyes not to spill as he leans forward. Our foreheads touch, and I release a shaky breath. For this moment at least, the fear and uncertainty fade away into the mist as Josiah's and my breaths mix in a moment of gratitude and love. For a time, as we stand in comfortable silence, I recall Da and Mother leaning into each other in front of the fire, Pru and myself all but invisible, as they held each other in their own intimate world. This, this peace, must have been what they felt for one another.

Somehow it feels right, here in front of Da's lamppost. Like I don't have to do this whole thing called life alone anymore. I allow myself to think this until Josiah releases a deep breath and I awake from this beautiful dream, stepping back into Warbler and the darkness waiting just on the other side of the fog.

Always just out of sight. Waiting to attack.

CHAPTER 13

There was no evidence of anything afoul at Gideon's workshop or his house."

Henry gulps down half of the glass of water Pru provides him. In the weak light of our single lamp on the kitchen table, Henry's eye sockets are dark, skeletal-like. He's a specter delivering unwanted news.

"Of course there wasn't." Pru glares at me as she pulls her shawl off and drapes it over the back of a chair. "Because there is nothing to find."

Henry shrugs. "Perhaps it was a trick of the light?"

I open my mouth to protest the ridiculous suggestion, but Josiah catches my eye before I can. He shakes his head and makes a downward motion with his hand. I need to tamp down my reactivity. I won't get far with Henry by lashing out in frustration.

Pru runs a hand across her face, tucking her loosened curls behind her ears. If the situation weren't so dire, I would laugh at her actions. At sixteen years, she's acting like a harried mother, disappointed with her child. Me.

"When Molly disappeared, Gideon wasn't home when I lit his lamppost." The memory flares up suddenly, catching others that respond in kind. "And I heard the scream coming from the direction of his workshop. It wasn't until later, when I relit the dead lanterns, that he was back home."

The intention to remain calm and collected disappears without a trace. I hear the intensity in myself, feel the passion of my twirling hands and pacing. It may not be evidence of his direct involvement, but it is suspicious he was missing at the same time Molly disappeared. Truthfully, I'm trying to catch a whale with a net, but instinct requires I at least try.

Pru's glare is scalding.

"This is a serious accusation you're making against one of Warbler's citizens." Henry's expression gives nothing away. "I cannot say how the council will react, especially without solid evidence."

I nod as the heavy implications his report will cause sink into me. "I understand."

Whether I am believed or not, the possibility of Gideon's involvement will be out for all to decide. As a member of the council himself, there certainly is a conflict of interest. One the other councilmembers will not object to, on account of Gideon's unnatural pull with them. But I cannot imagine Molly's parents will allow his possible involvement to be dismissed so quickly. If, however, his status in Warbler shields him from investigation, there is one thing in my power to do: refuse Pru's marriage with him.

In the meantime, I can only hope to retain my position as lamplighter. The possibility of losing it and marrying Josiah out of necessity feels like someone has tied a weight to my ankle and thrown me into the river. He says none of it bothers him, the extra mouths to feed and no additional income brought in. But the ones you put your trust in can hurt you the most if they abandon you. Life isn't easy, and you can't know a person, not really, until they've gone through difficult times and come out the other side a survivor.

Pru and I are survivors out of necessity.

I'll do everything in my power to make sure Josiah doesn't have to be tested like we were. Because what if he fails?

What if we're hurt all over again, left to fight to survive? Just like after Da.

After Henry and Josiah depart, Pru shrugs off any

care she might have had to preserve her calm. I follow her stomping gait into our bedroom, where she removes her dress and tears at the ties of her stay with an aggression most unlike her. She shakes her head, eyes anchored to the floor as she works, teeth gritted. "I cannot believe your audacity to accuse Gideon of this heinous crime. How could you do this to me, Tempe?"

"I didn't contrive this story with the intent to sabotage your relationship."

"No?"

"Of course not! My livelihood is at stake now. I would never place us in this position for a superficial reason." I cross my arms and glance back through the doorway. Mother is in her rocker, sipping a glass of water, staring into the burning embers and whatever memory she tucks herself into. Her head is tilted, though, as if listening in on our conversation. I could be wrong.

I turn back to Pru, unable to hide the disappointment on my face. "I must confess I never thought you selfish. Don't you care about Molly? The safety of everyone in Warbler?"

"Of course I do!" She runs a brush through her hair so intensely I expect her to pull a chunk out.

"Then what is it? You act as if I am going out of my way just to hurt you. What is the matter?"

"No, it isn't that." The brush clacks as she places it back on the dresser. She sets her hands on her narrow hips and glares at the floor with the intensity of a whaler looking to catch sight of a whale.

I bite the inside of my cheek before blurting out a terrible epiphany. "Are you truly so unhappy in your life here, you cannot wait to escape?"

Pru lifts her gaze to me. The slight downturn in her lips is a nail hammered into my heart.

"You would leave the safety of our home and walk straight into danger's arms, just to be rid of us?"

"Stop being so obtuse, Tempe. Of course not." She shakes her head. "I love you. But I want to have a home of my own, a love of my own. You have to let me go, and you aren't."

"The day you meet a truly good man, you will have all my support. I swear to you. But Gideon is not that man. You choose to see the good in people, while ignoring their darkness. And there is darkness in Gideon."

"Maybe you"—she points her finger at me—"should have more faith in people. Give them a chance."

"I gave him a chance, Pru. And I shouldn't have. He's a bad man and no one seems to understand, so I'm forced to make the hard decisions for our family."

Pru lets out an exasperated groan and climbs into bed. "Stop acting like such a martyr."

"Excuse me?"

She turns onto her side, presenting her back to me. "You cannot control everything."

"I'm all too well aware of that." I brush away angry tears she will never see and leave the room. We are at a standstill. The fire requires stoking, and I do so as Mother watches. The embers have retained their heat, and it isn't long before flames begin to dance once more.

"None of this would be happening if Da were still here," I mumble.

The creaking of the rocker ceases. Mother gazes up at the likeness of Da on the mantel. It's but a smudge in the poor lighting, but I am positive not even Mother needs a picture to remember him by. It's easy to recall his narrow nose and strong chin with its single dimple. The thin lips and curve of his smile. His raspy laughter and thick brogue as smooth as syrup.

He was an easy man to be around. Confident and welcoming. Known to tell a tall tale or two and chat your ear off if you let him. You could always count on him. Rely on him. And if he made a mistake, he was defended. Pardoned.

It was easy to forgive him. Everyone wanted to because they respected him.

Warbler and his family hold different standards for his eldest daughter.

My mind refuses to rest, unease frantically crawling in my stomach. I take my energy outside and walk my route through Warbler. I'll keep an eye out until I need to extinguish the lampposts. Might as well put myself to good use under the circumstances.

The Gathering continues until just past midnight, when those still celebrating stumble home in drunken stupors. The tables and chairs have all been left behind until morning, as well as a smattering of plates and overturned cups. A white cat sits on one of the tables, licking frosting from a fork. A shawl lies forgotten on a barrel, a dirty handkerchief on the ground. The lanterns still lit around the perimeter hold the location in a hazy island.

Walking up to the abandoned celebration is strange. With no one here, an overwhelming sense of wrongness stands in their place. Like they were swallowed up in the fog by some beast, only a remnant of life left behind. To remove the discomfort that thought provides, I put out the oil lamps, each of the metal knobs a cold bite to my fingers. The creak of wood on the water reaches out to me as melancholy returns once more. The hulking whaling ships are mere outlines in the fog.

With each pass I make on my route, I spend extra time around Gideon's lamppost, but the workshop and house remain dark. All of Warbler, in fact, is at a standstill. No movement to be seen. Just one, long held breath. That is, until around four in the morning when I reach the Green. A dark shadow appears, fog swirling with the movement. My heart stops as the shadow becomes a figure. With theories of Molly's disappearance spinning in my head, all I see is Gideon's face grinning back at me.

When the fog shifts, I realize my mistake. Henry's blunt features emerge, replacing the sharp lines of Gideon, who must be asleep at home. The constable's urgent steps sink my heart. I open my mouth, but he interjects with his usual brassy voice, "Susannah Culver is missing."

Disbelief fills my lungs. How is this happening again? Not eight hours ago she was dancing at the Gathering, an irritatingly beautiful vision in pink, embracing all the attention she could garner from her partners. I do not care for her pretentious attitude, her clear disregard for those she feels are beneath her. It does not mean I want her to come to any harm.

"When was the last time you saw Susannah?" Henry asks, brow furrowed. He doesn't pull his pad out to write. Whether he is in too much of a hurry or believes we are past note-taking at this point, I'm not sure.

"At the Gathering. She was dancing," I say, my jaw tightening at the memory of her in Josiah's arms. I am immediately slapped with guilt. She's missing, possibly hurt. Or worse. Then I remember, and dread pulls at my limbs. "She was with Leonard."

Henry nods as if this is not new information, but mere confirmation. He asks, "Have you noticed anything out of place on your route?" at the same time I blurt, "Have you spoken with Gideon about it?"

Henry doesn't respond, doesn't blink. Waits.

"No," I concede. "Nothing all night."

His gaze turns to the great skeletal shadows of the trees standing just outside the lantern light. There are dark circles beneath his eyes, his beard is unkempt, and lines crack his forehead. For the first time, it hits me: I'm not the only one whose job and actions are being scrutinized by Warbler.

"Please investigate Gideon further, Henry."

He turns back to me and shakes his head. "I know you believe you saw Molly's basket at Gideon's. But it's no longer there, and I have no reason to believe anything is amiss with his story."

"I don't *believe* I saw it. I did see it."

"Be that as it may, Molly didn't go missing until this new whaling crew sailed into our seaport. Now Susannah has disappeared with one of them, which I've verified with multiple witnesses. As you said, Leonard left with her last night."

Surprise blows my previous accusations away. It's like putting the final hoop on a bucket to solidify the staves and allow the bucket to hold its shape. His new theory is as clear and cold as the water in the river, and I cannot deny it holds merit.

Leonard did have that strange run-in with Gideon. Could he have planted the basket to try and frame Gideon? I wouldn't put it past him, having suspected Leonard of ill intent from the beginning. Gideon could have found the basket after I left and hid it, panicking over any accusations he would receive.

A stretch, but perhaps not entirely so.

We haven't had a local go missing from the village since Da was the lamplighter. And Molly went missing the night I had my confrontation with an extremely volatile Leonard. I even told Henry to look into it, and he assured me he would check the time frame.

His normally bright eyes are hooded, inevitability lowering his eyelids into acceptance as an epiphany strikes me.

"You never looked further into Leonard."

His thick silence is confirmation. We both stand for a heavy moment, acknowledging the harm our choices have caused. I should have reported the scream and the lampposts going out. Henry should have double-checked Leonard's whereabouts. We've both failed.

Henry adjusts his baton in the loop on his belt. "Leonard is notorious among his crew for getting into trouble in port. The night Molly disappeared, he slipped away about half past six. Turns out his shipmates and captain were covering for him when I questioned them all."

There is no need to express my disappointment. I can see it in the lines on Henry's face. The droop of his shoulders.

We stand with our regrets, a strange camaraderie neither of us want.

"Stay vigilant. If you see Leonard, do not approach him." Henry points a finger to himself. "You find me."

After I've acquiesced, he disappears down the street. My thoughts keep me company, their weight a brick on my chest. The leaves do not crunch beneath my feet like they do during the day; moisture has saturated them so completely they stick to the soles of my boots, then fall back to the ground with an unsatisfying hush. Some hairs have come loose of my braid and tickle my throat, my cheeks. Their delicate touch sends goose bumps down my neck.

I knew there was something not right about Leonard. A feeling of wrongness each time he pressed in too close, stared too long. There is no doubt now he was the one watching me in the fog that night. He extinguished the lampposts to get me into trouble. It must have been him. I pull my jacket closer.

But why would Leonard have kept Molly's basket for so long? Sure, he could have wanted to incriminate Gideon after their run-in. But their confrontation was several days after she'd disappeared.

Leonard may have come to our seaport with the intention to do harm, but there is a darkness here in Warbler and the ship carver is part of it. I know it.

Stay away from Gideon.

Da's warning has steered me clear of Gideon's path as often as possible, a promise instilled in me for years now. Gideon has a weakness for young women. I learned that firsthand. And now he wants Pru.

Could he have also been pursuing Molly?

What about Susannah? Leonard seems a plausible enough suspect. Molly's and Susannah's disappearances could be completely separate from each other, however unlikely that might feel under the circumstances.

Could we really have two men with intent to do harm in Warbler?

My troubled thoughts accompany me until morning. The fog lifts, leaving behind frozen dew-like crystals scattered amid the autumn chill. The sun lifts into the blue and pink of dawn. Light kisses the tops of the trees and works its way down them until finally the grass, dirt, and cobblestone paths of Warbler too are within her grasp. I extinguish the lanterns one by one and refill the oil wells.

Many of Warbler's villagers are late to awaken after last night's celebration. The wharf, however, is business as usual with the crabbers and fishermen, though their gaits are a bit slower. After extinguishing the lampposts along the wharf and shipyard, I hold my head high as I round the corner, willing his absence beneath my breath. My wishes are futile. The workshop door is open. Gideon stands in the doorway, a cup in his hands, steam rising languorously into the cold air. His long, dark hair is unbound, framing his sharp face and adding to the intensity of his gaze.

I tighten my grip on my ladder in an attempt to stop my fingers from noticeably trembling. The Warbler Wood Shop sign creaks in the slight breeze. Out of the corner of my eye, I see his head turn to follow me. I make quick and diligent work of the lamppost, though time slows with an audience such as him. It is an unsettling contradiction.

His footsteps crunch behind me. "I regret that you misunderstand me so."

A slight rasp in his voice hints at intimacy. My mouth dries up as I climb down the ladder and turn to face him. "I do not misunderstand you. I dislike and mistrust you."

"You have made that quite evident, Temperance."

My name on his lips sends a tremor cascading over my skin while simultaneously burning my throat as if I swallowed a mouthful of lye. I steady myself. This well-mannered, generous, concerned persona of his is a farce. I refuse to enable it. "You briefly fooled me. Made me believe you've changed. But I saw Molly's basket in your workshop."

I hate that my voice is shaking, but being so abrasive to a well-respected member of our society, let alone a man, has my mind and body at war. My mind presses on; my body shies away. But I will not stop.

He does not move, but I swear his eyes change. Must be the morning light. I force myself to take a step forward. He does not retreat. "Prudence will not be marrying you. And I know the truth will come out, your involvement in Molly's disappearance."

"The truth? What, pray tell, have I done?" He takes a sip from his drink. Standing this close, I get a hint of mint. He's taunting me.

I cannot respond because I do not know. His continued denial chips away at my certainty. No, I am not biased because of our history. It would be easy for anyone to assume so if they knew of our past. But he wasn't home when I heard her scream. And the theory that Leonard planted the basket? Gideon's status in our community would ensure he'd receive the benefit of the doubt. The more I think on it, the more plausible it seems. He would not be judged so quickly, so why panic and hide it?

Because he was telling the truth. You've made it up in your head. There was no basket. The crack in me grows larger.

"I've joined the search parties and permitted my home and business to be searched. I've offered marriage to Prudence without any caveats, kept a roof over your head after your father's death, and vouched for you so you and your family do not become destitute while your competence as lamplighter is questioned. As far as I can tell, I've done nothing but help."

I practically snarl. "You will never marry Pru."

"Is that so?"

The corner of Gideon's lips curls up as he reaches into his pocket. He withdraws a piece of paper, and my stomach drops. He unfolds it gently, one handed, in no hurry, and begins reading aloud. With each word, I'm dragged beneath the undertow a little farther.

"I, Temperance Byrne, in signing this paper agree to the marriage between Gideon Virtanen and Prudence Byrne."

My letter. I forgot it when I ran from the workshop last night. How could I have forgotten something so important? Realization closes a fist around my heart, fear and desperation setting it pounding.

My letter wasn't on the desk when I returned with Henry and Josiah. Gideon pocketed it before we arrived. Proof that he actually had returned to his workshop, seen the basket, and hidden it.

Gideon lied.

CHAPTER 14

Gideon rubs his thumb along the edge. "This is binding, Temperance."

Back and forth, like a caress, he continues the motion as my world collapses. Only after he returns the letter to his pocket can I rip my gaze back to his face.

He leans into me. "The town council would find it ill-favored of you to retract your written word. Especially with no evidence to back your wild accusations of my person. They will be particularly upset after it has been announced that another young woman has gone missing. Mr. Culver's daughter, I hear. He has substantial pull over the council, if not as much as myself."

Gideon lifts his cup with calloused fingers and nods over my shoulder. Mr. Landon strolls past on his way to open the general store. The older man smiles at us, completely unaware of the threats anchoring me in place as the crow that is Gideon picks at me bit by bit.

"There has been a great deal of mention, concern rather, of whether or not you are fit for this work. It must be difficult walking in your father's footsteps. Seeing the place he died every day. Perhaps harder than you originally thought when you took on the position. Emotions can be . . . difficult."

I flinch, his implication a physical blow. While I might have had my doubts earlier on, there is no questioning my sanity now. "I am not mentally unfit. And neither was Da. He was respected."

"He *was.*"

The word hits with two blows. I know the whispers about Da's character after he took his own life. Since Molly's disappearance, I don't need to hear what they say about me under their breath. I can see their thoughts in their faces when they think I'm not looking.

People do not stand by you when the road becomes rocky. The truth is we're all alone in this world. You can only count on yourself.

Gideon hooks his thumb behind one of his suspenders and leans closer. "Your job inefficiency and wavering manner have carved quite unattractive marks on your character. I would think twice before doing anything else that might jeopardize your position or your family's prospects."

His eyes are icy fog, swirling in mystery, his lashes so dark it's as if his eyes are lined with kohl. I take a stuttering breath. "Are you threatening me?"

"Of course not. I merely have your best interests at heart. After all, we will be family soon."

To this man, I am not a valued individual. I am merely a woman who must follow commands because how could I know better than he? His quiet, unassuming nature is merely a front. Gideon is as deceptive as a crab trap to roving sea life. Pru's happiness and Mother's care were bait. I walked right inside his trap.

There's more going on here. I feel the ache of it in my bones. Molly and Susannah are still missing, and I now know without a doubt Gideon hid Molly's basket. He must be involved in her disappearance. Henry's theory sounded plausible—Leonard is a bad man. But it's the quiet threat that does more damage. Sea worms burrow into the hull of a ship, slowly destroying its integrity. Who knows how long Gideon has been playing others, let alone myself. Like the ships built in the shipyard, copper plating nailed to the hull, Pru and I also need protection.

A dog bark cuts the air. I jump, nearly bumping into Gideon.

"Tempe?"

Josiah stands in the street, Ruby beside him, her ears perked, attention on me. Josiah's expression is hooded, and my heart stutters back to life. I grab my things, stepping around Gideon as if he were a great hole in the ground, and hurry to the welcome of Ruby's wagging tail and Josiah's presence. Sadly, I find no warmth in the latter.

"What was that about?" Josiah nudges me.

I look up at him as we walk and open my mouth to explain, but nothing comes out. How do I tell him I am convinced Gideon is a villain of the worst sort and yet I have no usable evidence? The only evidence I have, confirming Gideon lied to Henry, damns me instead: a note I wrote giving Gideon permission to wed Pru only to change my mind less than twelve hours later. My competency will be questioned by the town council. Again. The letter also proves I lied to Henry about why I entered the workshop in the first place. I told him I noticed the door was open.

Henry's sure to take Gideon's word over my own now.

Will Josiah stand by me despite it all?

Da killed himself, and Mother isn't well. What if he thinks I too am destined for a path such as them? Josiah has always had a confident and joyful demeanor. I, on the other hand, challenge it constantly with skepticism and practicality. Why would he want to stand by someone like me? Already there is mistrust in his sideways glances. There is too much to risk when I cannot guarantee the outcome. Playing it safe and keeping my head low may be the only option while I figure out my next steps.

"It is nothing." I swallow the acid crawling up my throat and manage to turn my grimace into a weak smile. "What are you doing here?"

Josiah's expression is unreadable. I haven't convinced

him, but he doesn't press me either. "I was hoping to find you. Susannah Culver is missing, and they think the whaler, Leonard, may have hurt her. They searched the whaling ship, but he's nowhere to be found. Until then, no women are allowed to walk alone. Henry doesn't want to take any chances the whaler will get someone else."

"They're sure it's him? No one else helped him?"

Josiah shrugs and keeps pace as I reach the next lamppost. "It's the only theory with any real weight to it."

I bite the inside of my cheek. I don't believe it was intentional, but his words sting. If only I could find the proof needed to change the course of the search. But who would believe me? A man can make mistakes. A man can change his mind. A woman? No. If she makes a mistake, she is unfit. If she changes her mind, she is fickle.

Incompetent.

It's an honor to bring light to the dark. You're a natural, Tempe.

I clamp my eyes shut and see Da's smiling face looking up at me. Eyes proud. I don't want to let him down, and the only way to do that is to take matters into my own hands. There is nothing to fear of solitude nor of being my own advocate. I've done so for years now as he did before me. When the waves come, I ride them out, keeping the fire burning in the dark until the storms pass.

This is a particularly bad storm. But people should always be able to rely on the lamplighter. On me.

More importantly? I cannot let myself down.

Josiah and I do not speak much for the rest of my shift. Ruby ambles alongside us like a young child, completely oblivious to the stilted air between their parents. I'm not sure what to do about us right now. My thoughts are too consumed with more pressing matters. Like breaking into Gideon's workshop tonight.

To find Molly's basket and steal back my letter.

All day I wait at home with bated breath for Gideon to arrive and inform Pru I gave them permission to wed. The slightest sound of any passerby has me wincing. I press my face against the window, breath clouding the glass, only to see neighbors walking by. With no company and no reason to leave the house, Pru, Mother, and I resume our usual activities in a stilted silence. There are no arguments. Nor is there laughter or comfort. Mere formalities. Pru's brightness has dulled, and my nerves are strung taut as a bow string.

I breathe a sigh of relief when the light darkens outside the windows and Henry arrives. With the understanding that women are not to be outside alone until Leonard is found, Henry accompanies me as I light the lampposts. But by the looks I receive, it's clear others think he is with me for another reason entirely: ensuring I do my job correctly because once again, a woman is missing.

It makes me want to scream.

The air is solemn as Henry shares with me the current happenings in Warbler. The foreign whaling ship departed this morning with Gideon's siren leading the way. After the ship was searched and no trace of Leonard found, the assumption is he is either hiding out somewhere within Warbler or, more probable, has left altogether.

One more soul added to the hundreds that have disappeared in Warbler's fog.

Susannah's father is out for blood, and with no present sign of Leonard, Henry and I have become the target of his fury. A constable who cannot catch a criminal and a lamplighter who neglected to report a possible attack. Fortunately, there is no real weight to his accusations, and this morning the council agreed that now was not the time for rash actions. Henry does not share with me whether or not Gideon weighed heavily in their decision.

I believe it more than likely and swallow the fact down like a chunk of ice.

When I return home, I do not dwell on my plan to steal my letter back but stay occupied repairing a tear in my jacket. After Pru and Mother go to bed, it isn't until the sounds of their soft snores ease my nerves that I decide to step outside.

The fog provides all the cover I need to reach Gideon's workshop unseen. Most of Warbler should be asleep, but Henry will be out patrolling with volunteers. I should be out here doing the same. The lamplighter also serves as watchman, but now that Susannah is also missing, I was told my assistance was not needed. To the eyes of Warbler, I cannot be counted on to help. If this is their idea of reprimanding me for not reporting the scream, they've hit their mark.

Best to look at it as an opportunity rather than let anger burn through me, however. I avoid the streets, the soft glow of the lampposts slipping away entirely as I wind along the tree line. The thick fog consumes most of Warbler's sounds, turning them into mere afterthoughts, a disorienting sensation. It matters not because I know my way as well as a celestial navigator on a clear night.

That confidence doesn't prevent my heart from pounding nor myself from shivering, clothing damp from both precipitation and sweat. As I weave between residences, chimney smoke permeates the natural odors in the fog. I can barely hear the burble of the creek as I cross the bridge outside of the church, the water low this time of season. Candlelight from the windows barely kisses the headstones closest to the building, their subtle curves a reminder that death is never far away. The others have been consumed in the fog's greedy appetite.

Shortly thereafter, Gideon's property draws underfoot. I approach the workshop from the back, avoiding the lamppost in the front. One moment there is nothing, just my own hands held out before me. The next, a wall wet with condensation. I let out a quiet breath.

It's as if the building has been merely waiting for me to find it. The lines of the structure reveal themselves, the fog thinning as I glance up the wall to the branches scratching it above. Assuming Gideon will be asleep in his house, checking his workshop first seems like the wisest course of action. Perhaps luck will be on my side and both the basket and letter will be here. I know it is unlikely, but I will it to be possible all the same.

I move to a window on the east side of the workshop. Shoving my gloves into my pocket, I place my hands on the window, my warm skin sticking to the cold pane. The window slides up with pressure. Outlines of my hands appear on the glass only to fade away as quiet as ghosts. I move slowly and with care, conscious not to knock anything over as I climb through onto a table just below the lip of the window. The table wobbles, the small *click-clack* of the legs moving beneath my shifting weight sounding like thunder. The workshop is swallowed in darkness, but I still feel exposed. I clench my eyes closed, waiting.

Breathe, Tempe.

After a count of three, I open my eyes and slide off the table. I withdraw a candle and box of matches from my pocket. With a scratch and a gentle *whoosh,* the small flame exposes my hand. I bring it shakily to the candlewick. Vague suggestions of my surroundings appear but only within an arm's length away from the candle.

It will have to do.

Methodically and slowly, I make my way through the workshop, opening cabinets, peering beneath tables, looking inside barrels. Small worlds bloom beneath my light only to fade into darkness as I step away. I check the back cabinet near Gideon's desk once more, hoping he returned the basket after Henry's search. No such luck. The smell of linseed oil, metal, and wood is heavy in the air. The floor in front of the door groans as I walk over the boards. Moisture has warped the planks.

Someone whispers.

I freeze midstep, stomach dropping. My heart pounds as I wait, breath held, to hear it again.

There is only silence.

Slowly, I take a breath. There is too much black space surrounding me. Too many places for someone to hide. I lift the candle up. Faces push through the darkness. Figureheads. Their blank stares watch each step I take. As light moves across their faces, some grin, others glower. They know I'm not supposed to be here. I shiver and look away. My imagination is getting the best of me.

I hear the whisper again.

It's barely there. Like the faint scratching of a lock of hair being rubbed between fingertips. I creep over to the elongated table taking up the center of the workshop. I hold my free hand out, fingers sliding along it for guidance. The candlelight inches along the table with each step I take, a reticent accomplice.

The closer to the whispering I get, the clearer it becomes. No, not whispering. More like air being blown between one's teeth. The delicate whistle sets me at ease. It's only a crack in the wall. My shoulders sag with relief, and I brush a bead of sweat from my brow. I've been all worked up over wind whistling through the walls.

My candlelight spills over the long piece of wood lying on the table. I lift the candle higher, adjusting my grip to avoid the burning wax dribbling down its sides. Gideon has begun to work on the exaggerated curves of the piece. Tools lay beside it; a few shavings and chunks have fallen underneath.

The siren's figure is easily discernable through the natural twists of the wood. One doesn't require much imagination to see how Gideon will shape it. The log is in the perfect position to be shaved down here, cut out there. The siren's back arches drastically, her arms held far above where the head is being carved, wrists and hands wrapped up in one another.

A blush suffuses my cheeks. She looks as if she should be with a lover, wrists pinned above her head as she is kissed. I glance up to where I know the figureheads are watching me just out of the light's reach. One of their own is on display, being carved on before their very eyes. A piece to be sold and placed at the front of a ship long before most of them will leave their perches on the walls. The hairs stand up on the back of my neck as I think of the ones behind me.

I clear my throat to disturb the growing feel of unease. I bring the candle closer to the prone figurehead. Gideon has smoothed out the wood already, as if he was merely discovering her within the bough, rather than creating a design from scratch. I reach out to touch the warm wood, and pull back abruptly upon contact.

The whistle is back.

It isn't coming from the ceiling or walls. I take another step and lean closer to the wood. Candlelight spills over the face taking shape. No, not taking shape. Done. It's so lifelike my heart skips a beat, believing a woman actually lies on the table. She has delicate features, a slight upturn to the end of her nose, large eyes. The details are remarkable. There are even lines in her thin lips. She feels familiar.

The whistle is coming from her mouth.

Goose bumps spread up my arms, over my skin, the feeling of thousands of crawling ants. Bells ring in my head. I lean closer to the wooden mouth. The whistle. There—a barely perceptible line between the top and bottom row of carved teeth. A tiny crack in the wood.

I bring the flame right next to it.

Something pink gleams in the light. Something shiny. It moves.

A tongue.

CHAPTER 15

I scream.

Lurch backward, dropping the candle. It falls to the ground. Darkness returns. I whirl around, breath catching in my chest. My shin bangs against a stool, and items clatter to the ground. I trip, stumble to the floor, knees stinging. Floundering against my surroundings, my hand falls on the handle of a chisel. I grip it, scrambling until I reach the corner of the workshop, where I curl over myself, forehead to the ground, arms over my head.

Eyes are on me, watching. Everywhere. Whispers.

The figurehead is pulling itself up, I just know it. Climbing off the table, wood creaking with each clunking step, tongue flicking behind its wooden jaw. Coming closer. My gasps resonate off the floor, loud enough to give away my position. I wait for the hot, unbreakable grip to clutch my neck. Rip me off the ground. Spin me around to stare into its stoic face.

Nothing happens.

I count to three before looking over my shoulder. It's too dark to see much of anything, but through the faint light outside the windows, it's clear no figure stands over me. The figurehead rests on the table, motionless. I stand up, heart pounding, chisel still in my hand. I edge around the center of the room, refusing to turn my back on the horror lying on the table.

The frail whistle perforates the quiet, like someone breathing down my neck, waiting expectantly. This is a bad dream. A nightmare. This cannot be real. There must be some evil work at play here. I've never been one drawn to the comfort of prayer, but if there really is a God, that means there must be evil as well. For what else could this be?

What does it want?

What does *she* want?

I inhale sharply.

Faint understanding falls like snow only to be swallowed up into a river of fear. It isn't possible. It cannot be. I take one step forward, eyes on the figurehead's face. I can see the familiarity in memory. The pert nose and large eyes. The delicate features. I don't dare touch the figurehead again, cannot bring myself to do so. Instead, I shove the chisel into my pocket and wrap my arms around myself. As I lean over the figurehead, the vanilla scent of white oak fills my senses. I release a shaky breath. "Susannah?"

The tone in the whistle changes, a note of desperation in its trill.

My chest constricts. Complete disbelief weaves into a rope around my neck, stealing all breath away. How is this possible? I don't understand. The wooden face of Susannah slowly emerges from the retreating darkness, as if responding to my sudden perception.

Or to a light spilling through the window.

I jerk from my frozen stasis, panic thrumming through my chest. My pulse pounds in my ears as I turn and pull myself up onto the wobbling table. The legs *thunk* against the floor so loudly I flinch. The door swings open across the room, instantly filling the workshop with light. I scramble forward, knocking tools over in my haste. The floor groans beneath weighty footsteps quickening their pace. I've one leg out the window, hands bracing the frame. I'm going to make it.

The fabric of my jacket tightens. Yanked backward, I hover in the air for a brief moment before my back slams onto the floor. A flash of white. The wind's been knocked from me. I'm drowning above the ground. My mouth opens and closes like a fish caught in a net, pulled ashore. I'm going to die here.

The click of a door shutting. Then a window.

Constriction loosens inside me. Air. I suck in a huge gulp of it. Cough as I roll onto my hands and knees. *Breathe, Tempe. Breathe.* Tears wet my cheeks. I brush them away after a few greedy breaths. The table is a salvation as I pull myself up, weak and unsteady.

Gideon stands between the front door and myself, an oil lantern propped at the end of the table beside him. Half of his face is lit, the other in shadow, but there is no mistaking the fervent grin beneath his hooded eyes.

"Wha—" I stammer, still trying to catch my breath. I grip the table with one hand and push the other into my pocket. The solid handle of the chisel helps stabilize me as Susannah's desperate whistle pierces the air once more. I swallow before trying again. "What did you do to her?"

Gideon doesn't move. Doesn't give any indication he heard me at all.

Denial. Outrage. Elucidation. Anyone else would come up with an excuse to explain what was going on. Not Gideon. No. I'm not dealing with just anyone, and he isn't going to answer me. At least, not that question.

"How?" I glance down at the figurehead, at Susannah, and back up. "What are you?"

Gideon tucks a strand of hair behind his ear as the corners of his lips fall. "You know what I am, Temperance."

"A ship carver. But this—" I gesture down at Susannah, hand shaking. "This is something else. Something evil."

His chuckle folds over me like a swarm of bees.

"You are too young, your life too short, to truly know evil." He takes a step forward, pushing me deeper into the workshop as I am forced to take a step back.

I nod toward Susannah, careful not to look away from him, whatever he is. "What do you call this?"

"Maintaining the balance between Warbler and its human population."

"By torturing and killing a young woman?"

"Torturing and killing? No. I've merely recognized and incapacitated a worthy opponent. In truth, it is a compliment." He reaches out to Susannah, touching the curved wood of her legs. His fingers trace her lines as he edges toward me. The tenderness in his touch makes me sick. He looks up at me. "She will live a very long time. I see to it that they always do."

They? Other so-called *opponents?* But who could that . . .

Yesterday I saw another realistic face. A new figurehead being attached to the foreign whaling ship. A siren whose lips were parted as if at the end of singing a note.

Or screaming.

Molly.

Understanding widens my eyes as I look back at Gideon. The tiny hope that Molly will be found dies suddenly. A butterfly overcome by winter's freeze. Susannah's wooden face draws my attention as I mourn the loss of the naivety I'd clung to so fiercely.

A ship carver who carves stunning sirens known for their good luck. Each said to be the spirit of the ship, guiding the voyage and keeping its passengers safe.

Seafarers' superstition. Gideon's reality.

He's turning real women into wood.

The table groans as he leans against it, a new smile splitting his face as I try to make sense of things. I have no better explanation, no tools of removing it. Logically or otherwise. He considers women a *worthy opponent* and he must *maintain the balance between Warbler and its human population.*

Women are capable of creating human life. It is a power

that even the most misogynistic man can recognize and value. Without women, there can be no sons. No daughters. Men certainly play their part as well. But they do not grow and support that life with their own bodies.

Gideon recognizes that power as a threat.

But what is Gideon? And what is Warbler if not the people who live here?

He takes a step forward, the lantern light completely at his back. Shadows douse his face, and Da's voice is in my head. *Stay away from Gideon. Stay away from Gideon. Stay away from Gideon.*

STAY AWAY FROM GIDEON.

He snatches my wrist, gripping it within his long fingers. I'm too stunned to move, to do anything. It's two years ago all over again, only this time I know I'm in real danger. This has nothing to do with inexperience, anxiety, or crippling fear. This is life and death.

Something sharp jabs into my palm. It's the same pain as that night. I look down and for a moment don't understand what I'm seeing. Something dark is piercing my palm, blood welling around it. I try to jerk back, but Gideon's hold is a vise. The dark tendril is coming from the underside of his wrist. A scream pours out of me the second I realize what it is. His free hand slaps over my mouth, cutting off my scream and smothering me with the smell of sap and sweat as he shoves me back against a table. I watch, terrified, as the root continues to grow out of Gideon's skin, like a shard of bone, and sink into my flesh.

It burns like fire, and I cry out behind Gideon's hand. An intense determination bordering on crossness overtakes his expression. As if whatever is happening is requiring a great amount of effort. I try to pull away once more to no effect.

But I still have the chisel.

Gideon's eyes are on my hand and the root connecting us, unblinking, darkening. A bead of sweat falls from his temple. He hisses beneath his breath, struggling, and somehow the sound awakens me.

In one swift motion, I lift my hand with the chisel from my pocket and jab it into Gideon's side with a crunch. He grunts and releases me, wincing as he grabs his wound. I brandish the chisel in front of me. Blood drips from my stinging palm.

"I knew it." The chuckle beneath Gideon's breath breaks through the ringing in my ears.

He's breathing hard, panting almost, as he lifts up his linen shirt, revealing a pale abdomen and the narrow lines of his hips. A small blood trail creeps down his side. He presses against the injury, pointer finger and thumb framing the open puncture.

A sharp inhalation as he pushes. The skin knits itself back together before my very eyes. No, not knits. Grows. It grows back together. One moment there is an opening, exposing red muscle and tissue; the next, the opening is gone. No evidence that anything had been amiss but a soft pink mark and a trail of blood he wipes away with a rag. He tucks his shirt back into his pants, still breathing heavily. For a moment he rubs his wrist, brows furrowed. Gone is the root, drawn back into his flesh.

Whatever thought is running through his mind, he seems to tuck it away as he straightens up, eyes free of the anger I expected as he scrutinizes me like a piece of wood for one of his projects.

"You are exceptional, Temperance. A fire in your blood. In your spirit. You and Prudence both." A shudder rolls through him as he mutters, "I must have it."

I'm completely and utterly stunned, a rabbit frozen before a fox. He's on a path I cannot follow, speaking another language entirely. But whoever and whatever Gideon is, he's dangerous.

Repulsive. Wicked.

I hold my chisel up high. "I'm leaving. You can stay here or run. But I'm bringing back Henry and the others."

"And what will you tell them?" He tilts his head, motioning to the table. "That this piece of wood is Susannah? That I did the same to Molly? Do you realize how peculiar that sounds? Far-fetched? All they will see is a young woman who went out of her way in the middle of the night to visit her sister's betrothed. And when he denied her, she created a fantastical story to save her pride and reputation."

I shake my head, refusing to accept it. "They'll see what I saw."

"No. By the time you return with anyone, there will be no sign of Susannah. In fact—" He leans over her, eyes narrowed as he inspects her. I want to shove him away from her, but fear stays my hand. "It's already done."

He takes a few steps back and gestures to her, as polite as if he had opened the door for me and was waiting for me to walk through it. I gingerly move forward, glance down. The crack between her teeth is filled in as if it never existed. Only a figurehead lies on the table. Resentment burns through me. I readjust the chisel in my hand and take a step toward him.

Gideon frowns. "It would be in your best interest not to act rashly, Temperance."

There it is again. I shouldn't act *rashly*.

The workshop is small, all the figureheads crowding in like sharks on chum in the water. Am I surrounded by other victims of Gideon? Have I passed by them, completely unaware, every time I lit the lamppost outside? As soon as the thought enters my head, though, I know it isn't true. Only Gideon's sirens are special. They cost extra. If he kidnapped a girl every time he carved a figurehead, there would be no one left. Surely, he'd have been found out by now.

As if he can read my mind, Gideon shakes his head at

me. "Give it time, and all of this talk of missing girls will go away. It always does."

"How do you get them?" I cannot believe so many young women fall victim to this monster, and with no one the wiser. It just doesn't make sense.

"Young women are impressionable. Show them a little kindness, a little interest, and they're happy to please you. They rarely say no, even when they want to." He glances at Susannah and smiles. My stomach flips, and he lifts his gaze back to me. An intrigued smile crosses his face. "But you did."

The memory flashes through me like a brush fire, stirring up all the emotions. Loneliness and longing, guilt and fear. Shame. I was taken advantage of. We all were. But I still don't understand how he got them here. Before Pru and before my own encounter with Gideon, I'd never seen him with another woman. Not alone. "Why would any of them seek you out?"

"You're an intelligent woman." His voice crawls along my skin like a worm. "Perhaps it is time we come to an understanding. Like your da and I had."

The floor plunges out from under me, and I nearly drop the chisel. I shake my head so violently my teeth rattle.

He nods. "Your father was smart too. He kept his mouth shut when I had a new commission. You know how dangerous it can be, wandering in the fog. Warbler is lucky to have such reliable lamplighters to guide the way. Accidents do happen from time to time, though. Lights go out." Gideon's eyes sparkle. "Or are forgotten."

Lies. He's lying to hurt me. Da would never commit such malicious acts. Never. He was a good man. The best. As my mind tries to explain Gideon's insinuations away, suspicion twists my spirit. I take deep breaths to try and settle my stomach.

Stay away from Gideon. Promise me.

Da knew. He knew what was going on and didn't tell anyone. The memory of Da, his generous smile, shatters like a mirror, warping his image until it is something monstrous. Inhuman.

Like Gideon.

My vision swims as I look up at him. My grip loosens on the chisel.

"Your father wasn't a bad man. But life became too much for him. The guilt, I think." Gideon runs his fingertips on the table, fitting them into the grooves, and frowns as if recalling an unpleasant memory. "He decided to abandon his family and leave his mess behind for someone else."

My lip trembles, heart breaking all over again as I see him hanging from the lamppost. Neck red where the rope was embedded. Tongue hanging out. Red eyes staring at nothing. But rather than the usual grief and regret that tickle my eyes, there is anger and betrayal.

"But you're stronger than him. You would never give up because you aren't selfish. You put your family first."

I close my eyes, exhaling through my nose. Inside I'm screaming. Screaming from within a locked trunk that has been thrown overboard. It sinks in the icy Atlantic, deeper and deeper, swallowed by the dark and the cold, where no one will be able to hear.

"You do as I say, and your family will never go without. Your position will be forever yours."

"And if I don't help you?" I know what he will say, but, like one of the traveling troupes that comes through Warbler once a year, it feels like a line I must speak.

"I will take possession of your home, leaving you homeless. And then I will hurt everyone you have ever loved. Your mother, Josiah, and we mustn't forget sweet Prudence." Gideon walks up to me, each creaking step the swing of a pendulum, and grabs my chin with rough fingers.

He tips my head back, and all I can see is the icy promise in his blue eyes. "I can be the best thing to have ever happened in her life. Or I can be the worst."

As I look up at him, a fire begins to burn inside me. It starts at my chin, beneath his touch, and spreads through me like a scorching oil spill. A barely contained seething rage. It wants to consume every inch of Gideon. Burn him. Hurt him. It's a barely restrained violence, challenging his threat until freezing understanding dampens it.

Da left us to this monster.

The quiet memories of Da were always a comfort to me. Now those precious moments have been stolen and twisted into something else. Something unrecognizable. My eyes fill with tears that soothe my burning face. Gideon smiles and releases me, seeing only what he wants to see. Fear and submission.

He sees what I let him.

"I will escort you home." He reaches out for my arm. "Women aren't to be out alone right now. It isn't safe, you know."

We walk arm in arm out of the workshop, the very picture of decorum as he whispers into my ear, "Do not let me discover you in my workshop again. There will be consequences."

He shuts the door behind us, and the prison walls close around Susannah. With each step we take away from the workshop, she pulls at me like the moon to the tide. But there is a gap that will never be bridged, a distance too far. Only in dreams will the moon feel the ocean's touch. I fear now Susannah is too far to be reached.

And it is Gideon's fault.

Together we walk in the muffled silence of the fog. When we pass Da's lamppost, I barely spare it a glance. All I see is red.

CHAPTER 16

For two days I manage to avoid all social interactions beyond lighting and dousing the lampposts with either Henry or Matthew as my unnecessary escort.

Every minute of every day feels as if I'm walking along the bottom of the river. A heaviness in my movements, an all-encompassing cold. When I'm not working, I'm in Pru's and my bedroom. I only come out to brew willow bark tea to help with the aching bruises blooming on my body from my confrontation with Gideon, and I take the cup back into the bedroom to drink. By the sideways glances Pru offers me, it is clear she thinks I am pouting, unable to handle the criticism I received for my accusations against Gideon the other night.

All day I lie atop my quilt, eyes tracing the swirls and lines in the wall beside my bed while I try to find a way to shed light on the dire situation in Warbler. On somehow helping Susannah. I cannot begin to fathom what Gideon is. Aside from the gullibility and imagination of childhood, I never put much stock in Da's folklore, Warbler superstition, or the concept of angels and demons. Maybe I should have. Whatever Gideon is, he isn't human. Not exactly.

The fishermen and whalers will be happy to know they have another believer of the uncanny in their midst.

Now that there is no doubt of Gideon's guilt, I must find a way to convince the others. They all believe Leonard is the culprit. But I don't believe Leonard was involved. With no sign of the man, I can only assume he abandoned his post and disappeared into the fog to pursue life elsewhere like so many whalers before him.

I do not foresee successfully sneaking into Gideon's workshop anytime soon. He undoubtedly has everything locked up now. Susannah is out of my reach, and she is the only evidence I have of anything amiss. Even further, as Gideon said, there's only a wooden figurehead now. Nothing suspicious about that.

On the third day, there is a faint knock on the front door. The sound echoes through the house, an ominous warning, reaching out to me in my stillness. Footsteps cross the kitchen and move into the entry room. The pitch of Pru's voice goes up. I cannot hear the visitor's voice. Only Pru's shout of elation bounds back to me through the wall a moment later.

Gideon has finally come.

I clench my teeth, close my eyes, and cover my ears. I simply cannot handle any stimulus after the encounter in the workshop. What I saw. Learned. My hand stings as I press harder over my ear, but I ignore the pain, unwilling to hear the delight in Pru's voice. Having Gideon in my home is difficult enough, even if I don't have to see him or speak to him. I cannot imagine being trapped on the table in his workshop, unable to escape his presence. A piece of wood, frozen in a moment. Can Susannah hear him? See him?

Did Molly see everyone dancing at the Gathering from her wooden prison at the bow of the foreign whaling ship? Or could she only see black as she dreamed of what could have been, the last touch of her lace and ribbon the closest she would ever get to that final dance.

Suddenly, the quiet dark behind my eyelids is repulsive. I sit up. My eyes water when they open to the stinging light pouring in through the window. I couldn't help Molly. She's long gone.

Is it even possible to help Susannah?

I look down at my palms. There is a small red stain in the wrap over my injured hand.

"Tempe?"

Pru's voice is hesitant. A tiny bounce graces her steps as she crosses the room to stand in front of me. I glance over my shoulder at the doorway, bracing myself.

She sighs. "He left."

Relief will be short-lived, but I'll take what I can get.

"I just wanted to thank you." A new edge has entered her voice that wasn't there before. "Whatever is going on with you, I still appreciate the effort you are giving."

I bite my tongue. Gideon told her about the letter. I cannot forbid their union now, but neither can I feign joy. Not to her. He has made it clear if I don't do as he says, he will take our house and hurt my family. A lie of omission is the best I can offer.

The flicker of pain in her eyes at my silence strikes me, but it is a mere glancing blow.

"With Mother and me gone"—her voice quivers—"you can have the life you deserve with Josiah."

"I don't want either of you out of my life, Pru." I shake my head, wishing my voice didn't sound so tired. All of this feels second tier to the real conflict at hand. There is so much more to this than dislike over a suiter.

"Then what do you want?" Pru hugs herself, and I can see the effort it takes her to stay composed. Such distance has grown between us in our misunderstanding, and I have only myself to blame. Her question is a fair one. Far more cognizant than I expected.

What do I tell her, though? I want the world to make sense and Gideon to be gone. For us to laugh together again. I want to be with Josiah without worrying about Pru's safety and happiness. I want to be able to count on others. Even more than that, I wish I never knew Da helped Gideon kill people.

Because that's what he did. He may not have touched those girls himself or wanted to hurt them. But they're trapped in their wooden prisons above the ocean because of his participation. Their lives are over. Molly, Susannah, Miriam, and others who'd disappeared under Da's watch—they are as good as dead. Da helped Gideon do that for years, never once speaking up or helping them. And who knows how long Gideon was at this before Da, back when only volunteers lit the lampposts.

Now Gideon expects me to take Da's place.

Pru raises her eyebrows, a soothing earnestness in her blue eyes. I reach out for her hands and squeeze them in my own. "I want our family, all of us, to be fine."

We sit in silence for a time, comfortable enough.

"What do you want, Pru?" I finally ask.

Her eyes are bright. "I want to marry Gideon."

I look away from her and at my hands holding her own, at the wrapping hiding Gideon's attempt to penetrate me.

"You're not alone here, Tempe. You could confide in me if you wanted," she says quietly. "I want you to be able to trust me."

How I wish I could too. But I've lied for so long, there is no way she would trust me in return. I cannot fault her for it.

When she leaves, I lie back down, just as lost as before. I cannot lose Pru like this. Our family can only survive if Gideon is no longer a threat. What does a person even call what he's doing? Speaking to our minister may guide me in the right direction. Perhaps he has some explanation for what Gideon is? Then again, he might direct me to an asylum just as quickly. Gideon's threat was credible. I lost Da to suicide. If I begin spouting notions of evil and black magic, others will no doubt assume I'm mentally unsound and need help.

Something must be done before more girls are hurt.

Evidence is required. Enough proof there can be no refuting it. I admit, a part of me needs to see evidence as well. I need to know for sure Da was involved. That Gideon wasn't just saying it to hurt me. He obviously knows where I am most vulnerable.

Hopelessness is exhausting.

And lonely.

Pru's words trickle through my mind, challenging assumptions I've built up to protect myself. I want to confide in her, but how could she possibly understand? She's made of sunshine and smiles, a soothing balm to any negative thought, forcing a person to look at the brighter side. She would never believe me. Besides, she may be an optimistic and encouraging presence to anyone in Warbler, but she's *my* sister.

A sister can be your biggest advocate or your deepest wound.

Eventually sleep takes me into her arms like the mother I used to have. But rather than the sweet oblivion I yearn for so desperately, I'm back on the riverside of my nightmare.

The blackness lightens, a deep red warming my skin. Soon the warmth begins to burn. The sand and pebbles shift beneath the legs of my chair. I cannot make any substantial movements other than to glance up at the fire traversing the river.

The flames part as a ship pours out of the darkness. The *Miriam.* She comes closer and closer, the flames eating up her sides, devouring her as she approaches. When she's close enough for me to see her blink, the scream that tears out of my throat eats up my insides, awareness elevating the terror of this nightmare that isn't a nightmare. Because it's true.

The *Miriam* was named for the woman who disappeared ten years ago while Da was the lamplighter. Known for the beautiful embroidery on all of her gowns, she was envied by all the other young girls for the talent she possessed with a needle. Many argued she'd left of her own accord, for surely someone with her talent could make a profitable name for herself in the big city. Her family disagreed, adamant she would never leave without a word.

After a year of no answers, however, her family left. Whether to chase down the least offensive theory or because they were unable to live a moment longer in the place their daughter disappeared, it was never clear.

For the first time, I awake without Pru standing over me, rescuing me from my nightmares.

Of course!

I cannot get to Susannah easily, but the *Miriam* waits on the river. Out in the open for anyone to see. Evidence of Gideon's evil.

The river smells of wet earth, wood, and the musk of fish. The fog is a thick, gray presence, motionless and stalwart. Even my lampposts cannot break through the unmoving mass, offering only a hint of differentiation in the distance. A mere barnacle beneath dark waters.

All sounds of tavern merriment have bedded down for the night. Normally I'd find the lack of such sounds reassuring, knowing I do not need to interact with any drunken whalers. Instead, the silence only reminds me how alone I am. I stop along the wharf at the dock lying alongside the *Miriam,* the weak light of a single lantern on board the only visual confirmation of her presence.

I tread lightly on the dock in order to prevent any sound from echoing across the water to alert the ship watch. A small part of me wants to stop, go back home. I have no doubt about what I saw in Gideon's workshop. The dark magic he used to ensnare Susannah. But I need to be certain this is bigger, that it has been going on for a long time.

Gideon says Da was involved. I need tangible evidence.

At the end of the dock is a gangplank leading up to the ship. A path to be taken on mere faith, its existence unproven in this soupy cloud of fog. I reach out, careful not to lean too far, and breathe a sigh of relief when my hand touches the railing. The wood is wet and icing over this far out in the river. Water splashes against the rocks along the shore as well as the dock. By the time I get to the lip of the ship, my gloves are soaked through. A small lantern hangs on the quarterdeck, providing enough light for me to assess my surroundings as I step on board.

I try to imagine what living here must be like for six months or more, working atop the ocean with no land in sight. Just the swell and drop of the waves, the spray of salt water, a regimented routine day in and day out, the same food over and over. But for the sudden thrill of the chase, the life of a whaling ship and her crew is protocol and ennui. Constantly on the lookout for the spraying signal of a whale just on the horizon. Praying for good weather, good fortune, and a safe return.

Though I'm fairly certain no one is here, I do not tarry long with my thoughts. I wind through crates and casks, around rigging, past whale boats and a giant whale hook, and reach the bow of the ship to look out over Warbler. The seaport could be a ghost village. The weak lights of the lampposts are hazy stars in a blurry galaxy. The lights shining from within the tavern hint at little worlds just out of reach. Or open graves. The mildew and wet odor in the air coat my thoughts with darkness.

After a quick glance around, I remove my gloves and heave myself up onto the railing. I swing one leg over, hooking the other just so. The air is cooler over the water, but whether I tremble from cold or fear, I cannot say. For a second, I see myself slipping, a resounding splash shooting across the wharf as I fall through the fog and into the water below. That thought only invites trouble. I shake the nerves from my hands and readjust myself, confident in the anchored position of my legs.

Within my jacket pocket, I curl my hand around the chisel I stole from Gideon's workshop. The grip is perfect. I withdraw it and try to ignore the ache already blooming in my thighs as they squeeze the banister. It's now or never. I lean over, gravity pulling at my torso and my right leg burning at the new weight. I stretch out and downward, left hand reaching, and make contact. My fingers feel the curve of her nose, the smooth shape of her eyes, the curl of her hair. Miriam.

Burning fire spreads through the muscles in my thigh. If I move ever so slightly to the left, the pressure should shift. My right ankle slips. I gasp, swing down a few inches. My stomach falls into my throat. My body tightens, hands gripping Miriam's face.

I stop slipping.

Every muscle in my body is taut, too scared to relax. Blood rushes to my head, the pressure building steadily until it feels like my head has been replaced with a cannonball. If I don't hurry, my body is going to give out and I will surely fall to my icy death.

Little by little, my grip loosens on the figurehead. On Miriam. The rest of my body stays put. Slowly I pass the chisel into my right hand. I feel her face once more with my left to give me some idea of where to aim. Before I lose my nerve, I swing my arm and jab the chisel into Miriam's head. The sound rebounds off the wood and bounces off the river, much too loud.

I hold my breath, listening, pulse throbbing in my temples. I jab again. Two more times until I hear the slightest *crunch.* Chisel still cupped in my palm, I extend my finger out, feeling for the chip in the wood. It's there, just above her ear. The divot is small, maybe half the size of my fingernail. It's all I can manage. My legs are numb, no life in them. With my free hand, I reach up and around my torso to grip the railing. I heave myself up and swing my numb leg and body over it. My legs nearly give out as I stand once more on the deck. Feeling sludges back into my muscles, an uncomfortable tingling rolling down my legs. With the chisel returned to my pocket, I grip the railing for support as I hobble back to the lantern on the quarterdeck. Even weak light is welcome.

My finger is wet. Not from sweat nor precipitation. A dark smear. Grim reality gleams before me.

Blood.

I gag, placing the back of my hand to my mouth, and close my eyes. What I once accepted as reality and truth pours out of me like a tapped cask, leaving a hollow ache. It's real. It's all real. There's a woman hanging off the bow of the ship.

She is the figurehead. The figurehead is she.

Miriam has been there for ten years, and I just jabbed a chisel into her head. Her blood is on me. I wipe it against the side of the ship. The blood soaks into the wood and moisture. Deep down, I knew it was all real. That Gideon truly had done something monstrous and his threats were not empty. That Miriam disappearing under Da's watch was no coincidence.

I still had hoped to be wrong.

There must be some way to save these women. If there is some sort of magic or ability to turn them into wood, surely they can be turned back. Blood means she's still alive. But is she still human? Would she want to come back after everything she's been through? It's hard to believe these are the thoughts running through my mind. Not a dream.

Concern weighs me down as I return to the wharf. A small splash pulls at my attention, perhaps a fish hunting for food. I cannot be sure in the weak light.

"Up to no good, eh?"

I all but jump out of my skin before I note the familiarity of the voice. The slur. "Benjamin! You gave me such a fright!"

He sways on his feet as he chuckles. "Ain't no spirit here. I only drink 'em."

I see no harm in conversing with the man now that I know he'd nothing to do with Molly's disappearance. I almost feel guilty about accusing him until his gaze settles on my chest. I cross my arms and clear my throat. I'm not sure how old Benjamin is, but with the deep lines in his face, sag in his skin, and thin hair, I'd wager he's been around awhile. Long enough to know better. "Speaking of spirits, have you heard any stories about wood spirits?"

"Wood spirits?" he all but shouts.

I signal for him to lower his voice. I'd rather not draw the ship watch's attention. "People being turned into wood. Or trapped in it, perchance."

His expression is imperceptible in the weak light, but his head turns from me and in the direction of Miriam. For all his drunkenness, Benjamin remains observant. Already I can see the wheels turning in his head.

He stumbles toward me and speaks in what only a drunk man would believe is a whisper, his hot breath a combination of sour and yeast. "You saying someone's in there?"

I take a step back. This was a terrible idea. "No, of course not. That would be silly. I couldn't help but think of ghost stories out here in the fog. You know how it is."

The last thing I need is to draw attention to Miriam. More than likely she would be viewed as a cursed object that needs to be destroyed, rather than a woman trapped by the ship carver. Superstition guides the hands and hearts of most of our villagers, and I don't know that I can trust them not to harm her before I can back up my claims with more proof.

After the incident with the basket, I doubt I can convince Henry to visit Gideon's workshop again and inspect

Susannah. Showing him Miriam first might convince him otherwise, however. But would he act quickly enough, if I immediately accused Gideon? Henry's already suspicious of my motives after what Gideon said. Timing will be everything.

Clearly, I need to think on this more.

Benjamin remains quiet, longer than I like. Finally, he scratches his head, hiccoughs. Footsteps click in the fog, hazy light blooming from their direction. The ship's watch. I point it out to Benjamin and wave. He nods as I slip away in the other direction. It would be no surprise to the watch to find him there. Benjamin is like a seabird. So long as he isn't taking anything, he's disregarded. I just hope he keeps his mouth shut, and if not, well, the ramblings of a drunk man shouldn't get too far.

Only when I've returned home do I remember it was Benjamin and his ramblings that got me into trouble in the first place.

I step over the threshold and see the likeness of Da on the mantel. I feel him everywhere. His ghost is walking through the room and grabbing his coat from the pegs on the wall beside me. He's reading the *Warbler Newspaper* to me from the kitchen table. He's dancing with Mother in front of the fire. The faintest scent of oil and smoke is in the entry room as if he just stepped out. His raspy laugh is outside in the garden, his deep brogue in the bedroom, and the whistle that is Susannah's desperate cry for help never stops through it all.

My hurried strides take me to the fireplace, where I pluck his likeness from the mantel and toss it onto the embers. It takes only a moment for the canvas to flare up.

Perhaps Gideon threatened him with our family's life, as he did to me, in order to keep Da's mouth shut. To ensure he let the lights go out when Gideon asked. But how could Da not even try to stop Gideon? And then to go and kill himself because of the guilt, leaving us to Gideon after all? My eyes fill with tears, blurring the fire in front of me. The hungry flames are eating the empty frame, Da's picture gone.

Only then do I bury my mouth into the nook of my arm and sob.

CHAPTER 17

They find Benjamin's body in the river the next morning.

"Thought he'd outlive us all."

"Was out of his mind."

"Stinking drunk more than likely."

"Slipped and drowned."

I stand, stupefied, amid the gathering crowd, watching as they pull Benjamin's body up from beneath the third dock. Guilt sidles up to me like a stray cat, bumping me over and over. Did he stumble into the water just after I'd left him? He hadn't appeared to be *that* drunk. If anything, he was better off than on his usual benders. It isn't uncommon to find him leaning on a building for support or crawling down the street. The constables go round and round with Benjamin.

Not anymore.

As his body is placed on a stretcher, another group catches my eye and I feel an all too familiar tug. Guilt is chased away, quickly replaced by suspicion. Unease whispers in my ears soft as barnacles chattering during low tide. The group climbs aboard the *Miriam* carrying ropes, boards, and mallets.

I reach out and tug on the arm of my escort, David. It's clear now why both constables were unavailable. When David looks at me, I nod to the ship. "What are they doing on the *Miriam?*"

"Benjamin damaged the figurehead last night. Best guess is he was drunk and confused. They're removing her for repair." He shrugs and turns away to what he finds more interesting, Benjamin's body.

As ropes are thrown over the bow of the *Miriam*, one worker, familiar, is still. A shock runs through my spine upon meeting Gideon's eyes. He removes his cap and inclines his head.

He was waiting for me to look.

I clear my throat, regaining David's attention. "Did they find any blood on her?"

"Blood?" He frowns, clearly annoyed.

Did they not question the blood on Miriam?

They carry Benjamin's body past me, hair plastered against his pale face like dark worms. Beyond him, Miriam awaits to be removed, the small divot I created with my chisel invisible from this distance. The timing of Benjamin's death is suspect. On its own? Possible. But with Miriam being removed by Gideon only hours after my scrutiny, and for damage that could easily be fixed on the ship or ignored? His death is no accident.

I glance back up at Gideon, at the shrewd smile on his face. He must have known I spoke with Benjamin. That I was here, checking Miriam. The question is how?

The answer comes swift as the breeze. He was in the fog. Those footsteps weren't from the ship's watch. It was Gideon.

Benjamin must have drawn his attention, said something. The ramblings of drunk men are often dismissed, even their truths. I underestimated the depths of Gideon's commitment. There is no line he will not cross. Believing I could honestly find some evidence to build a case against him is laughable. Pathetic. A child's naivety in a harsh reality.

Regret weighs on me, an anchor threatening to pull me down into the river's depths.

"Tempe?" I start as David's voice pulls me from my spiraling panic. His eyes narrow, wary, before he continues.

"No, no blood. Benjamin took a chisel to her but slipped and fell into the river. He was too drunk and the river too cold to find his way out in the fog. It's no surprise he drowned."

Gideon cleaned up the evidence before others could see it, then. By the suspicious look I receive from my escort, it's clear Gideon was hoping I'd ask. I can already hear David's nonchalant comment at the tavern now. *Temperance sure is an odd one. She thought the figurehead was bleeding. You think something ain't right with her head?*

Gideon nods at me before he turns back to Miriam. He is enjoying playing me. There is no outsmarting him. No answers to be found while he stands vigil. Benjamin is dead, and Miriam is to be removed. What he is going to do to her, I don't know. I've no solution for stopping him.

I'm a ship with no tail wind, stagnant and helpless on the great ocean.

David and the clunking of the mallets loosening Miriam from her perch follow my retreat from the wharf.

I'm ready to begin my evening shift, lantern in hand, when I swing the front door open to find Josiah. "Josiah. What are you doing here?"

"Henry's busy." His voice is flat, no inflection to be found.

Something's wrong. He could never keep anything from me for long as children, not that he ever tried. He was never one to shy away from his feelings around me. It's one of the attributes I love about him.

"Hello, Josiah!" Pru calls from behind me.

He looks over my shoulder and offers a small smile. "Evening, Pru. Well, aren't you chipper as a flower. Special occasion?"

"I'm to wed Gideon. Tempe has given us permission." Her cheer is a knife in my gut.

Josiah's smile widens, but it isn't genuine. I can tell. "How wonderful. Congratulations."

He tips his cap at her, turns, and proceeds down the path. Pru shuts the door behind me as I jog to catch up to him. Since the Gathering, sunset has become a cold, unwelcoming time. Where before there would have been voices of cheer and comfort as people returned home for the evening, now there is quiet. Suspicion and fear in the women's eyes. Accusation and helplessness in the men's. There are no more shouts for Molly's name. Not even Susannah's. It is the silence of anxious observance. Of waiting. For whatever might happen next.

Josiah waits as I retrieve my equipment and ring the bell to let all of Warbler know I am here. Although I am no longer confident it provides the comfort it once did. It's been over a week since Molly disappeared. So much has happened since that night. The only thing weighing upon me at the time was concern over Josiah's return. Now he's home. Safe. Yet the distance feels all the same. I miss us.

I lay my hand on the arch, on the carved whale, and glance over my shoulder. "Remember when—"

But he's already moved on, propping my ladder against the first lamppost. I tuck the hurt away, refusing to let him see it as I hurry over.

"I'm sorry I haven't come to visit you, Josiah." I climb the ladder and wipe down the lamppost's glass panes. "I haven't been feeling well."

It isn't a lie exactly. He mumbles something beneath his breath as I light the wick and shut the door. I climb back down. "What did you say?"

He shakes his head. Rather than press him, I continue on, taking care of each lamppost we come to in a stilted quiet. Josiah has never been one to withhold his thoughts. I'm not sure what to make of his silence. It becomes heavier and heavier with each lamppost. Once we are in front of the tavern, he speaks, his gaze on the fog curling around our legs. "You were adamantly against Gideon and Pru marrying. What's changed?"

"I am still against it." My teeth clack together as I shut my mouth, the words out before I can stop myself.

"Then why allow it?"

I see Benjamin's cold, pale body on the stretcher and shudder. Josiah would be in danger if I ever told him the truth. I clean and light the lamppost, aware of his eyes on me the entire time. Patiently waiting. When I get back to the ground, I shake my head at him. "I don't want to speak of this right now."

His brow furrows, the openness to his expression darkening as he crosses his arms. "I would like to."

A sound comes out of my mouth, half sigh, half groan, as I yank the ladder off the lamppost. Josiah makes no effort to move as I step around him. "It doesn't concern you, Josiah."

Bumping into him is an accident, but he recoils as if it was intentional.

"It doesn't concern me?" He scoffs. "Tempe, I love you. Pru is my family. Of course it concerns me. Why are you closing yourself off from me?"

"I'm not!" Why? Why is he doing this right now? I don't need this on top of everything else. I shake my head and stomp toward the next lamppost along the riverfront. A few whalers are loading up the last of the supplies onto the *Elizabeth*. She sets out tomorrow morning for a new expedition, this one meant to last eighteen months. The fog is already so thick it has consumed the dock. The whalers disappear into it as if through a curtain and into another world.

"Then tell me." Josiah hounds me, disregarding all my personal space as he crowds me.

"I'm working, Josiah." I don't even bother cleaning the lamppost. Wick alight, I'm moving on to the next one, barely keeping the anger inside from boiling over as he keeps pace with me. His chest is rising and falling steadily, his breath loud through his nose.

"What is going on between you and Gideon?" he grits out when we stop.

His question would have knocked me off the ladder if I were on it. "Nothing. Why are you even asking me that?"

"Then tell me why you do not like him." Josiah lifts his chin, settling his stance, a tree bracing against a storm. "Are you upset he is marrying Pru instead of you?"

"What?" I scoff at the absurdity of the idea and the conviction in his tone.

Water droplets gleam in the wool of Josiah's jacket. The flame from my lantern reflects in his bright eyes. "You were in his workshop during the Gathering. And then again, the other morning."

"I only went into his workshop during the Gathering because the door was open and I happened to see Molly's basket inside." I know he heard me tell Henry this. My insides begin to tighten and twist. "And I was on my shift when Gideon struck up conversation the other morning."

I feel sick at the look on Josiah's face. The revulsion and anger. And hurt. His expression matches my own.

"And the other night?"

My heart stops. "Pardon?"

"Four nights ago. I had to take Ruby out, and I saw you two leave his workshop. You were not on shift, and you appeared to be . . ." Here he pauses, and I can see his Adam's apple move as he has to swallow the word down. "Comfortable."

I can only gape as disgust rolls through me. I spin away from him, anger moving my feet.

"Don't walk away from me." He grabs my wrist and jerks me back.

I cry out at the sudden sting. Josiah's eyes widen. Before

I can move, he pulls the sleeve of my jacket up. There, on my wrist, are two bruises. Long, like fingers.

"Who did this to you?" His voice is dangerously low.

I glance up into his eyes. Comprehension hardens them, flares his nostrils, purses his lips. I tread thin ground here. Josiah is a cannon ready to explode. The slightest incorrect movement and he'll be gone. "Please release me."

He does, but he doesn't break eye contact. Josiah said he would wait as long as I needed. I can see that no longer applies now.

It's now or never.

"Do you remember when Gideon mentioned he and I had a history?" I rub away the ache of his grip.

"You said it wasn't what I thought."

"Yes, well. Not exactly. When I was sixteen, he invited me into the workshop for shelter from a storm." I don't want to tell him more. I don't even want to go back there myself. Navigating this situation is like wading barefoot along the riverside, trying to avoid the sharp rocks. But I need him to understand. I owe him some portion of honesty. "I was having a difficult time—emotionally. I wasn't thinking straight, and I . . . I . . . kissed him."

I look down during my confession, a sour taste in my mouth, waiting. How is it that three simple words—*I kissed him*—have the power to destroy a future? Mustering my courage, I peek up from the swirling fog to Josiah's face. He hasn't reacted; I get the feeling his very muscles have frozen.

"And then he hurt me. Threw me into the wall." My current aches flare at the memory of the first assault, the pain of vulnerability. Of being brutalized. Seeing stars. Hair pulled. My burning hand.

My hand—Gideon had pressed something sharp into my hand. Like the other night. I just didn't see what it was at the time, a root growing out of a monster. He had tried to turn me like the others. It failed, though, the touch merely burning and awakening me from my shocked state. Enough so that I spit in Gideon's face. If the root is what changed Molly and Susannah, how was I able to stop it?

What does that mean?

You are exceptional, Temperance. A fire in your blood. In your spirit. You and Prudence both.

A laugh in the fog pulls me from my thoughts. The whalers have left the dock and are heading toward the tavern. Josiah is still watching me. Now isn't the time to try and figure things out. Right now I have to tell him as much of the truth as possible, but not enough to put him in danger. "I didn't want Pru to be with him because of what happened to me. I was protecting her."

"Why didn't you tell someone? Why didn't you tell me?" His voice is calm. Too calm. Warning bells ring in my ears.

"I was ashamed." My voice quivers. "For kissing Gideon despite you and me. I was scared what would happen if you found out. If anyone found out."

"That a grown man hurt you?"

Unable to hide my frustration, I shake my head. How can he be so obtuse? "It wouldn't have been seen like that."

"You should have given me a chance."

I release a shaky breath, casting my eyes away and toward the next lamppost waiting to be lit. "Perhaps."

The fog grows, and I shift my weight, looking pointedly back at Josiah. This is an unfortunate time to have this conversation, one I'd never intended to have with him. His perceptiveness and patience, two qualities I've always admired, have caught up with me. I incline my head down the road, and he nods, releasing me from his uncomfortable stare. Together we move to the next lamppost, but I know there is no escaping his questions.

My ladder is heavy and cumbersome, my hands shaking. Josiah stands an arm's length away from me, but the river might as well be running between us. Tears are flowing freely by the time we reach the lamppost in front of the shipyard. Prop, climb, open, clean, trim, light.

Breathe, Tempe.

He waits until I've climbed back down before speaking again. "You haven't told me why you went to him the other night."

"It's difficult to explain." Josiah snorts and turns away. I snatch at the back of his jacket, and he stops, shoulders hunched. "Please, Josiah. I broke into the workshop to find Molly's basket."

He lets out an exasperated sigh and takes off his cap to run his hand through his hair. It's as if it is taking every ounce of his patience to stand here with me. Cap back on, he raises his eyebrows. "And?"

"I didn't find it." I shake my head and shrug. "And Gideon caught me. He grabbed my arm to pull me out. That's it."

It sounds plausible, but already I can feel the heat climbing my neck, the red staining my cheeks. He must believe me. He has to. I do not doubt Gideon when he says he will hurt the ones I love should I tell anyone about Susannah and Molly and the others. Not anymore. And I have no proof to support my story about them, so why would Josiah believe me? *Especially* after all my lies. How would anyone believe me if I told them what I saw? It sounds made-up. I rub my sweaty hands on my trousers.

"So he escorted you home because he cared so much about your safety?"

"He promised not to report my break-in if I gave my permission for him to wed Prudence." It rolls off my tongue so easily, this rancid lie. "So I did."

"Gideon is threatening you." Josiah shakes his head, eyes wide and mouth parted with incredulity. "You have to report it."

"No."

"Then I will."

He turns away, and my heart jumps into my throat.

"Absolutely not." I run around him and place my hands on his barrel chest. "If you love me at all, you will forget about all of this. Let it go. I'm begging you."

His chest heaves beneath my hands, heart pounding through the fabric. The anger in his eyes scalds the very air between us. I know he will not harm me just as I know fire burns, but for a small moment I see true fury in someone once so even-keeled. I have to recalibrate my understanding for a moment. Because this is the moment I've been dreading.

Josiah can give up on me right now. Go home. Leave me to continue on with his life and he would be perfectly within his right. It's what I've always expected.

I curl my fingers into the fabric over his chest, the strip of linen on my hand bright beside his brown jacket, and release a shaky breath. "Please, Josiah."

The hardness in his gaze falters, and my heart leaps. It is a moment of tenderness. He reaches for my hands.

He grabs my wrists instead, pulling them away from his chest.

Josiah lets go of me.

One second he's there, and the next there is only the faint scent of cedar. Then even his smell is gone as I stand frozen by disbelief while the *Elizabeth* creaks and groans on the river. I'm left with the wet fog, smoke, and oil fumes, unable to chase after him because Warbler is smothered in danger and there are lampposts waiting to be lit.

I continue on in a dazed state. As I light the lamppost in front of the workshop, Gideon leans against the doorway, watching me. He is the only witness to the shattering of a heart I had thought was already broken in the first place. A rot, steadily creeping through the foundation of my life.

The trees whisper behind the fog, or maybe it's the fog itself? Feeding on my sanity like termites.

Da's lamppost is void of his ghost tonight, which I would

appreciate any other time. He is trivial when the living are the ones truly hurting. I go to bed without eating and ignore the concerned frown on Pru's face in passing. There I lie with a gaping hole in my chest only Josiah can fill. To chase after him now would only cause irreparable damage. If there is anything worth salvaging left, I must wait. There will be time to fix it.

There has to be.

"Tempe?" Pru stands in the doorway, a trim silhouette, haloed in light. "Are you all right?"

I shake my head, unable to get the words out. She approaches slowly, hands gripping her skirts, before sitting on my bed. Love and concern emanate from her as she reaches out and wipes a tear from my cheek. The dam threatens to burst inside me.

"Did you and Josiah quarrel?"

I nod.

"Would you like to talk about it?"

Her tenderness threatens to undo me. I want so badly to open up to her, but nothing and no one in my life is safe anymore. How much time before another woman comes under Gideon's claws? How long before I misstep and get another person killed? How long can I watch him infiltrate my family and destroy everything and everyone I love?

I shake my head because as much as I want this moment with her, to connect and share my fears about the man I love, I cannot. Because Gideon is part of that, and in Pru's head, Gideon is part of her now. I always thought as sisters, we could count on each other. That no one and nothing would come between us. Pru will want nothing to do with my accusations, though. She'll either not understand or merely refuse to do so.

With the light behind her, I cannot see her expression. But the earnestness and vulnerability in her posture, the attempt to get close without getting too close, breaks my heart.

"No." My voice is gruff.

Her small shoulders drop, but she squeezes my hand affectionately nonetheless before leaving the room. She is the best of all of us Byrnes. No one deserves her.

When the door shuts behind her, darkness rushes in. With the absence of light, there are no shadows in the room, no lines. Pitch black. Is it like this for Molly and Susannah? Miriam? The countless other sirens trapped on the ships?

As I lie in the dark running through frightening emotions, it feels like I'm being buried alive, slowly fed on by worms. I'm trapped with no clear way out, and I can't breathe.

I fling my quilt off and reach for the bedside table with shaking hands. I light my lantern.

The darkness dissipates, chased away by the delicate flame. Warmth emanates from the glass, a reminder that I am home. In my room. Pru singing softly to herself on the other side of the wall. There is still something in my control, even if it is at its most base level.

I'm the one who brings light to the dark. Braving the fog and its misdirection in order to guide others. Light—fire—is power.

If Gideon *is* some sort of wood demon, fire must be his weakness.

Action is the only option left. Gideon made that clear this morning as they lifted Benjamin's body from the river. I refuse to live like this, unable to make my own choices for fear of retribution. Allowing an evil man to control, confuse, or scare me into submission. I'm strong and capable. I earned the right to be the lamplighter. This is my life. Warbler is my home. Who am I to let women be harmed when I can do something about it?

Even if that means becoming a monster myself.

I'm my father's daughter, after all.

At a quarter past two, after Pru is fast asleep, I dress as quietly as possible. When I step outside, matches in my pocket, I picture Susannah trapped on the table, encased in wood. Gideon's painful grip on me, the root in his hand, his wound growing back together. A demon with the power of wood. Well, I have a power too. I lift my chin and make my way down the path and begin to creep my way in the direction of the town hall to retrieve my backup oil cannister.

The fog thickens with each step as if it knows what I'm about to do and seeks to discourage me.

It matters not. I am sure-footed.

CHAPTER 18

There are no lights on in Gideon's workshop, nor any in his house.

Still, I wait, bending an ear for any sounds of movement from within or out on the street. Confident no one is nearby and that Gideon must be sleeping, I circle the house twice, peeking in through the three windows on the ground level as well as confirming the number of doors. Two. The front door and a back door that opens outward. I debate finding a rock to roll in front of it, or something to wedge against it, but common sense stops me.

The fire cannot appear suspicious.

Doubt freezes me for a moment, the confidence I felt earlier waning as I stand here. This is no longer merely an idea. Am I actually to do this? Can I truly justify taking a life? Gideon will always hold the upper hand, and so I must do what I can to protect not only the ones I love but all of Warbler. There is only one path I see out of this hopeless place.

But it still is a life.

The fog has coated everything in a wet blanket. Fire thrives in perfect conditions, and soaked wood is far from that. The only way the fire can spread is if it starts inside. Thankfully, the back door into the house is unlocked. I slip inside without a sound, holding my breath.

I'm in the wolf's den now.

There is no sign of Gideon. I let out my breath but have no control over my pounding heart. The house is frigid, unlike the balmy warmth of his workshop. I wasn't sure what to expect upon entering his home. But as I creep through it, stopping to gaze into the shadows, should he be tucked away in them watching me, all I can discern is that for all his organized and put-together demeanor, there is no rhyme or reason to any of his furniture or layout. Everything is made from different wood. Tables, chairs, settee, bench, stools, picture frames, vases—all dissimilar. Dark and light woods, large grains, small rings, knotted, smooth.

I suppose there is beauty to the chaotic and clashing differences. Not dissimilar to Warbler's forest, made up of different trees and foliage. But more than anything, it's crowded and uncomfortable. Pretending to be a welcoming home but just missing the mark.

An overwhelming smell of finish and mustiness hangs in the still air. Wooden bowls filled with flower petals sit on the tables, the perfume long dried out. Different herbs and flowers are strung from the kitchen ceiling, hanging like the draped branches of a willow tree.

Woven rugs muffle my footsteps as I pace, trying to figure out how to start a fire without waking Gideon. It's too big a risk to go upstairs. Do demons sleep heavily? Or is he up there listening to my every step, waiting to spring a trap on me?

I gulp down a wedge of fear and stop beside the fireplace. No warm embers burn within, but there is a perfect stack of wood ready to be lit. I reach up and inside to find the damper already closed. Perfect. Who's to say he didn't just close the flue too soon? That he didn't put the fire out all the way?

As quietly as I can, I pull the rugs together, creating a woven path from the fireplace to the table and chairs. Handfuls of the petals are scattered around the room, their barely perceptible rustles like a sprinkle of rain.

Any moment I expect to feel Gideon behind me. Hot breath on my neck. Hand twisting into my hair, ripping it at the roots. His whispered cadence in my ear, as his hand latches onto mine, root tearing through my skin. With a quick glance over my shoulder, I confirm I'm alone. It doesn't stop my hands from shaking, increasing the chances I accidently drop something and wake Gideon. My plan to eliminate his insidiousness from Warbler will be over, and I will spend the rest of my life in prison, or worse. I could hang like Da.

My resolve hardens.

Oil pours easily from my canteen, the smooth viscosity calming my fraying nerves. I douse both doors and all the window ledges on the ground floor, ensuring no possible escape once lit. What's left in the canteen goes to the rugs and stairs. The musty air is quickly overtaken by the thick, fishy odor of the whale oil. I cannot imagine being on the actual whaling ships while they boil and render the whale fat. Josiah said after experiencing such a putrid scent, he would rather sleep in a pile of manure than smell it ever again.

Just thinking about him rips a stitch in my heart.

Once the cannister has been emptied, I set it outside the back door before returning to the fireplace. The heart of his home. I'm about to take a life from this world. Can I live with myself after this?

Da couldn't.

A new knot forms in my throat. I shake my arms, rub my hands along my thighs. I pull the book of matches from my pocket and choose one, rubbing the small wooden bit between my fingers. Unlike Da, I'm doing this for the right reason. He was allowing people to be hurt.

I'm saving them.

It takes a few minutes for the flames to spread from the tinder and onto the logs. As it does, I wrap my scarf around my mouth and nose. Smoke is already spreading through the room, the damper blocking its escape up the chimney.

The rug beside the hearth is next. Oil ignites, and the flames spring alive with a *whoosh* as they race along the fueled path. Flower petals burst in orange and white light, their edges curling only to be gone a second later. It's almost beautiful.

The floorboard above my head creaks. Slight movement. A cough. My already catapulting heart leaps into my throat.

"Not yet," I whisper.

I hurry to light the front door and windows. Flames ignite the oil so fast the heat blisters my fingertips. The smell of burning pine, oak, and cherry woods joins the oil. A thick black smoke slinks in the air, puddling against the ceiling. As I move through the rooms, the fire crackles and hisses as it feeds, steadily growing. Smoke oozes up the stairs, a black fog of death.

Sweat drips into my already burning eyes. The house is sweltering, smoke replacing any breathable air. Each breath I take sends a burning current down my throat. I strike my last match and lift it up to the drying herbs hanging from the ceiling in the kitchen. They light with a hiss, and just as fast, embers rain over me. Hell's dangerous fireflies. Crouching low, I hurry to the back door and slip through. Just as I do, a small ember flutters down to the doorway, igniting the whale oil. I shut the door right as a wave of fire roars against it.

Canteen in hand, I run to the tree line behind the house, relishing the wet air as it cools my steaming skin. I never expected to be grateful for the fog. As a deep glow emanates from the house, I wait for the wave of peace to crash over me. I am safe. Pru is safe. Josiah. Mother. Warbler. But the peace I hoped for never comes.

Instead, I feel only ill.

I hold on to the trunk of a maple for support as smoke begins to filter beneath the door and through cracks in the walls. Eventually, bright flames flicker behind the windows on the second floor, the corrosive and violent spirit peeking out from within its cage. There will be no escape from within. If the smoke hasn't taken Gideon already, the fire will.

It must.

I shouldn't tarry.

In no time, the fog envelops me. The creaking trees whisper as I move among them. Their voices reach out into my subconscious, poking and prodding with accusatory fingers. The fog, which for a moment gave me cool relief, suddenly becomes cloying, soaking my clothes through to my skin. I feel trapped as the tree trunks close in around me like an angry mob.

We saw you. We know what you did.

I trip over a root, fall through the blurry void and into the decaying leaves and dirt. A heavy presence leans in above, the dark silhouettes of the trunks fading in and out. I can't seem to catch my breath, the wet earth crawling into my lungs, fog soaking through my skin, trees pinning me in. In my peripheral, the air becomes a soft orange.

I have to get out of here.

I regain my footing and stumble through the trees, toward where the villagers' homes are. It's too risky to use the street, the chance of being seen in the lamplight too high. But at least there is more air here near the buildings, away from the deep woods and the feeling of being watched. I'm passing behind Susannah's home when someone calls out from the street. I duck down behind a shed.

Warbler's Bell rings a cacophonous cry in the distance.

The single shout on the street becomes many voices as the word no one wants to hear cries out across Warbler. *Fire.* I can just make out figures running through the lamplight on the street. People carrying buckets of water. The chaos provides enough distraction I manage to avoid being seen.

Back home, I stoke the fire until it blazes up and I can heat water for washing. It's normal to have some aroma of fire on one's person and clothes in the colder months. Too much, however, under the circumstances, may be suspicious. It takes me most of the night to rid myself and my clothes of the overpowering smell of arson.

Once done, I drape my clothes on the backs of the chairs by the fire and sit while I wait for my hair to dry. The dancing flames are mesmerizing. Curious how something so comforting can at the same time be so dangerous. In the quiet and stillness, all I can think about is boiling and charred flesh. I can still taste the smoke at the back of my throat.

I see it three ways. Gideon succumbed to smoke inhalation and died before the flames could feed on him. Or, trapped, he died a terrible and painful death. Lastly, and the least welcome option, he survived. He got out.

Only dawn will tell what befell Warbler's ship carver.

As the embers pulse in the hearth, I make a vow. I will find a way to free Susannah and Miriam from their wooden prisons in the workshop. I will help all of the sirens I can find and spend the rest of my life living right. Doing what I can—if not as penance for the life I've taken, then to show I did not make this choice lightly. It will be all right. It has to be.

Sleep escapes me, nerves stringing me up like a tanned hide, as I wait to start my morning shift. I fling the door open the moment footsteps scuff up the front path. It isn't Henry. A puff of smoke clears, revealing David as he works his lips around the bit of his pipe. "Morning, Temperance."

"Good morning, David." I nod, instilling a light tone into my voice.

He grunts, pipe clacking against his teeth as he takes his cap off and rubs a big hand over his bald head. "There was a fire last night."

I cover my mouth, infusing shock in my expression.

The fisherman nods, his eyes grave. I fight the elation building in my chest while maintaining the appropriate response. "Where? Was anyone hurt?"

"Ship carver's residence. Still searching for a body." He winces. "Hard to think a person could survive that, though."

"How awful. I cannot believe I didn't hear the bell." I shut the door, grateful my shift starts while Pru still sleeps, and hurry down the path, David trailing a step behind.

"You weren't the only one." He pats my shoulder from behind. It is an awkward gesture, but it is his way of comforting me, I suppose. "Fire was early this morning. Most were asleep."

Each lamplight winks out at my touch, leaving the post dark and lifeless. I try not to appear overanxious, but I cannot help it. David seems not to notice as he puffs away at his pipe in the pink light of dawn. I glance at the trees along the street, their forms still. They're watching me, aren't they? Silent with disgust.

The closer we get to the business district, the heavier the scent of smoke becomes. Flower petals flash before my eyes, their delicate bodies curling up and consumed in devouring flames. How long will they have to search through the rubble before they find his body?

I don't bother filling the oil wells, patience escaping me entirely. I'm up the ladder and down in less than five breaths and moving on to the next lamppost. I'll fill them later today. Do whalers feel this antsy when they've spotted a whale spout on the horizon? Anxious to close the distance?

Finally, we reach the end of the wharf. Just past the inn, a breeze carries the scent of char and smoke, thick and powerful enough to overpower the fishy smell of the docks. Where Gideon's house once stood is the most basic framework, now charred and smoldering rubble surrounded by an iron fence. The stone fireplace is half-crumpled but remains a suggestion of what once was. Mounds of unidentifiable material fill the space, a blackened and pulpy mess.

Small areas still smolder, the wet air barely touching the heat. A group of men are gathered before the debris. They look like they climbed out of the fire themselves, nearly unrecognizable, layers of gray and black covering them entirely. They must have been the ones to respond to the fire. I can just barely make out Henry in the bunch, his large beard so grayed by soot he looks thirty years older.

"Lord have mercy on his soul."

I glance over at David. He's removed the pipe from his mouth and holds his free hand against his heart. I follow his gaze back to the group. Only now do I notice the curled form on the ground through their legs. It's charred, blackened, bits of pink peeking through. The distance doesn't allow for an easy identification, but there is no doubt.

It's Gideon.

A relieved sob escapes my lips, startling me so I jerk back, ladder slipping through my fingers. The clatter draws Henry's gaze to me as an emotion I've never felt takes over my body. I think it might be elation. Light is finally bursting through the dark.

It's done. Gideon is gone.

We're safe.

David pats my back. I can tell by the uneasy pressure and wooden movement how awkward he feels. "There, there."

I shake my head, stand up straight, and wipe my eyes. "Sorry."

"Don't be. Life is cruel. All we can do is fight her for survival. Lucky the fire didn't spread beyond the workshop."

Cold rushes through me. "What?"

David nods back to the rubble. Where the workshop used to stand is now a scorched piece of land. All of the figureheads are scattered ash and charred bits, lumps of wood like unmarked graves.

Susannah and Miriam.

I burned them to death.

CHAPTER 19

The moment I return home, Pru rushes over and takes me by the arm to sit beside the fire.

I feel as if I have been dragged behind a ship for the entire breadth of the ocean. Exhaustion weighs me down so that even lifting my head to meet her eyes is a struggle. I'm an eighteen-year-old murderess. I've taken three lives, two of them innocent.

Now I'm to break my sister's heart.

A log shifts in the hearth, crackling as sparks skip out onto the floor. They die without fuel, unlike in Gideon's workshop, where Susannah and Miriam lay, doomed to a fiery death, wooden prisoners trapped in a hell I caused.

Pru squeezes my knee. "What's happened?"

I rip my gaze from the treacherous flames and look into Pru's earnest face, reach out for her hands. They should be small in my grasp. Younger sisters are always that. Little. But she is a woman, and as I look down at her hands, I see the same long, slender fingers as my own.

She is safe. Pru is safe. The mantra loops in my head in an attempt to keep the terrible reality of what I unintentionally have done at bay.

"There was a fire."

My throat is scratchy, the volume weak. Pru nods her encouragement, and I take in her strength while it lasts.

"Both the house and workshop burned down."

Pru's expression does not change, but her grip tightens. Specificity is not necessary. It is clear in my tone, in my hesitation. It is the moment when a person's world is on the cusp of shattering. They always know it's coming.

"Gideon is dead."

Saying the words aloud should be a triumph filling me with indescribable relief. But the words have no weight. Instead, they are lifeless, colorless, flakes of dead skin. Yet they carry all the weight of the world for Pru.

She crumples into my arms, and we sink to the floor together. The heat of the fire reaches out to warm her while at the same time searing me. Out of sheer obstinacy, I refuse to move. Susannah and Miriam weren't capable of moving. Why should I for a little discomfort? They are only biting sparks.

I rub Pru's back and make soothing noises between her sobs. Just enough energy exists within me to be here for her. Melancholy sits on my shoulders, holding me down. But for Pru, I have strength in reserve. I will always find it for her.

The rustle of fabric pulls my attention from her shaking body. Mother stands beside us, her fingers fidgeting along her skirt. Hesitation opens her lips; uncertainty battles in her eyes. I cannot think, only watch, as she reaches down to us. Her left hand pats Pru's back, cautious in its delivery. Her right hand sits atop my shoulder, so soft I wouldn't have known it if I hadn't been watching. She squeezes and nods at me, her eyes bright and connecting.

A sob escapes my lips as a crack in the wall I'd built up around my heart spreads. Hope flutters delicate as a feather. I want to reach out to her, but I cannot let go of Pru. Mother resumes her seat in the rocking chair long before Pru is able to catch her breath, unaware of the miracle that just occurred.

For two days, Pru walks in a daze. I cannot say I am any better, each of us mourning for the same and yet also very different reason. Lost life. For Pru, it is a man and the life she could have had with him. For me, two young women and a former life where I was devoid of blood on my hands. If there is something good to come from our sorrow, it is that for the first time in two weeks, Pru and I are leaning on each other. As equals. Sisters. She may not know the whole truth of my grief, but there is comfort in being there for another, if only a small break from your own pain.

I had forgotten what it felt like to let someone comfort me, and it strengthens my resolve to be there for her.

She cries at night, trying to hide the noise as she sniffles into her pillow. When I crawl into bed beside her and hold her, I'm not sure how much comfort it gives, but she never turns me away. It reminds me of when we were children and the spring storms shook the house. Or when we heard frightening tales from children at school that we couldn't rid from our imaginations. We used to always have each other's back, and it feels right reaching out to her, even if it isn't her who needs the comforting.

We have each other, and in our somber movements, in our unyielding support for one another, the guilt tugging at my skin for what I've done begins to lessen. It's still there. Will always be there. But when I remind myself that my family and all of Warbler are now safe, it becomes bearable.

By the third day, much of the site of the fire has been cleaned up.

The state of Gideon's body dictates he cannot be put on display for the funeral, nor can it be held at his home as there is no home left. Instead, he's buried in the church graveyard, where the minister speaks of his life to the villagers attending the service, myself and Pru included. Nothing he says illuminates how Gideon came to be the evil I have come to know, but I listen all the same, hunting for some sort of explanation.

"Gideon arrived in Warbler over thirty-five years ago, employed as the cabin boy on a Dutch whaling ship. Solemn but with an easy smile, his curiosity took him to the storefronts along the wharf, where he asked every question imaginable about each trade, jumping out of sight anytime his fellow crew members happened by. When the ship set sail, everyone assumed the boy had left with them, but the next morning Gideon stepped out of the forest in the dissipating fog, hungry and dirty, but with a relieved smile on his face." The minister chuckles and smiles at two other villagers old enough to remember this moment.

"It was clear he wasn't keen for a life on the open sea. Warbler, still young at the time and in need of able bodies, welcomed him with open arms. But no one welcomed him more than Charles Keesling, our old ship carver, after the boy showed a keen interest in his workshop. With an apprentice, Charles no longer had to trek into the forest to locate and carry out wood for his commissions or head out to the lumber mill. He also appreciated Gideon's admiration for his craft. A quick study, it wasn't long before Gideon's skill surpassed his assistants' and then his own.

"When Charles died five years later, he left his workshop and home to Gideon, having grown fond of the smiling, enthusiastic boy. The old man had become much like a surrogate father to Gideon, who took his loss hard."

I know well the feeling of losing your innocence. The death of a loved one, a father, is not something you can explain. Only feel. That being said, I still cannot reconcile the boy the minister speaks of with the man I came to know.

The minister continues on. "A determined work ethic, a constant study of his craft, and a seriousness replaced the boyhood charm and laughter Gideon once had. He matured and grew to be an integral part of our community, the devotion and passion he put into his work admirable, the quality astounding. He was a natural talent. An artist."

Of nightmares, I want to say.

"While he was an eligible bachelor, there wasn't a single woman who appeared to catch his eye. His love was only for his craft." The minister does not seem to notice the strangled sob escaping Pru's throat, nor the flood of tears pouring down her face.

My heart hurts for her, but there is also relief, cloaked in guilt, that Gideon hadn't publicly announced his intentions to marry Pru. Only Henry, Josiah, Pru, Mother, and myself know.

The minister ends his eulogy by highlighting how much value Gideon brought to Warbler. He does not say it out loud, but I'm certain we all are having the same thought. It will be difficult for our economy to absorb the impact of Gideon's death. His skills brought many ships to our seaport. We will have to rebuild the workshop and hire a new ship carver to continue supporting our shipyard. Mayor Albright is sure to attempt to capitalize on the idea of our lucky figureheads as long as we can get away with it.

At least we won't have to worry about any more of our young women going missing now that Gideon is dead. Being the only witness privy to the dark underbelly of Warbler is strange. I will have it no other way, though. No one need ever know what the ship carver did.

Or its lamplighters.

After a murmured prayer, everyone departs the service. I remain beside Pru, watching as she props a small embroidery hoop against the wooden marker baring Gideon's name. Until his gravestone is finished, the wood will be the only sign. Pru decided to make her own flowers as none are alive to be placed this late into the season. The delicate threadwork looks out of place over the freshly turned earth and the dark wooden marker. She whispers something I can't quite catch before stepping back. Arm in arm, we make our way out of the cemetery. Neither of us ask to stop at Da's grave, Pru too distraught in her thoughts while I cannot even bring myself to look at it.

Back on the road, Pru takes a handkerchief from her

pocket and dabs at the corners of her eyes, clearing her throat. "I haven't seen Josiah lately."

I wince.

"You should talk to him, Tempe."

"I don't think he'll want to."

She halts our progress, stopping and turning to face me. "We don't have forever to be with our loved ones. You should take a chance."

She manages a small smile, but there is no joy in her eyes. Only grief. I want to tell her she will be all right and her heart will heal. That she should find joy in her book club, in discussions with her friends, in the little pleasures of everyday life while she figures out what matters most to her. Where her passions lie. That it's possible to take other paths and still fall in love someday. Instead, I step back from my role as the older, all-knowing sibling, and allow her words to sink in.

She is right.

We do not have forever in this life. I have always known this, and yet I always pushed it aside for what felt more pressing at the time. Shouldering the burden so that my family didn't have to. Preparing so the worst wouldn't happen. And if it should, ensuring it did not take me by surprise. And yet it has happened again and again.

No matter how hard I wish, I cannot control everything.

In my attempt to do so, I've lost so much precious time. I've kept Josiah at arm's length for too long, hurting him deeply with my agenda.

He is a kind, wonderful man and friend. Someone I want to spend my life with. I clear my throat. "Will you come with me?"

Pru nods, her presence all the support I need.

Decision made, I steer us in the direction of the cooperage. What is Josiah working on today? A new cask? Butter churn? Trough? We have never had an argument like the one the other night. Aside from his recent adventure on the *Miriam*, we have never gone more than a couple days without speaking. Dread fills me at the thought of him shunning me the moment I reach out. I have taken his patience for granted.

What if it's too late for me?

We make our way down the street, pulling our cloaks tighter around ourselves. It seems autumn crumpled overnight and became a fine dust blown away by the winter winds. The trees are bare. Gray, white, brown, and rust reign supreme in this motionless world, the river a ribbon of navy winding through the forest. A few colors pop out along our walk: a pink bonnet, green cloak, blue ribbons in a little girl's hair. Small joys to get us through the frozen season.

One thing I am grateful for in the colder months is that the clear, frigid air strips some of the pungent scent of cod, clam, and crab. Not completely, of course. That would take nothing short of a miracle. But it allows the more desired smells to come through. The cinnamon and nutmeg of pies, the fresh ink from the printer, and the warm woods burning from the cooperage.

Smoke floats lazily from the cooperage's chimney when we stop at the door. I rub the fabric of my skirt between my fingers and shift my weight between my feet.

As soon as we open the door, heat ushers us in.

"Just a moment," George calls out from the back as Ruby greets us with a breathy ruff. Her tail thunks the ground as she heaves herself up and out of her barrel bed. We rub her snout and back, producing the appropriate affectionate noises that leave her glued to our sides and gazing up at us with her adoring brown eyes.

When George comes out, mug in hand, a smile splits his face.

"Tempe, Prudence! What a pleasant surprise this chilly

morning. It's been far too long since you've stopped by, Prudence. You're a sight for sore eyes."

Pru ducks her head. "It has been. Please forgive me."

George waves his free hand at her but still manages to slosh coffee out of his mug. "Nothing to forgive so long as you promise to remedy it."

"Of course. I'll bring Mother with me next time. It will do us both good to step out of the house every now and again." Pru laughs as Ruby nudges her hand for more pats. It is a welcome sound after the past few days.

"Wonderful." George nods. "Ruby and I will welcome the extra company what with Josiah off again."

"What?" Gravity vanishes. The only thing grounding me is the smile disappearing from George's face.

Lines appear between his eyes. "Didn't Josiah tell you?"

"Tell me what?" Ruby pushes against my hand. I step away from her and cross my arms.

"He left. Signed on for the *Elizabeth*'s whaling expedition."

My lungs deflate. Pru grabs my arm and squeezes, the only thing preventing me from crumpling to the ground. I close my eyes, blocking out the pity-filled grimace on George's face. I'm too late.

I see Josiah standing in front of me, eyes gazing down at me with compassion, devotion, love. I feel the warmth of his cheek in the palm of my hand. He was wearing a mask, after all, wasn't he?

My eyes sting. I bite my lip.

"I'm so sorry, Tempe." George sets his mug down on a stool and reaches out for my hand. His hands are rough, the knuckles knotted. A cooper's hands. Josiah's hands. "I would have told you myself, but I thought he already did. He left here early to catch you before your shift the other night. I thought I saw you walking together."

It takes me two tries to clear my throat. "He did walk with me. It just never came up."

Josiah had been so angry when he retrieved me for my shift that night. It's clear he had already planned on leaving me. But why didn't he tell me? He could have at least said goodbye. My thoughts race through our conversation. His questions of clarification. The hurt in his voice. Maybe he wasn't sure yet about parting from me.

Would he have stayed if I hadn't told him about kissing Gideon?

"I don't know what to say." George shakes his head, his bright eyes filled with concern. He looks at Pru helplessly.

"Let's go home, Tempe." She turns me with a nod to George, who looks like he wishes he were anywhere but here. We walk home, but everything feels wrong. I don't recognize anything. None of it holds any meaning. Only Pru's reassuring grasp is keeping me tethered to this world.

Doing everything to prepare for the best chance of survival makes failure hurt even more. I want to be furious with Josiah. Angry that he would prove my fears correct and leave when our situation got difficult. But the truth is I cannot be surprised. The only person I can be mad at is myself because there was a chance, however slim, I could have prevented it.

I wasted too much time.

Back home, Mother has set our teacups on the table. She sits in her rocker, sipping from her own. Sending curious glances Mother's way, Pru pours tea for us from the teapot. Mother still hasn't spoken, but she doesn't have to be prompted or encouraged to participate like usual. It's as if observing her daughters hit rock bottom has reawakened her maternal instincts, even if they are a shadow of what they once were.

"Do you think he will ever forgive me?" I whisper, keeping the fragile concept safe.

Pru joins me at the table. Her hand is warm as she places it atop my own. "You're worth forgiving."

"Am I?" I don't feel like it. If Pru knew the truth about everything I'd done, whether it was with good intentions or not, she wouldn't think so anymore. I wouldn't if I were her.

I didn't forgive Da.

He's gone, but I still feel him everywhere, unable to escape the memories nor my own feelings. For the first time, I do not have to wonder about what Da would have done in my situation. I have no doubt Gideon threatened our family in order to get Da to help him. He must have. Da would never have done anything so terrible without a reason.

He did what he felt he had to do even though it was wrong.

After four years, our family found ourselves under the same circumstances again. But I chose a different path than Da. I am not proud of my choice, but it was the better of the two. It's my fault two women are dead. And Benjamin. And Gideon, of course. Perhaps Josiah is God's way of punishing me. And I deserve punishment. But in refusing to succumb to hardship and guilt, in refusing to let Gideon win, I have the opportunity to live my life. To do right by it, and just maybe remedy my mistakes and live the life I want.

I will wait for Josiah. For the eighteen months of his journey. For as long as he needs. He is worth it.

The tea is bitter, but it begins to warm the cold suffusing my body. Pru is lost in her own thoughts, thumb tracing the rim of her teacup. Mother rocks in her chair, gaze on the flames, a faraway look in her eyes. There is a stillness here, a pause between heartbeats, not unpleasant or worrisome. Simply quiet. Life carries on around us in Warbler. But here, we all navigate our thoughts, mulling over futures, pasts, present.

We will be okay, us three. In time.

The next morning, Matthew is my escort. I had hoped for Henry, so will need to find him after my shift. With Gideon dead, I worry whoever takes ownership of our house may turn us out. No one has said anything yet, and I'm not sure who I need to speak to about it. Hopefully Henry can give me the guidance I need. At least I can count on him not to disregard me like the others.

With these new worries keeping me company, I extinguish the lampposts and we greet the other early risers. The fishermen, crabbers, storefront owners, ship workers. The fog drains out of the woods, the streets, the wharf, and sinks into the river. Frost crunches beneath our boots; the cold of the handle on each lamppost burns through my gloves.

By the time we reach the end of the wharf, I cannot feel my ears and my nose is red. I loathe winter. Climbing out of the warmth of bed to step into the frigid dawn is beyond unpleasant. New England winters are brutal on the body and spirit. I wear Da's coat over my own, which barely takes the edge off the biting cold. I'm grateful for Pru's masterful sewing and knitting skills to safeguard my hands, neck, and head.

Is Josiah managing to stay warm while the Atlantic coats the *Elizabeth* in a freezing layer of ocean spray?

A small commotion arises just out of eyesight, tugging at my attention. Henry's booming voice rolls down the street like thunder. Hurriedly, I extinguish the lamppost, fill the well, and then pursue his gruff tone. Matthew appears as curious as I. We turn the corner and see a small crowd just outside of where Gideon's workshop and house used to be. A horse and wagon are stopped in the middle of the street, a hoof stomping the cobblestones nervously at the raised voices.

Curiosity has me sidling closer to the crowd, trying not to appear too eager to learn of whatever has piqued everyone's interest. Matthew doesn't bother with courtesy and ambles straight into the group. A combination of nervous tittering, angered gesticulating, and perplexed expressions clash against Henry's attempt at order. Onlookers peek out at the ruckus behind curtains in the neighboring homes. Their guess is as good as mine.

At last, Henry gains the attention and control of the crowd, slicing through them with a piercing shriek of his whistle. The echo of it cuts down the street and across the water, bringing everyone's hands to their ears. All but one person flinches in the crowd.

At the center of the hunched group, still as a figurehead affixed to a ship, stands my waking nightmare.

Gideon.

The air freezes in my lungs.

He's a ghost. He must be. Or a neighbor with a similar profile. Please.

Deathly still, the man stares at the charred lot, the iron fencing all that remains of his home and workshop. Henry says something to him, too muffled for me to hear. The simulacrum's head turns to acknowledge the constable, and I see him clearly.

All doubt is gone.

The air begins to dance as if filled with fire sparks. My soul has up and left my body, leaving me weightless. Everyone around Gideon blurs while he appears clear, the target of a looking glass. Our eyes connect with the impact of a blow to my stomach. I stumble back, ladder clattering upon the road as I land on my buttocks. A stinging bolt shoots up my spine, through my arms, and out my fingertips. It's nothing compared to the all-consuming enmity in his eyes.

He knows what I've done. Somehow, he knows.

Self-preservation screams through my blood like a banshee. I tear my gaze away from his and scramble to my feet. There is no need for discretion. Ignoring the muttering crowd, I run through Warbler as fast as my feet can carry me, unable to catch up to any explanations.

Gideon died. I saw his body.

Except that must not have been his body. But where has he been all this time? And whose body was it?

Scenarios spin in my head, rolling in a circle with no clear answer or end, like a child hoop trundling. Warbler blurs by, the businesses and homes, villagers and visitors, all blissfully unaware of the evil in their midst.

By the time I reach home, my throat is raw and dry from the cold, and I cannot seem to catch my breath. A bench rests beside our garden, dead vines curled up and around its legs. After setting my tools and ladder down, I collapse onto its frame and sit in the stillness. Confusion and despair flap around in my head. Two birds stuck in a room with no windows.

I'm trapped.

Eventually, the blue morning light warms into a soft peach pouring over the rooftops. Tiny crystals melt off windowpanes, the stalks in the garden, the stone walls. The air holds a crisp wet smell only broken by the smoke floating lazily out of the chimneys. If I just stay here for a while, sit in this moment of peace, I cannot be touched. For a time, I can pretend the world will carry on without hardship. Without any darkness to feed off it.

"Temperance."

The façade shatters. Gideon sits down beside me, his thigh pressed up against my own. I cannot respond. Breathe. Recoil at his touch. Nothing. A tear slides down my cheek, leaving a cold trail in its wake. The calm before the storm, and I do not know if I will survive the impact. I destroyed his home, his livelihood. The only thing I did not take from him was his life.

And I will pay for it all.

I can feel it in his silence. We sit in front of a frozen lake, and I must traverse the icy surface to get away from him. I blink back the threat of more tears and take the first step out onto the ice. "Where were you?"

He stretches his legs before him, ankles crossed, hands in his lap. "New Bedford. I was delivering a commission."

A commission? His commissions are only ever sirens. That can only mean one thing. I let out a shuddering breath. I did not kill Susannah at least. She escaped the bite of the flames. The relief is short-lived, however. She's away on some ship, doomed to spend the rest of her life locked above the waves.

And Miriam is still dead.

"It seems I narrowly escaped a terrible death by fire. Alas, my home and workshop are destroyed. But I will rebuild. I will endure," he murmurs, turning his gaze to something I cannot see.

There is something I still need to know. I take another step, the ice groaning beneath my weight. "Someone died."

"Yes." He looks back at me. This close, I can see small hairs growing outside the clean cut of his goatee. The strangely disheveled look does not suit him. But the thought of him doing something so mundane as shaving seems so at odds with what I know about him. He tilts his head. "The constable's best guess is it was arson and the perpetrator was unable to get out before the fire blocked them off."

At the word *perpetrator*, his eyes narrow. We both know who did it, but it will never be heard coming out of my mouth. The question is, will he use it against me now in retribution for his losses? Or will he stow it away to be used later? The safety of shore is still far ahead with each creaking step on the ice.

Who did I kill? "And does Henry know who it might have been?"

"There is a theory a certain whaler might have been the culprit. Henry was not aware of the complaint I made to

Leonard's captain after his unprofessional advances toward my betrothed. He knows now."

My betrothed. I close my eyes but cannot unsee the gleaming pleasure on his face. And a man is still dead by my own hands. I had all but forgotten about Leonard after all that has happened.

If Gideon told Henry about Leonard, I can only assume it really was him who I killed. I am not sorry Leonard is dead, may God strike me down for my wicked thought. I am, however, sorry I did it. But why would Leonard have been in Gideon's house?

When I saw them interact, Leonard appeared scared. I'm surprised he would approach Gideon again of his own accord. I think back on the last time I saw Leonard, the night he disappeared with Susannah.

Did Gideon take him then too? Has he been with Gideon this whole time? But why would Gideon have kept him around?

I clear my throat. "Why was he in your house?"

"He stormed in as I was packing to leave for New Bedford. Threatened my life."

That doesn't make sense. I frown and cross my arms.

"Oh! You mean Leonard?" Gideon raises his eyebrows. "No, no. He wasn't in my house."

A lone gull cries out of sight.

"While Henry's theory does hold merit, it is far from the truth." Gideon chuckles, each huff of air stolen from my own lungs. "No, I'm talking about the young cooper who fell entirely too hard for someone who didn't return his affection."

The ice cracks beneath my feet.

"He burst into my home that evening and . . . well . . ." Gideon shrugs as easily as if he were speaking about a disagreement over the price of wood. "We had words. He believed I acted inappropriately toward you. When it became clear he would not listen to reason, I had to make sure he understood in another way. I do regret our altercation. I did not want to kill him."

No.

No. No. No. No.

The front of Gideon's jacket is in my grasp, my knuckles aching, my ears ringing, the house and garden blurring at the edges. "But I heard someone upstairs. I heard a cough."

"Oh dear. I must have been mistaken, then." Glee alights in Gideon's eyes, and a weight like a ship slams into me. "Do you suppose Josiah screamed while he burned to death?"

My insides shatter. The ice opens up beneath me.

Darkness swallows all of my pieces.

CHAPTER 20

Days flutter by, a moth in the breeze.
Then weeks.

The pendulum swings.

Something is broken inside of me.

Each of Gideon's visits to our house sets a tremor beneath my skin, but the hate and loathing I once felt have all but simmered into acceptance. There is no pushing back on the immoveable. I live life in a circle. I maintain the lampposts, greet passersby, return home to sit before the fire, eat, sleep. Repeat.

There is nothing else.

Nothing I've done has altered the course of the future for the better. Each choice I made, each action I took, only made life worse. Sweet Molly is gone, trapped forever over the ocean. Benjamin is dead. Susannah is gone. Miriam is dead. Pru is to marry Gideon. Josiah, my best friend and love, is dead. Buried in a plot under someone else's name.

I killed him.

Now there is only the circle.

I cannot scream. Cannot cry. There is simply nothing there. Nothing left. Who I used to be, who I wanted to be, is now obsolete. Nothing makes sense, and it doesn't need to. All I have to do is go through the motions to get through this life. Repeat. Repeat. Repeat.

Believing I ever had any control was a fallacy. Apathy is the only action I can take to keep my loved ones safe. Everything else made it worse. It's all I have left anyhow.

Something is broken inside of me.

Two days after Gideon's return, construction began on his new workshop with his living quarters above it. He informed us it was so he could keep a better eye on his business, and he asked for Pru's thoughts on the design. A none-too-subtle reminder of their upcoming nuptials. As if I could forget. She embraced the opportunity for happiness like a woman given a second chance at life.

Chatting nonstop, she showed me different patterns and fabric samples for the curtains, blankets, and cushions she planned on making. Clearly her attempt to connect with me again after her world was put back together while mine stayed crumpled. I smiled and nodded, offered a thought here and there. I said all the right things, went through all the motions. However, the delay in her reactions and concern in her eyes told me she knew my heart wasn't in it.

But she never asked, too absorbed in her own overdue happiness. A part of me believes it is because she is young. It's hard to put others first, even for someone so compassionate as Pru. The truth is, though, I cannot blame her. Who am I to steal away her happiness so long as Gideon does no harm to her?

As far as she's concerned, I am grieving over Josiah's eighteen-month-long voyage on the *Elizabeth.* Over missing my chance to start my life with him. Over pushing him away. Losing him to life at sea. I will have her believe the fire in me has faded on account of the time I lost with him. A flame at the very end of a wick.

"He'll be back, Tempe," she says one day, squeezing my arm affectionately as I stare into the fire. "Just you wait and see. It'll all work out."

Only Gideon knows the truth. One more dark secret between us.

An ugliness connects us.

Though he stays at the inn, he makes a point of joining

Pru for a meal every day. Her eyes light up every time he squeezes her hand. When he tucks a strand of hair behind her ear. I watch the ease with which she's begun to graze his shoulder as she leans in to pour his favorite tea, an earthy blend. She serves it every day whether he is there or not. A reminder he is part of our family now.

I see it all.

I should feel something.

I don't.

Leaves fall every day only to be whisked away by the river. There is nothing the leaves can do about their fate but to ride the current.

I should want to fight it, though. Shouldn't I?

What would be the reason? There is no one willing to jump in the river with me.

I am tired.

So I drink my tea and accept something is broken inside of me.

The unease within Warbler has passed.

With Leonard presumably dead, women no longer require an escort, and I am permitted to resume my shift without a shadow. I suppose I am grateful for that. There is no need to wear a mask. To pretend nothing is wrong and that the security everyone feels is not a farce. The patronizing comments by the council and many of my peers have finally begun to fade away. There will always be the few who struggle to accept my competence as the lamplighter, but for the most part, life has gone back to normal.

However, I steer clear of Henry and his curious eyes, the astuteness in his gaze that will bring me nothing but trouble. An encounter with him is best avoided. I wish I could do the same with Gideon.

Currently, he is working in the shipyard while his

workshop is being built, carving a new figurehead to crown the *Miriam*. The captain thought it fitting to honor the loss of the previous one by requesting she be carved as an angel rather than the siren she once was. Both relief and sorrow war within me.

I dread the day Gideon receives a new siren commission. What he will ask of me.

Families have begun embracing the winter season and the icy winds that never fail to blow up off the half-frozen river and strip the warmth right off a person, leaving them entirely exposed, like a skinned animal. While no one looks forward to the all-encompassing cold, however, there is one thing that seems to raise Warbler's spirits. The holidays.

Thanksgiving approaches, and as such, Pru has begun planning the special meal, prattling on and on about all of the special dishes Gideon has offered to pay for. It's only in the early morning before my shift that I can escape her chirping and be in the silence. I don't want to think about Thanksgiving. Of Gideon joining us and taking Josiah's seat.

The thought hits me so suddenly, I stumble midstep into the kitchen.

I catch hold of a chair to steady myself and inhale through my nose. Exhale through my mouth. Again. Again. Again. It takes me a minute to realize I am not alone. Mother stands before the front window, arms crossed, hair pulled taut into a bun. A wool shawl is draped over her narrow shoulders. Standing beside her, we are the same height. She reaches for my hand, gripping it tightly as we watch the sky lighten.

The morning quiet and warmth of her hand is a lullaby long forgotten. She and Da used to sing early in the morning, harmonizing beautifully as they readied for the day. I loved listening to them, warm and snug beneath my covers, as Pru softly snored beside me. Da sang always, but Mother would only ever sing with him. She said a butterfly couldn't fly without its wings. Da was her wings. Perhaps that was the reason she gave up after he killed himself. She just didn't know how to live without him.

As the fog thins, the houses across the street come into focus, their windows great eyes staring back at us. I never believed there could be someone out there who might understand what it feels like to lose yourself. Yet here she is. I was angry at Mother for so long. For abandoning us and retreating inside herself. I never considered it wasn't a choice she made. Perhaps she was incapable of healing whether she wanted to or not.

Does she replay their last night together over and over? The last time she lay eyes on Da? I think back on what I said to Josiah. On the pained look in his eyes. The touch of his hands. And what it felt like when he let go. I'll never forget it.

What is the memory Mother can never forget?

The house creaks around us as it settles and shifts. Neighbors walk by on the road, blowing into their cupped hands. Another cold morning. Mother pulls her shawl tighter and shivers. In the weak light, I can barely see the silver in her copper hair. Other women her age are graying, but not Mother. She has a sprite-like beauty with high cheekbones and bright eyes. There are very few lines on her face. She appears untouched by the years.

But not all scars are on the outside.

I feel Mother's eyes on me once I leave the house, but I don't glance back. I cannot bear to see her standing still as a gargoyle. A ghost haunting a past life. My breath puffs out with each exhalation, like David smoking his pipe. I spend extra time at each lamppost, cleaning every nook and cranny within the cast iron and wiping down the glass panes until they are so spotless they become invisible. Each oil well is left nearly brimming. Allowing myself to do mindless work, keeping my hands busy, enables me to forget about the world. It's all right not to feel anything right now. There is no guilt in that.

George greets me as I climb down the ladder in front of the Green, his words interrupted by a rattling cough.

I wince. "Oh no. Are you coming down ill?"

He nods, eyes miserable. Nose and cheeks rosy as a cherub's.

"Why don't you stay home?"

"I've to let Ruby out. My apprentice has too much to do today, and I've been putting off a walk for far too long for her."

Ruby. How could I have forgotten about her? I pull my bag onto my shoulder, shifting the weight to a comfortable position. "I'll take her for a walk as soon as I'm done with the lampposts. You just leave her to me."

It's clear how terrible he feels when he doesn't even argue. Poor man. He nods and continues on to open the cooperage. Hopefully he will lie down on the bed in the back for a spell rather than walk back home. New task set for the day, I finish my shift and then return to the cooperage after dropping my tools off.

Ruby pulls herself out of her bed, tongue lolling out, and hurries over as soon as I call her name. Her cold, wet nose presses into my hand. Peter, George's newest apprentice, greets me as I hurry outside with Ruby, waving over my shoulder. It's warming up late in the morning, a day free of clouds and wind. The streets are busy with everyone taking advantage of the brief respite from the cold. Ruby relieves herself on everything she can find.

The frost is melting, water dripping from rooftops and tree branches. Ruby's nails click on the cobblestones as she trots happily beside me. People smile as they pass. It is calm here. Peaceful even. A seemingly perfect day.

I leave the street and cut into the woods. Ruby's side presses into my legs as we push through foliage and pass by naked trees, her tail wagging at the adventure of the day. Josiah loved taking her for long walks. When they returned, he would be covered in a sheen of sweat and she would usually have a new stick to add to her collection on the side of the cooperage.

She bumps into me as we push through the flora to find a clearer path. Without the leaves on the trees blocking the light, it's easier to see farther. A few birds scatter, wings flapping as sticks break beneath my boots and Ruby sniffs around, huffing and barking at sounds only she can hear. The sides of my pants are covered with yellow dog hairs by the time I stop in a glade I've never seen before.

The clearing is large, at least four acres. I think we've wandered onto Gideon's property. These are the trees that provide the lumber for Gideon's figureheads, other projects, and firewood. He has numerous signs put up near the workshop and street forbidding entry. People are not allowed to traipse through his precious trees.

Great oaks line the perimeter, standing guard to the young trees planted and now growing in the clearing. Life continues on. Ever the spinning circle. Ruby nudges my hand, and I squat down to gaze into her brown eyes and simple grin.

Gray and white hairs leading up from her mouth to her eyes remind me she isn't long for this world. She doesn't seem to mind. She's out in the woods with a friend, receiving pats. Her eyelids droop over her trusting eyes as I scratch her ear. Groaning, she leans into it with all of her weight. Completely trusting me to support her.

The woman who killed her father.

Tears trail down my cheeks, drip from my chin. She has no idea Josiah is gone. That she'll never hear his voice again or feel his touch. A sob splits me wide open, and I wrap my arms around Ruby as it hits me with the force of a hurricane.

I'll never feel his touch again.

Josiah stood up for me. He had no idea what he was up against because I didn't tell him. I didn't trust him. I thought I was protecting him.

Instead? I killed him.

Every move I make, every single thing I try to do, Gideon twists into something ugly. It isn't fair. It isn't right.

I'm so angry. Sad. Desperate. Frustrated.

Alone.

The clearing emphasizes my sobs so greatly it sounds like an entire crowd grieves along with me. Not just one woman. One stupid, naïve young woman at the end of her rope. Ruby pulls away from me and trots off, leaving my hands to grasp at dirt and dead leaves. I cannot blame her. I wouldn't want to be around me either.

She snuffles into the earth, pushing leaves, pebbles, and dirt around with her pink nose. Huffing and puffing in her excitement. I roll back onto my heels and release a shuddering breath.

I'm so worn out I could curl up here and sleep until life passes by. I don't have any answers or ideas, but somehow crying has replaced whatever piece was missing. I feel again.

Wretched. Awful. Hopeless. But at least I feel something *more.*

"Come on, Ruby." I slap my thigh, the sound loud in the clearing.

She ignores me, digging into the mound of earth surrounding a young tree. Kicking dirt out behind her hind legs. I groan and look to the sky, inhaling the fresh winter air. She's caught the scent of something. Lord, what if it's another dead fox? I hurry over.

"Ruby!" I grab the scruff of her neck and tug.

A deep grumble vibrates her chest. I shy back for a split moment, heartbeat accelerating. The smell from the object of her attention hits the back of my throat and makes me gag. Ignoring her growl, I wrap my arms around her chest and pull. "No, Ruby. Bad girl."

POP

Ruby and I stumble backward. I recover faster than the old girl and grab her scruff, pulling her around me so I'm between her and the freshly dug hole. A flap of gray hangs from her lips. She tosses her head back, jaws clacking, cheeks smacking as she attempts to swallow it. Without thinking, I hold her jaw and shove my hand into her mouth, getting a better grip. The limp object tears as I pull it out, victory in Ruby's eyes as she manages to swallow the larger piece.

Covered in Ruby's saliva, the gray flap is slimy and rank. Oh God, what dead animal am I holding? Lips locked, I glance at the freshly dug hole. Ruby managed to dig down to the base of the tree. Roots dangle down like little veins or tendons. The hole is not empty.

There is a body. A human body.

Ruby has managed to uncover an arm, its angle unnatural and most likely the explanation for the *pop*. She's also unearthed the upper portion of a torso, neck, and face. The flesh of the forearm is sloughed off, a small chunk missing, exposing deep red and purple, a thick yellow like curdled milk. The wet slime in my hand sinks in.

I cry out, flinging the flesh away. The corpse's green-and-gray-hued face draws my gaze. It's dirty. Soil caked into the corners of the eyes and the mouth, beard, eyebrows. The eyes are moving; the green lips part.

Maggots.

They fall like yellow grains of rice, cushioned in the soil. Wiggling. There is still plenty of flesh and shape to the man's face. Enough to recognize exactly who he is.

Leonard. He's been here the whole time, wrongfully accused of crimes he never committed.

Ruby whines, struggling against my hold. I have to get

her away from here, but the sight of the dead whaler has me engrossed. There are tree roots embedded into his body, gripping him like a child would their favorite toy. He was obviously buried here first, the tree placed afterward.

Except—a tree wouldn't grow through him so quickly in mere weeks. It's impossible.

But there is no impossible here in Warbler. Not with Gideon.

The smell has me breathing through my mouth as I drag Ruby away. I get her to the edge of the clearing before I turn back to see Leonard. Decomposing in the ground, mere carrion. The surrounding trees shielding him from the wind. The sun observing from up above. The dark mound of soil a blanket over his body. The tree roots intertwining with his own limbs.

There are eleven other mounds in the clearing similar to Leonard's. Yet I know the property continues beyond what my eyes can see. Young birches shoot out of the mound centers, like flags atop their own little islands in a sea of faded green. Or grave markers.

Oh God.

I now know the reason Gideon doesn't allow people onto his land, into his grove. Nausea curdles within my stomach the longer I look at them. For weeks I have felt nothing. Mere acceptance.

Fear has arrived.

It blooms within me, a toxic garden feeding off my insides, poisoning my bloodstream. There is evil in Warbler, and I am the only one who knows about it. Young women are being turned into figureheads. People are being murdered and buried in the ground. But who are they? Where did they come from?

It strikes me suddenly. The whalers.

Warbler is known for its fog, and with that the opportunity for whalers to abandon their posts. What if we were only led to believe that? What if they never actually left? Has Gideon been bringing them all to this grove?

But to what end?

Something has to be done.

I can't do this alone.

The thought comes so suddenly and completely it's as if someone stood beside me and said it aloud. It's so clear and obvious. The only option I haven't tried is to reach out for help. In my hopes to keep people safe, I've isolated myself, and Gideon, in his turn, has threatened me into silence. I can't help but wonder, if I had just trusted Josiah with the full truth, could he have helped? Would he still be alive?

You should have given me a chance.

Blue sky peeks through the branches above my head. Josiah should be here. I still see the hurt in his vulnerable gaze, the mole just under his left brow. I feel him let go of me. Tears pool in my eyes.

I should have learned from Da. He tried to do this alone. Kept it all to himself until the weight of it drowned his light, snuffing it out, and he left us. I too tried to do this alone, and in a way, I left our family too. Maybe not physically, but emotionally. I cut myself off from my loved ones, thinking the right thing to do was to not burden them with my heavy thoughts and fears. But Josiah was right.

You should have given me a chance.

It's too late for him, though not for my sister. I don't want to do this alone anymore.

Maybe I never had to.

CHAPTER 21

"Pru, may we speak of something important?"

We sit at the kitchen table with Mother, three cups of steaming tea before us. I'd rather not drink the tea, Gideon's earthy brew, but this is a delicate matter to ease into. Refusing to drink will only set Pru's defenses up. As I take a sip, I see the clearing. The trees. The mounds. Roots growing into Leonard's body.

My teacup clatters onto the saucer as I return it with shaking hands.

Pru frowns and sets her own down. "Of course."

"I know the past months have been difficult." I run my hands on my trousers, the monotony of the constant movement holding me steady. "We haven't exactly agreed or seen eye to eye."

Pru nods as Mother takes a delicate sip of her tea.

"But I need to be honest with you about something that isn't going to be easy to hear."

Like clouds passing in front of the sun, Pru's welcome dissipates. She leans back in her chair and crosses her arms.

I set my palms on the table, pushing into the wood, an anchor. "I was walking Ruby in the woods, and I found a body. The missing whaler. He was murdered."

Her eyes go wide. "Good heavens! Did you report it to Henry?"

"Not yet." I shake my head.

"Why?"

Now that the moment is here, my courage begins to falter. "I need you to hear this from me first."

She frowns. "I don't understand."

I focus on the chip in my teacup as I work up the resolve to say my truth. "Leonard disappeared with Susannah the night of the Gathering. All this time he's been dead. I believe he was murdered the same night Gideon took Susannah and turned her into a figurehead."

Pru doesn't react. Uncertain whether that is good or bad, I continue.

"The night after the Gathering, I found Susannah transforming into wood on Gideon's table. He's the reason women go missing in Warbler. He takes them and turns them into his figureheads. The special commissions, at least. The missing girls . . . Molly and Susannah . . . and he was doing it while Da was alive too. He takes advantage of them and then traps them forever using a root that grows out of his hand."

Her eyebrows rise, and I hurry on before I lose her to disbelief.

"There's something wrong in his head. He thinks women need to be controlled or maybe defeated. It's some sort of strange power struggle. When I found out about what he was doing, Gideon threatened to hurt our family if I didn't do as he said. Particularly you."

Out of the corner of my eye, I see Mother turn her head toward me, but I cannot look away from Pru. It feels like the small thread connecting us will break if I do. I lean toward her, her silence encouraging me to continue. "Gideon has attacked me twice, but I was too scared to tell anyone because who would believe me? Gideon is a well-respected man and member of the town council. His business helps Warbler's economy. I'm the lamplighter, yes, but I am still a woman, and because of that, my motives will always be questioned. He has used it to his advantage to keep me quiet. Even you have questioned my motives. My own sister."

I raise my hand when she opens her mouth to deny it. "You know it's true. And I cannot live like this any longer. Da couldn't either."

Mother flinches.

"Da was helping Gideon. I'm not sure why, except that maybe Gideon was threatening us like he is me. But Da couldn't live with it anymore and took his own life."

Pru's neck is splotchy red, her breath coming fast. She glances at Mother and back at me. I'm losing her.

Time to play to Pru's strength, which is to help others. "After finding Leonard, I can't help but wonder if Gideon is also the reason men have gone missing. I'm scared, Pru. He needs to be stopped, and I need help. I'm going to go to Henry, tell him everything I know. But I had to tell you first because you're in danger, Pru. And I cannot bear the thought of you coming to harm. It's the only reason I've made the choices I have so far."

The words are barely out before a sob escapes me.

Oh, Josiah.

I reach my hand out on the table, palm up. Beseeching. "I love you, and I never wanted to hurt you. Please, believe me. Trust me. I beg of you."

The air is still, the pops and cracks from the burning logs in the fire absurdly loud. We three sit, still as the dead, waiting. Finally, Pru stands up and takes a deep breath before letting it out and shaking her head. There is no anger. No surprise. No fear.

Only disappointment.

I pull my empty hand back into my lap.

"Tempe, I don't understand what is happening to you. But this fantasy of yours is not healthy. I—" She shrugs, helplessly. "What do you want me to say? Because all of this sounds like nonsense. Sick, hurtful nonsense. And to bring Da into this as well?"

She shakes her head, a hint of anger flashing before it's tempered by resignation. "It's cruel. I think you might be sick. Truly. I know you have struggled since Da, but this is getting out of hand. Stop creating scenarios to get me to stay."

"Listen to me, Pru. Yes, you are part of this and why I've done some of the things I have done. But this is bigger than me. It's bigger than you."

"I'm being selfish. Is that what you're saying?"

"Pru, just listen for God's sake and stop acting like a child."

Fury explodes from her blue eyes, and I know I've lost her. Insulting her was the worst thing I could have done. I wasn't thinking.

Her hands curl into fists. "I am listening. I've been watching as well. And unlike you, I haven't shut myself off from the world. You've isolated yourself for years and it's starting to catch up to you.

"I"—she points a finger at her chest—"have reached out to others while still living my life. To other women in particular because you're right. It's difficult being overlooked, our value disregarded. But even *you* treat us like silly women. My book club doesn't merely read romances and gossip. We've supported each other, discussed so much, listened, learned from each other and our different experiences. Not once have you taken us seriously or accepted an invitation from me. Always insistent you don't need anyone when clearly you do."

Her words gut me over and over. She's been taking care of herself, approaching hardships and problems differently than I. She has always had a positive demeanor, been a hummingbird flitting this way and that, socializing and participating. Figuring out how to meet her needs in ways I never gave much merit to.

I suddenly feel like the younger sister. Chastised. I took on too much instead of sharing it with the one person who would have understood. We have our own strengths, but we are the same blood. We're sisters. That should have meant something more to me.

For a moment, there is a breach in the wall she's put up. Vulnerability as she bites her lip. I lace my fingers together. Begging. "Well, I'm reaching out for help now. It's a matter of life and death."

Pru wipes her eyes, tucks a stray curl behind her ear. "Gideon was right. You'll say or do anything to get what you want. Even if it means hurting people."

"That isn't true at all. He's a liar."

"No. He's worried about you. And so am I. If I were you, I would keep this fantasy to yourself. Anyone else who hears of this might not take it so lightly."

My knuckles go white.

Pru stands up and squeezes Mother's arm. "I'm sorry you had to hear that."

She leaves the room, shutting the bedroom door on me and any chance of reconciliation. I feel like I've had a limb suddenly severed, and bewilderment floods my logic. We've been all each other has had for years, and I took it for granted. She once looked up to me. Now I'll never be able to forget the shame on her face so long as I live. A wound that could only be delivered by her.

I worry my lip in an attempt to keep my composure. I had hoped that if anyone were to stand by me, it would be her, but I'm too late. And I can't blame her.

Hope bleeds from me, fed on by a leech of doubt.

I must act before I lose all my resolve. There is no time to waste now. I push myself up from the table, but before I can turn away, Mother's hand presses down on mine, holding it to the wood.

She squeezes so tight I wince. "Mother, please."

Her gaze is glued to the table. Her knuckles go white as bone, grip tightening. Something's happening; the pent-up emotion swirls inside me like a tempest.

I lay my other hand atop her own and squeeze. "Mother?"

"Your da didn't kill himself." Her voice is soft as a wisp. As delicate as my grasp on reality, surely, because this can only be a dream. For the first time in four years, Mother is speaking. I hold my breath, watching her lips part again as a voice I only hear in memory tumbles out of her. "He would never."

"Pru!" I cannot risk looking over my shoulder to see if she reenters the room. This connection with Mother is tenuous at best.

The chair scrapes the ground as I scoot it beside her, pull her hands into my lap. Her fingers are frail beneath my own, a porcelain doll's. My cheeks are wet.

"But he did, Mother. He was caught up in something bad, and he saw no other way out. I'm sure he didn't mean to hurt us . . . or you." The words coming out of my mouth are hollow—as if I am reading them off a piece of paper—because I have no compassion for him after what he did to us. But she doesn't need to know that. I squeeze her hands, infusing them with all the strength I have for her, while keeping none for myself.

"He wanted to stop him."

A log shifts in the hearth with a loud *crack*.

Mother lifts her gaze to my own. Her eyes are bright, wild even, lines of consternation set between them. "Your da wanted to stop Gideon."

Her body trembles, a near manic intensity to it. It takes me aback, this woman so different from the shadow of a mother who has sat in this room for years, unattached, hidden deep in the recesses of her mind. I can hear the *whoosh* of my own pulse in my ears. Feel each nerve in my skin. I'm scared to breathe, to hope, to understand. Is she saying what I think she is saying?

"Did Gideon kill Da?"

Her blue eyes are bright in their pool of tears. When she nods her head, they spill down her cheeks, and a sob parts her lips.

And I know like I know my heart beats in my chest that she speaks the truth.

The weight of four years evaporates and with it my strength. I wrap my arms around myself, squeezing tighter and tighter to hold myself together as I'm hit with a bewildering barrage of both shame and joy. Da didn't abandon us. Every choice I've made since that horrible morning was built off a lie. A farce. Pru's voice slips softly into my thoughts. *Even lamplighters fall victim to the fog.*

Gideon's lies.

How could I have ever doubted you, Da?

The grief and anger over the wasted years of my life burn inside me as hot as tar. I've made so many mistakes. All of my choices were wrong. Misguided.

It has been no way to live. But behind the grief is something else. Awareness. A cleansing lightness. Because Da never left us. He fought. He wanted to stay.

Da didn't abandon me.

I wipe the tears from my face, my cheeks hot, and lift my chin higher than ever without the weight of that wound. Mother watches me, shoulders shaking, looking smaller than I have ever seen her. For a moment, the heat of anger catches in my chest. For years I was led to believe Da died by suicide. I saw his body, a construed hanging, and it has haunted me to this day. Mother could have prevented all of it.

"Why didn't you say anything?"

She merely shakes her head and squeezes her eyes closed, chest heaving with her ragged breaths. I clench my teeth together, unable to make an excuse for her. My hidden longing of being held tight in my mother's arms closes up once more. A flower briefly touched by the sun before the storm clouds return. Gideon has been in our home, courting Pru. Not once did Mother speak up. Warn us of the danger.

But that's not entirely true, is it?

I think back now on all the idiosyncrasies in the last few weeks. Of her eavesdropping on our conversations about Gideon. Flinching when Gideon arrived at the Gathering. Reaching out to me after we thought he had died in the fire.

She tried to connect. In her own way. As her narrow shoulders tremble and her sad blue eyes beseech me, I know it came down to one reason. She was scared.

I take a deep breath, release it with my frustrations. "Why are you telling me this now?"

Mother grabs my hand, grips it in my lap so tight my bones rub together. "Don't go."

I shake my head. "I cannot let him hurt anyone else. Someone has to protect our family."

The tears falling are filled with fear. But also love. She sees me. She cares.

Someone listened.

"I have to go now. But I'll be back. Everything is going to be all right, Mother." It's an empty promise, but feeling the desperation in her grip, I would promise her anything she wanted if only to soothe her.

Prying her hand off is difficult, but once I do, she puts her hand back in her lap as if nothing happened between us. At the front door, I pluck my hat off the dowel and place it onto my head, shrug my jacket on, all the while telling myself to keep going. Gideon has to be stopped.

Is this how Da felt? Am I walking the same footsteps as his ghost?

I open the door and step through the doorway, glancing back at Mother. She remains seated, eyes on the tabletop. She never looks at me. Pru never stepped out of our room, unaware of what has occurred. Of Mother's secret. But for now, she is safe.

There is no time to waste. The door clicks behind me.

"What is going on, Temperance? This is Gideon's private property."

Henry's voice rumbles behind me as he follows me through the woods. I grabbed two shovels from the stable with the promise to return them later and now carry them over my shoulder, the faint whiff of manure on them. I didn't tell Henry what I found, only that he needed to follow me posthaste. I had to get him away from unwanted eyes and ears, uncertain about what will happen when word gets out about the glade. I need to be positive Henry is on my side before the whole of Warbler knows.

I glance over my shoulder. "Please listen before you react."

He scowls as I lead him around the trees. When we reach the edge of the clearing, I stop and point. Henry's expression hardens as his gaze lands on Leonard. From all the way over here, it looks as if the whaler is trying to crawl out of the ground, but the tree won't let him go.

We approach, and Henry crouches in front of the grave, eyes taking it all in. I explain how I uncovered Leonard with Ruby. If she hadn't been with me, would he have ever been found? More than likely, he would have rotted away here on land no one is allowed on, a buried secret beneath Warbler's feet. "Gideon did this."

"Why? How do you know?" Henry reaches down, brushing away some of the hanging roots, but all they do is tug at Leonard's body, embedded into his flesh.

Secrets are ugly, and it's time I share my own.

"Gideon has been threatening me for weeks. He kidnapped both Susannah and Molly. He's been kidnapping women for years." I take a deep breath and let it out slowly. It's now or never. "He turns them into figureheads, Henry. His sirens."

Henry's expression remains impassive, but I know what he must be thinking.

"It sounds ludicrous. I know. And I do not have proof for you. All of it burned up in his workshop or sailed out to sea. But I'm asking you, as the lamplighter and someone you once trusted, to keep an open mind. Clearly, Leonard didn't hurt Susannah or Molly and run off. He didn't set Gideon's workshop on fire. He's right here. Someone killed him."

"Did you kill him?" Henry stands up and looks at me directly. He doesn't make any move for his baton, but there is a stillness in his posture suggesting he could grab it quickly.

"No. I didn't like the man, but I didn't kill him." I pull the shovels off my shoulder, Henry's eyes watching closely, and prop them against my hip. "There's no one else I can talk to. You're it. I brought you here to be honest with you."

I take a deep breath and tell him everything. In detail. The night Gideon assaulted me when I was sixteen, sneaking into the workshop and finding Susannah, the truth about Da, Gideon threatening me with Mother and Pru's welfare, Benjamin, the *Miriam* . . . and Josiah. My sweet Josiah. Throughout all of it, Henry remains silent, an effigy of patience, as I expose all my dark secrets, lay down my soul for him to do with it what he wants. I wipe my eyes with trembling fingers, an overwhelming feeling of despondency consuming me.

While reliving everything, it's as if I'm also inside someone else's head hearing a terrible story. I see myself explaining it all and cannot help but wonder *why*? Why did this young woman take all the weight onto her shoulders?

It's all too much for one person to handle, and yet I thought I had to.

But there is no going back to the moment those choices were made. They are over and done with, consequences rippling through lives and time, stopping here in this clearing with Henry and myself. There is nothing to question because there is only one action to take now, and I am doing it.

Asking for help.

When I'm done, I'm wrung ragged, but it's all out in the open now and somehow, I feel a little better. This vulnerable honesty is freeing. I have no more lies. No more secrets. Henry runs his fingers through his beard, eyes assessing me. No doubt looking for some façade or trick.

"This sounds bizarre, Temperance. Beyond, in fact."

"I know it does, but I would never contrive something so hideous as this. Telling this to the wrong people could be dangerous for me. But you know me, and I think—" The word gives me pause, Pru's rejection earlier still too fresh in my mind. It doesn't mean I shouldn't at least try. "I *hope* you will hear me out. Give me a chance before placing judgment."

We stand in silence for a few beats before he finally nods to the shovels, eyebrow raised in question.

Now that he hasn't dragged me back into the village to be placed under arrest or taken to an asylum, confidence rushes through me. I motion to the glade, invigorated by the opportunity to prove my theory. "I have a suspicion, but I thought it best to investigate with a witness. And one with some standing in the community."

"For now, at least," he mutters, the stoic, hardened expression he wore earlier replaced by fatigue.

"I think there are others here, which is why Gideon is adamant about no trespassers on his land. Just look around us." I wait for Henry to take the scene in, the eleven other mounds nearby. The exhaustion melts into alarm. He reaches out his hand for a shovel. My heart leaps. He hasn't any clue how so small an action can have such a great impact. I wish I had trusted him, anyone, sooner.

Is it possible to get through life without any regrets?

Shovel in hand, he approaches the mound beneath a tree that looks to be a few seasons older than Leonard's. *Leonard's Tree.* Heaven help me.

Without a word, he begins digging into the earth. Soon, I join him. It takes time. Winter has not frozen the ground completely, but it prevents the task from being achieved quickly. We manage to fall into a simple rhythm of crunching earth and the soft whisper of dirt sliding from our blades. There is a short pause when we catch sight of the first bone. We proceed more delicately. The sun slips farther from her perch, dipping out of sight and behind the clouds. Once uncovered, it becomes clear roots have completely engulfed the skeleton. A stained and ragged shirt stretches taut over a sternum and rib cage like diseased skin.

By the time we finish uncovering a second body at another mound, this one with some flesh still on its bones, there is no need to continue. It's clear what we will find. Henry sits back, wiping the sweat from his brow and leaving a dirt streak behind. I shiver in my damp clothing. The physical labor warmed me enough I had removed my jacket. But now the breeze cuts like glass as it blows through the creaking branches and darkness settles in the air.

Henry appears at a loss for words. I am not surprised at what we found, but even I cannot shake off the incredible and horrible evidence before my very eyes. How old are the bodies buried here beneath the trees? Are there more bodies in the woods or just in Gideon's grove? Why is he killing people? Reasons elude me once again for his sinister actions.

Do monsters have reasons for the things they do?

The magnitude of the situation we find ourselves in has me feeling more than a little deficient. What could I possibly do to remedy the horror being inflicted here? At least Henry knows now.

I put my jacket on as he gets back to his feet. "Well?"

"I'm going to need to think on this."

"You believe me? About everything?"

"I cannot come to terms with your theory of the figureheads." Some of the wind is taken out of me as he shakes his head. "But this here is evidence enough of evil. I'm not dismissing you. I hear you. I just . . . I need some time to think. All right?"

Henry's acceptance is everything and more. Vindication needs no flourish. Its mere existence is a balm to my soul. My shoulders drop as I lean my head back and inhale deeply. Wet air.

I look down at my feet. Fog covers the ground, just thin enough to escape immediate detection. In the blink of an eye, it has filled the uncovered graves; the fine lines of the bodies within ebb and flow like vegetables swirled and smothered in stew. The fog pours out from in between the trunks to the west. Dusk is already upon us.

I'm late.

With everything that has happened today, all the revelations and hurts, my shift completely escaped my mind. I should have brought my tools with me. Shovels in hand, Henry and I turn as one, both of us lost in our concerns, duties, and thoughts.

In the weak light, a branch shifts in the breeze as if in greeting. Except it isn't a tree.

Gideon steps out of the tree line.

CHAPTER 22

Henry. Temperance." The ship carver inclines his head to each of us before his gaze flits to the bodies in the ground. He sighs and folds his hands before him. "This is private property."

I grip my shovel handle and glance at Henry before clearing my throat. "How did you know we were here?"

"We could feel you. Like a wood borer."

We?

Gideon doesn't clarify, but Josiah had explained wood borers to me one day when I accompanied him to the lumberyard for a purchase. They are insects that feed on the inner bark of trees when in their larvae stage. Considered a pest, they could weaken and even kill trees if not caught in time.

"Best to eliminate you before more damage can be done." He hasn't moved, but I feel jaws closing around me nonetheless. I take a step back.

"Now see here, Gideon. I'll have none of that." Henry takes a step forward, handing me his shovel. His voice has gone deeper, slower. "We have a lot to discuss, you and I, and I need to get someone out here to help remove these bodies. You need to come with me."

"I'm afraid that will not be happening, Constable."

The fog thickens, the tension between us an entity all its own. Henry pulls his baton out, slipping the leather loop over his wrist. My heart races as he signals for Gideon. "Come now. Let's not make this difficult."

"I do not want to hurt you, Henry." Gideon's tone is unnervingly apathetic. "But the bodies, as you see, cannot be easily moved. We have already claimed them, and therefore it is in your best interest this matter stays between us. If you agree, I can ensure you will not want for anything."

There's that *we* again.

"I do not take kindly to bribes."

"Merely stating a fact is not bribery." The man has the gall to shrug. "If you do not accept my offer, you will have to die just as Temperance's father did."

The casualness with which he speaks of Da's death has me clenching my teeth together. Having learned the truth earlier doesn't make it any easier to hear it out of his mouth now, but I refuse to let him see my pain. Gideon's frown only bolsters me. He did not expect me to know about Da.

The fog has engulfed the clearing entirely, smudging out all details. We three stand as ghosts in a dream. Gideon tucks a strand of hair that had fallen out of his leather hair tie behind his ear. "Her father foolishly decided to go to the authorities, knowing his family's life was on the line. It was a selfish choice to help clear his conscience, and one which—"

"How did you know?" I cut him off, refusing to listen to him slander Da's name anymore. "How did you know he was going to the authorities?"

Gideon must have found out from someone. So, who did Da tell? If Gideon was never arrested, it must mean that person was killed as well. Are they buried inside one of these mounds? I glance over at Henry, whose gaze remains glued to Gideon. Henry's reaction to everything has felt genuine. It wasn't him. And I don't think Da would have gone to Matthew before Henry.

Gideon tilts his head, lips quirked in amusement. "Your mother, of course."

I see his lips move, but the words are far away. As if he is speaking from a ship while I wait onshore. When they finally reach me, they crash over me, a never-ceasing cacophony of shock and betrayal.

Mother. It was Mother.

I was so surprised by her opening up about Da I didn't even think to ask her how she knew. I can imagine Da now making his plan to talk to Henry. Perhaps go to the council. He would have gone to Mother first, though. Confessed everything to her. They had no secrets. He would have warned her what might happen. To try to keep us safe. Exactly what I tried to do earlier.

Then she told Gideon about Da.

He chuckles. "We've found humans quite easy to manipulate."

My tears fall unimpeded as my brain tries to make sense of it all. "She loved Da. She wouldn't be able to live with herself."

Then it hits me. She barely is.

"It is fascinating what a person will do to protect the ones they love. I made it clear to your mother that should your father tell anyone, I would hurt her daughters in such a way that killing them would be an act of kindness."

I think back on the morning Da's body was found, trying to recall any tension in the air, any overwhelming sense of wrongness with Mother. She must have known Da wasn't going to return. But trying to recall anything other than the moment I saw Da's body hanging from the lamppost is like attempting to locate a specific pebble in the riverbed. Impossible.

Gideon could have made Da disappear in the grove like Leonard and the others, leaving Mother only to guess what had happened. Instead, he left Da's body in the open for all of Warbler to see. A suicide. But for Mother?

A warning.

Just like Benjamin was for me.

My hand burns where she squeezed it earlier. Mother

tried to warn me. In her own way. I wish she had just told me.

Like I should have told Josiah, Pru, Henry, anyone about what happened the night I kissed Gideon. And all of the missed opportunities that came later.

I cannot fault Mother for trying to protect her family the only way she could think of and all on her own. Because I did the same thing. We have more in common than I ever realized.

Gideon turns back to Henry with a shake of his head. "What say you, Henry? May I count on your discretion?"

The fog twists and rolls. The trees creak. I can smell Leonard's sour rot creeping from his grave. My eyes remain on Gideon, but the bodies buried around me call to me like the buzzing of bees, a hum in the air. Gideon has killed again and again. The evidence is all around. How can one man and one woman stop him when no one's succeeded in stopping him before?

Something slithers over my boot. Nudges my ankle. I shift, trying to peer through the fog, but all is obscure. Something is out here with us.

We're in danger.

"Henry?" I whisper.

He shakes his head, dismissing me as he walks up to Gideon. "Now, Gideon, I think it best—"

Henry swings the baton over his head.

The air whistles. Gideon has just enough time to rush forward into the arc of the baton. He catches it with a *CLAP* that echoes in the clearing before the fog absorbs it. I flinch and drop both shovels. Henry drives his left fist into Gideon's kidney. Gideon grunts, curling in with a wince. It happens so fast; I barely finish a breath.

Henry is much larger than the ship carver, but the hit doesn't stop Gideon's forward motion as he drives his body into Henry. They fall to the ground with a thud. Fog billows around them, unveiling the ground covered in tree roots that weren't there before. Surprise and indecision lock up my muscles as the two struggle, Henry's back to the ground. The baton loop is still around his wrist, but Gideon maintains control of the baton. Holding each end, he pushes it into Henry's neck. Straddling him while leaning all of his weight into the baton.

Henry bucks beneath him, grunting, hands pushing up against the baton. His legs kick out in desperation, stirring up clods of earth in the fog. Spit flies out onto his beard as the grunt becomes a gurgle.

Gideon is going to crush Henry's throat.

My fingers find the handle of a shovel. I lurch forward, barely keeping my footing as I trip over a root, stopping beside their struggling bodies. Gideon murdered Da. Took him away from my family, shattering us all. And he's going to kill again.

It's now or never.

I swing with all my strength. The shovel slices through the air, the blade embedding deep into the back of Gideon's thigh with a squelch and crunch. The hit rebounds up the shovel and into my hands. He throws his head back with a pained roar.

Gideon kicks out. His boot slams into my shin with the force of a ram. Quick and brutal. My feet fly out from under me; the world rushes up to meet me. Stars burst behind my eyes as my head slams into something hard.

The world is fuzzy. Silent.

Fog creeps up to bury me with the rest of the bodies. The languid movement after such brutal chaos is almost hypnotizing. Like a flame. For what feels like hours, years even, I struggle against a desire to lie here in its calm embrace.

A sound, soft as a whisper. It grows. Higher and higher. A ringing. It shatters the stillness, turning into a splintered frenzy. This is wrong. I shouldn't be here. I must fight harder. I take a deep breath and immediately begin to cough. It feels like the first life-saving breath after breaking the surface of water. My head is on fire, but as I catch my breath, the ringing subsides. Other sounds return. Henry and Gideon struggle somewhere in the distance.

I turn my head slowly, nausea roiling in my stomach. No, they're right beside me. Gideon looms over Henry, a giant shadow. An outline of the shovel still embedded in his leg, wiggling with his struggle. Everything is moving slowly, as if underwater. Cartilage pops. Bone crunches. Gideon drops a few inches down.

Henry stops moving.

Gideon is panting, hair hanging in sweaty strands around his face. All urgency has left his body as he leans back.

Henry isn't dead. He can't be. But the constable does not move, and though my mind denies it, the tears blurring my vision tell a different truth.

Gideon reaches around and rips the shovel out of his leg with a snarl, chucking it away to be swallowed by the ether. His calm and collected composure has fallen away, exposing a side of him I've never seen. The mask is off.

Move, Tempe.

A whimper escapes my mouth unbidden. The movement sends a knife through my skull as if my head were a mere clam to be cracked open. Struggling to sit up shoves the knife in farther. Any second it'll pry me open, exposing the meat of my brains. It hurts so much I just want to hold still, disappear. I need to throw up.

I cannot stay here.

Gideon remains silent until I pull myself to my hands and knees. Dusk has wiped his expression away completely, but I can feel the glower in his dangerously soft voice. "I might thank you for bringing both the shovel and feed."

Still straddling Henry, Gideon rips open the dead man's jacket, sending buttons flying. A tear splits the air as the front of Henry's shirt is next. His pale torso glows in the dark, and I almost look away, embarrassed. But he is dead. Henry cares not.

Besides, I cannot seem to rip my gaze away. Gideon holds his hand just below Henry's sternum, a few inches above his stomach. The dark root comes out of Gideon's wrist and presses into Henry. It pierces through his skin, a wiggling worm, going deeper and deeper. Watching it happen before my very eyes is horrific. I want to scream. Drag Henry away. But all I can do is stare with a combination of helplessness and dread.

The root pulses like the beating of a heart. Once. Twice. Thrice. Then it withdraws, retracting back into Gideon's wrist. I can still feel the ghost of a tickle against my palm. My gorge rises, but I swallow it back down. My vision is slowly gaining clarity, though the pain in my head and leg continue to radiate with the rhythm of my heartbeat. The pulse of the root.

I shudder, drawing Gideon's attention once more. He turns my way, eyes gleaming through the strands of his dark hair. Ice floods my body, goose bumps covering every inch of my skin. Gideon turns back to the fresh mark on Henry's torso.

And then the earth begins to shift.

CHAPTER 23

Dark tendrils wiggle beneath the surface of the fog. A scream is trapped in my throat as roots nudge my legs, slithering past like snakes. More roots push out of the ground.

The never-ceasing current of fog wipes away all the trees, the stars, and Henry's body as he sinks below the surface, submerged in soil. Gideon tilts his head, considering, and then gingerly crawls off Henry, sending the fog swirling around us. The wound on the back of his leg still gleams red. For anyone else, a serious injury.

Gideon isn't just anyone.

His funeral painted a fairly generic picture of him, with few details of any merit that couldn't be gathered through basic observation. There was one detail in particular, however, that was glazed over without much pause. I cannot repress a shiver as I recall the minister talking about Gideon disappearing into the woods as a boy. Then later, how he seemed to change overnight after the old ship carver died. Did the woods do something to him?

I would reject the thought as ludicrous if I did not feel more roots brush up against me as the trees watch me through the fog. A malevolent entity finally showing its face.

This forest is sentient.

I wrap my arms around myself. "What did the woods do to you?"

Gideon's eyes widen, the stark blue piercing. For a moment they appear vulnerable, bright and pure in this dark and blurry world. He shifts himself up with one arm and stretches his wounded leg out, panting. Then the branches begin to creak in the breeze.

Except there is no breeze. The fog is stagnant.

The creaking of wood comes from not only above, but below. Gideon's lips turn up as he leers at me, any vulnerability I thought I'd seen long gone.

CRACK.

I flinch, gaze pulled to Henry's body. His moving body.

For a moment I think I am wrong. That Gideon hasn't killed him. But then the skin of his torso shifts. Henry isn't moving—something is moving *inside* of him. More *cracks* and *pops.* Henry's bones. Horror curls my lips, widens my eyes. A sapling rises out of the wound in his chest. It grows, roots shifting and curling beneath his skin as others wrap around his ankles and wrists. They pull him down into the disturbed soil as the sapling continues to grow.

Gideon said I brought him a shovel and *feed.*

The trees aren't growing around the dead bodies. They're growing *out* of the bodies. I think of the pigs in their pen at the barn. Of the scraps thrown into their trough. Henry, Leonard . . . all of the bodies are scraps for the trees. It was just like Gideon told Henry: *We have already claimed them.* The bodies are part of the trees now.

I watch the thin trunk grow up from Henry's chest at an unbelievable speed as Susannah's whistling cry for help rings out of the recesses of my memory. Gideon said he wanted to maintain balance in the human population. Now I know he's been killing men, using them like fertilizer. The young women he overtakes, controls, and contains so that they may never have children to add to the population. Their wooden prisons a symbol of his power.

But the figureheads are so renowned, they bring more people to Warbler. Doesn't that go against what he wants?

Another *crack* comes from Henry's corpse as roots

continue to curl up inside his chest, breaking another rib before pushing through his skin to anchor him farther into the ground. One more skeleton to add to the body count.

It slowly sinks in.

The more ships in our port, the higher probability of strangers becoming lost in the fog. Everyone assumes the majority of missing whalers have jumped ship, escaping life at sea by taking advantage of our fog. Disappearing without a trace. A plausible explanation for anywhere else. But not here. Not in Warbler.

Only cursory investigations are done for missing people who are not Warbler citizens. And when our own go missing? Unlucky happenstance. Or local folklore. We investigate the disappearances to a point, but when no bodies are found . . .

One, two, three leaves unfurl from the tiny branches, blooming before my very eyes. A vibrant green quickly flares to red . . . rust . . . brittle brown. The changing of the seasons in mere moments. Birth, growth, and now dormancy until the spring.

Our economy thrives off visiting whaling ships coming for Gideon's lucky siren figureheads, but our population is stable—*has been* stable, for years. With its sustainable population, Warbler hasn't needed to expand its borders by cutting into more of the forest. And with Gideon managing the acreage of forest granted to him by the council, he's maintaining that balance. Replenishing Warbler's trees through these men's deaths. Curating Warbler's population by eliminating young women of birthing age when needed. But waste not, want not. The girls still provide for Warbler in their own way.

As bait.

With Henry stuck in the clutches of the roots, more roots begin to nestle up against me. Trailing their ends against me like fingers. Immediately I am brought back to

Gideon's workshop. Recalling his finger running sensually along Susannah trapped in the wood.

The weight of realization threatens to drag me under with the rest of the bodies.

I have to get out of here.

Somehow, I get to my feet, then nearly crumple back to the ground. My shin feels like a mallet has pounded it into pieces. But I cannot let the trees take me, nor can I watch them feed off Henry's body. I will not stay a second longer in this forest of the dead. In the dark. Alone.

I refuse to die here.

"Where do you think you're going?" Gideon's voice whispers in my ear as I limp away. I gasp as his breath heats the back of my neck. I look over my shoulder. He is still propped near Henry, his face deep in shadow. I can hear the grin in his voice. "You will not get far. We can feel you."

An unwelcome thought breaks through the chaos in my brain as the roots continue to tear through Henry's flesh and pull him into the soil. They spread and connect tree to tree, encompassing the whole woods. The revelation spreads its own roots out into my understanding, settling in, smothering within as outside the fog consumes my body.

A fog that always originates in these woods.

I hear Benjamin's voice in my head and close my eyes for a brief moment. *Was the fog. Watching me, speaking to me.* The words had sounded like the ramblings of a drunk man at the time. Nothing to be taken too seriously.

The uncanny rarely is.

Gideon is everywhere. The fog his conduit as the roots are for the trees. He knows where people are. Always. He could feel Henry and me digging up the bodies, disturbing the roots. Wait. No, that isn't right. Not *he*. Gideon had said *we*.

Keep moving, Tempe.

The fog thickens. A root pulls at my ankle as I turn

away once more, but I manage to shake it off. I try to hop, but each landing is jarring, hammering a thousand nails into my bone. My retreat is painfully slow as I clench my teeth together with each limping step, heart pounding, hands shaking. I wait to feel more roots snatch at my legs or Gideon's murderous hands on me, but they never come. Only his chuckles shadow my departure, and the sound of a shovel scooping earth.

My courage curdles.

The fog has soaked into every inch of my clothing. It drips down my face. Or is that blood from my head wound?

It doesn't matter.

I know which way to go, but the confidence in my footsteps is gone. The fog is different now. Gideon may still be in the grove, bone, muscle, and flesh growing back together, but the fog all around me is part of the woods. Part of Gideon. He's with me still. He caresses my skin, soaks my hair and clothing, and is inside me with each of my breaths.

All of the whispers, suspicions, disappearances, and deaths our unnatural fog has caused . . . they all boil down to one entity. The woods. And Gideon is part of that. We've rearranged our lives for him, the diseased heart of Warbler, totally unaware he was the mouthpiece for something bigger.

Maintaining the balance between Warbler and its human population.

He'd told me from the beginning. Warbler isn't the seaport. It isn't our community. It's been the forest all along. A cognizant forest that unleashes a nightly fog like a net, waiting for stray life to get caught in it. Quiet as a drowning.

I shiver, barely holding back my scream as I continue to limp into tree trunks and foliage too crowded for me to pass through. Intuition has me changing directions, finding new routes toward where I know safety lies. At least, a semblance of safety. But the forest seems to be changing. I don't see the trees or roots moving, yet they are in new positions when I turn around, blocked in once more.

I'm being corralled.

Branches pull at my jacket, scratch at my cheeks and hands. The uneven ground threatens to trip me with each step. How many bodies have I trodden over?

The absence of sound but for my own breaths is a claustrophobic pressure pushing in from all sides. I feel eyes on me from everywhere. If I can just make it to the street, I'll be free of this wooded maze. The trees cannot touch me there. The cobblestone is safety. As I move beneath the maples, zigzag through the birches, and push through undergrowth, it doesn't seem possible, but the fog thickens all the same. The wet decay of forest mush and dirt crawls up my nose like hungry maggots looking to consume the pulpy meal inside.

All hint of light is gone, dusk spent. The air is so thick a person could suffocate in it. Not once in my four years as lamplighter have I experienced a fog this substantial. I suppose now that I've learned Gideon's secret—or is it the forest's?—there is no holding back when it comes to prey.

In the fuzzy gray, there are dark shapes, trees. Here one second and gone the next. A stick breaks to my left. Another *crack* sounds just behind me. It could be Gideon, but instinct tells me it isn't him. At least not physically him. The forest is playing games. Attempting to herd me back to danger like a mindless sheep.

Despite the fear feeding on me and the pain radiating through my head and leg, I reach deep within myself. I refuse to fall victim to the fog. I know my way through the darkness better than anyone. It isn't the magic trick Josiah believed it was as a child. It's a sense, engrained deep within me as it had been in Da, leading me onward to where I need to be. I close my eyes and listen for it. Ignore the groaning and cracking of the woods, and the trail it tries to set me on.

The compass burns within me, and I feel the path burning to the right, tinder waiting to be lit. I follow it.

When my feet finally hit the cobblestone of the street, I know I should go to the first house. Ask for help. Instead, all I want to do is go home. Get out of the fog. Be shielded by the house built by Mother and Da. Feel Da around me and know he loved us. That he tried to protect us. That he didn't choose to leave us.

I cannot disappear without Pru knowing the truth. She needs to know I would never leave her. And Mother . . . she has to know I understand why she did what she did. It was horrible. Wrong. She should have given Da a chance.

But I understand.

No one is out on the street. I never lit the lampposts, nor did I ring the bell. The man who would have covered for me is back in Gideon's glade, dead. Feed for the trees. I've failed Warbler and feel the loss of the lights like they are my own friends. The streets have disappeared into the gloom without any light to illuminate them. Walking past the lampposts' dark husks goes against everything Da instilled inside me.

It's an honor to bring light to the dark, Tempe.

There are no landmarks as I limp down the streets, the scuff of my boots loud in the haze. The knife twists in my head when my foot catches on a cobblestone and I stumble. A whimper tumbles from my mouth as I attempt to quicken my pace. I can sense home like birds migrating in the winter. But soon the agony of each step becomes a weight I can no longer carry.

I have to stop at the northwest lamppost. Da's lamppost.

It supports me as I hold my throbbing leg up and close my eyes. I imagine Da's hand covering my own, picture his grin, the joy alighting his face. He never left me. It all seems so silly now, the time I lost trying to plan for the worst. The isolation of believing I needed to take everything on my shoulders, unable to trust or reach out to others. That was never what Da would have wanted for me. Why is it so easy to allow the darkness to take precedence in our lives? To shape us?

Footsteps in the fog.

My time is up. It didn't take Gideon long to follow after all. Tears spill out as I shake my head. I'm not ready. I now know Da wasn't either. Here I stand in his footsteps, unable to escape inevitability. We made mistakes along the way, but we both tried to do the right thing. It's not the ending I wanted, but it's one I must live with.

However much longer that will be.

Gideon's dark shadow walks around the post and stands tall in front of me, no hint of a limp, of any sort of injury. Long pale fingers cold as death reach out and clutch my chin. I pull away from his grip. He laughs. "Such fire in you, little lamplighter. A family trait I require."

Disgust turns my lips. "Why?"

This close, I can see the thin blood vessels beneath his pale skin, a root system all on their own. "We've lived long and learned that in order to survive, we must evolve. This body has been a great conduit, but it will not survive forever."

I know where this is going.

"There is a fire coursing through you that burned us when we tried to gain control of you. That fighting nature runs in your family. I did not recognize it for what it was when your father defied me. Only when you did."

The switch in his perspective is unnerving. Who am I talking to? The forest or Gideon?

"Lucky for me you have a sister because we need that fire. That Byrne strength."

He looks into the distance, at this obsession of his built out of corpses. Growing tree after tree, cultivating a forest that was gutted with the creation of Warbler over forty years ago. An evolved amalgamation of survival. This cannot be real. His eyes gleam with obsession bordering on madness. Whatever Gideon is, whatever is inside of him, a sickness drives it, and I am at his . . . *its* mercy.

Gideon flips his hand over, and I watch as the skin tears in his wrist, like splitting jerky. As the tip of the root emerges, trepidation seizes my core. "When this body fails and no longer has the strength to go on, my children will. With the power of fire in the bark, Warbler will be that much stronger."

"Your children can only be monsters."

He tsks, shaking his head. "Do not worry. Your niece or nephew will never know of your disapproval. They will only know of you through the lovely stories their mother tells them. Because my legacy will be around for a long time. And so will you, dear lamplighter. Perhaps they'll even visit you when your ship comes into port."

Quick as a snake strike, he grabs my wrist. I tug back, but his grip is unyielding. Strong as the roots of a tree. And now I can feel it. The root pressing against me once again. It burns. Gideon grimaces, a bead of sweat rolling from his temple. I clench my teeth together, feel the heat overtake my entire body.

No. I've fought him off once before. I'm the lamplighter. He cannot change me.

A scream is ripped from me as the root pushes through. My body recoils, energy depleted, and I drop to the ground. Stunned. Gideon's grip is unbreakable as he follows me to the cobblestones.

He smiles victoriously as the root crawls through my palm and up my forearm, shoving everything aside with an intense pressure not unlike a nail driven into flesh. I watch the root move beneath my skin, a dark pumping vein of fire. Revulsion rolls through me. I try once more to pull away, but I've no fight left.

It's gone.

"You've been drinking my tea."

My lids are heavy, but I manage to look up into Gideon's blue eyes. No. They aren't blue. They're fog. They're nothing. His tea? Gideon's favorite tea, an earthy brew we've been drinking for weeks. Fire continues to scorch all the way through to my bones.

"You've let me inside you for weeks. Willingly," he murmurs, free hand stroking my cheek, his gaze unblinking. "Your defenses aren't quite what they were."

I envision leeches latched inside my stomach, sucking out my blood, protected by my own traitorous body. But no. It's bigger than that. Whatever was in his tea, some piece of himself, I drank it without question. I may not have been aware of it, but I consented and in doing so allowed him in. Past the fire and fight he spoke so yearningly of.

"We find a way," he murmurs. "We always do."

Gideon lets go of my wrist, root withdrawn, but I can still feel him. Inside me. A splinter of himself. A seed. Suddenly it gets bigger. Growing. Around me. Everywhere. My muscles harden around the piece he left behind. My skin. My nerves. Everything.

He leans in close, a sweet putrefaction on his breath. I can hear voices in the distance. Responding to my scream maybe? But the fog is thickening, tucking us away from searching eyes.

Gideon's words are a whisper in my ear, a barbed caress down my neck. "You're mine."

I'm dragged to my feet, my arm pulled out in front of me. The pain in my leg is a dull throb fading away. So too is the pain in my head. He holds my hand, wrapping my fingers around his as if I am showing off a wedding ring. And perhaps in a way, I am. Because I am trapped forever with Gideon. He and I are one now. My skin goes taut. Darkens. It's happening fast. Too fast.

The never-ceasing swing of the pendulum slows after all.

There is a fuzzy light in the fog, growing larger. Brighter. Is this what the others saw before they were changed? A last glimpse of what was forever taken from them? But as it grows closer, a shape emerges with it. I take a breath, unable to mask my surprise. Gideon turns.

The oil lantern bursts upon impact.

Glass shatters in a spray of flaming oil, dousing Gideon in a second skin of heat. He screams, a sound both human and uncanny. It is the groan of a tree being ripped up during a storm, the roar of a rockslide, the shriek of a monster being burned alive. His hair goes up first like the petals in his house. Pale skin bubbles, reddening, then charring.

Fire really was his weakness, after all.

The street lightens, the fog a soft cloud, swirling around the screaming sun. Gideon's body blocked me from most of the deadly spray, but I still feel the burning bite of a few droplets. I cannot seem to do anything about them, my body unresponsive.

Mother appears, batting at the droplets of burning oil beginning to feed on my clothes, the splash on my outstretched hand. Terror alights her face, eyes wide with shock. At what she has just done or whatever repercussions her actions may cause. Either way, my heart bursts at the sight of her.

There is a stinging deep in my nose as a breeze carries the odor of singed hair and melting flesh. Burning cotton and leather. Pungent whale oil followed by the sharp sweetness of burning birch.

The fire monster that is Gideon spins around and stumbles toward us. I take a deep breath, bracing myself for the inevitable agony of being engulfed in flame. Then time freezes, and my nightmare flashes before me like the aftermath of a strike of lightning, blinding in its outline.

The ship in my nightmare was always on fire, the figurehead screaming amid the flames as I sat frozen, watching inevitability approach me. Like now. My pulse thrashes, I lose all breath, and the epiphany lodges a stone in my throat. Miriam burned in reality just as she did in my dreams.

Now the evil that is Gideon is coming for me as I watch helplessly, unable to move, just as in my nightmare. But I always woke up.

This is the ending to the nightmare I never got to see.

Mother turns and throws her arms around me, a loving shield. For the briefest of moments, her warmth surrounds me with the smell of sweet soap that is distinctly her.

The heat of the flames caresses my face.

Mother is ripped away, the echo of her touch dissipating just as quickly. Gideon falls atop her onto the cobblestones in a heap, and my heart takes its final plunge. Flames spread, engulfing her completely. The fire roars, an invisible wind stirring up the flames. Her shrieks grow desperate as she flails and kicks, her movements weakening as she asphyxiates. Her face twists in anguish in the orange light. Eyes bright, lips moving.

Forgive me.

Everything is occurring so fast while managing to be excruciatingly slow. A dichotomy warring within my thoughts as I process everything as if two very different people in one skin.

I watch Mother burn alive and think of Josiah. Of the pain he suffered alone. Of Da being surprised by Gideon. Did he know it was Mother who betrayed him as Gideon strangled him? I hope not. Maybe he is watching her right now, forgiveness in his heart as she atones for her choices. Trying to save her daughters.

While a part of me watches the fiery struggle, another part of me glances away for self-preservation. There are more voices and shadows in the distance. Are they close by? The fog conceals all perception. Gideon's and Mother's screams direct those brave enough to have ventured out into the fog.

But her screams have gone silent now, and so too have Gideon's.

I glance over to them. With the flames still feeding upon Mother's motionless body, I know the voices in the distance will not be here in time. The fog is thick as oil, a cyclone of confusion, capable of baffling the moon itself. It slithers over Gideon like a bed of eels as he crawls toward me. What's left of his clothing is smoldering; the joints of his body, his knees and elbows, glow red as burning embers.

He reaches me, his viselike grip snatching hold of my waist as he heaves himself to his feet. Logic tells me his great weight should pull me over, but instead there is only the suggestion of pressure. By the time he is standing before me, I cannot feel anything. I watch Gideon's mutilated face, the blistered and black skin, simply heal. No, not quite heal. It's like his flesh is sealing itself back together, leaving lines of red behind, like scars. Like that night in the workshop, Gideon's skin stitches back together. His hair grows back. All but the burned and singed clothing returns to normal.

His eyes find focus on me once more, the swirling white a flash of hazel before the blue returns. In the hazel swirled madness. Fury. Hatred.

But in the blue, there is grief. Determination. Endurance. The person he once was maybe, before Warbler took him too? I feel all of it pulsing within me. From the piece Gideon put inside me. I do not know where he begins, where the forest is, where I end.

A freezing breeze blows through the clearing, the smell of the river on it. It thins the fog just enough to see the swaying oaks and maples lining the street. I can hear the water sloshing in the creek somewhere through the trees.

I'm out of my body, riding the fog. No. I too am the fog.

We drift over the villagers, their homes and businesses scattered along the river like a child's building blocks. Then over the piles of wood stockpiled in the lumberyard to the south, and the scarred land around it that goes on for miles. Stumps sticking out of the earth like bone fractures.

The leftover violence of it presses a bruise inside us. We roll over the farms and fields covering the land cleared in the west, a new type of life cultivated. The wrong type.

Deep satisfaction infuses us as we caress the seedlings sprouting from the ashes of a small forest fire to the northwest. The roots feeding from the bodies buried in the grove. The trees grown from even older skeletons throughout the entire forest. We feel the young women trapped on their ships, miles and miles away over the ocean, encased forever by our strength, their own power and gift of life frozen forever.

They are the sirens luring our food back to us.

I'm brought back to my body as Gideon lifts me up with unnatural strength. He carries me away from Mother's burning body. Away from the voices calling out in the fog, neighbors looking to help one of their own, not knowing what they will find. Not knowing they are too late to save anyone.

I'm so sorry, Pru.

I wish I could protect her from the horror lying in the street, the seeming abandonment from her sister, and whatever hardships lie in her future. Most of all from Gideon. But the truth is, Pru will be all right. She has adapted to each new hardship placed before her with grace and optimism. She has made sure she was never alone, drawing other women to her for support. What's more? Not once has she stopped moving forward. She is the best of all of us. Of Da, Mother, and me.

She will find her way.

Like she told me once, you have to have faith in people.

Every inch of my body has fallen asleep. Trying to move proves futile. Even tears refuse to fall. I'm trapped in this moment and cannot open my mouth to breathe. To scream for Pru. To say *I love you. I forgive you. I'm sorry for everything. I am so proud of the woman you're becoming. Never stop shining. For you are the sun.*

My arm is still stretched out, but it isn't mine. It's a long and slender limb, the fingers curled down as if holding something. Perhaps a lantern will hang from her wooden hand someday.

For she is the lamplighter, after all.

Maybe she will show others to look for the light rather than the dark.

I wish she had done so in her own life.

The farther Gideon carries me, the thicker the fog becomes among the trees, but not for me. I feel it rolling steadily through me now, like the syrup tapped from the maples. Syrup as dark as Josiah's eyes.

Are you watching me, Josiah?

I am so sorry.

The wood continues to pull at me, altering me on the inside now. A high tinny sound in my ears, a *pop.* And then nothing. Shadows push into my peripheral, crowding closer and closer. Inevitability is tireless. You think you have so much time. A slow decay you can prepare for. But that is the Great Lie. Time. Life . . . it is here, and then it is gone. Over. Too fast to understand.

Was it like this for Miriam, Susannah, Molly? For all the others taken over the years and used as bait? How many are we? Thinking of them gives me comfort for a brief moment, this terrifying experience shared between us.

Yet we are all still alone in our own darkness.

I am afraid. So afraid of this dark. It comes like a great wave, taking me to depths unimaginable. I'm going under.

Someone squeezes my hand beneath the surface. The touch is comfort. Strength. Love. A promise.

Da.

Then he is gone, but I feel the ripples carried through me in this growing abyss of darkness where there is no ending and no beginning. I am the wood. The wood is me.

Pru's face is a shooting star above the water, but

I can still feel her,

a warmth that comes and goes

the lighting and extinguishing of a lamp.

These moments are

a reminder of existence.

Time cradles me

in this burning darkness,

and I wait.

I will wait.

Holding out

for

the light

to catch.

EPILOGUE

By the time Pru reached the dock, her hemline was soaked, and her bodice was covered in Constance's muddy handprints. The baby giggled as Pru adjusted her wiggly weight onto her other hip.

At not quite one, Constance was a curious child with a tendency to find herself in all sorts of trouble. Pru supposed this was the prerogative of most infants, but she couldn't help thinking her child had a larger than normal propensity for getting into things. Which, if she were being honest with herself, she was quite happy with. Constance was highly entertained joining Pru in the front garden while she worked. She loved to play in the dirt and had a penchant for gripping tomato stalks in her chubby little fingers in order to stand, and tugging green bean vines with a strength found in only the most determined of babies. Pru had lost many a plant thanks to her little girl's curious fingers, but she didn't mind.

But motherhood had not been an easy role to step into.

When Constance was first born, Gideon demanded Pru soothe their child the moment she cried, never let her out of her sight, stimulate her with activities, and attend to her every need. While Pru had every intention of doing so, sometimes she needed time to herself. Constance was safe, cared for, loved. Yet Gideon had watched Pru like a hawk in those early months, criticizing her for wanting a few spare moments to herself without their baby. When she'd asked him one day to take Constance so she could enjoy her book club, there had been a brief moment where she felt like she had made a grievous error in judgment, a stillness in her husband's eyes that made her almost take it back.

She'd stood her ground, however. If she hadn't, Pru was confident she wouldn't be in the healthy head space she was today. She loved being a mother, but she couldn't lose herself, and she almost had. Just like everyone else in her family.

Thankfully, she and Gideon had worked through their rough patch. Her friends, many of them mothers themselves, had been a great support when she'd vented at their weekly gatherings. Not surprisingly, most had been able to relate, and it helped her feel a little less lonely. Less isolated. Nonetheless, she could not always avoid the moments of darkness in her heart. Of uncertainty. She always found a way through them, however. Giving up was never an option for her. In truth, she didn't know how. It was one of the traits Gideon said he loved so much about her. He called it her fire.

Though they were doing much better now, things were becoming rocky again. Despite his adoration for Constance, Gideon was pressing Pru for another child, the hope being she would give him a son.

Pru wasn't ready for another child. And truthfully, she wasn't sure she ever would be.

"Da-da!"

Constance stretched her pudgy fingers out over Pru's shoulder. When Pru turned around, it was to see Gideon approaching, an appreciative smile stretching the pink raised scars near his lips. The smattering continued farther up his cheekbones, contracting the skin near his left temple. A freak accident while he was out of town two years ago that could have blinded him. Pru believed it gave even more of an edge to his striking looks.

He plucked Constance out of Pru's arms and tossed their little girl up into the air as if she weighed no more than a loaf of bread. Pru's breath caught in her throat at the sight of the suspended little body as Constance's delighted shriek sent a seagull flapping from the moored ship.

Only after Constance was once again safely in her father's arms could Pru convince her heart to slow down. Gideon chuckled as he looked her over, and then back to Constance's muddy dress and hands. "I see you two made a visit to the creek this afternoon."

"Whatever gave us away?"

"Intuition."

Gideon wrapped his arm around Pru's waist and pecked her cheek as their daughter struggled between them. Gideon smelled of birch, a familiar and comforting smell, mixed with the distinct odor of wet earth splashed over their daughter. It made Pru think of home. She brushed a shaving of wood from Gideon's shoulder. "Did you finish the new one?"

"Not quite. Still have work to do on the face. Been struggling with her expression." He shifted Constance in his arms as they turned toward the river. "Have you seen her yet?"

Pru shook her head, exhaling a shaky breath.

"Bo!" Constance chirped, struggling in Gideon's arms.

"Yes, daughter. That is a boat." Gideon pointed to the front of the whaling schooner, to the figurehead perched on her bow. He began making his way down the dock, not bothering to mask the concern in his eyes as he glanced over his shoulder at Pru. Their footsteps echoed, reverberating beneath them and across the water splashing up against the dock. She could see the shadows of small fish flitting beneath the teal current.

She swallowed down the knot in her throat as her eyes began to tickle. With each step closer, the details of the figurehead became clearer and clearer. The arm stretched out into a slender wrist and long fingers. The lantern they grasped swayed in the breeze. The face was lean, with delicate features, parted lips, and a coronet braid wrapped around her head like a crown.

"Bo!"

"That's right, sweetie." Prudence took a shaky breath. "She's called the *Lamplighter*."

Pru looked up at the figurehead, at her lines, the haunted look on her face. A look of acceptance and grief. Yet it was also as if she were searching for something. But perhaps that had something to do with the lantern held out before her. Part of this figurehead's story.

Before long, Constance began to fidget in Gideon's arms. His grip tightened, which, sure enough, set their daughter to fussing even louder. Pru lay her hand on his upper arm, squeezing it. "Would you mind taking her home?"

He frowned, uncertainty in his eyes. Pru hoped he didn't notice her pounding heart. After a moment lasting an eternity, he finally asked, "Are you all right?"

"Of course." She smiled, hoping to set him at ease. "I could just use a few moments alone."

Gideon switched the arm holding Constance. This appeared to appease the child, whose grumbles turned into giggles. "Don't stay too long."

Pru watched her family until they disappeared down the street, before turning back to the figurehead. She remembered when Gideon had showed it to her for the first time. It was a gift he'd said, something to remember Tempe by.

Pru had hated it.

Two years ago, Tempe had lost her mind, spouting outlandish theories about Gideon, Da, and the missing women. Mother, already of unsound mind, had believed her and died by suicide at the same location Da did. The villagers had heard her screaming but were too late when they finally found her in the fog, the lampposts unlit.

Tempe should have been out lighting the lamps. Perhaps

she could have stopped Mother. But instead, she'd run off with the constable, which they only knew because Henry had left behind a note, admitting to their secret affair.

For a long time, all Prudence had felt was rage. It was an emotion she hadn't quite known how to handle. She'd been exhausted of putting her best foot forward only for everyone else to leave her behind. Again.

Eventually, time had brought unexpected healing. Slowly, the anger had lessened, and Pru had recalled the good memories. The tender and sweet moments between her and her sister. She thought on them often, actually. But she never discussed them with Gideon. Something inside her, perhaps a selfish side of her, wanted to keep Tempe to herself. Keep her safe in her memory.

It didn't make the slightest bit of sense.

But the more she thought of Tempe, the more confused she became.

Gideon consoled her after Tempe left. He'd been there for every tear, every shout—the logic to help balance out her emotions. Pru had never taken Tempe's accusations of him to heart. They were absurd. They certainly didn't match up with the Gideon she knew. That was, until she'd given birth to Constance and seen a different side of him. Controlling, dismissive. She'd tried to explain his overbearing demeanor away, as just a side effect to becoming a new parent.

But when the *Elizabeth* returned without Josiah, concern began to squeeze Pru's ribs like the harshest of stays. Per the captain, Josiah had never boarded, and they'd been forced to pick up a cooper at another seaport down the river. Gideon had brushed away Pru's concerns, suggesting Josiah had more than likely up and left after his fight with Tempe.

It was an explanation that carried no weight. Once time had passed and grief no longer blinded her, Pru knew without a doubt that Tempe would never have abandoned her. Not like Da had done to them. And to run off with

Henry, no less. Henry was a good man, but Tempe loved Josiah. She would have told Pru if she had had feelings for someone else.

And Josiah would never have given up on Tempe. He would have never left his family—Tempe, Pru, George, and Ruby—without a word.

When Pru had finally worked up the courage to discuss her concerns with her friends, they agreed with her. It didn't seem right. Pru had not realized how heavily her disquiet over Tempe's abandonment and Josiah's disappearance had been weighing on her for so long. With her friends' acknowledgment, she felt a fire begin to burn inside her, a rekindling after her feelings were finally validated.

Pru wasn't ready to accept Tempe's preposterous story about Gideon so easily. To do so would be a betrayal to her husband. However, if she wanted to put to rest the uncertainty that had begun to wedge itself further into her marriage with each passing day, she had to be sure. Especially now that the *Lamplighter* had returned to port as Warbler's most successful whaling venture in history.

The luckiest of Gideon's figureheads.

Pru glanced over her shoulder and back at the bustling wharf. No one was paying any attention to the docked ship, emptied of its cargo the day before. The only whalers in the vicinity were busy speaking with Gertrude and Sara. Her friends had drawn their attention, discussing some matter of unimportance, to keep the men distracted. When Pru met their eyes, they nodded, barely perceptible. The whalers wouldn't notice anything amiss, and Gideon would be nearly home with Constance by now.

Heart racing, Prudence turned back to the ship.

To the lamplighter reaching out to her.

And pulled the chisel from her pocket.

ACKNOWLEDGMENTS

Telling stories has been a passion of mine since I was a little girl. It wasn't until 2010, however, that I began writing in earnest with the intent to get a book published. Ten years later, in the middle of the pandemic, I wrote *The Lamplighter*. It was my sixth book and the one to finally land me a publishing deal. Everyone's journey is different, and I must admit, burned out and emotionally beat up, I nearly gave up on the dream of being published. Then Michelle Hauck, my (now) literary agent, emailed me in August 2021 and everything changed.

So, Michelle, thank you for pulling my book from the slush pile and taking a chance on it. You literally breathed life back into my dream. I'll forever be grateful you chose me and fought so hard for Tempe. You are an amazing champion, and I am so appreciative of your guidance in my career. Meg Gaertner, my incredibly talented editor: Thank you for helping my book baby be the best she could be. You understood my vision perfectly and somehow managed to pull even more out of it. *The Lamplighter* wouldn't be what it is today without your wonderful and astute editing eye. Grace Aldrich, my phenomenal illustrator: You captured Tempe and Warbler so beautifully and in the most unsettling manner. I never dreamed I'd have such a stunning cover. You are a seriously talented artist. To everyone with Flux Books who played a part in placing *The Lamplighter* into the hands of readers: From the bottom of my heart, thank you for everything you did. I'll never forget it.

To my entire family: I'm thrilled to finally be able to show you what I've been doing all these years. Know that each time you asked how my writing was going, you made my day. I love you all so much. And to Daddio and Gi-Gi, I wish you could have held my book in your hands. Know that I miss you and will forever treasure your notes/texts of encouragement and enthusiasm.

Mama, you've been my number one fan since day one, supporting me in every way imaginable and encouraging my love for reading from an early age. Thank you for your love, generous spirit, and poetic soul. You helped give me the confidence to do what I love. Jeremy and Taylor, thank you for all your support and excitement. I'm lucky to have you two for brothers and know you're always here for me . . . even when I beat you at spoons. Pat, thank you for mailing me books and articles about anything nineteenth-century related to help my research. It may not have seemed like a big deal to you, but your interest and support meant everything to me. I won the jackpot getting you as my mother-in-law.

To my friends who have supported me over the years: Rachel Audette, Katie Burns, Laura Okun, Victoria Henson, and Jasmin Rangel: Thank you for talking books with me, writing together (Tori and Red!), celebrating my victories, supporting me in my low moments, and providing so much joy in my life. I'm blessed to call you friends.

To the talented women in my writing group—Maggie Boehme, Ellen O'Clover, and Taylor Roberts: You three have played such a huge part in my growth as a writer. I value your critiques and love how much we've been able to celebrate and support one another not only as writers, but as friends. How did we get so lucky to find one another?

To those in the writing community who showed me such kindness: It can be lonely being a writer, particularly in this day and age of social media with its ever-prevalent comparison game and vicious imposter syndrome. A big thank you to Ari Augustine, Yasmin Angoe, Anna Britton, Jeni Chappelle, Roselyn Cronin, RL Martin, Kara Seal, and Destiny Smith. For beta reading one—or multiple—books for me, trusting me with your own, providing chapter critiques, check-ins, and your overall camaraderie. I'll never forget it.

And finally, to Patrick, my husband and best friend: Thank you for believing in me, brainstorming with me, letting me vent and holding me while I cried, going on walks with me so I could talk out plot design, and supporting our family so I could commit myself to a career as a writer. Without you, I never would have visited the East Coast, never would have walked the historic streets of Mystic Seaport, and never had the seed of an idea that became this book. Through the awful lows and amazing highs in this life, I'm so grateful to have you with me through it all. I love you madly.

ABOUT THE AUTHOR

Crystal J. Bell is a writer and videographer who calls the Rocky Mountains her home. After graduating from Colorado State University with her BA, she began writing in earnest and hasn't looked back since. When she isn't drinking up autumn like the elixir of life, she can be found on the back patio with her laptop and a book, out on the reservoirs on her stand-up paddleboard, or cooking in the kitchen with her husband. Most likely pasta. *The Lamplighter* is her debut young adult novel.